Isle of View

**Also by the same author,
and available from NEL:**

Man from Mundania
Heaven Cent
Vale of the Vole

About the author

British-born Piers Anthony now lives in a forest in Florida and devotes all his time to writing. He is the creator of many bestselling series including *The Magic of Xanth*, *The Apprentice Adept*, *Incarnations of Immortality* and *Bio of a Space Tyrant*.

Isle of View

PIERS ANTHONY

NEW ENGLISH LIBRARY
Hodder and Stoughton

The right of Piers Anthony to be identified as the author of this work has been asserted by him in accordance with the Copyright, Designs and Patents Act 1988.

Printed and bound in Great Britain for Hodder and Stoughton Paperbacks, a division of Hodder and Stoughton Ltd, Mill Road, Dunton Green, Sevenoaks, Kent TN13 2YA (Editorial Office: 47 Bedford Square, London WC1B 3DP) by Clays Ltd, St Ives plc.

British Library C.I.P.

Anthony, Piers, 1934–
    Isle of view.

ISBN 0 450 57113 0

CONTENTS

Chapter 1. Chex's Challenge

Chex was desperate. Her darling foal, Che, was lost, and she feared the worst. He was only five years old, and though he had her lightening magic, his wings were not yet developed enough for flight. So he contented himself with extraordinary leaps, and was a happy little centaur— now inexplicably gone.

How could it have happened? She had been inside their cottage stall, using rushes to close the crevices that let the draft in. They were near the region of the Element of Air, and often there was some leakage of wind from it. That was fine on hot days, but chill at night. So she used the rushes, but she had to work quickly and pay close attention, because they were always in such a hurry. They would wedge into any place, not waiting for the right one. So she had concentrated and gotten the job done and somehow hadn't checked on Che for a while.

Now he was nowhere to be found. She had called to him and flown all around the glade, searching with increasing alarm. There was no doubt: he was not here.

Cheiron was away at a winged monster convention and wouldn't be home for another two days. She was almost relieved; how could she face her mate with the news that she had lost their foal? Of course she couldn't do that; she simply had to find Che soon.

1

She circled the region several times, peering down intently, but all she saw was forest around the glade. She had liked this region because it was private with the trees hiding most of what went on, but now they were hiding her foal from her. She had to get under the canopy of foliage.

She glided down and landed near the cottage. Then she trotted in a complete circle around the glade, looking for signs. The ground was pretty well scuffed in the center where Che had been prancing, but the grass remained green at the fringe. He must have wandered out into the forest, though he knew he was supposed to stay in view of the cottage.

She made another circuit, this time walking at the verge of the trees. Suddenly she spied a little hoofprint. She saw that it was headed out into the forest. He had come this way!

But why? Che knew the rule and had always been a good little centaur. He knew that there were dangers out in the deep forest of Xanth, such as dragons and tangle trees and hypnogourds. He shouldn't have walked out this way.

Yet evidently he had. She searched out the prints. They seemed hesitant at first, as if he had been looking for something. Then they became purposeful and moved straight toward the thickest section of the forest.

Chex followed, her alarm increasing. She had hoped that Che had merely wandered and was somewhere close by, perhaps caught in a bramble and unable to extricate himself. But now she feared something worse: he had gone somewhere, and that could only be because something had lured him. There was unlikely to be any good purpose in that.

In a moment her worst suspicion was confirmed: there were signs of an ambush. Something had been lurking here, waiting for Che, and had captured him. There was a bit of cut vine, evidently used to tie up the foal, and the ground was scuffed. But something had gone over the ground with a brush from a nearby brush bush and wiped out all the tracks. She couldn't tell who or what had kidnapped her foal. All she knew was that it had been accomplished quickly and silently.

She searched all around, but there were no tracks of any kind leading from the ambush area. Yet this was not a spot for flying by any creature large enough to carry a little centaur; the vines were tangled in with the foliage of the trees, with several hangman's nooses just waiting for some unwary dragon or griffin to make their day. It was as if kidnapper and foal had vanished at this spot.

Chex shuddered. That meant magic! Che must have been conjured to some other part of Xanth.

But why? She could understand a predator crunching its prey, awful as that concept was in this case. But to lure Che into a trap and conjure him away? What use could anyone have for a winged centaur foal who couldn't yet fly?

At least it meant he was alive. She had suppressed her fear of the worst, because it was unbearable. But how long would he remain alive? Maybe his captor didn't realize that he couldn't fly, and when it found out—

She had to get help. Che had to be found before anything worse happened to him.

She trotted back to the glade, then spread her wings, flicked herself hard with her tail, and took off. She could make anything light by flicking it with her tail. That was how she got rid of biting flies; the moment her tail touched them, they became too light to remain sitting and were launched into the air, where they had to buzz for some time to get things under control again. When she wanted to make herself light enough to fly, she used her tail on her body, and then it was easy for her wings to carry the reduced weight. When the effect faded and she began to get heavy, she just flicked herself again. But she tried not to do that near the end of a flight, because it could be hard to stay on the ground if a gust of wind came along.

She flew high above the forest and turned south. Soon she was passing over the great Gap Chasm, where Princess Ivy's friend Stanley Steamer had gone for patrol duty. She knew the kidnapper wouldn't have taken Che in there, because Stanley knew Che and would have steamed anyone who tried to harm him. But where *had* Che been taken? That was the awful mystery.

She continued south, heading for Castle Roogna. That was where King Dor was, and if anyone could help, he could. He was able to talk to inanimate things, so nothing was secret from him.

She spied the castle, with its pretty stonework and turrets, and glided down for a landing in the orchard. There was a young woman there gathering fruit, and Chex knew who that would be.

"Chex!" the girl called, waving violently. She had freckles and light brown hair in two braids and seemed younger than she was, because she acted younger. She looked fifteen.

"Electra!" Chex responded as her feet touched the turf. Then she braced herself.

Sure enough, Electra came charging in for a hug. She collided with Chex, her impact shoving the light centaur back. It was awkward, but exuberance was Electra's second nature, maybe even her first nature. She was Prince Dolph's Betrothee, and a wonderful girl.

"But where's Che?" Electra asked, her freckled face concerned.

For an instant Chex had almost forgotten her misery. Now it returned with force. "He's gone!" she said. "Something kidnapped him! I must get help to find him, before—" Here she found herself unable to continue.

"That's terrible!" Electra exclaimed. "You must tell the King!"

As if that wasn't the reason Chex had come here! "Yes, I must," Chex said.

They walked on up to the castle. "Oh, I forgot!" Electra exclaimed, her braids flinging about her head as she turned to face Chex. "King Dor's away!"

"Away?" Chex asked, alarmed. "Where?"

"Ceremonial call on King Nabob of the Naga."

"Oh? What's the ceremony?"

"Well, they are allies, and maybe soon there'll be reason for getting together. Nada, you know."

Suddenly Chex appreciated the girl's diffidence. Nada Naga was Prince Dolph's other Betrothee, and in her human form a truly lovely young lady. It had been a political liaison, but everyone knew that Dolph preferred the Princess Nada to Electra. The time was approaching when Dolph would have to make his choice between the two, and it did not look good for Electra. She was a wonderful girl, but Nada was a beautiful princess.

Unfortunately, Electra was under an enchantment. Not only did she love Dolph, who had rescued her from a very long sleep, she would die if she didn't marry him. No one wanted that! There was a further irony: Nada did not love Dolph. She was five years older than he and regarded him as a juvenile. But she had given her word, and intended to carry through, in the manner required of a princess. It was obvious to everyone that Dolph could make both girls happy by marrying Electra—but that would not make Dolph happy, and he was not adult enough to do what he didn't like. It was a difficult situation.

However, Chex had a pressing problem of her own at the moment. "Then Queen Irene—"

"She went with him. She wanted to meet King Nabob and Nada's handsome big brother, Naldo."

"Then Princess Ivy—"

"She's off with Grey Murphy at the Good Magician's Castle."

"There must be somebody in charge!" Chex exclaimed, exasperated.

"Oh, sure. Magician Murphy."

"Then I'd better see him." Chex wasn't quite satisfied with this as she had never completely trusted Murphy, but she couldn't wait for one of the others to return to the palace.

Magician Murphy was a graying but otherwise ordinary older man. "Yes, I can help you, Centaur," he said. "First, I will organize a search for your missing foal. Second, I will set my curse on the party responsible for the abduction, so that that effort will foul up in devious ways. That should provide additional time for the searchers to complete their mission.''

This was more than Chex had expected of this man. But she reminded herself that on occasion evil magicians did become good ones. King Emeritus Trent was the most notable example. Murphy had sworn to uphold the current order, and if King Dor trusted him, she could do no less. ''Thank you, Magician,'' she said.

Murphy spoke to a magic mirror. ''Now hear this,'' he said. ''This is King pro-tem Murphy speaking. Chex Centaur's foal has been abducted by a party unknown, and must be found and rescued ASAP. All personnel not otherwise occupied get your butts to the castle pronto for organization into search parties. That is all.''

Chex listened with a certain surprise. Evidently Murphy had picked up some Mundanish terms during his exile. However, his general meaning came through.

They walked to the front of the castle. From every direction folk were coming: shoe tree farmers, milkweed maids, P and Q nut growers, and even a young ogre who was evidently tired of twisting trees into pretzels. Some were coming from the castle, too: Prince Dolph, Nada Naga, Grundy Golem, and a ghost or two. There was even a puff of steam from the direction of the Gap Chasm: Stanley Steamer was coming in. It seemed that everyone wanted to help.

''Very well,'' Murphy said when a suitable group had assembled. ''We have no idea where Che may have been taken, but we have reason to believe that nothing bad will happen to him for a while. Our best course is to cover as much of Xanth as we can in the next few hours. Because it is not safe for folk to go alone into the jungle—'' He paused, for the ogre was looking perplexed. ''Ogre's excepted of course,'' he said, and the ogre's confusion eased. ''Most parties will consist of two or more folk, at least one of whom should be able to defend them until help can come. Here are magic whistles from the castle armory; these can be heard far and wide, so each person will carry one and use it if threatened."

He passed out the whistles. The ogre, being typically stupid, blew his immediately. But there was no sound.

Startled, the ogre looked up. "Me blow, hear no."

"That's because you aren't far or wide yet," Murphy explained. "We are all standing close and narrow, which is out of range. Try it from far."

The ogre charged to the horizon, knocking down a stray tree accidentally. He blew again. This time the sound was piercing.

Soon the parties were organized and heading out in every direction. "Grundy will go with you, Chex," Murphy said. "You can act as liaison between the search parties, so that you will be the first to know if your foal is found. Grundy will help you by questioning any plants or creatures as needed. First I think you should question the plants in the vicinity of the abduction; they must have seen something."

"Yes!" Chex said, feeling foolish because she hadn't thought of that herself. Murphy was doing a great job!

Grundy scrambled up on her back. He was a tiny man, easy to carry even without lightening. He had been a real golem originally, made of rag and string and wood, but now he was a real man, though still the original size. One other thing had not changed: he still had a big mouth and made enemies with an ease that left others awestruck. Chex flicked herself, spread her wings, and took off. She was glad to have such an efficient search proceeding; if anything could find Che, this would.

"Where's Rapunzel?" she inquired as they flew north. For Grundy had finally found in her a woman to his taste— or maybe it was the other way around. Rapunzel could assume any size she wished, being descended from both human and elven stock, but preferred small. She was a lovely lady, with—oh, yes—magically long hair. Chex didn't envy her the chore of brushing it! Normally Grundy and Rapunzel were together.

"She's seeing about a new house," he said.

"Oh? I thought you were satisfied with that birdhouse you converted."

"I am. But she says it's too small."

"Too small? But you haven't changed, and she can be any size she wants."

Grundy shrugged. "I don't understand women. Do you?"

Chex laughed. "No!" But then she got a faint notion, and began to understand. The two of them might remain small, but if the family changed sizes . . .

She glided down to the glade. It had been her home for several years, because she hadn't wanted to risk having Che fall off the edge of a mountain before he was able to fly. Now it seemed alien, because it had turned out to be unsafe in another way. Whoever or whatever had kidnapped her foal—would it have been possible had Che lived in a mountain retreat? Just how smart had she been to avoid the mountain?

She trotted into the forest where Che had been lost. "Here," she said, coming to a halt at the place.

Grundy talked to the plants in the vicinity. Chex heard only a faint rustling, but in a moment he had his report. "There was an awful smell, as of pastry baking, and—"

"That's not awful!" she protested. "Che loved fresh pastry!"

"What's it made from?" the golem asked.

"Why, fresh flour from sea oats, and— oh." For of course plants like oats would not like the smell of their brethren being baked. Breadfruit trees and pie trees did not mind giving up their wares, but when grains were stripped from the plants it was another matter. "An awful smell," she agreed.

"The foal sniffed it and followed it right here," Grundy said. "But here there was only a bit of cloud, an evil fog. The smell came from that. The foal went in, and there was the sound of a struggle, and then the fog lifted and nothing remained. The plants didn't see what happened, only that Che went in and didn't come out."

"Magic!" Chex exclaimed. Other centaurs often didn't

like magic. She had thought them old-fashioned and unrealistic, but now she was beginning to appreciate their
view. Magic had taken her foal from her!

"Must have been. And that fog sounds like Fracto. He's
always interested in doing something nasty."

"Fracto!" she cried, remembering the worst of clouds.
It was true: wherever there was mischief to be done, there
was Fracto. "We should search him out and make him
talk!"

"We might find him, but even if we spoke his language,
he probably wouldn't tell," Grundy pointed out.

He was right. There was no point in giving Fracto the
satisfaction. They would have to find some other way to
investigate.

This was evidently a pretty sophisticated abduction. It
had been set up so that it could not readily be traced. Why
such an effort—for one flightless little centaur? It didn't
seem to make a lot of sense.

They left the forest and took off from the glade. Chex
was mystified and dispirited. The early shock of the loss
was wearing off and being replaced by the grim certainty
that there would be no easy resolution. She still had no idea
where Che had been taken.

"We had better see how the others are doing," Grundy
said, sounding dispirited himself. "Che has to be somewhere."

He was trying to cheer her, and successfully failing. But
it was good advice anyway. She was supposed to be the
liaison between the teams.

"Closest is the ogre," Grundy announced. It seemed that
he had a list of the assignments. "Checking the Goblinate
of the Golden Horde."

"The Golden Horde!" Chex exclaimed, horrified.
"Those terrible goblins!"

"They're your closest evil neighbors to the west," he
pointed out.

They certainly were! They liked to catch creatures and
torture them before cooking them. They lived around a hate

spring, which perhaps accounted for their extreme meanness. If Che had fallen into their grubby hands . . .

It was good that the ogre was going there. An ogre knew how to handle goblins. It was said that goblins who attacked an ogre would find some of their number orbiting the moon—and those were the lucky ones. Still, if they had Che, the foal could get bashed right along with the goblins, because ogres were justifiably proud of their stupidity.

She angled west. Soon she observed a path of trees being knocked down as the ogre traveled the only way he knew how—straight ahead, bashing any obstacles out of the way. The average tree didn't like the average ogre much, but didn't have much choice about contact if the ogre came its way. Some trees, however, did fight back, like the tanglers. It was said that an ogre-tangler battle was worth watching—from a distance.

She flew on past the ogre to the goblin camp. The goblins spied her and shook their little fists at her. But there was no sign of Che. That was reassuring—

"Unless they cooked him already," Grundy remarked.

Chex almost fell out of the sky. What a genius the golem had for the wrong thought!

"But they don't have a pot going," Grundy continued. "They couldn't have done it in this time."

Maybe it was the right thought after all! He was right: there was no smoke, no fire. So either Che had not been cooked or he wasn't here at all. She wasn't sure which to hope for.

She flew back to the ogre. "They're right ahead," she called. "Keep an eye out for the foal!"

"Me goal save foal," he agreed.

Well, he had the right attitude. But she felt better now that it seemed unlikely that the foal was there.

"Next group is human, checking the centaur village north of the Gap," Grundy said.

Chex knew why no centaurs were participating in the search: they did not accept her as one of them. Indeed, they considered her a monstrosity, a degenerate crossbreed. She had been welcomed by the winged monsters but not by her own kind. But she tried not to dwell on that; there was nothing to be gained by it. In time there might be an established species of winged centaurs, needing no affiliations with the ground-bound centaurs, just as the winged dragons survived nicely independent of the land dragons. But not if Che was lost!

The human party consisted of three milkweed maids. They must have been given some kind of speed-up spell, because they could not have gotten this far this fast otherwise. They were crossing the invisible bridge, seeming to be in midair, and giggling as they teased each other about what monster below might be seeing up whose skirt. There was no monster below; the Gap Dragon had joined the search effort. But milkweed maids tended to be silly anyway; it was said to be one of the features that made them attractive to men. Chex did not quite understand that, but of course she wasn't human.

She swooped low. "Have you seen anything?" she called.

"Just trees!" one called. "But we haven't started looking yet, because our assignment is the centaur village. Someone else is checking the forest south of the Gap."

"Good luck!" Chex said. But she didn't think Che would be at the centaur village, because though the centaurs did not approve of winged crossbreeds, they were honorable folk who would not interfere. They would not have cared to use so much magic, either, or to conceal their activity, for pride (some said arrogance) was a centaur's nature.

They continued their check of the various parties. They were all searching diligently, but without any success. To stave off her developing gloom, Chex pondered her relationship with Che.

It had all started with her wedding, really. She had met Cheiron, the only other winged centaur in Xanth, and probably would have fallen in love with him even if he hadn't been handsome and strong and smart and experienced. They had agreed to mate—the human folk called it marriage—

and the Simurgh herself had flown in to officiate. The Simurgh was the largest and oldest of birds, who had seen the destruction and regeneration of the universe three times and was probably good for one or two more times. She had handled things competently, of course, and made one passing reference that astonished Chex and Cheiron. FROM THIS UNION, she had said in her powerful mental projection, WILL COME ONE WHOSE LIFE WILL CHANGE THE COURSE OF THE HISTORY OF XANTH. Then she had required all the attending winged monsters, and even Prince Dolph, who had managed to sneak in by assuming the form of a dragonfly, to make an oath to protect that one from harm. It had become clear why the Simurgh had come: to ensure the safety of the future foal.

In due course Che had arrived. The stork had not delivered him, and he hadn't turned up under a cabbage leaf; the centaurs, being realistic about natural functions of all kinds, had more direct if uncomfortable means of acquiring their offspring. After all, storks were notoriously myopic, and sometimes misdelivered babies. Maybe that was all right for human folk, but no centaur would care to risk it.

Che was beautiful from the start, with his dark brown pelt and soft little wings. The winged monsters had looked out for him, so that no griffin, dragon, roc, or anything else that flew, right down through harpies to little dragonflies, was any threat. In fact, young flying dragons had flown in to play with him, though he could not yet fly himself, and they had spread the word to the landbound dragons. The land dragons were not bound by the oath, but many of them had vestigial wings and identified with their flying cousins, so they were careful of Che also.

Their family had led an almost idyllic life, here in the glade. When she and Cheiron wanted to go somewhere alone, or to help some of their friends, they never lacked for foal-sitters. Even Draco Dragon, the terror of north-central Xanth, had come in once, and not just because of the oath. He had a special debt to the skeleton Marrow Bones, who had saved his nestful of pretty stones, and

Marrow was Chex's friend. Dragons had a keen sense of loyalty to those they respected, though fortunately there were not many of these. So Che had never lacked for company and was a happy little centaur.

What was it that the Simurgh saw in Che's future? How could he change the history of Xanth? Though Chex loved him overwhelmingly, she knew, somewhere in the nonparental reaches of her mind, that he was, after all, only a winged centaur like his parents. The regular centaurs would not acknowledge him at all, and the human folk thought him a mere curiosity. There was no indication that he was destined for greatness—or even, at this moment, for survival. Yet the Simurgh would not have made a mistake; she was the keeper of the seeds, and there was little if anything about the tides of life she did not understand.

Then Chex had a horrible thought. Suppose Che wasn't the one the Simurgh meant? He was the result of Chex's union with Cheiron, to be sure, but perhaps not the only one. Also, it wasn't clear exactly how he was to change the history of Xanth. Could it be by getting himself abducted and killed, and setting off the winged monsters in some sort of rampage?

No, she couldn't accept such notions! She had to believe that Che would survive to grow into an adult flying centaur, and that in that state he would accomplish something undreamed of in the philosophies of those who presently ignored him. She had to see that he was cared for and educated in the ways that he needed, so that when the time for greatness came upon him he would be ready.

And surely she would do that, for the Simurgh would have known, if Che were destined for an untimely end. Someone had kidnapped him—technically, kidnapping applied to little goats, but it remained the best word—but would not kill him, and they would rescue him and the prophecy of his greatness would be back on track. That was the way it had to be.

Reassured for what she realized might not be a fully objective reason, Chex flew on her round, checking the search parties that were radiating from Castle Roogna. Grundy knew where all of them were, approximately, and when they weren't quite where he expected, the neighborhood plants were glad to give him reports.

They came to a party consisting of two pretty young women: Nada and Electra. They were going to the Good Magician's castle to ask him where Che was. Chex was ashamed to admit that she hadn't thought of that obvious method. The Good Magician, traditionally, knew everything and told it for the price of a year's service. Of course the original Good Magician, Humfrey, wasn't there now, but his apprentice, Grey Murphy, was, and he was trying hard to fill the post. The Princess Ivy was there to Enhance him when he needed it, and that helped. Could he answer? Chex hoped so!

She went on back north of the Gap, where Prince Dolph was checking the Elements. The Elements were five special regions in north central Xanth: Air, Earth, Fire, Water, and the Void. Each was dangerous in its own way, as Chex knew well from her nearness to Air, but Dolph could assume any living form. That meant he could become a creature that could handle any Element he entered, so that he could explore it safely. She didn't see him, which was probably good; it meant he was in some other form, deep in an Element, and if Che had been taken there, Dolph would find him and probably rescue him.

She had completed the circuit. All the search parties were busy, but none had found Che. She would have to stop at her cabin and rest and eat, before going out on another circuit. She would keep doing this until she had risen to this horrible challenge: that of finding and rescuing her foal.

As she came down, she saw something in the clearing. Was it Che? Her heart leaped, which caused her body to rise and almost made her overshoot her landing. But it was not. It was only a little elf girl. Her heart sank, which caused her to drop and almost undershoot her landing. She came down solidly on all fours and folded her wings. Then she approached the elf, who was staring at her as if astonished.

"Who are you?" she inquired. "What are you doing so far from your elm?"

The elf scuffled her feet. She was young, a child really, yet was unusually large for the elves Chex had seen. A normal elf stood a quarter the height of a normal human being, while this one was half human height. She had a turned-up nose, a few freckles spattered across her cheeks, and ragged brown hair that couldn't quite make up its mind between chestnut and butter. Her eyes were brown, and seemed nearsighted. That reminded Chex of Arnolde Centaur and Good Magician Humfrey, who used spectacles to correct their vision—which was even odder, because she'd never met either of them. "My cat—" the elf child said.

"But elves don't have cats," Chex protested. "In fact, nobody does; there are no straight cats in Xanth, only punnish variants like the cat-o'-nine-tails."

"Xanth?" the girl asked, seeming perplexed.

Chex was tired and in a hurry, but she realized that something was wrong here. "Yes, Xanth, where we all live. Don't try to tell me you're from Mundania!"

"No, I'm from the World of Two Moons. My cat—"

"I told you, there are no—" Then Chex saw the cat. He was an orange fluff ball, that did seem to have an elven cast to his features. He was lying stretched out on the ground, tail extended behind, looking like nothing so much as a speed bump: a hump in the trail designed to trip up speeding centaurs. "How—?" she asked, somewhat at a loss.

"Something strange here," Grundy murmured. "There are no elf elms close by. She should be too weak to stand. And look at the size of her! She's as big as a goblin!"

"Sammy can find anything, except home," the elf said. "Only usually I never know what he's looking for. So he gets lost. I have to keep up with him so I can bring him back after he finds it." She paused, looking at the cat. "I think he was looking for a feather, this time." Indeed, the cat had a feather between his tawny paws.

"That's not just a feather," Chex said. "That's a first-molt wing feather from my foal, Che. There are very few like it anywhere.''

"I guess he wanted a special feather, then," the elf said. Then, seemingly with an effort, she raised her face to look at Chex. "If you don't mind, please, could you tell me— what are you?"

Chex was taken aback. "I am a flying centaur, of course! A winged monster, technically. Haven't you ever seen a centaur before?"

The girl shook her head. "No."

"Your elm must be far from civilization!"

"What's an elm?"

"A tree, of course."

"We don't have many trees in the World of Two Moons. At least, not ones I can see well." She looked around, blinking. "Are those trees?"

"Yes, of course. It's all forested here. But how can you not have an elm? All elves—"

"I don't have an elm, not even a wolf friend, though I think one day I will be with Lone Wolf. So right now I just have a cat," the girl said, "who finds things, but gets lost, which is how I met him, because there aren't any others like him in our world—and this time I think I'm lost too, because this is a very strange place."

"But all elves are associated with elms!" Chex protested. "Where did you say you were from?"

"My holt is at—"

"Your what?"

"My holt. It's—"

Chex realized that something was not merely odd, it was decidedly strange, just as Grundy had said. "I think we had better start over. Let's introduce ourselves. You are . . . ?"

"Jenny of the World of Two Moons."

"And I am Chex Centaur of Xanth. Now I think we should—" She broke off, because she had noticed something even stranger. "Are those your ears?"

The child touched her left ear. "Yes. Is something wrong?"

"It's pointed!"

Jenny was perplexed. "Aren't yours?"

"No. Can't you see?"

"Your head is sort of fuzzy, from here."

So it was true: the elf could not see well at a distance. "My dear, we must get you some spectacles," Chex said. It was as if she had to mother someone, while her foal was missing. "We have a spectacle bush here, and we haven't harvested any of its fruit, so there are plenty." She led the elf to it. "They correct vision, and fit magically, of course. Here, try this pair." She picked it and set it on Jenny's face, carefully. It was rather big for her, but the side pieces closed around her head and hooked behind her phenomenally pointed ears. Her hair had masked the effect somewhat before, but now there was no doubt. There were no ears in Xanth like that! Not on humanoid folk.

Jenny's eyes grew even bigger than they naturally were, magnified by the spectacles. "I can see everything!" she exclaimed, amazed.

"Well of course. That's what spectacles do. They enable you to see every spectacle in sight. I'm surprised you didn't have a pair before."

"There are none at home," Jenny said, lifting a hand to touch the amazing device.

Chex was surprised yet again. "Your hand—you're missing a finger!"

Jenny looked at her hand. "No I'm not. All four are there."

"But other elves have five fingers!" Chex protested. "All humanoids do. See, I have five." She held forth her hand.

Jenny stared. "How odd!"

"You're really *not* from Xanth!" Chex said, realizing why the girl was confused. "You look like an elf, but you're quite different in detail."

Jenny shrugged. "I guess you can call me an elf if you want," she said. "I'm just a person, really."

"Yes, of course. But here in Xanth you are considered an elf. How did you get here?"

"I didn't see." Which made sense. How could she have seen where she was going, if she could not make out details of the landscape as she passed them? She was as lost as Che!

"I think you will have to stay here until we find out what happened," Chex decided. "You are here looking for a feather, and I am looking for the one that feather came from, my lost foal, Che. Now perhaps we should—"

But she broke off, because at that point the little cat came alive and bolted for the forest. "Sammy!" Jenny cried, running after him. "Wait for me! You'll get lost again!"

"Jenny!" Chex cried in turn. "You'll *both* get lost! That forest's dangerous!"

But cat and elf were already disappearing into the jungle, heedless of the danger. Chex realized that they must have come through it, somehow escaping the predators.

"We'd better find her," Grundy said. "Maybe it's co-incidence that she appeared right when Che disappeared, but maybe not."

Chex hadn't thought of that. Could her foal have been turned into—? No, impossible! But it was true that this was a remarkably strange business.

She trotted to the center of the glade, spread her wings, and leaped into the air as she smacked her body with her tail. In a moment she was climbing up past the trees. She flew over them in the direction the elf girl had gone, but the canopy was too thick and she could see neither the ground nor anything on it. They were gone.

"We can alert the others about the elf," Grundy said. "If she really is from elsewhere, she can't stay hidden long."

Chex agreed, but remained disquieted. Why should a strange elf girl show up here, right at this time?

She looped about and glided back to the glade. She had better things to do than loop helplessly around the forest! She had to find Che and could not afford to waste her time or energy pursuing strangers. But it was certainly a curious encounter!

Chapter 2. Jenny's Journey

Jenny ran after the cat. "Wait for me! You'll get lost again!" But of course Sammy didn't listen; he never did. He wasn't trying to run away from her, he just got so caught up in whatever he was chasing that he lost track of everything else and often got himself into trouble. She couldn't let that happen; they were already in a very strange region, and if it got any stranger they might never find their way out!

Sammy plunged into the thickest foliage of the jungle. Jenny had no choice but to plunge in after him, though the brush threatened to ruin whatever remained of her clothing. It was bad enough getting her hair all tangled in a knot from burrs and things in her desperate effort to keep up. If she ever lost sight of him, she might never catch him again!

She heard the centaur lady calling after her. "That forest's dangerous!" That was the strangest looking creature Jenny had ever seen, like an animal and a bird and a woman all jammed together, but she seemed nice. She had a foal, she had said, which meant she was somebody's mother, and that was a good sign. Mothers were a class unto themselves, a good class. It had been very nice of her to find the magic spectacles; Jenny had never known such things existed. They made all the difference in this strange world! But she just couldn't stay and talk when Sammy was taking off.

She tore through the brush, and in a moment spied Sammy ahead of her, running up a slope, dodging around bushes that grew pretty colored pillows. Pillows? That was crazy; pillows didn't grow on bushes, they had to be made of bird down and cloth, sewn together and all. When the hunters and their wolf friends brought back birds for eating, they always saved the feathers. Nothing was wasted. But those certainly did look like pillows growing!

Sammy ran on over a ridge and down the other side. Here there were cornlike plants, with their ears getting ripe. Jenny brushed by one, and it exploded, sending bits of puffed corn out. It was popcorn! She snatched some out of the air and stuffed it in her mouth, because she was hungry after chasing Sammy this far.

Now the cat got on a nice little path through the jungle, leading to a giant tree with hanging tentacles.

"No, Sammy!" Jenny cried in alarm. She had seen one of those trees before. The tentacles had tried to grab her, and she had been lucky to escape them. In fact she had lost her knife in the process, which upset her considerably. "Don't go near that tree!" At least now she could recognize it from a distance, instead of blundering into it. She would have to thank Chex for the spectacles, once Sammy stopped and they could go back.

Sammy jumped off the path and scrambled back through the thick brush. For once Jenny was glad for that; she didn't want him getting caught by that dreadful thing!

They came to a region of larger but more peaceful trees, and it was easier going here, because the thick leaf cover above shaded the ground and there wasn't much brush. Sammy slowed to a fast walk, but didn't stop moving; she could keep up but not catch him. She would just have to follow until he found what he was looking for this time, and then see what to do next. She was tired, but still had no choice; she just couldn't let Sammy get even worse lost alone.

As she hurried along, she thought about how she had come to this weird region. She was just an ordinary girl of her holt, nothing special at all. In fact she was unspecial, because she just couldn't see well; without sending she would have been in constant trouble. She liked to paint and weave and make jewelry, and was learning how to decorate pottery. Those hearthside skills did not suffer from her myopia. She hoped to grow up to be a good weaver, making rugs of special beauty with designs and pictures that every elf would want. She also liked to make berry pie, mainly because she liked to eat it so much. The main problem there was all the time it took to pick the berries, because the berry patches close to the village were all picked out and she had to range fairly far afield, and that was hard because she was lost the moment she strayed from the main paths. She couldn't count the times she had had to call for help, mentally, just to find the path again. When she got a wolf friend she would be able to go out farther, more safely. For now, she had her cat friend instead, and she could do her hearthside practicing. Her fingers were long and nimble, but she still had a lot of skill to develop. While she practiced with these things, alone, she liked to sing to herself. She always stopped when any other elf was near enough to hear, of course. But Sammy liked it, and that was most of what counted.

She had gone out looking for berries in the cool morning, with Sammy. The cat had seemed bored; the truth was, he wasn't much interested in berries. "If I had a feather, I'd tickle your whiskers," Jenny said teasingly. Then the cat had taken off, and she had known she had to follow, no matter what, because when he got into one of his moods and set out in pursuit of something, he didn't stop until he found it. She had no idea how far the chase was to take him, this time!

He had cut through a section of the forest she was unfamiliar with. It was said to be haunted, but she doubted it; spirits normally didn't waste time with simple trees. Mainly she was afraid of poisonous serpents or other hungry wild things that would be lurking to gobble Sammy or her. Yet she had to keep going, lest Sammy be lost.

She ran and ran, her vision blurring as she struggled to keep up. All she saw was Sammy's fleeting tail, and bits of scenery whizzing by. She was better at seeing motion than things; otherwise she wouldn't have had a chance to stay near Sammy. Then, suddenly, the cat went over a ridge, and she followed, and discovered that there was no other side to it. She flailed in air for a moment, too scared to scream. Then her feet touched ground again; it had only been a slight drop, shrouded by fog. She ran on, still barely keeping the cat in sight.

But now the scenery was strange. She didn't have time to stop and examine it closely, but she knew this wasn't like anything she had seen before. She would have to come to this forest some time when she wasn't chasing her cat to see just what there was about it that was so different.

Sammy skirted an odd green tree. Jenny ran by it—and the tentacles snapped up and tried to grab her. One hung on to her flaring dress, and as she tried to pull free others grabbed her, but she drew her knife and sliced the awful green things and was able to pull free. Unfortunately, her knife got caught in the last tentacle, and she lost it. That was her first experience with the aggressive tree, and the confirmation that she had wandered into a very strange region.

Then Sammy scampered into a clearing in the forest and stopped. He had finally found what he was looking for: a big white feather.

"You dragged me all the way here for a stupid feather?" she demanded, not really angry with him, but having to exclaim about something to someone before she burst. The truth was that she was frightened by the strangeness of this region, and still shaken by the way that tree had grabbed for her. She had never even heard of a kind of tree that did that! But now she realized that this business had started with her, because she had teased Sammy about tickling him with a feather. He had oriented on "feather" and gone in search of one—and what a feather he had found!

A shadow had descended, and the amazing animal-bird-

lady came down. She seemed almost as surprised to see
Jenny as Jenny was to see her. She said she was a checked
centaur, or something, and talked about elms. Jenny learned
that an elm was a tree; she wasn't sure why the centaur
thought she should have something to do with it.

The centaur lady was looking for her lost foal, called
Chay. But Jenny hadn't learned any more, because Sammy
had suddenly taken off again, and she had had to follow.
She hoped it wasn't going to get even stranger, because she
wasn't at all sure she could find their way back as it was.

Now Sammy slowed. Maybe he was approaching what
he sought. Maybe it was another feather, and she could
carry it for him, and they could go home. No, not another
feather, because he never looked for the same thing twice
in a row. Maybe a—

Jenny paused, amazed. There ahead of them was a little
winged centaur! That must be the foal! The centaur lady
had said she was looking for it, and Sammy had taken off
to find it, just like that.

But the poor thing hadn't just wandered away. He was a
captive. There was a rope around his neck, and his hands
were tied behind his back, and his legs were hobbled so
that he could hardly stand. He was fluttering his wings
helplessly, and he looked very unhappy. That was all Jenny
needed to see; she knew she had to help Chay get back to
his mother.

However, there were mean creatures around the foal.
They looked a bit like people and were her own size, but
their heads, hands and feet were larger and knobby. They
were dark, and their scowls were darker. There were three
of them, evidently guarding the foal. They weren't doing
anything to him, but it was obvious that they would if he
made any real effort to escape.

Jenny put her hand on Sammy's back. He had paused,
satisfied not to go farther now that he had spotted what he
had come for. "We have to rescue Chay from those mean
folk," she whispered. "I could untie him, so he could run,

but they'd only tie me up too. I wish I had something to make them go away, just long enough!''

Sammy took off. "No!" she whisper-cried. "I didn't mean for you to—'' But of course it was too late, as it always was with Sammy. When would she learn not to speak carelessly when he was listening?

Well, there was no help for it. She had to follow him, though it delayed whatever action she might take to free the foal. Maybe that wasn't too much of a loss, because she had no idea how to free him. Still, she hardly needed distractions right now!

Sammy led her to a tree. It had bright green leaves and bright red berries. Berries? No, those were cherries! It was a cherry tree. But she was in no mood to eat right now.

"What possessed you to come here, when I said I needed something to make the mean little men go away?'' she asked the cat, knowing he couldn't answer.

He merely stood by the tree, ignoring it now that he had found it. His joy was in the search; once he found whatever he sought, he usually did ignore it.

Perplexed, she reached up to pluck a cherry. It was round and red, but evidently not ripe, because its skin was hard, not soft. She touched her teeth to it, but could not dent it. The thing was like a wooden ball!

She plucked another. It was just as bad. These couldn't be real cherries. Maybe they were there just to fool hungry people—and she was a hungry person, even though she didn't want to eat at the moment.

Suddenly she was angry. Not only did she not want to eat, these cherries would be no good if she did want to! She hurled the two as far away from her as she could. They arced past the trees and came to the ground.

Boom! Boom!

Jenny stared. The two cherries hadn't bounced or rolled, they had exploded! There were two small craters in the ground where they had hit, and dirt and leaves were scattered around.

Amazed, she looked at the tree. Cherries that exploded?

And she had tried to bite into one! Suppose it had exploded when—

Then something clicked in her head. Sammy had led her here, and maybe this was why. What would happen if she threw a cherry at the mean men?

Jenny smiled. She did not regard herself as a mean person, but she thought maybe she could be mean for just a short time if she tried.

She gathered a number of cherries and put them carefully—very carefully!—in her pockets. She carried two in her hands, too. Then she walked quietly back to where she had seen the mean men. She hoped they hadn't heard the two explosions. The cherry tree was some distance away, so maybe they hadn't.

She was in luck: the party remained exactly as it had been before. The mean men seemed to be waiting for something, and of course the foal couldn't do anything.

Now she had to plan this carefully. She had to drive off the men, then run down and untie the foal so he could run away. His mother had talked to her, so probably he could too. She would tell him what she was doing. With luck, he would get away before the mean men knew what happened.

Jenny was scared, but that didn't stop her. She just had to rescue that foal!

She nerved herself, clenched her teeth, and hurled a cherry bomb down toward the party. She had a pretty good arm, and now she could really see where she was throwing. She aimed it so that the cherry wouldn't actually hit anyone, just land nearby.

It worked perfectly. The bomb exploded right behind one of the mean men. He jumped right off the ground, his stubby legs running while he was still in the air. He thought somebody was attacking him—which was the general idea.

Jenny threw another bomb. This one detonated behind one of the other men, and he ran off too. It was such a joy to see what she was doing! The foal was also alarmed, but he couldn't run, because of the hobble, so he just stood there looking scared.

Jenny dug a bomb out of her pocket and threw it behind the third mean man. He was already running away, and this made him run faster. In a moment all three were gone.

Jenny ran down to the foal. "Don't be frightened, Chay!" she called. "I'm here to help you!" Of course he was frightened, but maybe this made him less so.

She reached him, panting. "Let me untie your hands!" she gasped. "I don't know how much time we have!"

She worked on the knot, but it was very tight. She was good with knots, but knots were ornery things, and it just wasn't possible to rush it. Slowly it came undone.

But that was only the hands. She still needed to do the hobbles on his legs. "Oh, I wish I had a knife to cut these!" she exclaimed as she wrestled with the second ornery knot.

Sammy took off. But he stopped in a moment, by something on the ground. Jenny looked. It was a knife, dropped by one of the fleeing men! She hurried over to get it, and used it to saw through first one hobble rope, and then the other.

But then a mean man returned. "What's this?" he cried.

No, it wasn't a mean man; the voice was too high. It was a mean woman! She was a lot prettier than the men, with head and hands and feet much smaller, but of the same species, maybe. "Run, Chay!" Jenny cried.

The little centaur took an unsteady step. It was hard for him to move well after being hobbled.

"I'll help you!" Jenny said. She put her arms around his body where it changed from colt to boy, trying to steady him and urge him forward.

"An elf!" the mean woman exclaimed, swirling her great dark tresses about in a no-nonsense manner. "Well, we'll put a stop to this!" She waved a wand, and suddenly the foal and Jenny were lifted into the air.

"Eeeek!" Jenny screamed, totally startled.

"It's her magic wand," the foal said. "We can't escape."

For a moment Jenny was startled back into a normal state. "You can talk!"

"Well, I'm five years old."

"But you look less than one year old," she said, peering more closely at him.

"We centaurs age at the human rate, or maybe faster for the winged ones, because of our avian heritage. I think I'm about your age, in relative terms."

"Three hands? But you're not even half grown yet!"

"Hands?"

Jenny showed her spread four fingers, three times. "Each finger a year," she explained

"Oh, that's right. You're an elf. I mistook you for full human." Then, after a pause: "Four fingered hands?"

Jenny looked down. "This is interesting, and we really must talk some more. But right now we have to get away from that mean woman!"

"That's Godiva Goblin. We can't get away from her as long as she has the magic wand."

"Magic wand?" Jenny was beginning to understand the problem.

Below, Sammy heard and walked toward the woman, his tail twitching ominously.

"No!" Jenny cried, afraid of what would happen to the cat if he attacked this mean creature.

"Don't tell me no," Godiva said. "I will keep you suspended until you tell me what the elves have to do with this. Where's your elm?" As she spoke, she lowered the wand, and Jenny and the foal came down to float just barely out of reach of the ground.

"I don't know anything about an elm!" Jenny protested.

Then Sammy leaped. He caught the wand in his mouth and tore it out of the woman's grasp.

Jenny and the foal dropped abruptly to the ground.

"Come back with that!" the woman exclaimed angrily. Her long hair swirled around her body as she turned.

Sammy had snatched the wand, after Jenny mentioned it, and now the lady goblin couldn't use it against them!

"Find somewhere safe!" Jenny called to the cat. "Run! Follow that cat!" she cried to the foal.

The little centaur moved faster than before, the kinks

working out of his legs. He began to trot. Jenny ran along-side, her eyes on Sammy. It wouldn't do them much good if Sammy found somewhere safe, but they couldn't find him!

Now the male goblins were returning. "Moron! Idiot! Imbecile!" the woman screamed. "Catch them! Get the wand back!"

But the cat was moving swiftly, and the centaur was gaining speed. They got a lead before the goblins got or-ganized.

Sammy, with something new to find, forgot the wand. It dropped from his mouth. Jenny saw it, and swooped it up. "Maybe this will stop them!" she said, turning to wave it at the goblins.

Nothing happened. "You can't use it," the centaur said. "It's attuned to Lady Godiva and won't work for anyone else."

"Well, I'll keep it anyway so she can't use it against us," Jenny said, and ran on.

They plowed through more jungle, running as fast as they could. But the goblins kept after them. Every time the mean men slowed, the mean woman screamed at them and made them speed up again.

Jenny's breath was rasping. She was used to walking a lot and to hurrying after Sammy, but this was headlong running, and she had already been tired from the prior chases. She couldn't keep this up much longer!

Then they came to a river. It wasn't the biggest river Jenny had ever heard of, but it wasn't the smallest either. It was a good stretch across it. She knew how to swim, but she wasn't sure about the foal, and she was so tired that she really didn't want to try it.

But Sammy came up to a square log raft tied beside the river. What a relief!

Sammy jumped onto the raft. Jenny jumped on after him, and the foal after her. Quickly she untied the rope, then lifted the pole and shoved the raft out into the water.

The goblins burst upon them, but stopped at the waterline.

Jenny poled frantically, but the raft moved with agonizing slowness. "Oh, they can swim right across to us!" she gasped, dismayed.

"No, they can't," the centaur said.

"But it's only a little distance!"

He pointed to a ripple in the water. Suddenly a slipper bobbed to the surface. "Water moccasins," he said.

"But that looks like a shoe!" she pointed out.

"It *is* a shoe—but it bites the toes of any footed creature it catches."

Now she saw that inside the moccasin, where the toes would fit, there were sharp white teeth. The tongue curled, slurping around the edge. She wouldn't want to put her foot in that!

The goblins seemed just as reluctant to trust their feet to the water. Several water moccasins were waiting, licking their rims. This was after all a safe place, in its dangerous way!

The current took the raft, moving it downstream. Jenny relaxed, not having to pole anymore. "What river is this?" she asked. "Do you happen to know?"

"I believe it is the With-a-Cookee River," the centaur said. "I heard the goblins say they wanted to avoid it."

"With a cookie?" she asked. "What an odd name! Why would anyone call a river something like that?"

"It might be because of the cookies," he replied, pointing.

She looked, and saw toadstools growing on the bank. But as the raft drifted closer, she saw that they were indeed cookies, or something with a very similar appearance. She reached out and took one, fearing that it would be no more edible than the cherries had been, but it turned out to be what she called a sandie, sugary and crisp. She sat on the raft and ate the rest of it, savoring it.

The centaur picked one himself and tasted it. "Very sweet," he commented. "That's probably because of the sugar sand."

"The what?"

"The sugar sand. It is found throughout much of Xanth, and is excellent for growing sweets. Sometimes I eat it straight, but my dam doesn't like that."

"But sand isn't sweet!" she protested.

He glanced at her, surprised. "You, an elf, do not know of sugar sand?"

"There is no such thing, Chay!"

His brow furrowed. "Are you addressing me?"

Jenny borrowed a notion from the foal's mother. "I think we had better start over. Let's introduce ourselves. You are . . . ?"

"Che Centaur of the winged monsters of Xanth," he replied promptly.

"Che? I thought it was Chay! I'm sorry."

"Quite all right. And you are . . . ?"

"Jenny of the World of Two Moons. Where I come from the sand is made of crushed rock or something; we can't eat it."

"Crushed sugar crystal," he said. "From the big Rock Candy Mountains, I believe. I gather you are not a local elf. Where is your elm?"

"What's all this business about elms?" she demanded. "I never saw an elm!"

"But all elves are associated with elf elms," he said. "They never stray far from them, because their vitality is inversely proportional to their distance from their home elm. If you are far from yours, you must be feeling quite weak now."

"I'm not associated with any elm!" she said. "No elves I know are! I'm tired, yes, but not weak because of any tree!"

He pondered. "I assumed your land of two moons was merely one that my dam had not yet educated me about. Do you mean to say it is beyond Xanth? In another land where there are doubled moons?"

"Yes. My world is nothing like this one! I never heard of Xanth before, and I find it impossibly strange. All these

magic things like cherries that explode and man-animals
that fly—'' She paused. "Oh, no offense."

"None taken. Centaurs derive from the stock of the human folk and the horse folk—and of course my kind derives
also from bird folk, ultimately. My grandsire was a hip-
pogryph."

"A what?"

"You would call it a horse with the head of a bird."

Jenny shook her head. "If I weren't right here talking to
you, I think I wouldn't believe any of this. But I did see
your mother fly."

"Yes, my dam makes herself light by flicking her body
with her tail; then she can fly. But my wings are as yet
insufficiently formed for that, so I have to content myself
with leaps when necessary."

"You can make yourself light?" she asked, surprised.

"I can make anything light," he said. "But of course I
don't do it indiscriminately. That would not be polite."

"I wish you could make me light!" she said. "Then
maybe I wouldn't be so tired!"

"As you wish." Che flicked her shoulder with the tip of
his tail.

Immediately Jenny felt quite light. She got up—and almost sailed off the raft! "I really am light!" she exclaimed.

"Certainly. But be careful, because I cannot make you
heavy again. My magic is one-way. But the effect slowly
fades."

Jenny felt her mind spinning, and not because her head
was light. There really was magic here, practiced by ordinary folk instead of High Ones, and it worked on her!
That explained a great deal.

"I remain unclear how you came to Xanth if you are
from a foreign region," Che said.

"I'm unclear on that myself! I was following Sammy,
and when he found what he was looking for—which was
one of your feathers—we were here."

"Oh, that explains it. Sammy's a magic creature."

"No, he just has an uncanny ability to find whatever he looks for."

"Isn't that magic?"

Jenny reconsidered. "I suppose it is. Certainly it is now, because he's finding things much faster and better than he used to."

"Do you have a magic talent of your own?"

"Me?" She laughed. "I can hardly do regular things, let alone magic ones! I'm fortunate just to see straight, thanks to these nice spectacles your mother gave me."

"Do you mean to say you have not tried?"

Jenny was intrigued. "You mean you really think I might have some magic? Like making things light or heavy or something?"

"It seems possible. Human folk all have talents, and some other creatures have them too, if they have human lineage. Elves as a general class seem to be content with their tribal magic associated with their elms, but if you are not of that type, perhaps you conform to the human mode."

"I wonder what mine could be?" For the first time she had found a really positive reason to be here in this weird world.

"Oh—I forgot. Mundanes don't have magic. Only folk made in Xanth."

"What's a Mundane?"

"A person or animal originating in the dreary nonmagic realm beyond Xanth. My dam does not like to speak of it."

"But I'm not from there! Does Mundania have two moons?"

"I don't think so. Just one moon, like ours, only its green cheese has calcified into inedible rock."

"A moon made of green cheese?"

"And honey on the other side. My sire and dam went to the honey moon, where they conceived me. Perhaps that is where I obtained my taste for sweets."

"So if I'm not from Xanth or Mundania, then we don't know whether I have magic," Jenny concluded. "But if Sammy has magic, maybe I do too."

"Perhaps it is true," Che said doubtfully.

"Why did the goblins kidnap you?"

"I assume they wished to eat me."

"Eat you!" she exclaimed, horrified. "But that would be mean, cruel, and awful!"

"True. That is the nature of goblins. Yet I confess to bewilderment that they did not slaughter me immediately. They seem to be saving me for some future occasion."

"They certainly had you all tied up!" she agreed.

"They seemed to be taking me somewhere. The men are brutes, of course, but Godiva kept them from mistreating me. Goblin women are much nicer than goblin men, of course. The fact that she was put in charge of the party suggests that something other than incidental mayhem is involved. It is quite odd."

"How did they get you? Didn't you know to stay away from goblins?"

"Certainly I knew! But they tempted me with the smell of baking pastry and I couldn't help myself. If you think sugar sandies are good, you should taste fresh pastry! Then a horrible fog surrounded me, and suddenly I was all trussed up and the captive of goblins. I think they had a one-way path."

"A one-way path? But all paths go both ways!"

"By no means! Magic paths typically are unidirectional, and some can be used only once. I suspect that the goblins used theirs to convey me a distance from my home glade, so that my dam would not be able to follow my tracks. Now they have exhausted their path spell and must proceed in more ordinary fashion. But they seem not to be local goblins, for they do not know the local terrain. Godiva was exploring the region ahead when you came upon me."

Jenny decided not to argue about the directions of paths; when she saw a one-way path, then she would believe it, not before. "It's funny that they ran into such trouble. I would have thought they would just take you straight back where they came from."

"That was my conjecture. But apparently something malfunctioned, because when they stepped off the magic path, they seemed bewildered. They were supposed to be on the east side of the Elements, and instead they were on the west side.''

"But a path can't just change where it goes!"

"Ordinarily they don't, but that is by no means fixed. Because this was a speed path, the scenery around it was blurred; they must have assumed that they were going in the right direction. We walked for perhaps half an hour before coming to the end, and then of course we had to get off, and it was gone. When Godiva saw where we were, she said something almost unladylike, which is unusual for a gobliness.''

"She didn't sound ladylike to me!" Jenny said stoutly. "I heard her calling the men stupid, and worse."

"No, she was addressing them by their names: Moron, Idiot, and Imbecile. Stupid did not come on this mission."

"Goblins have funny names!" Jenny said, laughing.

He smiled. "I understand they consider our names to be odd, too." Then he glanced up. "Oh, I fear trouble!"

Jenny looked. "But that's just a little cloud! We have nothing to fear from that."

"On the contrary! That looks very much like Cumulo Fracto Nimbus, the very worst of clouds. He brings mischief to all good folk and even some evil folk."

"A *cloud*? Oh, pooh!"

But Che looked extremely worried. "I hope you do not receive more of an education than you desire, Jenny Elf. Perhaps Fracto is merely passing by."

But the cloud was not passing by. It loomed in close, becoming darker and larger. It seemed almost to have a nebulous face on it, with two big eyes and a bigger mouth. Then the mouth opened, and the cloud blew—and a cold wind rocked the raft.

Waves formed, and they advanced on the raft and rocked it. The cloud swelled up denser and uglier, and thunder rumbled within it. The wind whipped the foliage of the trees, and the first big raindrops spattered against the raft.

"Maybe we had better pole in to shore," Jenny said, worried. "I don't want to get washed off the raft, with those water moccasins waiting."

"Perhaps that is best," Che agreed.

Jenny lifted the pole. But she remained light, while it remained heavy; now it seemed heavier than she was, which made poling awkward. But that was readily solved: Che flicked the pole with his tail, and it became light.

She shoved them toward the shore. But as she did, evil little faces appeared. The goblins!

Hastily she shoved the raft back away. The goblins stood and waved their stubby fists. Some of them had stones, but they did not throw them. There were more than there had been before—six, at least, that she saw. They must have gotten reinforcements.

"We can't go ashore," she said.

"I fear we can't stay in midstream, either," Che said.

"Maybe it's safe on the other side." She poled across.

But the water got deeper in the center, making the poling increasingly difficult. The storm intensified, so that the waves washed over the raft. Sammy was not keen on involuntary baths, and jumped up to Jenny's shoulder to hiss at the water.

The raft spun around. Jenny lost her footing and felt herself sliding off. She screamed—but Che caught her arm and prevented her from landing in the water. His four feet gave him a better anchorage; he had his hooves braced against the ridges of the raft.

Still the storm raged. Jenny knew now that Che was right: this was no ordinary cloud, but a magically malign demon of a cloud, out to get them. She couldn't guess why it hated them so, but it was doing its utmost to dump them in the river. She had not believed in the deliberate malignancy of weather, but now she did!

A gust of wind caught the raft and shoved it to the bank Jenny was trying to leave. She tried to stop it with the pole, but the thing caught in the bottom muck and was twisted out of her grasp. She was after all no big human man; she was a little elf girl, not used to this sort of thing.

The waves gathered for one concluding effort. They lifted the raft and tilted it so sharply that elf, cat, and centaur slid off it and into the shallow water. Jenny screamed as she splashed.

But the water moccasins did not clamp onto their toes. It seemed that the storm had scared them too, and they were either stunned or elsewhere. The goblins charged in and grabbed Jenny and Che. In a moment both were hopelessly tied up.

"Find help, Sammy!" Jenny cried desperately, though she feared there was no help to be had.

Sammy jumped past the goblins and disappeared. Maybe he would find help—but how would the help find them? For she knew the goblins wouldn't just leave her by the bank of the With-a-Cookee River. What had she accomplished in her effort to save the foal? Nothing but a delay, she feared. Now she was in just as much trouble as he.

Chapter 3. Electra's Exam

Electra watched Chex fly away with Grundy Golem. She hoped Che was found soon, but she had a bad feeling about it all. The foal had been kidnapped, and that meant that someone was trying to hide him away. He would not turn up innocently wandering through the forest.

Who could want to do such an awful thing? Che was the only winged centaur foal in Xanth. If something happened to him, it would cut off the childhood of that entire species. That was even worse than an ordinary kidnapping, bad as that was. She wasn't sure that anything like that had happened in Xanth before.

Nada looked grim. She was such a lovely young woman in her human form that she looked terrific even that way! Electra envied her, and had no trouble understanding why Prince Dolph liked her better than Electra. *Electra* liked Nada better than Electra! She was a princess and a really nice person, too. If Electra could have chosen any woman to compete against, Nada would have been at the very bottom of her list. But for friends, the top of the list.

"We'd better get moving," Nada said. She became a giant serpent.

Electra got on the serpent's back. Nada moved, sinuously gathering speed. There was a certain similarity to the way she walked in the human form, but then it had more effect

on the eyeballs of any men in the vicinity: they practically
popped out of their sockets. As a matter of fact, the golem's
eyes had bulged similarly just now, perhaps because Nada
was not wearing her clothing. Grundy had a perfectly lovely
wife, Rapunzel, but like all males of any size he liked to
stare at whatever else was in sight. He had not given Electra
a second glance, and not just because she was clothed. No
man gave her a second glance when she was with Nada, as
she usually was. She was used to it.

It was too bad that Nada did not love Dolph the way he
loved her. But of course she was five years older than he,
now twenty to his fifteen. Nada was a poised young woman,
while Dolph—well, even Electra had to admit that he was
sort of unpolished. Electra loved him anyway; she couldn't
help it, because of the enchantment she had fallen into. She
had to love and marry the Prince who had kissed her awake
after her thousand year (well, almost) sleep. She had not
been the one who was supposed to make that sleep, and
she was certainly no princess. But Evil Magician Murphy's
curse had fouled everything up, and she had somehow bitten
the apple and fallen into the special coffin, and now she
was here.

Actually, Murphy wasn't all that bad, now that he had
renounced his claim to the throne of Xanth. He had used
his magic to help his son, Grey, get out of his horrible
obligation to the evil machine Com-Pewter. Maybe eight
hundred years in the Brain Coral's pool, pickled in brine,
had mellowed Murphy and twenty more years in Mundania
had finished the job. Electra had forgiven him what he had
done to her with his curse. She had sort of had to, because
if that hadn't happened, she would have been long since
dead and forgotten. Such things made a difference. Still, it
wasn't any great situation she was in now: in love with a
Prince who loved her best friend instead.

In fact, she was coming to a crisis. The Good Magician
had done some research in the Book of Answers and discovered that there was a time limit to her enchantment. If
she didn't marry the Prince by the time she was eighteen

years old, she would die anyway. Betrothal could hold her only until she came of age; then she had to perform. If she did not marry him and consummate the marriage before she was eighteen, she would die on the stroke of her birthday.

It was tricky judging exactly how old she was because of her most-of-a-millennium sleep, but they had figured it out: only her normal life counted. So her aging had halted the moment she fell into the enchanted sleep and resumed when she woke from it. By that reckoning, she would be eighteen next week. Dolph would have to choose. He couldn't avoid it, because if he did nothing she would die, leaving only Nada for him to marry. His parents had laid down the Word: he could not do it by default. He had to Decide, and then marry the one he chose, and it would be done. One way or the other.

In a way it was good to have this distraction of Che's kidnapping, because it took her mind from her own problem or at least made her remember that she wasn't the only one in Xanth with something to worry about. Many folk had problems, after all! She knew she was lucky to have come here, and lived these past six years in Castle Roogna with good friends and her great love. Even if it was magical in origin and hopeless, it was still a great wonderful thing in her heart.

She wiped the tears from her face with the back of her hand. Why should she be crying, really?

Travel was swift down the magic path, and before long they were there. Electra dismounted, and Nada resumed her human form and donned her dress, panties, and slippers, which Electra had carried in her knapsack. The dress and slippers didn't matter, but it was essential that no male eye see the panties. They were exciting pink, while Electra's were dull white, but no males were supposed to know that. What would Xanth come to, if anything like that happened?

Nada turned to her, as they stood outside the castle moat. "I wish he would marry you," she said.

"I know." But they both knew that their preferences

didn't count. Only Dolph's counted. He would choose, and the one he chose would marry him. That had been understood from the outset, ever since Queen Irene had declared that he could not marry both. One man with two wives? It just wasn't proper, for some reason.

They gazed at the castle. It looked ordinary, but the drawbridge was up. That meant that they couldn't just go in.

They exchanged most of a glance. Good Magician Humfrey wasn't here now, but Grey Murphy was doing his best to substitute in the interim. He had the Book of Answers and all the collections of vials and spells and things, and Ivy to Enhance him when he needed it. He had done well enough, all things considered, these past three years, though Electra understood he sometimes had to scramble for a difficult Answer. He had set up the same rules Humfrey had maintained: any applicant had to pass three challenges to get into the castle and then to give one year's service or the equivalent. That was to weed out those who weren't really serious. Even so, there were quite a number of folk with Questions. Several were sitting by the bank of the moat now, evidently trying to make up their minds whether their Questions were really important enough to warrant the price required for the Answers. That explained why the drawbridge was up; otherwise those folk might simply have walked on in.

Nada nodded, and her gray-brown tresses bobbed prettily. Electra's tresses were brown too, but somehow they never bobbed; they just hung there listlessly, no matter how she tried to fix them. "I think Grey can't afford to play favorites," she said.

Electra agreed. No favorites! Nada's other best friend was Ivy, and even Ivy got a trifle nervous when Nada got too close to her fiancé, Grey. Why Ivy and Grey were affianced, while Dolph, Nada, and Electra were betrothed, was a question none of them had ever quite worked out. So Grey couldn't afford to let Nada in without challenge, while others watched.

"Maybe I can go in alone," Electra suggested.

"Alone?" Nada's brown-gray eyes were beautifully perplexed. Electra's eyes were forgettable, whether perplexed or excited. Even she could not remember their color, if they had any.

"No one will notice if I go in."

" 'Lectra, are you going into another inferiority tizzy?" Nada demanded severely.

"Well—" Electra said guiltily.

"I won't have it! You're a great friend and a great girl, and only an idiot wouldn't notice you!"

"How about Dolph?" Electra asked wryly.

"He *is* an idiot!"

Then they both laughed, appreciating the painful truth of that.

"Anyway," Nada said after a moment, "it's not you or me, it's that the drawbridge is up and we can't ask favors. So we'll just have to forge in any way we can, just like anyone else. We do have a Question, after all."

"Not the one I'd like to ask."

"Maybe we can get Dolph to ask it."

"We'd have to dose him with a love potion first!"

Nada paused. "Now I wonder—"

"Forget it! Even if he loved me, he'd still love you too, and you're everything I'm not, so—"

"Now stop it, 'Lectra! Physical appearance isn't everything."

"Right. There's also the matter of royalty versus peasant, and niceness versus—"

"You're nice, 'Lectra! You're as nice as anyone, and—"

"And I have freckles too."

"Oh, you're hopeless!" Nada exclaimed in exasperation. She was lovely when exasperated, as Electra wasn't.

"That's what I've been trying to tell you."

Nada changed the subject. "So we'll both go in. Together. As soon as we figure out how."

Electra contemplated the moat. She didn't see any moat

monsters, but they were surely lurking somewhere. It would not be safe to swim, unless Nada became a bigger monster.

"Suppose you become a giant water serpent, and—"

"My thought exactly! Get on."

Nada shrugged out of her clothes, handed them over, and became the serpent. Electra stuffed the clothes in her knapsack and bestrode her, as she had when they traveled the magic path. Nada slid into the water and started across. Electra's feet and dress were getting wet, but she wasn't going to let that stop her; they would dry in due course.

There was a stir at the far shore. Electra peered forward. "All I see is shells," she reported. Then she laughed. "She saw sea shells by the sea shore! Only it's a moat shore."

There was a bang, and something flew toward them. "Duck!" Electra cried.

Nada ducked, and Electra got dunked. But the object missed, plunking into the water behind them.

Nada surfaced, lifting her head for a hiss.

"I don't know," Electra said. "It looked like a flying shell with the number point twenty-two painted on it."

Nada shook her head, unable to make much sense of this. Electra understood her confusion. Since when did shells fly? They normally lay on the beach or under water.

Then there was a bigger bang, and a larger shell came flying. This one had the number .357 on it. "Down!" Electra screamed.

They dived again, and the shell missed.

After a moment they resumed motion—and an even larger shell, marked .45, came flying at them. "Another!" Electra cried, throwing herself aside.

When she came up, something clicked in her head. "It's a challenge!" she gasped. "Those shells are the first line of defense!"

Nada looped around, and they headed back for the outer shore. When they got there, Nada changed to woman form and climbed out. A man farther around the moat fell over; evidently he had gotten too much of an eyeful and was stunned. Electra was sure it wasn't her own bedraggled wet-clothinged body that had done it.

"I never heard of flying shells!" Nada said. "How can we get past, when they keep getting bigger?"

Electra concentrated. "I almost remember something, maybe from when I visited Mundania. Some folk—they like to throw shells at targets, I think. Or at bulls. Something like that. The eyes—it sounds so mean—"

"Bull's-eyes!" Nada exclaimed. "I've heard of that. They aren't really animals, but big painted circles. Maybe if we make one of those, the shells will go for it."

It seemed worth trying. They scrounged around, and found a giant white pillow from a pillow bush, and a patch of Indian paint brushes. They used one of these to paint Indian designs—it wouldn't paint anything else—in a big circle that looked somewhat like an eye. Then they floated this in the moat, the eye looking up.

Sure enough, the shells went for it. And while the shells were distracted by the target, Nada and Electra quietly swam across and emerged on the castle side. The only one to see was another man beyond the moat, and he promptly went rigid and keeled over the way the first had. Nada did have that effect on men, even without her pink panties.

Nada dressed. Electra's knapsack was watertight, so Nada's dress was nice and dry and fresh, while Electra looked like a damp zombie. But she knew that even if her clothes had been fresh, and Nada's sodden, Nada would have been a sight for sore eyes, while Electra would have been a sight to make eyes sore.

But hardly were they through, when the next challenge was upon them. A swarm of flying red objects charged them. Each was roughly heart-shaped but not properly symmetrical; there were ugly tubes protruding from the tops, and great swollen veins around their bodies. Each pulsed horrendously.

"Oh!" Nada cried daintily as one of the grotesque things whammed into her shoulder. Even when under attack, she was ladylike.

"Yuck!" Electra grunted in unladylike fashion as another sailed at her face.

"What *are* they?" Nada asked, trying to avoid another that was threatening to splatter her nice dress with juice exactly the color of blood.

"Monsters of the next challenge!" Electra replied, as the thing missed Nada and scored on her own dress. Bright gore dribbled down it and dripped to her feet.

Nada became a big snake and reared up at the next red blob, her dress hanging awkwardly on her new body. In a moment she slithered out of it. She opened her mouth, showing formidable fangs, and hissed. The blob veered to the side—but another splatted her from behind. Her head whirled to snap at that one—whereupon the one in front splatted its gore on her.

"There are too many of them!" Electra cried. "We can't fight them; we'll just get hopelessly gored. We have to figure out the key to this challenge!"

The snake slithered down into the moat to wash off the splat. That left Electra as the main focus of attention. A huge blob smashed into her chest, trying to knock her down.

She grabbed it, and lifted it up, ready to hurl it into the moat. But she knew it would just loop around and attack her again. The thing was slimy with leaking blood, and worse, it was warm and pulsing. Just as if a living heart had been ripped from—

"*Aaarrghhh!*" she groaned with heartfelt horror. "It *is* a heart!"

The snake became Nada in her natural form: a naga, with the body of a serpent and the head of a woman. "A heart attack!" she exclaimed. "I've heard of them, but I never thought it would happen to me!"

"No one ever does," Electra agreed heartily. She ducked as a bold heart came at her head, and was caught in the rear by another.

She still held the big heart that had hit her chest. It was oddly passive now, though she wasn't holding it hard. She realized that her electrical nature might be affecting it. That heartened her, because it might offer a solution to this challenge.

Her magic talent was electricity. She was constantly building up a charge, and could discharge it all at once by delivering a hefty shock to some monster or gradually as when she made an electrolytic environment for the Heaven Cent. She had heard that hearts used electric pulses to time their beats or something. Maybe these wild hearts were just out of control, and so were attacking anything in the vicinity. If she could put her hands on them and use her electricity to get their pulses even, maybe that would tame them.

She let the big heart go. It floated away, passive, beating steadily, seeming at peace with the world.

She watched for the next, and when it zoomed in she grabbed it. The thing tried to slip out of her grasp, but she clutched it to her. It was hot, and it almost burned her, but she knew it was only heartburn. In a moment, as her hands retained contact, the heart became passive. Then she let it go, and it floated peacefully away. It was working!

"What are you doing, 'Lectra?" Nada called from the moat.

"I'm making a better pace for these hearts," Electra replied. "They're wild because they're out of control."

"You're a good pacemaker," Nada agreed, watching the orderly hearts floating away. "Don't break any!"

"We don't want any broken hearts," Electra agreed as she caught another. She doubted she could ever be a heartbreaker.

Finally every heart was tamed. Electra was a little sad to see the last one drift contentedly off, but she knew it was only heartache. She had surmounted the second challenge.

She went to the moat and washed off the blood. She hoped the tame hearts found good bodies to occupy, because they seemed very warm and friendly and would probably do good service if treated well. She couldn't blame them for being wild, when they were cast out into the world alone.

They emerged from the moat and walked on. Nada's dress was now as wet as Electra's, because she had had to wash

it, but it still looked ten times as good on her as anything
Electra had ever worn had ever looked on her. They came
to an arched gate and went through it, into the castle. There
was a long narrow hall ahead.

But there was something oozing from the far gate. It
looked lumpy and red and sticky, as if a thousand wild
hearts had been squished and dumped in a sodden mass.
Was this where the hearts had come from? No wonder they
had been wild!

Nada sniffed. Then she reached down and put a finger to
the mess, and tasted it. "I thought so: strawberry."

"You mean it's edible?" Electra asked, amazed. "We're
supposed to eat our way through it?"

"I hope not! Strawberry jam is horribly fattening."

"That wouldn't stop me. I can't put on weight no matter
how much I eat. That's my problem."

"That's *not* your problem!" Nada flared. "You're beautifully slender!"

"I'd trade my figure for yours anytime!"

"If I eat any of that jam, you won't want my figure,"
Nada said. "I'd be so fat I could roll without pulling in my
arms or legs."

Electra tried to picture that, and found it hilarious. But
it didn't come out as a healthy laugh, or even a girlish
giggle, just a foolish titter.

She dipped a finger and tasted the jam. "No, this isn't
strawberry, quite. It's too metallic. Not hayberry either.
And look—those aren't exactly berries. They're moving
around."

Nada peered. "You're right! Some are bigger than others,
and they're sort of square. They keep nudging up to each
other and stopping."

"Until something else gets out of the way," Electra
added. "Only things seem to be much better at getting into
the way than out of it."

"And the total effect is one of absolute gooey crawl,"
Nada said. "Not one berry can get where it's going before
all the others do, so they are all made maddeningly slow."

"I think I tasted something like this, once, hundreds of years ago," Electra said. "It was a kind of berry growing in a circle, a—a traffic circle. The berries just kept rolling around and around it until they wore out."

"Those must have been crazy berries!"

"Traffic berries. They're always moving around, except when they get stuck in—"

"Traffic jam," Nada concluded. "And this is one big mess of jam!"

"Yes, it's awful. How can we get by it?"

They watched the jam ooze its way onward. "There's no help for it," Nada said reluctantly. "We'll just have to slog through it. I hope I can take a bath at the other end."

Electra sighed. "I'll go first. I have less to lose."

"No, you don't! You have more to win." Nada stepped into the jam.

Immediately she slowed to a crawl. She tried to move her feet, but there was always something in the way. The jam wouldn't give her any chance to get anywhere.

"This is no good!" Nada gasped. "I can't move!"

Electra reached out to take her hand. "I'll pull you out." But though she did pull, Nada remained stuck in the traffic jam.

"There has to be a better way!" Nada said. "I'm just getting caught worse!"

"Change into a small snake, so I can lift you out," Electra suggested.

Nada did so. She became a garter snake, whose garters had nothing to attach to. Electra closed her hand carefully about the body and pulled, but the snake's tail was hopelessly caught. She just couldn't get free. Finally she changed back to human form, so that she could stand on her own without getting in deeper.

Electra put her hands to her head and ran some current through it, making her brain strain. This enabled her to force out an idea. "Maybe if we could get the jam to go somewhere else," she said, "and leave us here."

"But that's the problem," Nada objected. "It can't move anywhere very fast."

"The traffic berries in it can't move fast," Electra said. "But maybe the whole thing can—if it wants to."

"But what could make it want to?"

Electra fished in her knapsack. "I saw something in my calendar about a festival or something." She pulled out a battered copy of a Xanth calendar and leafed through it. "Yes, here it is! A jamboree!"

The traffic jam quivered.

"But isn't that—" Nada started.

"Yes. It will occur in the Gap Chasm."

The jam began to move. It slid slowly, then more swiftly out of the hall, carrying Nada along with it. Soon it was going at a respectable speed. Electra grabbed onto Nada again, and hung on, and the jam moved onward so rapidly that it lost cohesion and let her feet go.

A moment later they watched the jam sliding on across the moat. There was no question: it was headed for that jamboree. Electra had guessed right; no jam could resist something like that.

"Didn't you make a teeny fib?" Nada asked. "There's no party at the Gap!"

Electra showed her the calendar. "I didn't say it was a party. I said it was a Jamboree. And here it is." She pointed to it.

"The month of Jamboree," Nada said. "But—"

"Right here in the calendar," Electra agreed. "It occurs in the Gap, just as it does everywhere else in Xanth at the same time. The traffic jam is sure to find it, in due course."

Nada shook her head. "I suppose that jam wasn't going anywhere else fast anyway," she said, resigned.

"But *we* are—quick while the passage is clear." She hauled Nada along into the castle. The naga woman let herself be towed, deciding it wasn't worth further protest.

The passage ended in steps that led to a door, and beyond the door was Ivy. She was in a yellow dress that complemented her pale green hair. She was Nada's age, but not as luscious. In that respect she fell more or less between Nada and Electra. "Oh, how wonderful to see you two again!" she exclaimed, hugging each in turn. "Why didn't you tell us you were coming?"

Both Nada and Electra stared at her, caught between astonishment and outrage. Then Ivy's mouth quirked, and in a moment all three were lost in girlish laughter.

"Well, come on," Ivy said as they subsided. "I think Grey's had time to research the Answer now."

Electra nodded. There was reason for the challenges. Not only did they discourage those who weren't really serious, they gave the Magician time to get the necessary information. Few folk knew this, but Nada and Electra were Ivy's closest friends and were privy to some pretty formidable secrets.

Grey Murphy was in the upstairs chamber with the Book of Answers. There were those who claimed there was no such book, but that was just because they hadn't seen it. It had answers to every question; the only problem was figuring out how to read them and understand them. Grey had been working on it for three years now and was getting better, but he still had to scramble at times.

"We'll dispense with the year of service," Grey said with a smile. "Ivy says her friends are exempt, or else."

"We thought as much," Nada agreed with an answering smile. "Are you ready for our Question?"

"I think so. But I'm afraid you won't much like the Answer. Are you sure you want to ask?"

"Yes," Electra said. "We don't have much time."

"Very well. Ask."

"Where is Che Centaur?"

Grey stared at her. "What?"

"She said, 'Where is Che Centaur?'" Nada said. "You know, Chex's foal."

"But—" Grey looked baffled.

Nada frowned, managing to look beautiful at the same time. "What's the matter—did we ask the wrong Question?"

"I just researched the problem of your betrothals!" Grey exclaimed.

It was Nada and Electra's turn to stare. Then both burst into laughter. "We never thought of that!" Electra cried.

"That's next week's problem," Nada added.

Grey brushed his hair-colored hair back and looked sheepish. It was a fairly easy expression for him. "I guess I was too busy with technicalities. I just assumed—" He shrugged. "This presents a problem."

"You mean you don't know where Che is?" Electra asked, "because you were checking into our triangle problem? I guess that's a problem, all right."

"Maybe the mirror knows," he said. Most magic mirrors were fairly transparent, but some were brighter than others.

He rummaged in a drawer and brought out a hand mirror. "The problem with this one is that it has to be questioned in rhyme, and the format's limited, and it isn't always quite current." He pondered for a moment, then addressed it: "Mirror, mirror, in the desk, is Che Centaur picturesque?"

"That query is grotesque!" the mirror responded, matching the rhyme. But a scene showed on it, of the little centaur tied, hobbled, and guarded by goblins.

Nada, Electra, and Ivy stifled similar exclamations of horror. He had been stolen by goblins!

"But there are several goblin tribes," Nada said. "There're the goblins of Mount Etamin that my folk war against—"

"And the goblins east of the Element of Earth," Electra added.

"And the Goblinate of the Golden Horde," Ivy said with a shudder.

"There are goblins all over Xanth," Grey said. "There are references to them in many of Magician Humfrey's papers. Most of them live well underground. But the mirror showed a surface scene. That limits it somewhat."

"Can you ask the mirror to be more specific?" Electra asked.

"No, it will only answer a given question once. Also, this could be from several hours ago. I'm afraid I'll have to research it in the Book of Answers." He looked glum.

"How long will that take?" Electra asked, concerned.

"Probably several more hours. It's not the sort of Answer I'm good at finding, yet."

"But Che's in danger *now*! We can't wait several more hours!"

Nada leaned toward him, her wet dress clinging and heaving in the way that no dress ever did on Electra. "Isn't there some other way, Grey?" she breathed.

"Find a way," Ivy said quickly. Her mouth was momentarily grim. One might almost have thought she didn't want Nada having to ask him any more questions.

"What?" Grey seemed distracted for a moment. Nada's dresses tended to have that effect on men, even when dry. It was a good thing her pink panties weren't showing, Electra thought, or he would have been unable to speak at all. "Oh, yes. Maybe the ghost writer."

"Who?" Electra asked.

"He's a ghost doing his year's service for an Answer," Ivy explained. "But he's very shy, and doesn't speak or show himself to others. So when he has to communicate, he writes."

"But how would a ghost know about something like this? Isn't he tied to his place of death?"

"No, this one is able to travel," Grey said, "because he's not associated with any one locale; he can operate anywhere. He moves very quickly, so may be foggy on details, but he should be able to give us a general notion."

"Well, ask him, then," Electra said impatiently.

Grey frowned. "He may not answer."

"But if he's doing service—"

"He's nervous about goblins," Grey said. "It seems that

the Goblinate of the Golden Horde caught him and cooked him in a pot. That's how he died. He hasn't been the same since. He says it was a bad review. Writers don't like bad reviews.''

Electra was able to appreciate that. She wouldn't have cared to get potted like that herself.

"So we don't like to push him, where goblins are concerned," Ivy said.

Electra looked helplessly at Nada. What were they to do?

But Nada had a notion. "Is he here now?"

"In the castle, yes," Grey said. "I can call him. But—"

"Tell him I'll let him kiss me, if he can tell me where Che is," she said. "And give him a good view. I mean, review."

She had been right the first time, Electra thought. Nada's dress clung to her tightly, except where it was forced to jump the gap across her heaving bosom. If the ghost floated close enough to kiss her, he would get the best view available in Xanth.

"That might encourage him," Grey said. He looked into blank air. "Ghorge—" He paused, evidently waiting for the ghost. "We would like to know which goblins have captured Che Centaur. Nada Naga, the woman with the—" He hesitated, his eyes traveling across wet assets and valley-hurdling cloth, until Ivy made a frowning ahem. "The amazing, uh, dress, she, er, will let you kiss her, if you answer."

Actually, Electra's dress was wet too, but it didn't have to strain to cross her front, and nobody's eyes got hung up on it, and the promise of kissing her would not have excited a living man, let alone a ghost. She might have been resentful, if Nada hadn't been such a good friend and fellow Betrothee.

After a moment Grey lifted a sheet of paper from the desk. *Very well*, was written on it, in ornate script.

Nada walked to the center of the chamber, put her hands behind her back, lifted her chin, pursed her lips, closed her

eyes, and inhaled. Her décolletage went into terminal strain.
Ivy crossed quickly to Grey and put her hands over his eyes
just as the last event was starting. That was probably just
as well, Electra thought, because those eyes had been in
danger of popping loose.

After a moment Electra saw something. Writing was appearing on the sheet of paper, written by an invisible hand.
It said: *Go find Che, With a Cookee.*

"Ghorge's given the answer!" Electra exclaimed, jumping with excitement. She could afford to do that, even in a
wet dress; with Nada it would have been dangerous.

Nada opened her eyes. "He's really cool!" she said.

"Well, he *is* dead," Ivy reminded her. "But I think that
is a good review."

More writing appeared. *Never a cleavage like that short
of the Gap Chasm!* Electra didn't bother to call attention to
that message; it didn't seem relevant. "But what kind of
cookie do we need to find Che?" she asked.

Grey looked at the message. "I think he means the With-
a-Cookee River. That must be where he saw Che."

"Already?" Electra asked. "But he hasn't had time to
travel around!"

"Oh, he has, he has," Ivy said. "He's very fast, being
unlimited by mortal considerations. Now, Nada, let's get
some dry clothing on you. You too, 'Lectra."

They went with Ivy and got changed and snatched a bite
to eat. By that time the day was getting late.

"We have to be on our way," Electra said.

"We can get you there," Ivy said. "Grey has been re-
searching the gourd while we were eating."

"The gourd?" Electra asked, alarmed. "We don't want
to get caught in that!"

Ivy laughed. "Don't worry, you won't. The Night Stallion needed an Answer, and he paid for it by giving us a
few big gourds. We use them for emergency transport. All
you have to do is step in the one here, and follow the path
to the one near the With-a-Cookee River, and step out. That
will get you there almost immediately." She paused, look-

ing concerned. "But it's pretty rough country there, and the goblins can be bad. Maybe we should give you some extra magic to handle things."

Electra considered. "Nada can handle just about anything, in serpent form. But maybe we could use something to signal for help, in case we do get in trouble. We have a whistle, but if the goblins are listening, they might come before our friends and make things worse."

"We happen to have some sparkleberries," Ivy said. "A branch of them should do nicely." She went to a cupboard and brought out a small branch with round green leaves and little black berries. She picked several berries and handed them to Electra. "You activate them electrically; that will be easy for you. Just hold one and run a charge through it and throw it up, and it will sparkle enough to alert anyone in the area, especially at night."

"Thank you," Electra said. "We'll set one off when we find Che, if we need help in getting him away from the goblins."

Ivy led them to the cellar. Grey was there, standing before a huge hypnogourd. "This doesn't take just your mind, it takes your body," he said. "I have nulled its magic for safekeeping, but I'll free it long enough for you to enter. Hold hands as you step in, so you don't get separated. You must follow the right path or you will get lost. Since you are going to the With-a-Cookee River outlet, watch for a cookie or a symbol of one. That will show you the correct path, when there is any choice of paths. You will arrive in just a few minutes, if you keep moving. Don't tell anyone about the gourd; we prefer to keep this system private."

Electra was impressed. "I should think so! You must be able to get anywhere in Xanth in a hurry!"

"Pretty much," Grey agreed. "Wherever we have big gourds placed, anyway. Now, are you ready?"

Electra and Nada nodded.

"Don't be surprised by anything you see in the gourd," Ivy said. "Remember, it's the realm of dreams. Just stay on the cookie path, and you'll have no problem. Don't let any of the dreams tempt you away from that path."

"We won't," Electra promised.

Then Grey released the magic. The gourd seemed to glow faintly. The two girls stepped into the peephole.

Chapter 4. Dolph's Dilemma

Dolph pondered briefly as he approached the Element of Air. What form would be best for this? He was in young man form at the moment, having used it to take a stick and poke a suitable hole in the flypaper surrounding the kingdom of the flies, but he doubted that would do for Air. He knew there would be air currents of all kinds here, including fierce storms. He could become a squat turtle and let it all blow safely over him, but it would take him forever to explore it. He needed to check it quickly, because if Che Centaur were here, he could be in serious trouble, and time would be of the essence. But if Dolph assumed a flying form, he could get blown everywhere else but wherever Che was, and that was no good either.

He came to the border. On one side were green plants and manure and rotting things, suitable for the delight of flies; on the other was a turmoil of wind.

He decided that a flying form was best, but not one that could be blown about. So he assumed the form of a ghost. He wasn't a true ghost, of course, because he wasn't dead; he just looked like one and acted like one, and the wind couldn't touch him because he wasn't solid enough.

He floated through the border. The wind tried to take him and hurl him about, but it couldn't get a grip on him. It howled with exasperation.

This might once have been a nice region, but the wind had scoured the soil from the land and the clouds from the sky. Probably it had also blown away the stars of the night. But he wasn't here to appreciate the view; he had to find Che, if he were here, and to be sure he was somewhere else if he weren't here.

He floated around just inside the border, picking up speed. He would spiral in toward the center of Air, looking at everything; he didn't dare miss one spot, lest that be the one where a poor injured foal lay waiting for rescue. Actually, since Che had been foal-napped, he probably wasn't alone, but captive of some other creature. Still, that creature or creatures could be holding him here, so it was best to look for a house or shelter too, and inspect any he spied.

This was a dull region, once he allowed for the violence of the wind. There was no vegetation at all, just sand, and the wind was constantly whipping it up into sandstorms. If anyone sat on the ground long, he would be buried in sand. A captor shouldn't take Che here for that.

Then Dolph had another bad thought. Suppose someone were mad at Chex or Cheiron and wanted to make them suffer? He could steal their foal away and dump him here, and they would certainly suffer! He wouldn't care that the foal could not survive in all the wind and sand; that would be the point.

Did he really want to find Che, if that was the case? A dead foal buried under sand?

No, that was too horrible! Nobody would want to do that to the winged centaurs. The regular centaurs didn't like them, because centaurs had very strict notions about species purity, but all centaurs were creatures of honor who would not stoop to any such malice. The other winged monsters certainly wouldn't, because all of them were sworn to protect their own; Dolph had crashed Chex's wedding ceremony and knew how the Simurgh had impressed this on them, and on Dolph too. Of course the land monsters weren't bound, but most of them lacked the wit to foal-knap him; they would simply eat him and be done with it. So the chances were that this was a more organized effort and that the foal wouldn't be left in a place like this.

Little dust devils sported among the moving sand dunes, being watched by their parent tornadoes. They had fun sucking up the sand and throwing it around. This was one big sandlot, for them. But there was no sign of Che or any other living thing. Dolph was glad.

Then a dust devil swung in toward him. He veered to the side to avoid it, but it veered too. He moved the other way, and it matched him. It was following him!

Well, it couldn't hurt him. "Whaaat doo yooo waaant?" he called in ghost accent, realizing that this was something more than a freak of nature.

The whirling cone was replaced by another ghost. "So you are an intruder!" it said, with no ghostly distortion. "Who are you?"

"I'm Prince Dolph of the human folk," he replied. "Who are you?"

The ghost swirled and became devastatingly female. "Well, now, a living man! This is most intriguing."

"You didn't answer my question," he said.

"I am the Demoness Metria," she said. "I have had some limited dealings with your benevolent."

"My what?" he asked blankly.

"Your compassionate, gentle, humane," she said crossly.

"Oh, you mean my kind," he said, catching on.

"Whatever. What are you doing here, Prince?"

"I'm looking for Che Centaur, who was foal-napped by a party unknown." Then it occurred to him that the demons could be responsible. Maybe he had said too much!

"Oh, that," she said, disinterested. "He's not here."

"He isn't?"

"No, the goblins took him. I suppose they want him for food, and to feed the little goblins too."

"Feed the little goblin stew?" Dolph asked, horrified.

"Why else would goblins want horsemeat?"

"Horsemeat!" he exclaimed. "He's a winged centaur, a unique species!"

"Well, you don't think they want him for his proclivity, do you?"

"His what?"

"His bent, disposition, inclination, penchant, propensity," she said, annoyed.

Dolph concentrated, and after a bit it came to him. "His mind?"

"Whatever. What would a goblin care about that?"

"Nothing," he said.

"Precisely. So you might as well be on your way."

"Wait a minute, demoness! How can I believe you? Maybe *you* stole Che, and you're trying to distract me!"

She focused her ghostly eyes on him. "Listen, vacuum-head, if I wanted to distract you, I wouldn't bother with words. I have easier ways."

"Yeah? Like what?"

"How old are you, Prince?"

"Fifteen, going on sixteen. What does that have to do with it?"

"And I'm a hundred and fifteen, going on a decade or two more. I lose count. But my age doesn't matter; it's yours that is critical. Do you know how to summon the stork?"

"No! No one will tell me! Not even my Betrothee."

"Your what?"

"My fiancée, girlfriend, promised, engagée."

"Oh, you mean your prospective ball and chain."

"Whatever. Why do you ask?"

"Because it's more fun to pester innocents. Human folk are pretty dull creatures, but ignorant young men are subject to amusing temptations. Maybe I'll keep you with me for a while, so I can entertain myself. It's been a decade or so since I've toyed with a mortal man."

"Oh? Who was that?"

"I forget. An ogre, I think, only he looked like a man. Aristocrat."

"What?"

"Patrician, gentleman, esquire."

"Oh, you mean Esk Ogre!"

"Whatever. Why did you ask?"

Dolph opened his ghost mouth, but discovered that he had forgotten whatever they had been talking about. "Enough of this. I have to find Che Centaur."

"But I told you he's not here."

Now he remembered: that was how all this had started. "You're of the demon folk. I can't trust you. So I'm going to keep looking."

"Do you mind if I tag along on your futile search?"

"Yes! Go away!"

"Great! I'll stay right with you."

Oops. He had made the mistake of admitting that her presence bothered him. "I'll ignore you."

"Suppose I tell you how to summon the stork?"

He stopped in the air. "You will?"

"Of course not! Don't you know about the Adult Conspiracy?"

"But you're a demoness. You don't honor that stuff."

"Of course I do!" she said indignantly. "It's the best torment yet devised for children."

"I'm not a child!"

"You are until you figure out the secret."

She had him there. "So you won't tell me, you mare. Go away."

"I'm a what?"

"Ewe, doe, hen, sow, lioness—" He broke off. "Oh, now you've got *me* doing it! Female wolf—I can't think of the word."

"Ha! You're young and innocent. You don't *know* the word!"

She had nailed him again. "And you won't tell me. So go away and let me finish my search."

But she lingered, her shape becoming even more shapely. "I won't tell you the secret about the stork, but I might show you."

She had his interest again, but he still didn't trust her. "What's the catch?"

"You have to resume manform."

"Nuh-uh! Not until I finish searching the Elements."

Metria frowned prettily. "You're being unreasonable, Dolph. *I'm* the one who is supposed to be difficult! Why don't you give up this hopeless search and let me show you the stork's secret?"

"Because I don't trust you! Not only will you stop me from finding Che, you'll fade out without showing me anything, and leave me twice as frustrated as before."

She nodded. "You're getting smarter. But you know, there is something more important you should be doing now."

Again, foolishly, he paid attention. "What could be more important than finding Che?"

"Plugging the hole."

He couldn't make sense of this. "Are you referring to the stork again?"

She laughed so hard she dissolved into fragments of smoke, and it took her a while to resume her shapely shape. "I could have been, but I wasn't. What an *entendre!*"

"What?"

"Never mind; it's not in the dictionary anyway. The Muses are way behind the times. No, I mean the hole in Xanth where the foreign elf and her foreign cat come through."

"*What* foreign elf?"

"The one who's with Che now, helping him flee the goblins. How do you think she got here, otherwise?"

Dolph knew she was trying to confuse him, but he didn't want to admit how well she was succeeding. "Why should the hole be plugged?"

"Because alien monsters may come through it. The elf is harmless, but what else follows her is not. All Xanth could be threatened. That's not just a hole between two worlds, it's between a squintillion worlds, and the Simurgh only knows what connection may be next."

"Why didn't you plug it, then?"

She shrugged. "It would be tedious. But I'll show you where it is, if you wish."

"But if it threatens Xanth, it threatens you too! You wouldn't just let it be. You're just trying to distract me again."

She nodded. "That, too."

"I don't understand you!"

"Well, you're only human," she said condescendingly. "Worse, you're only male."

"So I'm just going to ignore you and go on with my search."

"Lotsa luck, obtuse."

"What?"

"Acute, right, oblique, reflex, angle—no, wait. I mean dull, uninformed, slow-witted, blunt, dense—"

"Stupid?"

"Thank you." She floated forward and kissed him on the forehead. "Stupid."

Somehow Dolph was not completely satisfied. But he realized that it was pointless to keep talking with her. He resumed his search for Che.

Soon he completed his spiral around the Region of Air, having found nothing. He approached the Region of Earth, and drifted through the border between them.

This section was just as violent, but in a different way. The air cleared and the sandstorm died out, but now it was the land in motion. It trembled, quivered, and even went so far as to shake. To the north was a giant volcano spewing out red liquid.

"That's boiling lava," the demoness said beside him. "I don't think you want to put your feet in that."

"It won't hurt ghost feet."

"But the hot gases may dissolve you."

Dolph thought she was just teasing him, but wasn't quite sure. He had never tried his ghost form—or any other form—in volcanic gas. So he steered well clear of the nasty mountain. He could see farther here, because the air was clearer, so could move more rapidly without missing anything important.

Yet as he moved, he wondered. Was it possible that the demoness was telling the truth? That Che had already been found? If so, he was wasting his time here. But if that was true, then what about the business of the hole in Xanth? If a foreign elf had come through with her cat, what else was likely to follow? He really shouldn't ignore that.

"You're cute when your ghostly brow furrows like that," Metria remarked.

"Go jump in a hypnogourd!"

"You're even cuter when you try to be clever. Does your future mate—the one who won't tell you about stork summoning—appreciate your cleverness?"

"No," he replied shortly.

"Why not?"

"Because she doesn't love me," he said, before remembering not to talk to the demoness. Oh, well, the infernal creature had probably already caught on to that.

"I thought you human folk didn't marry without love, foolish as that may be."

"We don't. It's complicated."

"I love complexity! How did it happen?"

What was the use? She would keep pestering him anyway, and maybe she would have an answer for his dilemma. "I needed help from the naga folk," he said. "They are serpents with the heads of human folk. Their king said I would have to marry his daughter, Nada Naga, so that my folk would help their folk against the goblins. But I was too young, so I was betrothed to her instead. She could assume serpent form or human form, because the naga have ancestry in both. But I can take other forms too, including serpent and naga. I liked her, and then I loved her. But she was doing it just because she had to; she never loved me."

"What, an animal girl failed to love a handsome human prince? How could she!"

Dolph realized that she was being sarcastic, demonfashion, but he ignored it. It helped him just to describe the situation. "She was beautiful herself, and a princess too, and half human. But she is five years older. To her I was just a child. So she couldn't love me."

"That's easy to solve. Just have her drink from a love spring in your presence."

"Yes, when I marry her next week she'll do that. But there's something else."

"You are full of surprises, Prince!" But the edge of her sarcasm was not as sharp; she was curious.

They completed the Region of Earth and floated into the next, the Region of Fire, which was surrounded by a tall wall of fire. Within the region flames reached hungrily for the sky, but no matter how hard they tried, they couldn't burn up the sky, quite. But the trees below were having a difficult time of it.

This search, too, was dull. So when the demoness floating beside him through the flames inquired about the something else, he answered.

"I have a second Betrothee."

"Now that I believe is unusual for your kind. We demons have no limits about such things—in fact we have no betrothals or marriages, we just do what comes unnaturally. But I never heard of a human man marrying two women." She considered. "In Xanth, I mean. They do it in Mundania, though usually one at a time. But that doesn't count. Mundanes are crazy."

"I don't know. Grey Murphy's Mundane, and he's not crazy."

"He's not in Mundania, now, either. He must have straightened out when he entered Xanth."

"That must explain it," he agreed. It did make sense. "Anyway, she had been fouled up by Magician Murphy's spell, long ago, and was sleeping in a coffin on the Isle of View."

"I love you too, Prince," Metria said. "Because you are a cylinder of laughs. But—"

"What?"

"A drum, round container—"

"Barrel. But I mean, I thought demonesses didn't love. So how—"

"We love to torment folk, and you are nicely tormentable. But you said it first."

"I did not! I was telling about the coffin on—oops."

"Yes, that's where, out of nowhere, you said you loved me. If that's what you did with that sleeping girl, I can see how you got in trouble."

"It's the island of V-I-E-W," he said, spelling it. He had learned to spell from his mother, who had absolutely refused to let his father teach him, for some reason. Irene was funny about such things as spelling and panties and marriages. "That's its name."

Metria made a moue. "You mean you don't love me?"

"That's right. I love Nada, and only her."

"Too bad. It's much easier to torment one who loves you. Well, maybe you'll love me when I show you how to summon the stork. It's been known to happen."

"You mean the stork has something to do with love?" he asked, amazed.

She eyed him slantwise. "Oh, you will be fun to educate!"

"No, I hate education," he said stoutly.

"We shall see. Go on with your history."

Disgruntled for no special reason, he resumed where he thought he had left off. "So Electra was sleeping, because she had gotten fouled up in the spell intended for the Princess, and took a bite of the apple. According to the enchantment, she would sleep for a thousand years or until a Prince kissed her awake, whichever came first. And I was the Prince who came and kissed her, so naturally she was instantly in love with me and wanted to marry me. I really couldn't tell her no."

"Why not?" the demoness asked mischievously. "All you had to do was say 'Read my lips, freckles: go back to sleep.' Then you could slam the lid down and get out of there."

Dolph opened his mouth in an O of horror. Then he

realized that she was teasing him in her demoniac fashion. He decided to plow on regardless. "She was already out of the coffin. She will die if she doesn't marry me. She's been on hold during the betrothal; I guess the enchantment understands about my being underage. After all, so is she. But in a week she will be eighteen, and if she isn't married to me by then, she will die anyway. So I sort of have to decide."

"But aren't you still underage?" Metria inquired alertly. "Or will you have your sixteenth birthday this week?"

"No, not for a few months yet. But my sister made Grey Murphy research that, and he found that it's the age of the girl that counts in Xanth: she has to be at least sixteen before she marries. It doesn't say about the boy. We think that whoever made that rule just assumed that the boy would be older. So I can marry now, if I marry a girl who is of age— and both my Betrothees are. So I have to choose, soon. My mother won't let me marry both of them, for some reason."

"What does your father say?"

"He keeps his mouth shut. I think it's not in his department."

"It isn't? Then what *is* in his department?"

They had covered the Region of Fire, and now were entering the Region of Water. It seemed to be one big lake, but Dolph knew there were some islands and shores in it, and the foal might be on one of them.

"He handles the big things, like Kingly Policy. She handles the little things—"

"Like everything else," Metria finished. "Now I understand. It's a true matriarchy, all right, as it should be. I'll bet you aren't allowed to look at panties, either."

"How did you know?" he asked, surprised.

"It's Female Policy. No unmarried or underage men can see such forbidden things. It would zonk out their feeble minds. So which one are you going to marry?"

"I don't know," he said. There was the substance of his dilemma: he still could not make up his mind. "I'd really like to marry Nada and see her panties. But I don't want 'Lectra to die."

"Doesn't Electra have panties too?"

"Yes, I guess so," he said, surprised. "I never thought of that. But I don't love her, and I do love Nada."

"So marry for love, and let the other croak."

It became easier to argue the other side, when the demoness summed things up. "But Nada would be unhappy, and 'Lectra would die. I don't want those things to happen either."

"Then boot Nada and marry Electra and take a love potion with her."

"But I don't *want* to love 'Lectra!" he protested.

"And Nada doesn't want to love you."

"Well, she wants to, but not that way. We think it's better if it's natural. 'Lectra's love for me is because of the enchantment. I'd rather she took a potion to null it. But that's not the point. She has to marry me whether she loves me or not, or die."

Metria nodded. "Do you want objective advice from someone who doesn't care about any of you?"

He peered at her. "That depends. What kind of advice would it be?"

"Marry Electra."

"No, I don't want that advice."

"Then you'll have to survive without it. I wouldn't proffer it if I thought you'd take it, of course. I much prefer seeing you make fools of all three of you."

Dolph had the sinking feeling that he would oblige her in that. He knew it would make everyone else happy, including both Nada and Electra, if he married Electra. But she was like a pale glimmering starfish, while Nada was like a brightly blazing sunfish. Electra was great for playing tag with, or pillow fights, or getting-sick-eating-candy binges, but Nada, ah Nada, what a dream! He had never liked kissing or any of that mushy stuff, until he knew Nada; now he could do it all day, with her. Except that she preferred to be off doing things with Ivy. Fortunately Ivy did not feel easy about having Nada too near her fiancé, Grey, for some reason, so it was mostly Electra she was with. Whenever something interesting came up, like the sound of the invisible giant's footsteps, the two Betrothees would head out, and Nada would try to discourage Dolph from coming along, while Electra would encourage him. If only it could be the other way around!

"There's an isle," Metria said. "We'd better land on it and explore it physically."

Distracted by his chain of thought, Dolph didn't argue. He floated down, ready to change to solid human form when his feet were in reach of the sand. This Water region was really pretty nice, when between tsunamis.

Nada would marry him, if he chose, because it was a political bargain and a Princess never reneged on her word. She would do her best to make him happy, and that would be no trouble at all, because he would be happy just being with her. Electra would bid him farewell, and go away to die by herself so as not to bother anyone with the sight. Electra was really a very nice person; he had never doubted that. But it would not make any more sense for him to marry Electra than it would for Nada to marry him. The love just wasn't there. Maybe a love potion would do it, but that seemed like cheating.

"You're very quiet, Dolph."

He jumped. That was Nada's voice!

He looked—and there was Nada standing beside him, at the shore of a tiny island. He had not been paying attention where he was going and had just sort of followed the demoness. "How—?" he asked, agog.

"I thought I would stop by to see how you were doing," Nada said dulcetly. She stepped in close to kiss him. "Perhaps, since we are here alone, we should settle down to some serious romancing." Her arms went around him, drawing him close. Her gray-brown hair fell down around her face and tumbled about her shoulders as her brown-gray eyes gazed into his. She had been taller than he, when he first knew her, when she was in her normal human form;

that was no longer the case. She was the loveliest creature he could imagine.

Then something percolated through the unwilling recesses of his mind. How could Nada be here? She couldn't fly! She would have had to assume snake form and swim, and before that she would have had to get through the Region of Fire. It seemed unlikely. Meanwhile, what had happened to the demoness? "I don't think—" he started, half mesmerized by her beauty.

She frowned prettily. "Well, if you prefer . . ." Her features fuzzed, then coalesced, and it was Electra in his arms. She wore the same dress, but it was loose on her where it had been tight on Nada. "I can do it too, you know," she said. "Maybe not as lusciously, but—"

"Metria!" he exclaimed. "I should have known!"

"You should have," she agreed, her features becoming those of the demoness. She remained embracing him, and her dress was tight again. "I'm ready to show you about the stork, now. But perhaps it will be better without clothes." The dress dissolved into smoke and drifted away.

"It's done without clothes?" he asked. Somehow he wasn't really surprised.

"Usually. So let me get yours off." Her hands began to work on his buttons.

He looked down. Her body was completely bare. She wasn't wearing any panties. Rats! The demoness had been too canny to ignore them; she had dissolved them away with the rest of her clothing. He had hoped for a moment that she would forget, and he would finally catch a glimpse of the forbidden article. Even on a demoness, it could have been quite a sight. No such luck.

But that decided him. He knew she wouldn't really show him the stork's secret; she would just tease him with faint suggestions of it, until he burst from unrequited curiosity. Then she would laugh herself into smoke and drift away. She had already teased him with the panties, which she had never intended to show him. There was no trusting a demoness!

"No," he said, determined not to give her the satisfaction of making him burst. "I'm going on with the search."

"But the foal's not here!" she exclaimed. "I told you, he's at the With-a-Cookee River with the goblins."

"You also told me there's a hole in Xanth," he reminded her. "I don't believe you." He was pretty sure she *hadn't* told him about the river, but he didn't want to get into another dialogue with her.

She sighed, and her clothing reappeared. For a moment it was faintly translucent, but when he tried to see through it to catch a glimpse of her panties, it turned opaque, and he saw nothing. She was still teasing him!

He resumed ghost form and floated across the isle, but there was no foal there. Could the demoness be telling the truth about this? That Che Centaur was in goblin clutches? If so, he shouldn't dally here; he should hurry right down to the river to help rescue the foal.

But he couldn't afford to believe the demoness, because the moment he did, it would turn out to be a lie. The same was true for her story about the hole in Xanth. He would just have to complete his search of the Elements.

They completed Water and approached the Void. The pleasant water ended abruptly, and beyond was nothing.

Metria drew up just shy of the line. "Look, Dolph, you're a ghost and I'm a demoness, but this is no ordinary region. It's not safe for even us to enter. This is the event horizon."

"The what?"

"Finis. Kaput. The point of no return."

"You mean there's no crossing back?"

"Whatever," she agreed, irritated.

"But what if Che Centaur is in there?"

"Then he'll never come out. You know that. So it's no good us going in there and getting trapped too. Why don't you do the expedient thing and believe me, so we don't get into trouble? That hole in Xanth still needs to be plugged."

Dolph looked at the Void. He knew he shouldn't believe her, but what she said did seem to make sense. He couldn't help Che by getting lost himself. Still, if Che *was* in there . . .

"You fool!" she exclaimed. "You're still thinking about stepping across that line!"

"Well—"

She became canny. "If you agree to go the other way, I might forget to keep my panties hidden."

He was sure she was lying. She probably never wore any panties anyway. But the notion was demonishly tempting, regardless. "All right. Show me your hole."

She paused for just half a moment, and he realized that she must have found something funny in what he said. Then she lifted from the ground. "It's south."

They zoomed back through the four regions until they were just south of the Region of Air and west of the territory of the flies. The demoness dropped down into the jungle. There did seem to be an odd section, between trees. "See, a monster has come through already," she said, pointing.

Indeed, there was something there. It looked a little like an ogre and less like a man. It seemed to have been patched together from scraps of people, with pegs holding the pieces fast at the joints, and a couple more pegs holding the head together. It was marching around in a wobbly circle.

Dolph landed before the thing and assumed his natural form. "What are you?" he asked. "Where are you from?"

The jaw hinges cranked open. "I'm the monster," it rasped. "I'm looking for my master, Frankenstein."

"Well, he's not here," Dolph said. "He must be on the other side of the hole. Why don't you go back and look for him?"

Without further word the thing turned and marched into the hole. This was a shimmering ragged circle just above the ground, with flickering darkness inside. From above it had looked like a line, but from the ground it looked like a tear in the scenery—which was probably what it was. The demoness had been telling the truth, maybe.

The thing disappeared beyond the hole, as if it had never

existed. But Metria was right: they didn't want any more such things coming through.

"How do we plug the hole?" he asked.

"I wouldn't know."

"But you brought me here for this! What was the point, if you can't tell me what to do about it?"

"I brought you here because you're interesting in your assorted naïvetés and idiocies, and it amuses me to watch you tackle things you know nothing about," she said. "I'll be as satisfied to show you the way of stork summoning, because I know you'll make fumbles and blunders never before dreamt of in your kind's philosophy, and that will be more entertaining than anything else I could think of at the moment. But you don't want to play, so this is next best. I don't much care which problem you care to tackle first."

She was baiting him again. The question was, how much was true and how much false? Was this really a hole in Xanth or just some odd natural effect she was using to confuse him?

"Maybe I should go on over to the With-a-Cookee River and help rescue Che," he said, hoping he could learn something from her response.

"Yes, that might be best," she agreed. "I understand it's getting pretty messy there, and your Betrothees are headed right into trouble."

"Nada and 'Lectra?" he asked, alarmed.

"Who else?" she said carelessly. "They went and asked the Good Magician where Che was, and he—" She broke into a chuckle.

"What's so funny about that? I think it made sense to ask him, in case the rest of us didn't find the foal."

"But he thought they were going to ask a different Question," she said, still jiggling with the mirth of it.

"*What* Question?" he demanded, knowing that if she responded, he wouldn't like the answer.

"How to resolve the problem of your betrothals."

He stared at her. Of course Grey would think that! Why

else would the two young women come to him a week before Electra's eighteenth birthday? This business with Che's foal-knapping had come up so suddenly that Grey Murphy had probably been working on something else and never heard about it. The real Good Magician, Humfrey, would not have been caught unawares like that, but Grey lacked age and experience. Also, he had Ivy pestering him all the time; that would drive anyone crazy. Dolph knew that from long experience as her brother.

"So how did he answer, then?"

"He got an indentured ghost to check around and spy the foal," Metria said. "But he couldn't tell them exactly, just approximately. So they're probably going to get captured by the goblins too. That's a bad region, you know; that's where the Goblinate of the Golden Horde hangs out."

Dolph knew. The Horde liked to torture and cook captives. He and Ivy had once had a run-in with them. If they caught Nada and Electra . . .

"I'll get right over there!"

"Aren't you forgetting something, Prince?" the demoness inquired.

"Yes, the hole in Xanth! But you're probably lying about that."

"How do you know I'm not lying about your Betrothees?"

That brought him up short. It was impossible to tell when she spoke truth. "If you are, I'll—"

"You'll what?" she asked, interested.

That was a problem. She was a demoness. He could not touch her unless she wanted to be touched, and he could not even insult her unless she chose to be insulted. What could he threaten her with that would make her take note?

The only thing he could think of seemed too dumb to work. So he tried it. "I'll refuse to play your game any more," he said. "I'll tune you out, so that nothing you can do or say will have any effect. You'll expire of absolute boredom."

"Ha! You threatened that before. You can't do it."

"The stakes were not as high before. Now I can do it." He hoped he could—and hoped that if he could, she would capitulate. He was really worried about Nada and Electra, but worried about the hole in Xanth too. If one of her statements was correct, he needed to know which one, in a hurry, so he could do something about it. He knew that if he guessed, he would guess wrong; he always did. So he stood there and concentrated on ignoring her, knowing that it was his only chance, and not much of a chance at that.

"Suppose I do this?" she asked. She solidified into her most lusciously luscious shape and approached him.

He reminded himself that it was Nada he loved, and that Nada's shape was just as good as this one, and a lot more honest. He put his hand to his mouth and yawned.

"Suppose I do this?" she asked, embracing him and kissing him on the mouth. It was disgustingly pleasant; she could kiss as well as Nada could.

He stood there, not reacting. He was amazed that he could do it, but he reminded himself that this was not Nada but a mere pesky demoness, who would laugh at him if he fell for it.

"Or this?" Then it was the image and form and feel of Nada embracing him.

She's only the demoness! he thought full blast, and somehow managed to not react.

"Well, then, I think I'll just strip down to my panties," she remarked, stepping slightly away.

He hung on, knowing that she was bluffing; she didn't want to violate the Adult Conspiracy. Somehow he managed to lock his eyes in place and not look.

"In Nada's form, yet," she said. "I wonder what color her panties are?"

That almost got him! But he clung to the fading belief that Metria didn't actually know what color Nada's panties were, so could not duplicate them. He felt as if his eyes were yanking themselves out of his head, being so eager to look, just in case the demoness wasn't bluffing. If he lost this contest, the real Nada might be in deadly danger. That kept him firm.

There was a pause. "Very well, Dolph, you win," she said after a bit. "Stop ignoring me, and I'll tell you the truth, this one time. Demon's honor."

Was that to be trusted? He suspected that if it wasn't, then nothing about her was. He gambled. "Okay. Which is the true threat?"

"They both are. But the hole is more immediate and worse. Your Betrothees are threatened with being cooked in maybe a few hours, but if a monster comes through that hole, all Xanth will be threatened with worse."

"But a monster might not come through that hole," he argued. "Then I'd be better off going to the girls right now."

"I suspect that this is a significant trial of conscience for you, Dolph," she said. "I am always interested in observing such things, having no conscience myself. You know you should marry Electra, but probably won't; you know you should do what is good for Xanth, but probably will go seek your girls instead. With luck you might time it so that the goblins have captured them but not yet eaten them; they might be in the process of stripping them down for the pot, and you could see Nada's panties just before you rescued her."

"You're tormenting me again!" he accused her.

"You promised to react, if I told you the truth. Well, this is the truth, isn't it?"

He had to admit it was. He knew that his secret motives were unbecoming, but they were there. "So what should I do? " he asked lamely.

"You should plug the hole."

"But then if I did the right thing and married Electra, I might never get to see Nada's panties!"

"True, Prince."

"Oh, fudge!" he exclaimed, wishing he knew a fouler word. But somehow all the centaur education he had received had not added anything to his childhood vocabulary in certain respects. Some men could turn the air blue with their language, and a harpy could make a painted surface blister with a single fowl-mouthed expletive, but the best he could do was bring the trace of a smile to a lady's lips. He couldn't even get rid of a curse burr without changing to a form with scales that the burrs couldn't cling to.

"You're so cute when you struggle with right and wrong," Metria remarked. "Would it help you to do the right thing and remain here to plug the hole if I assumed Nada's likeness and donned panties?"

"Hey, yes!"

"Forget it, Prince! I'd rather see you struggle."

Somehow he had known she would say that. She would not help him at all, except to encourage him to do something he would regret, whatever that might be. She delighted in seeing his dilemma.

But maybe there was a way out of it. There was no obvious way to plug the hole, so maybe he couldn't do much here anyway. He could assume roc form, fly to the Good Magician's castle, and tell them about the hole. Then he could fly to the With-a-Cookee River and rescue the girls. That way he could do the right thing and still maybe catch a glimpse of—

Something showed at the hole. It looked like a cross between a man and a demon, but worse than either. Its arms looked like tentacles, and its three huge eyes glared out with such malevolence that Dolph was terrified. The demoness had not been fooling: this was a monster that could wreak havoc in Xanth!

"Maybe you're right," Metria said. "It's time to get out of here!"

"No way," Dolph said, walking toward the monster.

"But you could get hurt here—and, worse, so could I. That thing is part demon."

"Then get out of here and stop distracting me," Dolph gritted. What form would be best to tackle this thing? Maybe an ogre.

"I don't understand you," Metria said. "Suddenly, without thinking at all, you're doing the right thing.''

"Of course you don't understand: you're not human. Are you going to help me deal with this thing?''

"Yes. Not because it's the right thing to do, but because I might learn more about the mysterious workings of the feeble human mind.'' She became a grotesque horned demon with outsized claws and came at the monster from another side.

The monster swiveled one eye to orient on her, while the other two focused on Dolph. Metria froze in place, while Dolph felt a huge and awful chill. The monster was monstrous in mind as well as body and was mesmerizing them both!

Dolph couldn't move, but he could still change forms. He became a basilisk, whose very gaze was deadly to mortal creatures. That should set the monster back!

The two giant eyes blinked. Then a tentacle arm reached for Dolph. A toothy maw opened. The thing was going to eat the basilisk!

Metria, meanwhile, remained immobile. That third eye held her fixed where she was.

Dolph became a picklepuss, with pickly green puss and brine-moist eyes. Anything it touched would be pickled, and anything that tried to eat it would find it disgustingly bad tasting.

More tentacles came and wrapped around the picklepuss. The monster was going to eat it anyway! Maybe it even liked being pickled. Dolph was hauled in to the maw.

He became a sphinx, with the body of a lion and the head of a man. Sphinxes ordinarily were peaceful creatures, not much for combat, but they were very big. The monster's mouth closed on something that was many times its own size. The sphinx hide was too thick for the teeth to puncture; they got stuck, and the monster couldn't let go.

Dolph sat down. Since the monster's mouth was fastened to his backside, this meant that he sat on the monster's face. His bulk spread out to cover all three eyes.

"I'm free!" Metria exclaimed, moving at last. "You broke its eye contact!"

"Go fetch some tangle vines," Dolph told her with his huge human mouth. "We'll tie it up and plug the hole with it."

She vanished. Would she do it? She might decide that she had better folk to torment elsewhere. He could hold the monster as long as he sat on it, but he couldn't leave without freeing it. He didn't want to sit forever.

Then the demoness reappeared with a squirming mass of vines. She used them to wrap around the monster. Some she put over its eyes, their suckers fastening the eyes closed. Then she hammered the teeth that were embedded in Dolph's posterior, so that he could get up.

He assumed ogre form, picked up the trussed monster, and jammed it into the hole. Then the two of them used more vines to anchor it there, so that it could neither enter nor exit Xanth. It had become the plug.

"That was very brave and smart of you, Prince," Metria said. "I am amazed."

"So am I," he admitted.

"But how did you manage to be so manly, when you had been so boyly before?"

Dolph pondered. "I'm not sure. I guess I just did what had to be done."

She shook her head. "You remain as much of a mystery as ever! Each time I think you are hopeless, you evince a modicum of amplitude."

"Of what?"

"Dimension, magnitude, scope, largeness—" she said fretfully.

"Potential?"

"Whatever. I am disgusted."

"You should be," he said, obscurely satisfied.

"Now I suppose you feel free to go rescue your Betrothees and try to sneak a glimpse of someone's panties."

"Right," he said, and assumed the form of a swift hawk. He launched into the air and headed west, toward the With-a-Cookee River. He was pleased to see that the demoness did not follow.

Chapter 5.   Chex's Checks

Chex was about to resume her circuit, when a ghost appeared. "Oh, hello, Ghorge," she said, surprised. "What are you doing away from the Good Magician's castle?"

The ghost opened his mouth, but there was no sound. "He needs a sheet of paper," Grundy said. "He's a ghost writer, remember."

"Oh, that's right!" Chex hurried to fetch the paper. She set it on the table.

In a moment the handwriting appeared, in Ghorge's fancy script: *The foal is at the With-a-Cookee River. Nada Naga and Electra are going there now.*

"Oh, I must go there right away!" Chex exclaimed, vastly relieved.

But the ghost hadn't finished his message. More writing was appearing on the paper: *Magician Grey believes there may be danger if you go. Che is the captive of goblins—*

"And if the gobs see a winged centaur flying in," Grundy said, faster than the ghost could write, "they'll know whose mother she is."

"And if they are the goblins of the Golden Horde," Chex concluded grimly, "they'll cook first and argue later."

"Or dunk him in their hate spring," Grundy agreed.

"They would find it very funny, if you rescued him and he hated you."

"Very funny," Chex echoed hollowly. Grey's warning was unfortunately well taken. She dared not show herself there until Che was out of their grubby hands. Certainly Nada and Electra would do their best; one could assume the form of a deadly serpent, and the other could shock anyone she touched.

"But we can tell the other searchers," Grundy said. "At least we know that Che is all right and that help is on the way."

"Yes," she agreed, a sinking feeling in her heart. "Thank you, Ghorge, for your message."

Welcome the ghost wrote, and was gone. There was one remaining note on the paper, in a corner, evidently a doodle: a crude sketch of a valley between mountains, and the word *Cleavage!* Maybe the ghost had been impressed by the Gap Chasm as he zipped over it.

Chex picked Grundy up, set him on her back, and trotted outside. She flicked herself so hard it stung, and launched into the air. She was going to make this one fast circuit! Then she was going to fly to Mount Rushmost, where Cheiron was at the winged monster convention, and tell him. He would certainly want to be advised, at this stage, and anyway, she needed the moral support.

The ogre was still crashing his way north. "The goblins do have him!" Chex called, hovering low, "somewhere near the With-a-Cookee River."

"Me no mind; me find," he replied cheerfully.

If he did, the goblins would surely forget about Che, because the oncoming ogre would be bad news for them. Chex flew on, somewhat reassured. Yet she wondered how the goblins could have the foal, when there had been no sign of that before. She was not about to question Grey's message; she just wondered. Maybe Che had fallen into their hands later. But in that case, who had abducted him? Disquieting questions remained.

She found the milkweed maids without trouble, but didn't

urge them to go to the river; they were innocent girls who had no business near goblins.

Chex moved on around the circuit, advising the searchers, then cut north. Was Dolph still in the Elements? She hardly cared to go in there to tell him! He would just have to wait for the news until he emerged. None of them had really expected Che to be in there anyway.

Now she could head for Mount Rushmost. She turned and flew south. Her wings were tiring, because she had been flying a lot today, but she was determined to reach Cheiron. Only then could she relax, slightly.

There were some scattered white clouds in the sky. They were harmless, and even friendly in their fashion. Then she spied one black one, angling as if to cut her off. She hoped that wasn't—

"Fracto," Grundy said. "Should have known! He must have seen the activity and wants to interfere."

Cumulo Fracto Nimbus, the worst of clouds! The last thing she wanted to encounter at this stage. There was little doubt, now, that he had spied her, for he was swelling up like the gaseous toad he was and sending out ugly vapors. He might not know why she was flying south, but he intended to mess her up regardless. The worst thing was that she was tired; she doubted she had the strength to fly straight through him.

"Maybe go to ground and trot a while," Grundy suggested. He didn't want to get blown out of the air any more than she did.

"That will take too long," she replied fretfully. "It's deep jungle there, not even any magic paths. We could run afoul of ground monsters. If I don't dare fly because of the storm, they could be a real problem, as well as slowing us."

"True," he agreed. "I could ask the local plants for the best route, but it would still be slow." He pondered a while. Fortunately he was small, so his pondering was short. "And just as bad trying to fly around Fracto," he said.

"I'm afraid so. He can expand at a great rate. In fact, he's doing it now."

"Then that leaves us only one route, if you're up to it."

"I'm up to anything that will get us safely through!" she said. "What's your notion?"

"Fly over the cloud. He may not have much strength up where the air's thin."

Chex glanced up, suddenly uncertain. "What about *us*, where the air's thin?"

"It doesn't get *that* thin, does it? Didn't you fly to the moon when you married Cheiron?"

"The honey side of it," she agreed, remembering it with fondness. "But there's a channel there; the air clusters around the moon, especially when it's low in the sky."

"Well, it's low now," he said. Indeed, the day was late, and the moon was venturing out into daylight. "Even if you didn't make it too high for the cloud, you could land on the moon and rest for just long enough to get your wind back. Fracto won't hang around the moon much, because he knows he can't blow it out of the sky, and he doesn't like to look silly trying."

"Could be." Certainly no better prospect offered.

Chex flicked herself again, making her body so light that it just about floated up by itself, and pumped her wings strongly. She rose. She hoped it would not be necessary to fly as high as the moon. That route would be faster than the ground route, but it would be best if she could make it though without stopping.

Fracto saw her climbing. He swelled up even more rapidly, his cloud face forming eye patches and a frowning mouth region. He blew out a wet gale, trying to mess her up.

"Try that again, cabbage-breath!" Grundy called.

Oh, no! The golem just couldn't resist hurling a good insult. Grundy had battled Fracto before, and they had a long-standing feud. Now the cloud would try even harder!

Indeed Fracto did. Bubblelike excrescences formed on his surface, indicating the fury of his turbulence.

"Keep at it, toad-face!" Grundy called encouragingly. "You going to wet on somebody next?"

"Don't aggravate him!" Chex gasped as she tried desperately to climb out of reach.

"Aw, it's better to work him up," Grundy said. "Then he loses what little wit he has and is even easier to outsmart."

Fracto evidently heard that, because he sent out such a gust of sleet-speckled wind that Chex almost did a somersault.

"Is that your best shot, smog-rear?" Grundy demanded. "What made you think you could blow up anything more than a teakettle? Better go back for training—or training pants!"

"Grundy, I wish you wouldn't—" Chex started. But she was cut off by the cloud's furious blast of snow. For a moment she was blinded and wasn't sure which way was up.

Then her head emerged from it, and she discovered that she was higher than before. "It lifted us!" she exclaimed.

"That's the idea," Grundy said. "Might as well use Fracto's energy instead of yours." Then, to the cloud: "Is that what you call a squall? Even a dumb anvil head can do better than that!"

But Fracto was finally catching on. Instead of blowing again, he simply concentrated on building up his mass, higher and higher. The air was not thin, but Chex still couldn't get over the storm.

"What a view!" Grundy exclaimed.

Chex looked down. The panoply of Xanth lay beneath them, just like one of her dam's maps. Chem Centaur's magic talent was map projection, and she had explored most of Xanth in the course of perfecting her maps. Now the long coastal outline showed clearly, except where Fracto's grotesque burgeoning mass blotted it out and the nebulous region to the north where it was possible to cross into Mundania. Not that any sensible person would want to do a thing like that. The sea extended out, featureless except for the bits of cloud floating above it. Part of the great Gap Chasm showed, and it did resemble cleavage, just as the ghost writer had noted. The overall scene was beautiful. She should have done this before, just to enjoy the view. But of course she had remained mostly landbound, because Che couldn't yet fly. What an experience awaited him, when his wings formed well enough for the heights!

"I guess we'll have to stop at the moon," Grundy said, sounding not too regretful. "Well, I've always wanted to visit the big cheese."

Chex had had no intention of visiting the moon—not without Cheiron! But she seemed to be stuck for it. She was getting dangerously fatigued and had to rest; she doubted she could even get down to the ground without Fracto blowing her into the sea. So she angled to the side and flew straight toward it. Fortunately she was now higher than the moon, so the effort of reaching it was not great.

Fracto saw what she was doing and tried to stop her. But he couldn't grow fast enough to block both Mount Rushmost and the moon, and knew that she would zip past him and fly south if he gave her the chance. So he could only blow snow at her.

There was a crack of thunder. Then a lightning bolt zapped past her. Oops—Fracto had more than snow to hurl!

"You missed, sizzle-snoot!" the golem cried gleefully.

"Grundy!" Chex hissed.

"Don't worry, old diaper-bottom couldn't hit anything smaller than Xanth itself, and half the time he misses that too," the golem said reassuringly.

Then a bolt zapped just past his head, singeing his hair. "Lucky shot, vapor-brain!" he yelled, but his confidence seemed slightly shaken. He kept quiet while Chex winged on toward the moon.

The moon was somewhat larger than it appeared from the ground, because of the special inanimate magic called perspective. Each object and part of the landscape liked to think it was larger than it was, so it pretended that everything else was smaller, and the farther away anything was, the smaller it could safely be considered. Thus some quite large objects were made to seem quite small by those far enough away to get away with such belittling. The moon was at a serious disadvantage in this respect, because it was far away from everything else, so had no supporters. It got even by pretending that the whole of Xanth was small. The moon was actually big enough to walk and run on, and a number of flying centaurs could camp on it—if there only had been more than two to do it. But in time there would be Che—

Chex had a horrible thought. When Che got old enough to mate, who would there be? Certainly he could not do it with a sister! Before Chex, there had been only Cheiron, and Chex herself derived from mixed ancestry. Well, maybe there could be another mixed mating, to produce another winged centaur. But it seemed doubtful, because Chem had been unusually liberal for her kind, and perhaps no other centaur would consider crossbreeding. Unless one happened to run afoul of a love spring . . .

"Watch it, mare!" Grundy cried.

Chex realized that she was about to land in a big dish of thoroughly moldy semiliquid cheese. The smell was terrible! She pumped her leaden wings and lurched up, but came down almost immediately in another dish of cheese. This one wasn't moldy, but the smell was if anything worse. It couldn't be helped; she landed squarely on all four hooves and slid to a gooky stop.

"Ugh!" Grundy said. "Did you have to pick Limburger?" He was right: she saw the slimy little limbs embedded in it.

Chex folded her wings and stepped ahead. Each foot came out with a slurp and a belch of awful odor. Those must have been zombie limbs used to prepare this batch! What a mess! She had had no idea that the near side of the moon was this bad. She wanted to hold her breath, but was still breathing hard from her exertion.

A horse appeared. It was midnight black and not glossy; it was hard to see at all. It trotted toward them purposefully.

Suddenly Chex was dreaming. In her dream a jet-black

centaur mare appeared. "What are you doing here in my retreat?" she demanded.

Astonished, Chex could only answer "Who are you?"

"I am Mare Nectaris, and this is the Sea of Nectar, where I relax between deliveries. You are tracking it up!"

"You're a night mare!" Chex exclaimed.

"Of course. And you are out of your pasture, aren't you?"

"I'm Chex Centaur, and I was trying to fly to Mount Rushmost, but Fracto, the evil cloud, blocked my way, and I had to detour—"

"Fracto! No wonder! My cheese is all gooky from the last time he rained on it! And the moon is supposed to be dry. He has no respect at all."

"That's right," Chex agreed. "I have an urgent mission, and he—"

"Very well, I can see it's not your fault. Come over here to my fountain and wash off your hooves."

Then Chex snapped awake, and saw the black mare leading the way to a much smaller disk, where water squirted up. Relieved, she followed.

The fountain was big enough so that Chex was able to stand in it and get her feet entirely clean. Beyond was a region where the cheese was dry and hard, probably sunbaked Cheddar, so she could walk on it without getting gunked. "Thank you so much, Mare Nectaris," she said. "I really am sorry I landed in your cheese. I need to move on as quickly as I can."

She looked up. One of the odd things about the moon was that it made Xanth seem up instead of down. Probably that was more of the magic of perspective. But there was Fracto, staying right between her and Mount Rushmost. He wasn't going to let her get through without a hassle.

The dream reappeared. "We don't like Fracto," the black centaur lady said. "He tries to interfere with our delivery of bad dreams. He can't touch us physically, of course, but he fogs everything up so it's hard for us to see where we're going. That puts us behind schedule, so that the dreams may be delivered late in the night, and sometimes folk even wake up and remember them. That is bad form, and we get the blame.''

"I suppose there's nothing you can do about it," Chex said, worrying about how long it would be before she could get through to Cheiron. If only Fracto hadn't picked this occasion to get difficult! That was his magic: to appear at the very worst time for anyone else. How absolutely maddening it was to be stuck here like this, unable to get around the evil cloud! "I wish you could give *him* a bad dream!"

Mare Nectaris was so surprised that the dream dissolved. But in a moment it reappeared. "I wonder if we could? That would be a dream come true, if you will pardon the expression."

Chex had made the remark in an off-hoof manner, not taking it seriously herself. Now she reconsidered. "Well, are your dreams limited to living folk? Fracto is a demon, as I understand, who assumed cloud form and crowned himself king of the clouds. I suppose the real clouds are too fleecy-gentle to make an issue of the matter. But if you—I mean, do demons dream?"

"Demons don't dream," Nectaris said. "But Fracto is no longer exactly a demon, because of all the natural cloud substance he has clothed himself with. Maybe that would make him mortal enough to dream. Let me ask the Night Stallion." She trotted to a gourd she had at the edge of her sea of cheese. She disappeared—and the dream ended. Chex was standing alone, except for Grundy, who didn't count.

"So this is where the night mares spend their time off!" the golem exclaimed. "I never dreamed it!"

"I suppose it makes sense," Chex said. "They can't work all the time, and they do have the seas of the moon named after them, and this gives them a chance to peek at Xanth by day. I'm surprised I was able to see Nectaris."

"They must relax their invisibility here, as they do in the gourd. I'm glad to meet one when she's off duty; she doesn't seem at all frightening. But of course Mare Imbri isn't frightening either."

"Well, she's a day mare; she's not supposed to scare folk."

"But she once was a night mare. I wonder who has her moon sea now?"

Mare Nectaris reappeared. It was evident that the gourds served as a handy direct route to the realm of dreams, no matter where they were. The dream reformed. "The stallion says to try it!" the centaur mare exclaimed. "He doesn't like Fracto either!"

"Great!" Grundy cried. It seemed that he received the dream just as Chex did. "Give him a mental hotfoot, get him out of there, and we can go on to Mount Rushmost."

That was exactly what Chex wanted, but she was sensibly cautious. "How long will it take to fashion a suitable bad dream for Fracto?"

"Oh, not more than a few days," the mare replied. "We want this to be a truly effective dream; Fracto has a lot to answer for."

That was what she had feared. "But I need to get past that evil cloud now, or at least very soon!"

"But a dream can't be crafted in a hurry," Nectaris protested. "The workers in the gourd are craftsmen. No inferior bad dream receives the stallion's stamp of approval."

Chex stamped her own hoof in frustration. "I can't wait more than a few hours. My foal is the captive of goblins, and I must tell Cheiron, who will know what to do."

"That is not our concern," the black centaur replied. "We have no onus against you, but we cannot compromise our standards of dreamsmanship. The Night Stallion—"

"Maybe I had better talk to the Night Stallion," Chex said desperately. "I have to make him understand—"

"Ixnay," Grundy murmured at her ear.

"I don't care how fearsome he may be to others," Chex continued heedlessly. "My foal's in awful danger, and I must get through!"

"There are some big gourds that can be used for transport," the black centaur said. "But none on the moon. You would have to get down to the ground first."

Chex gazed at Xanth. Fracto waited, uglier than ever. She spread her wings tentatively.

The cloud rumbled. "I can translate that," Grundy said. "He says 'Make my day, clod-head!'"

Chex could have survived without that translation. Not only that, her wings were still too tired for more than the merest coasting. She needed more time to rest them, and she needed Fracto gone.

"Yes, I must talk to the stallion," Chex decided. "We need a dream crafted in the next two hours, and I don't care what it takes."

"Ouch," Grundy murmured. "You've done it now, wings-for-brains! The Night Stallion is Trouble with a capital offense."

There was a shimmer before them. This resolved itself into the statue of a giant stallion mounted on a pedestal. This was Trojan, the horse of another color. "What brings you here, quarterbreed?" the statue demanded without moving its mouth. This was a stronger dream; they now seemed to be in a fancy pavilion.

"Fracto, the evil cloud, blocks my way, and I had to land here to rest," Chex said bravely, though daunted by the dread apparition. "I want to drive Fracto away with a bad dream, so I can continue my flight to Mount Rushmost, so Cheiron can help me save our foal."

"I don't give one dropping about your foal!" the statue said. "You have no business on this side of the moon."

"Now we're in for it," Grundy muttered.

"And you, golem," the stallion said. "Did you not advise her against this trespass?"

"Leave him out of this!" Chex said. "We had no choice. A'' I want is a fast dream. Do I have to craft it myself?"

The stallion glowed slightly with ire. "It will cost you half your two souls just to get free of here. Do you wish to lose the other halves as well?"

"Half my soul!" Chex exclaimed, shocked.

"I told you," Grundy moaned. "He doesn't fool around."

"This is outrageous!" Chex fumed. "All I want is the chance to rescue Che!" But she remembered, now: that was the price of getting out of the world of the gourd, in certain circumstances. She hadn't realized that landing on this side of the moon would be so expensive!

The stallion blinked. His eyelids did not move; the whole statue flickered. "Who?"

"Che, my foal! The goblins have him, and I must get help to rescue him! If I have to throw away my soul in the process, then so be it, but I have to get on my way soon."

"The chosen of the Simurgh," the stallion said. "I had not realized. We must facilitate your progress without penalty."

"What a break!" Grundy whispered, his relief about twice as big as he was. "We keep our souls!"

"If I can just rest a little and then fly on to Mount Rushmost," Chex said, "that's all the facilitation I need. But if it takes a bad dream to move Fracto off—"

"It takes time to craft a proper bad dream," the stallion said. "The mares do not make the dreams, they only carry them, though at times they must add dreams from the common pool if the effect is not sufficient. An inferior dream would not properly disturb Fracto, who is bound to be a tough client. Two days is the minimum we can do it."

Chex saw that he was being candid. Now she realized that routine dreams of toothy dragons or ugly spooks would not do the job; it would require something very special to bother a cloud. It was a real problem. If she wanted fast service, she would have to figure out a way to craft an effective dream in a hurry.

Then she had a notion so bright that the bulb shattered over her head. Mare Nectaris flinched. "Fracto—he's not like other creatures!" Chex said. "He hates good things. He hates happiness."

"Yes," the stallion agreed. "That is why a phenomenally horrendous dream must be crafted. It will require the most terrible elements we can muster, integrated so as to leave no ray of hope or pleasure.''

"No it won't!" she exclaimed. "It will take a happy dream!"

"You're crazy, feather-face!" Grundy said. "If Fracto's happy, he'll stay forever."

"Not so," Chex said. "The happier it is, the worse Fracto will feel, because that's *his* nemesis: the joy of others. If he is faced with a happy scene he can't rain out, he will flee in high dudgeon."

The stallion was amazed. "Mare, I think you are correct! Reverse psychology! But we are not equipped to make a happy dream."

"Maybe I can think of one," Chex said. "I am a happy person, normally."

"And the sets," the stallion continued. "Every scene has to be recorded with the proper background, with talented models. We don't have happy ones."

"But you must have scraps and snippets cut from prior dreams that weren't nasty enough for your purpose," she said eagerly. "If those were collected together, there might be an almost-nice effect. You could use up all those wasted bits!"

"Perhaps," he agreed uncertainly. "But the time—"

"It shouldn't take much time just to assemble them," she argued. "They've already been made; they just need to be tied together. The real challenge is the main sequence. Something so sickeningly sweet that Fracto will be revolted."

"Our models could not manage anything like that," the stallion said. "It would make *them* be revolted!"

"But could they pantomime?" she asked. "If Grundy and I spoke the words?"

"Say!" the golem said, getting interested.

"Possibly," the stallion agreed reluctantly.

"Very well. Collect your sets and models, and I'll try to come up with a suitable narrative."

The stallion seemed bemused. "Do it," he said to Mare Nectaris, and shimmered out of view.

The dream sequence abruptly ended, and Chex found herself standing with Grundy, otherwise alone by the lake of cheese. The minions of the night were doing their part; now she had to come through with her part.

What kind of a dream could she make, which she and Grundy could narrate, that the horrendous actors of the gourd could pantomime? Her mind was blank.

"Grundy, you must have a notion," she said. "You've talked with creatures all over Xanth. What's the most sickeningly sweet story you ever heard?"

"That was your courtship of Cheiron Centaur," he said promptly.

She refrained from flicking him hard with her tail. They were not as heavy here on the moon, for some magical reason, and she was afraid that if she made him lighter he would fly into the air, and she would have to take off after him, and Fracto would get them both. That wasn't worth the effort, especially since it was now getting dark and it would be hard to see their way. Anyway, it was probably his notion of a compliment.

"Aside from that," she said.

"Probably the tale of the Princess and the dragon," he said. "The bird that told me that one swore he had seen it happen himself, but I'm not sure."

"Why not?" she asked innocently.

"Because he was a lyrebird."

This time she did flick him. Fortunately he hung on to her mane, and did not fly off into Fracto's waiting storm.

"Tell me the tale," she said grimly. She knew that she could not afford to be overly choosy at this point.

"There was a lovely Princess who met a strange handsome foreign Prince," he began. She listened attentively, until the conclusion. "And so they lived happily ever after."

"I think you're right," she said at the end. "That's so nice a tale it will drive Fracto right up the wall and into distraction. But we'll have to fit him into it, so that he identifies."

"But he'll just rain on it!" the golem protested.

"No, the beauty of a dream is that a person has to dream it its way, not his own way. Otherwise no one would even tolerate a bad dream. He will be there, but unable to rain on the proceedings."

Grundy nodded appreciatively. "You have a diseased mind."

"Thank you. Now we must rehearse our parts, so that when the Night Stallion gets his act together, we are ready to animate the dream. I will take the female parts, and you the male parts. Remember, don't overact; what we want is verisimilitude."

"What?"

"Plausibility. I thought you knew all words in all languages."

"I do. I wasn't sure you did."

Again she refrained from flicking him. All centaurs had competent vocabulary, as he knew. "Perhaps you confused me with a certain demoness who has trouble getting her words straight."

"No, you're not as pretty as D. Metria."

What an effort to keep her tail still! "And not half as mischievous, either," she agreed. "Now remember: this will be a narrated play, in essence. The stallion will provide the actors, but we must speak their parts because there is no time for rehearsal and we don't want to have to do it more than once. Some dreams are like that, so there is precedent. We can ad-lib, but we have to stay with the general story line. Can you play it straight, for once?"

"Look, Chex, I can do it if I want to!" he said, annoyed. "I know you have to do this to get to Cheiron and save your foal. I may have an offspring of my own some day!"

"Yes, of course," she agreed quickly. "I apologize, Grundy."

"Thank you." He seemed surprised; evidently he did not receive many apologies. "Now let's see just how good a dream we can do.'' And they worked on the details, waiting for the stallion's return.

In due course the stallion arrived, and with him a troupe of denizens of the gourd bearing assorted props. Soon the region was littered with painted scenes of pleasant glades and beaches, and little containers of dream fragments. A larger pavilion was erected, shrouded by cheesecloth, so that Fracto would not be able to see what was being done here.

"Just how is a dream recorded or animated?" Chex asked.

"We have camcorders," the stallion explained, showing a creature with a lenslike snoot. "They note all details of a scene, and the mares take the finished dreams to their recipients. When you are ready to record a scene, just say 'take one' and when you want to end it, say 'cut.' They will do it."

Chex wasn't sure about this, but had to assume that the stallion knew his business. "First we want some nice background scenes of a lovely castle and mountain with flowers. Can this be done so that it looks alive? I mean, not like a picture?"

"Certainly. How's this?" The stallion wiggled an ear, and a mare stepped forward.

Suddenly there was a dream. It was of an ornate mountain with a path spiraling up it, and Castle Roogna perched at the very top. That wasn't exactly what Chex had had in mind, but it would do. There were flowers at the base of the mountain, at least.

"And a separate scene," Chex said as the dreamlet ended, "an escarpment or barren rocky place where a dragon might live."

After a moment there was another dream scene of just such a place. It was by a raging sea, and evidently intended for a fear-of-drowning dream, but the overall scene was perhaps too pretty to inspire proper fear. Thus it was a reject and perfect for her purpose.

"Now the actors," she said. "We need a lovely Princess,

a sinisterly handsome man, a dragon, and a pair of unicorns, as well as some bit parts.''

They were available. "But not naked," Chex said. "Human folk are funny about such things; they are almost always clothed. The man must have a functional but obviously high-class suit, and the woman a quality dress with a revealing décolletage.''

"What?" the stallion asked.

"A low neckline." Chex drew a finger across her breasts to indicate where the line crossed the upper swell of them. "Human folk pay a good deal of attention to that line, as they do to the bottom line.''

"Ah, yes. We have a financial stress section where we fashion dreams for export to Mundania. Wrong bottom lines are—''

"I meant the hem of the skirt. The higher it is, the more intriguing it seems to be to human folk.''

"Yeah," Grundy breathed. "You ever look at Nada Naga's top and bottom lines, when she's in human form?''

"This is an odd business, exploring human desires instead of human fears," the stallion grumbled. But he rousted up the clothing, and in due course the naked actors were suitably clothed.

Chex had the Princess and man stand near the castle, said "take one," and started the narration.

It did not go perfectly, and they did have to do a take two for some of it, but overall Chex was satisfied with the session. In the course of two hours they had the dream in the can, as the stallion put it.

They ran the whole thing through one time to be sure that it was satisfactory. All of them watched, sharing what was perhaps the most positive dream the proprietors of bad dreams had made.

The Princess appeared at the base of the mountain, picking nice flowers. Suddenly the handsome sinister Prince appeared. "Oh!" she exclaimed in Chex's voice. "You startled me!"

"Fear not, lovely creature," the Prince said in Grundy's voice. "I have not come to hurt you, but to love you, for you are the most delicious princess I have seen."

The Princess turned her big shining eyes on him, flattered. "Others have not found me so. Indeed, I am not married, and I am almost twenty-one."

"I do not regard that as regrettable," the Prince said. "Come, we must get to know each other better."

Soon they knew each other better, for the weather was fair; the only cloud in the scene was so white and fluffy that it would not have been able to rain on anything no matter how hard it tried. Indeed, faced with such excellent weather, they fell in love. "I must tell you something," the Prince said gravely. "And ask you something, which I fear you will not like."

"Oh, I hope it is not that you are not a prince!" she exclaimed, horrified, "or that you do not love me!"

"No, it is neither of these things," he reassured her. "I am indeed a prince, and I do love you. But I fear your love for me will suffer when you hear what I have to say and ask."

The Princess thought that he would say that he was from an enemy kingdom, and that he wished to marry her. Since she was frankly bored with the local scene and found the daily return climb up the mountain to be arduous, she expected to express only token dismay at the prospect, even if her father the King were miffed. "Tell me and ask me, my love," she breathed. She was very good at breathing, and this had been so ever since she turned fourteen and donned an adult off-the-shoulder dress.

"I am not a man," he said. "I am a dragon. I assumed human form only to cause you to love me. It is one of three transformations I am able to make."

"But you told me you were a prince!" she exclaimed, dismayed.

"I *am* a prince," he replied. "A Prince of Dragons. Once I attain my majority, I will be the King of Dragons, for my sire was recently chomped by a hostile poisonous sea serpent and is indisposed.''

The Princess considered. "I really had not anticipated this development," she confessed. "But I suppose a prince is a prince. What is it you wish to ask me?" For it seemed to her that it was better to marry a dragon than a commoner.

"I must undergo a rite of passage in order to attain my majority and become King," he said. "I must resume my natural form, and consume a lovely innocent princess. This is a thing required of all royal dragons. Will you come to be eaten?"

The Princess experienced a somewhat greater dismay than before. She had not anticipated this development either. She had rather hoped for a different type of question. "I will really have to go and ask my father," she demurred.

"By all means," the Dragon Prince agreed. "It isn't wise to make a decision as important as this without consultation. I will depart, and await you one week hence at the escarpment by the sea. If you decide not to come, I will understand." He kissed her and departed.

The Princess made the arduous climb to the castle at the top of the mountain. She went to the King and explained the situation. "I met this wonderful prince, O sagacious father," she said breathlessly, for she remained exercised from the climb. "But he is a Dragon Prince and wishes to consume me. Should I go to him at the escarpment by the sea next week for that?"

"Well, that depends, O innocent daughter," the King replied. "Do you love him?"

"Yes, father."

"Do you love him enough to die for him?"

She considered, for it was not an easy question. She really would have preferred an easier question. "Yes, father, I suppose I do."

"Then I suppose you must go to him," the King said, evincing a certain regret. "But I fear we shall miss you. Perhaps you should consult with your mother the Queen."

That had not occurred to her, so the Princess thanked him

for the suggestion and repaired to the Queen.

"What!" the Queen demanded.

The Princess repeated the statement.

"Thank you," the Queen said. "I didn't hear you before. But I'm not sure I approve. What are the credentials of this dragon? Is he really a prince?"

The Princess assured her that he was.

The Queen considered. "I am afraid I still don't approve. I can not forbid you this thing, being only a woman, but if you insist on it, don't think to return to my region of the castle thereafter."

The Princess was saddened by her mother's disapproval, but realized that she was unlikely to have much occasion to return to the castle after her tryst with the Dragon Prince.

When the appointed day came, the Princess garbed herself in her finest raiment, wearing a dress whose décolletage was so low and whose hem was so high that the dragon should have little difficulty seeing the most delectable parts of her to bite first. After all, she loved him, and wanted him to be pleased with her. She brushed out her marvelously silken tresses and set a ruby tiara on her head, its color suggestive of the blood she proposed to shed for her beloved. She touched a bit of red rose perfume behind her ears and in the hollow of her cleavage, its odor also suggestive of that color. All in all, she thought, she had done a creditable job for the occasion.

She set out afoot, for though it was a fair walk, her father had informed her that he did not care to risk a fine horse too near the dragon. "After all, those creatures are notorious," he said. "Once they get the taste of blood, they are apt to attack anything in view." She had had to concede the validity of this caution.

In due course, tired and dusty but still bravely beautiful, the Princess reached the escarpment. The Dragon Prince had not yet arrived, for she had allowed sufficient travel time and was a few minutes ahead of schedule. So she paused to repowder her face and wipe the dust from her slippers, so as to be as presentable as was feasible. She wanted her beloved's last sight of her to be a pleasant one.

Something caught her eye in the mirror as she touched up her nose. There was something off to the side, behind the escarpment—something that had made a glint in the morning sunlight. She peered more closely at the reflection in the mirror, for it would be unbecoming to turn her head and stare directly. She saw that it was the shiny helmet of a mercenary soldier.

Curious, for there seemed to be no purpose in a mercenary deployment at this site, she used her mirror to check farther. Soon she was assured: there was an entire troop of mercenaries armed with swords and shields. This deepened the mystery: what could they want here?

Then the dragon appeared in the distant sky, winging his way toward the escarpment. Suddenly it occurred to the Princess that this could be an ambush sent by her father to slay the dragon. It was, she now recalled, the way his cunning mind worked. It was quite possible that the Queen had importuned him to Do Something, and though of course the Princess had no idea what sort of encouragement a woman could offer a man to do her will, she had on occasion seen her father change his mind after a night with the Queen. She had hoped some day to ascertain how such persuasion was accomplished, but that hope seemed academic now. At any rate, it did seem that the Dragon Prince was likely to be in trouble if he landed here.

She ran to the very brink of the escarpment, frantically waving her arms. "O Prince Dragon!" she screamed, though it was not considered truly princessly to scream. "Do not land! There is an ambush!"

The Dragon Prince heard her and shied off. He made a loop above the landing field, evidently in doubt how to proceed. He would not be able to complete his rite of passage if he did not land, yet it seemed distinctly awkward to do so.

"Curses!" the leader of the mercenaries cursed. "The tart (if you will excuse the term) has given us away! There'll be Lucifer to pay if the dragon gets away."

"Well, at least we can have our sport with the woman," a mercenary remarked with a certain enthusiasm.

The mercenaries marched toward the Princess. Alarmed, she retreated, but they cut her off. They looked hungry, though they surely had eaten well before the ambush.

The nearest one reached for her. The Princess screamed and fell helplessly to the ground.

The Dragon Prince, evidently disturbed by this spectacle, abruptly made up his mind. He wheeled and came directly in on a strafing run. He sent out a blast of flame that singed the Princess's lovely tresses as it passed over her, but bathed the standing mercenaries in fire. In a moment they were roasted, as it were, in the shells of their armor.

The Princess, perturbed by the smell, got up and tried to leave the scene. But the smoking bodies were all around her. So she leaped off the escarpment. "Catch me, O my beloved!" she cried as she fell toward the churning sea below. "My hair is burnt, but my flesh is not; I remain excellent eating, I'm sure, and if not, then you can drop me in the heaving sea and seek another princess."

The dragon maneuvered expertly and swooped down to catch her in his great jaws. But he did not crunch her in half, perhaps because at least one of the pieces would have fallen into the water. He carried her unharmed into the sky. There was a small dark cloud present, but the wind was wrong and the storm was unable to present any difficulties. The cloud seemed oddly perturbed at that. He bore her away to a distant isle, and there he landed and set her gently down.

"I am glad they did not get you," she said. "For I love you, whatever your form, and would not have you suffer."

"I cannot eat you now," the Dragon Prince said with a certain regret.

"But why not, O my love?" she inquired.

"Because you have lost your innocence. I must consume an innocent maiden princess to complete my rite of passage."

"But what did I do?" she cried, distraught.

"You betrayed your father's ambush."

"But they would have hurt you!" she protested.

"Undoubtedly. But a true innocent would not have betrayed them to an enemy."

She hung her head, ashamed. "You must be right, for I feel dirtied. Yet I fear I would do it again, given opportunity, for my love for you will not be denied. I am sorry I failed you in this; I had wanted so much to be pristine for you."

"Perhaps it is for the best," he said philosophically. "For I had already come to the conclusion that I could not eat you, and in that I betrayed my own trust."

"You could not? Why?"

"Because I love you as you love me. Now I dare not show my snoot back in Dragonland, for I have shown myself to be unworthy of my calling."

"I'm so sorry," she said sympathetically. "Now we both are in trouble, for surely I can not return to my kingdom after this. Whatever shall we do?"

"I think there is no help for it but that we marry and settle down to live happily ever after," he said with regret.

"But I can not marry you in that form," she protested. "Also, I would not enjoy living on this isle, without benefit of castle and servants."

"Are you sure you don't want to return you to your castle?" he asked. "There at least you will have the princessly things to which you are accustomed."

"No, for my father the King would be most wroth with me for betraying his ambush, and my mother the Queen told me not to return."

The dragon pondered. "I do have two remaining transformation spells," he said after a moment. "I could use them to transform us to similar creatures. Would you like to be a dragoness?"

"And eat people? I prefer not. What about a more benign form, such as a unicorn?"

"You are enamored of unicorns?" he asked, surprised.

"Naturally. All innocent young women are."

"Then I shall make us both unicorns," he said. "That

way, we shall be recognized by neither of our kingdoms and will be able to range here on the Isle of View."

"I love you too," she agreed.

Then he invoked the spells, and he became a fine handsome unicorn stallion who looked rather like the Night Stallion with a horn, and she became a lovely unicorn mare who resembled the night mare Nectaris. They lived happily ever after, and it never stormed there, for their love made all clouds fleecy and all rains gentle, no matter how ardently those clouds might wish to be otherwise.

"What do you think?" Chex inquired as the sweet dream ended. "Will that horrify Fracto?"

The stallion shook his head. "We have no experience with this sort of thing. You would have to ask the day mares."

"I don't think so," she said. "We are dealing with reverse psychology here."

"Fracto hates being balked," Grundy said. "And he hates sweetness. It should infuriate him."

"Let's hope so," Chex said. "We shall just have to try it. I thank you gourd folk for your effort, even if it does not prove effective."

The stallion glanced at Mare Nectaris. "Take that dream to Fracto," he said. "We shall watch its effect."

Mare Nectaris touched the dream capsule with her nose. It vanished. Then she leaped through the roof of the pavilion and galloped through the air toward the monstrous cloud.

The pavilion faded out. It was light on the surface of the moon, but there seemed to be a spell to make the group of them invisible, so Fracto would not know. Chex was interested to see that moonlight did not bother the night mares, but she realized that this was logical, as they had always gone abroad at night, whether the moon was in sight or hiding.

The mare disappeared into the darkness surrounding the malignant cloud, but Fracto himself remained visible. He was snoozing, which meant he was just right for delivery of the dream. Chex suffered increasing doubts: could this wild notion succeed? A sweet dream to a mean cloud?

Fracto flickered. The dream was starting!

Something flickered at the side. Chex looked, and saw the dream playing on the surface of a hard-cheese rock, as if it were a hypnogourd. She could monitor what Fracto was experiencing. That was nice.

The Princess was meeting the Prince. The weather was nice. Fracto, watching from the vantage of a dark cloud, was trying desperately to get over there and drench their encounter. They would not find each other nearly so attractive if her hair were plastered across her face and his suit was shrinking rapidly out of fit! But Fracto couldn't move; he seemed to be boxed in by adverse winds, unable either to get into the action or to float away from the scene.

When the Princess made her arduous climb up the mountain to the castle, Fracto strove to get above her and dump a bucket of water down her décolletage; that sort of thing really made princesses angry! But his motion was like molasses, and by the time he got there, she was inside the castle. He was so frustrated he hurled a thunderbolt at the castle, but it only bounced off harmlessly. Now, close to the castle, he couldn't get away, and had to listen to the Princess's dumb dialogues with her father and mother. He rumbled in rage, but no one paid attention, which made him madder than ever.

Then the Princess walked to the escarpment. What an opportunity to soak her down! But somehow he was able only to follow, his raindrops pattering harmlessly behind her. The Princess got hot, not wet, and didn't even hear his ominous rumbling.

Then she saw the dragon and warned him away from the ambush. Fracto tried to drown out her cries in thunder, so that her warning would not be heard, but he was frustratingly muted. The dragon heard her, and used his fire to scorch the soldiers, which was a fun scene. But what Fracto really wanted to do was blow the beast out of the sky, and he couldn't. The Princess leaped off the cliff, the dragon caught her, and the two flew away over the horizon, while Fracto followed helplessly. Even when they landed on the isle, he couldn't blow them away, because it was protected by enchantment. He was so frustrated that he was ready to explode.

Then they became two stupid unicorns and lived happily ever after, munching the sweet grass. And he still couldn't touch them: not with a lightning bolt, not with a frigid blast of air, not even with a stinging hailstone. It was too much; Fracto detonated. His vapors spattered across the landscape, and he was nothing but foul mist. Ugh! What an awful dream!

Chex peered into the darkness. All she saw was stars and the lights of houses in Xanth. The evil cloud had dissipated.

"It worked!" she cried. "The dream broke him up!"

"So it *was* a bad dream," the Night Stallion said, gratified. "I admit to having been concerned."

Chex was now well rested by her hours on the moon. "I thank you, stallion and mares," she said. "Now I must be on my way." She spread her wings. Night flying wasn't her favorite mode, but she could not afford to lose any more time.

"Many ill returns!" Grundy called as they took off.

The flight was easy enough, because it was mostly gliding. In due course she spied the landing lights of Mount Rushmost, and called out to the fireflies so that she was given clearance. Grundy, knowing that no nonmonsters were allowed here, hid himself in her mane and kept his mouth shut. That was a relief in itself.

It occurred to her, belatedly, that Magician Murphy's curse probably accounted for Che being near the With-a-Cookee River, instead of in the heart of the goblin camp. Whatever could go wrong with the goblin effort, was going wrong. Still, several wrongs did not necessarily make a right. She had to get some positive action!

Soon she was with Cheiron, telling him everything. Then at last she could relax, knowing that he would know what to do. It had been quite a day!

Chapter 6.   Jenny's Jeopardy

Jenny and Che were tied up but not hobbled, for the goblins didn't want to have to carry them. Their hands were bound and each had a rope around the neck; when one slowed or stumbled, a goblin would jerk cruelly on the rope, hauling them along.

Jenny was soaking muddy wet because of her dunking in the river, and her new spectacles were spattered with dirty drops. But they remained on her face, and they helped her vision enormously. She realized that her feeling was foolish, for she was in horrible trouble, but it gratified her to be able to see things so much better than ever before.

But even in her distress about being captured, she found something odd. These weren't the same goblins as before. Where was Godiva?

"Che," she murmured as they stumbled through the jungle. "Are—?"

"No, these are not the ones who foal-knapped me," the centaur replied. "I very much fear these are worse."

"Worse? Aren't they all just as bad as anything?"

"No. Some tribes are less worse than others. Godiva did not treat me cruelly. In fact she was looking for a more comfortable trail north when you rescued me. These goblins are brutal, and going south."

"Then where is the other group?"

"I suspect they are hiding. Goblins do not necessarily get along well with one another. Perhaps the others will suffer the same fate as we do, if they are captured."

"You mean I rescued you and only got you in worse trouble?" she asked, chagrined.

"That would be an unfair assertion. You tried to help me and suffered misfortune."

"I never realized!" she exclaimed.

The goblin holding her rope jerked it, making her lurch to the side. "No talking in the ranks!" he snapped.

Jenny could only hope that Sammy had found help, and that the help could find her and Che before they got wherever these cruel creatures were taking them.

The goblins soon found a well-beaten trail, and hustled them rapidly along it. It was as if they were a bit out of their territory, and felt insecure. That, coupled with Che's statement that these weren't the ones who had captured him before, made her wonder just what was going on. She knew just about nothing about goblins, but had somehow assumed that they were all the same: elf-sized monsters. Certainly, Godiva's party had seemed evil. If these were worse . . .

Her legs grew tired with the constant walking; she had been on them too much before any of this started. It was also getting dark now. But she had no choice; she had to keep walking, lest she be dragged along by her neck. Che seemed no better off. He had four legs, but more weight.

Finally, late at night, they came to the goblin camp. It was beside a dark lake, with crude earth and rock huts in a semicircle. The goblins pounded a wooden stake into the packed dirt and knotted the ropes that bound Jenny and Che to it. They were tethered.

Now Jenny saw something in the sky. It was huge and greenish white. "What's that?" she asked, amazed.

Che glanced up. "Oh, that's just the moon. It's almost full now."

"The moon? But it's so big! And where's the other?"

His brow furrowed. "The other what?"

"The other moon! The small one."

"There is no other moon. This is the only one. It comes out only at night, except when it's biggest and fattest, when it has the courage to show itself at the edge of day. It is made of green cheese, which would spoil if it got heated too much. The sun, in contrast, is afraid of the dark, so never comes out at night. The only other items in the sky are the stars, which are too small to accomplish much, and of course the clouds."

"I really *am* on another world," Jenny breathed, dismayed. She had known it before, but somehow this confirmation made it worse. How would she ever get home again, even if they got away from these horrible goblins?

Meanwhile other goblins were piling brush in a small fire pit. The snoozing coals discovered the food and licked hungrily up through it. Soon there was a ferocious blaze that made the entire camp bright.

"I wish I had been tutored more thoroughly in geography," Che said, gazing at the great fire.

"Why?" Jenny asked, because this seemed irrelevant.

"Because then I would know exactly what goblin tribe this is, and what its specialty of mischief is."

"Would that help us escape?"

"Probably not. But at least we would know what to expect."

Then the goblins hauled a huge black pot to the fire, and set it on a metal grate so that the flames licked up around it. They brought buckets of water and dumped them into the pot. The thing looked big enough to hold an elf girl and a small centaur.

"I think we can guess," Jenny said, feeling a chill despite the heat of the fire. She wanted to scream and run, but knew that it was pointless, so she just sat there.

"Can you untie yourself?" Che inquired.

Jenny tested the rope that bound her hands behind her. "No. They are good at knots."

"Perhaps I can untie you," he said, "if you put your hands where mine can reach them."

"What good would that do? We are completely surrounded by goblins, and I'm so tired I couldn't run very fast anyway.''

"If I can untie your hands, then you can untie the rope at your neck. Then I can flick you with my tail, and make you light enough to float. Then you can jump and sail away from here."

Jenny realized that her weight had gradually returned, after he had made her light on the raft. That was one reason she was so tired now: it was the weight. But that lightness had enabled her to walk far faster and farther than she could have managed otherwise. The same must have been true for Che. His magic didn't show to the goblins, but it had saved the two of them from getting cruelly dragged.

Still, she had questions. "What about you? If I could untie me, I could untie you too. But you said you can't fly yet."

"True. You should be able to grab on to the branch of a tree, and hurl yourself further up and away, escaping them, but I would be unbearably clumsy, and my body would get tangled in the branches, and they would soon catch me again. So I must remain here."

"But I can't go without you!" she protested. "They'll cook you!"

"Yes, I suspect they will. But at least you will be free. One escape is better than none."

"But I don't know my way around here," she said. "I don't even know where Sammy is!"

"Surely he is finding help, and if you remain clear of the goblins long enough, that help will reach you."

That made sense. Also, she realized that if she got free, she might be able to do something to get him free too. Maybe there was another cherry tree nearby. "Well, we can try. Maybe we can both escape."

She turned and put her hands back, and he reached down to work on the knot. But in a moment he desisted. "I should have known: it's a magic knot. Only the goblins can untie it."

After what she had seen here, Jenny didn't doubt it.

Somehow she wasn't all that surprised. The goblins weren't paying any attention to the two captives, which meant they were either pretty stupid or pretty confident. It seemed they weren't stupid.

Now the goblin chief tramped across to them. "Well, well, what have we here?" he asked as if surprised to see them. "A funny little centaur and a funny little elf wench. Har, har, har! Well, I'm Chief Grotesk Goblin, and I want you to know what kind of sport we mean to have with you."

Jenny couldn't help looking at the huge pot on the fire. "We already know, thank you," she said tightly.

"Oh, that's not for you two," the chief said.

Jenny perked up. "It isn't?"

"Not this week. Would you deny us our sport? We must see you bathe first."

It was true that Jenny was good and dirty now, but somehow she didn't trust this. "I'll wait, thanks."

"To be sure! Har, har, har!"

Jenny was unable to see what Grotesk thought was so funny, but decided not to inquire. She really didn't like the goblin chief very well.

"I suspect we shall not like their sport," Che said.

Jenny had already suspected that for herself, but she didn't point that out.

"Fetch the night's entertainment!" Grotesk exclaimed.

The goblins went to a hut, unbarred the door, and brought out two other creatures, who had evidently been taken captive on a prior day. One was a young woman with tight-fitting clothing; the other was a furry man whose feet ended in round boots—no, hoofs. Both were bound, but the goblins touched the knots and they loosened on their own. They two stood substantially taller than the goblins, which suggested that they were close to human size.

"What are those?" Jenny asked.

"They appear to be a dirty nymph and a faun," Che said, peering at them. "I know such creatures only by description, but the features seem to match."

"A what and a what? They look like a woman in stretchy

brown cloth and a man with shaggy trousers and funny feet.''

"A nymph and a faun," he repeated. "I believe they are together, and live in happy communities where the fauns chase the nymphs all day. That is all I know, except that neither wears clothing. What you see is his fur and the mud with which she is coated.''

Jenny looked down at her own muddy legs. She understood how it could happen. "I guess the goblins are going to cook them tonight and save us for tomorrow." She was surprised at her seeming calmness; she knew she would be throwing a fit if she had any choice.

"I fear it will be worse than that."

"Worse than getting boiled alive?" she asked doubtfully.

"Yes. My dam refused to tell me what goblins do to their captives. That means it is worse.''

Jenny would have shuddered if she hadn't been so tired. She hoped Sammy found help soon.

"Now here's the rule," Chief Grotesk said to the nymph and faun. "Faun, if you catch her before she reaches the pond, you go free and we cook her. If you don't, she goes free if she wants to, and we cook you. If you don't race, we cook you both. Got that?''

"That's cruel!" Jenny said. "Making them sacrifice each other!''

"They will surely make us do the same tomorrow," Che said. "I shall be very sorry, for you tried to rescue me and I like you.''

"We've just got to get rescued!" she said. "I know your mother's looking for you. Maybe she'll find you in time.''

"I certainly hope so.''

"So we must make sure you win our contest, because no one will rescue me anyway.''

His head turned to her. "That is very generous of you, Jenny. But since you would not be captive if you had not tried to help me, I feel that you should be the one to—''

"Maybe we'll both be rescued before the goblins get to

us," she said. It seemed better to believe that than to let the dialogue continue.

The action was starting with the others. The goblins released the nymph, and she ran fleetly away. Then they let the faun go, and he took off after her. The nymph screamed fetchingly and ran faster. They seemed equally swift, but the nymph tried to run out of the goblin circle, and the goblins wouldn't let her. She had to dodge back, and when she did, the faun gained on her. She screamed sweetly and ran off.

"Why doesn't she run to the pond?" Jenny asked.

"I am perplexed about that myself," Che said.

The nymph dodged again, but not toward the pond. She tried to get by the goblins a second time, and was thrown back. She fell, and this time the faun almost caught her. She screamed cutely and scrambled up just in time to avoid him, but he was hot on her heels. She had no choice but to go for the pond.

She did so, with seeming reluctance. She reached the end and leaped in. The faun stopped at the edge, disappointed. He did not touch the water; indeed, he seemed afraid of it. That was odd, considering his likely fate.

"Why don't they both just wade across to the other side?" Jenny asked. "There are no goblins guarding it there."

"It is indeed a mystery."

The nymph, thoroughly doused in the water, stood. Now her body was clean, and Jenny could see that Che had been right: there were no clothes. The nymph was a very pretty figure of a bare girl.

The nymph stared at the faun. Then her lovely face twisted into an unlovely expression. She screamed again, but this time it was not fetching, sweet, or cute; it was hateful. She surged out of the water, chasing the faun.

The faun turned and fled. The goblins laughed uproariously. They obviously found this surprising reversal very funny. It seemed that the nymph was angry with the faun for some reason and had forgotten that she could go free. She just wanted to catch him.

"I don't understand," Jenny said. "She could have gone on across the pond. Why did she turn back, and why is she so angry?"

"Now I think I understand," Che said with a shudder. "There are love springs in Xanth; it is reasonable to assume that there can also be hate springs."

"You mean it—?" But evidently it did. The nymph had been in the water of hate, and now hated the faun so much that she didn't care about anything except hurting him. The two of them must have known this, because they hadn't wanted to go in the water. It was indeed a terrible thing.

The faun ran, but now things were reversed. The goblins would not let him through, and he had to dodge back, and when he did the nymph closed the gap. Her delicate hands were curved into claws and her pretty teeth were bared in an ugly snarl; there was no doubt she intended to hurt him as much as she could. She was ferocious.

Finally the faun ran down to the water and plunged in. Then he too was transformed by hate. He turned on the nymph. In a moment they were fighting savagely, each one trying to drown the other.

Jenny looked away, feeling sick. She was hardly aware when the goblins hustled her and Che into the hut that the nymph and faun had used. She had never imagined that such mean creatures as the goblins could exist.

The hut was dark, except for a bit of light from the distant fire leaking in around the edges of the door and a thin shaft of moonlight from a round vent at the top. In a moment Jenny's eyes adjusted, and she could see well enough. The hut was empty except for them; there was no furniture, just the packed earth floor, which smelled of urine and worse.

They remained tied; evidently the goblins didn't care about their comfort. There was nothing to do but settle down and rest as well as they could. Che lay down in the center of the hut, as his body was not structured to do anything else. Jenny settled at the edge and leaned against the hard mud wall. She was hungry, but knew that this was the least of her problems; she could eat after she was rescued, and if she wasn't rescued, it would hardly matter whether she ate. She was tired, and this she could do something about simply by resting and sleeping.

Che leaned his human torso back against his animal torso, fluffed out his wings a bit, and closed his eyes. He breathed evenly, looking quite relaxed. Jenny envied him that ability; she was unable to relax despite the sense it made. Her mind was too busy with the events of the past day.

How far away and long ago her normal life on the World of Two Moons seemed! That business of the giant single moon—

She shook her head. There was no sense dwelling on that. Once they escaped, and she had Sammy back, and Che was safe with his mother, then she could see about returning to her normal and familiar world. But all that was so far beyond her present situation of fatigue, dirt, and horror that she would do best to put it out of her mind.

The trouble with trying to put things out of her mind was that then they just came right back into it stronger than ever. What were her folks thinking now? Surely they were wondering what had happened to her, and worrying—no, she *had* to stop thinking about that!

Unless—unless she could send to her holt and make her situation known. Sending was the mind contact between people of her kind that enabled them to find each other or to give warning of danger without shouting. Why hadn't she thought of that before?

She concentrated, sending. But there was no response. She was out of range of her kind, and the folk of Xanth could neither send nor receive. Now she felt more truly alone than ever before.

She had only one remaining resource, the one that was most private to her. She could invoke it only when alone, but she was alone now, for Che was asleep.

She began to hum, and then to sing. Jenny never sang in company, because it was just too complicated to try to explain what it meant to her. But when she was alone or with her friends, it was a great comfort. Her friends were

Sammy and the flowers and the colored stones around her holt, or maybe just herself when she had some chore to do. When she sang it made her surroundings seem brighter and warmer and nicer, and though she knew it wasn't real— that is, that no one else would see it that way—it was always a comfort to her.

In her fancy as she sang, there was a Princess, and a castle atop a mountain, and a strange handsome Prince, and a dragon who was somehow the same as the Prince. Jenny had never seen a dragon or known that any such creature existed, yet she somehow understood the nature of this creature and respected it. It was like a big winged snake with fire in its belly. And the Princess loved the Prince-dragon, but—

Feet tramped up close to the door. Jenny's song and fancy cut off instantly.

The door banged open. "Food," a goblin said in his harsh voice, and dumped down a big leaf on which were two chunks of meat.

Che lifted his head. "We can't eat if we remain tied," he pointed out.

Grudgingly the goblin touched his knot, and Che's hands came free. Then the goblin touched Jenny's knot, and it relaxed and let her go. "But don't try anything dumb, you dumbbells," he warned as he backed out the door and slammed it shut. They heard it being barred outside.

"I can't eat that!" Jenny exclaimed.

"Neither can I," Che agreed. "Unless the leaf is edible."

"Oh, you do not eat meat either?" she asked.

"I would not eat *this* meat. You do not recognize it?"

Jenny peered more closely. She screamed. "It's—"

"From the faun," he finished. "And the nymph."

Jenny tried to be sick, but there wasn't enough in her stomach to come up. She just heaved several times and stopped, gasping.

"I apologize," Che said. "I had thought you understood."

"No, I just don't like to eat meat or to hurt any animal,"

Jenny said, her tears blurring her vision. "I should have realized—" She was interrupted by another attempted heave.

"At least we are no longer tied," Che said. "I can make you light, and you can try to climb out the roof vent and escape."

"And leave you here to be—be—" She couldn't get past her choke. "No," she managed after a moment.

"I appreciate your generosity, but it is foolish. You should save yourself if you can."

"I never claimed to be sensible," Jenny said, unable to look in the direction of the door where the awful meat lay.

"Then perhaps we should rest again."

"Yes." She hoped it was possible.

They were quiet for a time. Jenny did not relax at all. The realization of that meat was haunting her, and she could not shove the horror from her mind.

"Jenny?" Che asked faintly.

"You can't relax either?" she asked, knowing the answer.

"Perhaps if you sang—"

A wash of another kind of chagrin left her cold. *He had heard*! She had thought he was asleep. "Oh, I couldn't do that," she protested, feeling the flush on her face.

"I apologize if I have transgressed," he said.

She couldn't answer, still feeling embarrassed.

After a time she heard a sniff, and then another. She looked at Che in the gloom and saw that he had his hands up covering his face.

Then she realized that he was trying to stifle tears.

She remembered that he was alone in much the way she was, having been abducted and roughly treated.

She remembered that he was only five years old. He spoke like an adult, which was apparently the way with centaurs, but he was only a child. A foal.

She remembered that they both faced a horrible fate. It was enough to numb her mind. What was it doing to his mind?

"I'm sorry, Che," she said softly. "I sing only to—to animals and things."

"Perhaps if you thought of me as an animal . . ." he said, his voice muffled.

"Oh, you're not an—" But what was he, if not an animal? A friend, in this terrible time.

He needed comforting. Could she withhold from him what she would grant freely to her cat?

"Maybe I can sing to you," she said doubtfully.

She tried it, uncertain what would happen. She had never before sung for anyone who understood what it was. She wasn't sure it was possible. Flowers and animals were uncritical; they never thought it was foolish or out of tune or whatever, or tried to critique it to be more conventional. They just accepted it as it was, and that was the way she could do it. Che might be a foal, but he had awareness beyond that of any animal or flower, and that was likely to interfere. Certainly he had a critical mind.

The sound didn't come. Her throat was tight; it just wouldn't let go. She just couldn't sing in this kind of company.

Still, a five-year-old foal . . .

She tried again, just breathing in tune. After a moment she was able to hum, and then her voice came, and she was singing as before. She was back in the fancy of the Princess, and the castle, and the dragon who looked like a prince.

There was a sound outside. Was a goblin coming? Che's head turned; he heard it too. But Jenny kept singing, hoping that the goblin was just passing by and wouldn't stop.

The sound faded; whoever it was was going away. Jenny kept singing, and her picture of the Princess became clearer and nicer. There were no mean things there, just pretty flowers and a beautiful day. The only dark cloud in sight was small and distant; it looked a bit frustrated.

But then something horrible happened, like awful meat appearing in the hut. The dragon wanted to eat the Princess! He wanted her to come to him when he was in his natural form, so he could eat her and be a king among his kind. What was she to do?

Jenny sang, and the words came naturally as the fancy developed of its own accord. It was almost as if someone were sending to her, so that she wasn't making up the story but receiving it. She was in it, in a way, as the Princess, and Che was in it too, as the dragon Prince, for both were winged monsters. Despite the horror of the situation, she knew that the dragon loved the Princess. He had a funny way of showing it, by her definition, yet she saw also that the love was true by his definition. Dragons were violent creatures who lived to roast and eat others, and the most perfect fulfillment of his nature was the eating of a pure and sweet princess.

So the Princess decided to go to the dragon, for she loved him and wanted him to be fulfilled, even if that required some discomfort on her part. Just as a girl might sing her most private secret song for a friend who needed it, when she had never done such a thing before.

Then mean men and a mean cloud tried to hurt the dragon, and the Princess cried warning to him, and he destroyed the mean men and carried her away to a distant and lovely isle. Because neither could go home again, they used magic to change themselves to unicorns and lived happily ever after. She had never seen a unicorn before either, but somehow in her fancy it didn't matter; she knew exactly what it was. She had no trouble recognizing the cloud, of course; that was Fracto, whom she had met.

It was a lovely fancy, and it made her feel warm all over, and she knew that it had calmed Che, even if he didn't know exactly what was in it. Yet she thought he did know, for he had been in it, and she was glad he had turned out good, and married the Princess instead of eating her. for all that none of it was real and they were only pretend parts.

She continued singing and humming, finding it easy now that she had worked into it. Che listened, and then he was asleep, and then she was asleep. She had done it, despite the horror they were in.

Steps approached the hut again. Jenny woke, hearing them, fearful. This time they did not pass; the door was jerked open, and a goblin showed against the declining fire beyond.

"What, weren't hungry?" the goblin demanded. "All the more for the rest of us!" He picked up the meat and took a big bite as he slammed the door shut again.

Jenny relaxed. She was glad to have the awful meat gone. She had never eaten meat, because she liked animals too well and she knew that it came from them.

But before she managed to sleep again, there were more and heavier steps. The door was yanked open, and Chief Grotesk was there.

"Not eating, huh?" he demanded. "Well, we'll just see about that. Come on out of there, you malingerers. We'll make you do your thing right now."

Jenny's heart sank down to her left foot. It was still the middle of the night, and they hadn't been rescued, and now there would be no chance! All because they had left the awful meat untouched.

They were led out to the subsiding fire. It seemed that some hours had passed, because most of the brush had burned down, and the monstrous cheese moon had traveled to another part of the sky. The goblins must have used up all their fresh meat, and now were ready for more.

"We want you healthy, so we can keep you a few days," the chief said. "If you don't eat, you'll be too weak to run, and you won't taste as good." He must have thought this was a reasonable statement.

"No, thank you," Jenny said. She hated being polite to this cruel goblin, but there seemed nothing to be gained by being impolite.

"Now you have a choice," Grotesk told them with a grimace he must have thought was a smile. "Eat your food or race right now." He showed them the two pieces of meat, one with a bite out of it.

Jenny looked at Che. She knew she wasn't going to touch the stuff, but he had to make his own choice.

He looked at the meat and at the pond a short distance away, and at her. "Sing to me," he murmured.

Jenny was astonished and chagrined. "I can't—" she protested.

"Yeah, tell her to eat it," Grotesk said, evidently mishearing. "So you won't have to race right now. We want to save you for another day, when we haven't just eaten."

"Before we die," Che said.

There was his answer: he wasn't going to eat. So they would have to play the goblins' cruel game, and hate each other, and be cooked. Che wanted to listen to her one more time before that happened. Could she say no?

But how could she sing before these horrible creatures? It had been hard enough to sing to Che alone!

"Come on, come on, make up your stupid mind," Grotesk snapped. The circle of goblins standing around them grinned, enjoying this.

She knew she had to do it. She had to give the centaur foal what little comfort she could. There would be no other chance. At least they would have this memory of their friendship, before the hate came.

She moved to Che and took his head in her hands. She wanted this to be just for him, because she just *couldn't* sing it for the goblins. She pretended that there was no one else here except the two of them. She put her mouth to his ear, closed her eyes, and hummed. In a moment she was able to hum louder. Her fancy began to form, a picture in her mind of the lovely castle on the mountain and the flowers at the base and the Princess picking the flowers and singing to them.

There was a goblin voice somewhere, calling something. "Well, haul some more wood in from the forest, then!" Grotesk said. "We need to keep the kettle hot, in case they don't eat."

Jenny sang louder, to squeeze out those awful words. The fancy firmed, and now the dragon was in it too, in his real form, but not being ferocious. She knew that Che had joined her picture, and that he was the dragon, hoping to carry her away to safety, if only he could fly.

There was a nasty cloud nearby, but even it didn't seem to want to make a storm. It was just watching, and perhaps would float away and rain somewhere else.

"Hey, Chief!" a goblin called. "Aren't we going to make them race?"

The cloud jumped. Then there was a heavy hand on Jenny's shoulder that jolted her into silence. The fancy faded away.

"What are you trying to do, you elven vixen?" the chief demanded. He seemed shaken. "Elves don't have that kind of magic!"

"Magic!" Che exclaimed. "That's it!"

"Now for the race!" the other goblin said.

"Naw, not right now," Grotesk said. "There's something funny about her. She's got magic. Look at those ears!"

The goblins clustered closer. Evidently they hadn't noticed Jenny's ears before. She had never thought her ears would save her from hate and death!

They were hustled back into the hut. As the door slammed, shutting them in, Jenny turned to Che. "You know I don't have any magic!" she said. "I don't even know what it is, really. Where I live, only the High Ones have anything like that."

"I think you do," Che said. "When you sang, I was in your dream about the Princess and the dragon, with Castle Roogna, only it was perched on top of a funny mountain instead of in the jungle where it really is. Then Grotesk was in it too, as the dark cloud. You have dream magic!"

"No I don't!" she protested. "I wasn't asleep, and neither were you, and certainly the goblin chief wasn't. I was just imagining it." But she realized that it couldn't be as simple as that. How could they share her daydream? She had never told either of them what was in it, and her song had not done it either; it had been just made-up words. Yet she had known when Che was there, and when Grotesk was—and they had known also.

"Night mares bring bad dreams to sleeping folk," Che

said. "Mare Imbri and other day mares bring good dreams to waking folk. Maybe you have day mare magic."

"I never heard of this!"

"Well, you haven't been in Xanth long."

He had a point. "These day dreams—do several folk share them?"

He frowned. "I don't think so. Also, the mares don't sing. But it must be something like that, because Grotesk felt it, and now he's not sure he wants to cook us until he figures it out. Perhaps he likes to exploit any captives fully before he eats them."

"But it didn't last," she said. "Otherwise I might have been able to keep singing, and we could just have walked out of here."

"That is an intriguing notion," he agreed. "Why didn't it last?"

"Grotesk put his brute hand on me."

"But if he was in the vision—and he was, as the black cloud—why did he break it up? That vision is pleasant. I did not wish to leave it, and I don't think he did."

"I don't know. I heard another goblin call 'Hey, Chief!' and—" She paused, remembering it. "The cloud jumped! Then he was out of it."

"Because someone disturbed him," Che said, "woke him from the dream, in a manner. That suggests that if that other goblin hadn't called, Grotesk would not have left it."

"I suppose so. It's too bad the other goblin wasn't in it."

"Maybe he was out of range of your singing," Che said, becoming excited. "Maybe if you had sung louder, we could have walked out of the camp!"

Jenny dreaded the thought of singing at all in such company, let alone loudly, but if it was that or their lives, she had to consider it. "I suppose—I suppose we should find out if that's it. Because otherwise they may cook us anyway."

"Yes. Sing to me now, and I will see whether I can break

out of the vision. If I can, probably the goblins can. But if I can't—"

"Yes!" She was excited too, for now they had a hope of escaping on their own.

She set herself, then began to hum. She just couldn't start singing cold; her throat balked. It was like plunging into cold water; she had never been able to do that and always had to go in gradually. But the humming got her in, and soon she was singing. It was easier than it had been outside, because there was only Che here.

Che watched her alertly. He did not go to sleep or even relax. He stood waiting to see what would happen, ready to break out of the vision when it came, if he could.

Her fancy formed, the castle and the Princess. But there was no dragon in it and no dark cloud. Just the Princess picking her flowers. It wasn't working! Che was not getting into the picture at all.

Then there was a sound outside. Che was distracted by it, probably afraid it was a goblin coming; they did not want the goblins to know what they were doing! Jenny kept singing, though ready to stop if it really was a goblin.

The dragon appeared. Now it was working! Then a small dark cloud appeared. That, she realized, must be the goblin outside; it must have come close enough to hear her singing.

Now it was time for Che to break out. She did not stop singing, because if she did the fancy would fade. That didn't count. They had to know whether others could break out while she maintained the fancy.

Che did not break out. He didn't even seem to be trying to. Finally, worried that some other goblin might come and discover what they were doing, she stopped, letting the vision dissipate.

"What happened?" she asked. "Didn't you try to get out?"

"No," Che said, abashed. "First I couldn't get in. Then suddenly I was in, and I just never thought of getting out. I just wanted to stay there and be part of it."

"But you were supposed to try!" she said. "So we'd know if this can hold the goblins."

"I know. Somehow I just lost interest."

"Well, we'll just have to try it again and this time make sure you try," she said severely.

"I certainly shall," he agreed resolutely.

She hummed, then sang again. But again the fancy formed without him. He was watching her, paying close attention, but it wasn't working.

Then the cloud formed. The goblin was back in, but not Che! How could that be, when the goblin surely didn't care and probably didn't even know about this?

Then she realized what it was. She stopped singing.

"But I wasn't in!" Che protested.

"I know. The goblin outside was."

"But—"

"You were paying attention," she said. "The goblin wasn't. And before—you only got in when you were distracted."

"When I was distracted!" he echoed. "I heard something, and looked away, and suddenly I was in the vision!"

"So maybe it only works when you're not paying attention!" she concluded. "And maybe you can get out only when you *are* paying attention!"

"That must be the case! But how can I not pay attention, when we are experimenting?"

"When you are distracted," she said.

"But that depends on chance events."

"I think so. But if that's the way it works, we must find a way to use it."

"Yes. We must try again, to verify this—and to ascertain whether I can leave it when I am in."

She sang again. He watched her at first, then deliberately turned away. He banged his hand against the wall hard enough to hurt, shook it—and the dragon appeared in the vision, limping.

There was no doubt that it took a distraction to get in! Now could he get out? Jenny kept singing.

But the dragon seemed to have no interest in getting out. Neither did two goblin clouds nearby. The peaceful, nice scene continued as long as Jenny sang.

Jenny stopped again, and the scene quietly departed.

Che was abashed. "I know I was supposed to try to get out, but I just couldn't bring myself to try. It was so nice in your fancy."

"But how can we find out, if you don't—"

"I think we have the answer," he said. "A person can not accomplish anything if he doesn't try—and the folk in your fancy don't try. They just enjoy it."

"But then how can *I* leave it?" she asked.

"Your situation is different. You are not just in it, you are generating it with your song. You have to keep singing, making your scene, and if you don't, the scene goes. The others are passive, while you are active, so you have control."

Jenny found that a little complicated to understand, but she was coming to respect the centaur's power of reasoning, so she accepted it. "So then the others can't leave it, because they don't want to—but they can be jogged out of it. But since we can't get them into it unless they are close enough to hear the song but aren't paying attention to it, it won't work on them when we need it to."

"Perhaps it will work. Grotesk was distracted when someone asked him about the wood, and he joined the vision before another goblin jogged him out of it. So if you are singing, maybe you'll catch the goblins anyway, the moment they aren't paying attention."

Jenny thought about how hard it was to pay attention to something steadily, even when it was important. Her mind was always drifting into other fancies, and sometimes she had gotten in trouble for it. Goblins didn't seem any better than other creatures in this respect. So maybe it would work.

Except that if there were constant distractions, there were also constant reminders. Grotesk had been distracted, then reminded, so his presence in the fancy hadn't lasted. "I don't think it will work well enough when there are many goblins,'' she said. ''Some of them will always be paying attention.''

Che nodded. ''That is true. I wish we could do it when they are asleep. Then any who heard us departing would join the vision, and any who did not hear us would continue sleeping.''

''Why can't we?'' she asked, her hope rising.

''Because we can't get out of this hut. The mud is too tough for us to break, and the door is barred from outside.''

Her hope sank again, to land with a silent thud on the floor. He was right. They would have to wait for a goblin to come to open the door, and then it would probably be morning.

They pondered a while. ''Perhaps when the next goblin comes,'' Che said, ''you can sing and lead me out, for I will not be doing anything of my own volition. If we are lucky, the others will not be paying attention, and we can escape before they realize.''

''It's worth a try,'' Jenny agreed doubtfully. She had nothing better to offer.

Then she sang them to sleep. They had learned a lot, and saved themselves from hating and boiling; now all they could do was catch up on their rest.

The sound of the bar being knocked out woke them in the morning. Jenny wiped the sleep from her eyes, trying to orient; where was she? But all too quickly she remembered: she was in trouble.

It was Grotesk himself. ''Are you two going to eat now?'' he asked, waving a cold awful chunk of meat at them.

''Sing!'' Che said.

''Oh no you don't, gamin!'' the Chief exclaimed. He evidently thought she was a boy, and she was not inclined to correct him. No, he had called her a wench before. Maybe he just didn't care. ''Gag her!''

Oops! Jenny tried to sing, but it was so hard to start. Especially when the goblins were charging in and grabbing her. Before she could do anything, there was a dirty cloth tied around her face, blocking her mouth.

"When I saw you had magic, I knew it wasn't safe to let you be," Grotesk said. "So now you two will eat or you'll run. The centaur will eat first."

Jenny knew that Che wouldn't eat that meat. They would have to race, and the result wouldn't matter, because the goblins would cook them anyway.

She couldn't sing, but maybe she could hum. She didn't know whether that would accomplish anything, but it was all she could do while gagged.

She hummed, starting faintly, then getting louder. She pictured the nice scene, with the Princess and her flowers. It was there for her, but could it extend to the others?

Grotesk looked around. "What's that?" he asked.

Unfortunately, it wasn't a distraction he heard; it was Jenny's humming. That meant he was paying attention, so he remained alert.

"Ha!" the Chief said. "The elf's trying to sing. Well, we'll stop that!" He drew back his huge gnarly fist.

Che lurched forward and yanked Jenny's gag down. Suddenly she was singing—but Grotesk was concentrating on her, swinging his fist at her face.

Jenny ducked, and the fist sailed over her head. But immediately the other goblins dived in, grabbing her arms. They hauled her up straight.

"Hold her," Grotesk said grimly. "This time I won't miss." And Jenny knew he wouldn't. She opened her mouth, trying desperately to sing, but her throat was so tight that not even a scream could squeeze out.

"Look at that!" a goblin cried, peering to the side.

"Don't bother me now," the chief said. "Wait till I punch in this elf's face."

"But she's—" the goblin said, amazed. Now others were looking there, their ugly faces going slack.

"I told you—" Grotesk snapped, finally glancing in that direction.

Jenny seized her moment. She forced the air through her throat and began to sing. If she could catch the goblins during their moment of distraction, maybe she and Che could still try to escape. It was, she knew, their last chance.

Chapter 7. Nada's Notion

Their hands linked, the two girls stepped into the huge peephole of the huge gourd. Nada led, for she had been in the gourd before. Actually, so had Electra, but that wasn't the same; Electra had been asleep all those hundreds of years.

It awed Nada to think of just how old Electra was, if her age were measured from the time of her birth. So she generally didn't think of it; she accepted Electra as she was now, which was just barely under eighteen, though she looked fifteen. In appearance she was a good match for Prince Dolph, who really was fifteen, going on sixteen. It was too bad that she lacked the qualities that would turn such a teenager on, such as a buxom torso and freckle-free face. Electra was a good girl, without doubt, but men of any age were more interested in appearances than in qualities. Maybe if Nada worked with Electra to make her more interesting—

Her thought was interrupted by the scene inside the gourd. They were in the middle of a village—no, a town—no, a city—of plants. Plants rustled along the streets and climbed up steps to buildings, while assorted animals and human folk stood decoratively in planters.

"Plant City," Electra said, letting go her hand, now that they were safely in the same scene. "What fun!"

Nada envied her that quality of delight in odd things. Nada would rather have been back at Castle Roogna reading one of the romance novels from the castle library. One of the ghosts had shown Zora Zombie that section of it, and Zora had told her, as they both liked such books. There, romance was always fresh and wonderful; the men were always handsome, strong, and older than the women. But Electra hardly cared about reading; she was always out and about, doing things, making new friends, and in general being a buzz of innocent activity. Part of it was because she wasn't a princess, so didn't have to uphold princessly standards. She could wear blue jeans and pigtails and play tag with the moat monster and ride Donkey Centaur at an indelicate gallop through the orchard and use slang expressions, and never get in trouble for it. She could flop down in the dirt and make mud pies. Nada had to pretend she wasn't interested in such juvenilia, but if she had ever had a secret place where no one would ever know what she did, she would have made mud pies. Most important of all, Electra didn't have to be constantly on guard against anyone seeing her panties; there was no risk, in blue jeans, and no one was interested anyway. She had such a carefree life, because of what she wasn't.

Except that in another week she would die, if she didn't get what Nada would gladly give her: marriage to Prince Dolph. One would never know Electra's tragedy by looking at her or watching her constant activity, but it was there and looming closer every day. Now Nada wished she had had the courage to break her betrothal to Dolph, when given the chance to do so without hurting her folk. But she hadn't realized that there was a time limit on Electra. She had thought something would happen, eventually, that would settle the matter. Now she knew it wouldn't. Dolph would have to choose between the two of them, and neither of them trusted that.

If only there were some way to force the choice! To take it out of his grubby hands. But that seemed impossible, while both of them lived.

While both of them lived. Suddenly Nada had a notion.

"There's a cookie!" Electra exclaimed in her enthusiastic way. She had been doing what Nada should have, looking all around to find their way. "See, there by that greenback buck."

Nada looked. Sure enough, there was a big male sheep with green wool on its back, standing in a planter, and beside it was a sign with the picture of a chicolate chop cookie. There was another thing: Nada didn't dare eat such a cookie, because it was Fattening, while Electra could eat anything she pleased and remain athletically slender. Consequently Electra had far more joy of appetite than Nada ever did.

They walked down the street in the direction of the buck. So far this seemed all right; there was no threat to them, and no horrible sights were inflicting themselves on them. But Nada didn't trust this; the realm of the gourd usually would not let strangers through without trying to get at them somehow. Something unpleasant, or at least strange, was bound to happen sometime.

Nervously, Nada looked back at the buck as they passed it, fearing it would act like its cousin the battering ram and charge them. But the scene remained placid. Nothing had changed. Except—

Except that the cookie picture was gone.

Was this a one-way path? If so, they had better not deviate from it, for once they lost it, they would not be able to backtrack to pick it up again.

The plants ignored them, perhaps from politeness, or perhaps simply because plants noticed animate folk no more than animate folk usually noticed plants. They were just there. Soon they came to an intersection, where something with three round little windows hung. The top window seemed red, and the bottom one green, and the middle one yellow. As they reached it, the red one brightened, becoming a rose.

"Do you know what that means?" Electra inquired brightly.

"I have no idea," Nada said.

"I think I have a notion. When Grey and Ivy and I went to Mundania, there were similar boxes hanging above the roads. They always flashed red as anyone came near, and that meant that everyone had to stop. After a while they would flash green, and then it was all right to go. Maybe this works that way."

"What happens if we go when it is red?" Nada asked.

"I don't know. Something awful, I think, because we always stopped and cursed at the red light."

Nada pondered briefly, and decided it was best not to risk it. She hoped there wouldn't be trouble if she didn't curse; that was another unprincessly thing.

After a minute the rose abruptly faded and a bright green lime flashed. Nada was ready to proceed, but Electra held her back. "We haven't seen the cookie," she explained. "I wonder—"

Sure enough, after only a few seconds the yellow window brightened, and it was a big vanilla cookie.

They hurried on before it could change its mind.

Nada glanced back, choosing her moment when Electra was proceeding eagerly ahead, for a notion was percolating through the reptilian aspect of her mind. Sure enough, the next time the light flashed yellow, it was no longer a vanilla cookie, but a lemon. The marker was gone.

This *was* a one-way trail, or at least a one-use trail. The moment a marker was used, it disappeared.

Now they were on a spiraling path that Nada somehow hadn't noticed before. It squished as they walked; in fact it felt swampy. But there was nowhere else to walk. So they followed it around and down, squishing all the way.

"It's a corkscrew swamp!" Electra exclaimed, catching on. She enjoyed squishing, of course.

The thing seemed to continue interminably. Nada's royal slippers were getting horrendously soiled. "I've had enough of this," she declared at last. "I'm changing."

She looked around to make sure no one was watching, then quickly got out of her clothing and handed it to Electra.

It would be devastating if any man were to catch a glimpse of princessly panties, but Electra would guard them with what was left of her life. Then Nada assumed her natural form: a serpent with her human head. Now she could slide along the muck without any problem.

"I saw! I saw!" someone cried just behind them. It was a man in an eerie cloak with hair standing straight out from his head. "I saw your pan—"

Nada shifted to full serpent form and whipped her head back, striking at the awful man. But her jaws passed right through him. Her momentum carried her on over the edge of the spiraling swamp path, and she started to fall.

"Nada!" Electra cried, diving to catch hold of Nada's tail. But too much of Nada's body was over the edge, and Electra was hauled along with her as she fell.

"You shouldn't have done that," Nada reproved her, returning to her natural form. "Now we're both falling to whatever horrendous fate awaits us below."

"But I couldn't let that stage fright do that to you!" Electra protested. "Especially when I know he didn't see your panties. I was facing that way all the time, and he wasn't there until he yelled."

"That's a consolation," Nada said. "But what I meant was, if something happened to me Dolph would have to marry you. But it's no good if we both—"

"That's horrible!" Electra protested. "I don't want you to die instead of me!"

"Look," Nada said reasonably, "we can't both marry him, and I don't even want to. But it's his choice, not ours. Since we know he'll make the wrong choice, it behooves us to make the choice for him."

"But we're friends! I couldn't think of—"

"Your niceness is all too likely to cost you your life, and me my happiness," Nada said. "It is time for desperate measures. We have to eliminate one of us, and we just had an easy way to do it. But now we may have eliminated both of us, and that's no good either."

"Maybe you're right," Electra said, biting her lip in the

way that wasn't permitted to princesses. "I guess I just wasn't thinking. But oh, Nada, I just had to try to save you!"

"I would have tried the same for you," Nada confessed. "Still, we have to get sensible sometime."

They were still falling, but it seemed to Nada that their descent was slower now. She remembered that this was the gourd, where things were not necessarily quite what they seemed. Was it possible that they were not both about to be dashed to pieces below?

Electra peered down. "There's a river!" she said, some of her brightness returning. "A very pretty one."

Nada looked. There was indeed a river, which glistened in the sunshine. At the moment Nada wasn't inclined to question how there could be sunlight way down here below the corkscrew swamp path; the river was beautiful in a crystalline way, with many perfectly-cut facets. "I agree."

They continued slowing, until at last they came to rest on the river bank. Now the crystals of the river were large and bright, sending lovely splays of light in a number of directions. "What a beautiful Crystal River!" Electra breathed.

"But now we are off the cookie path," Nada reminded her, getting practical. "We shall have to look for it, for we don't want to be forever lost here in the gourd, no matter how beautiful this part of it is."

"Yes, of course," Electra agreed, chastened. "But I'm sure the corkscrew is here somewhere."

They looked, but there was no corkscrew swamp path. Evidently they had fallen beyond it and were lost. "We shall just have to look for a cookie sign," Nada decided. "You look upriver and I'll look downriver. That will double our chances of finding the correct path."

"But we shouldn't separate!" Electra protested. "We might never find each other again!"

"And if only one of us emerges from the gourd, where does that leave us?" Nada inquired softly.

"But—" Electra started, flustered. Then she caught on. "You mean—?"

"I mean it is one way to resolve our dilemma, without prejudice to either of us."

"Oh, Nada, I don't like this way!" Electra cried.

"Make me this pact," Nada said firmly. "Whichever one of us finds the cookie trail will follow it straight out, so as to waste no time in rescuing Che Centaur. The one who doesn't find it can backtrack and pick up the trail later."

"But if we both make it through, then who marries Dolph?"

"The one he chooses, of course, as always."

Electra looked troubled. She evidently had a suspicion what Nada intended to do, but didn't want to accuse her of it openly. "I suppose."

"Very well, it's decided," Nada said briskly. She slithered downriver. She made it a point not to look back, so that Electra would have to do the right thing and explore upriver.

She hoped Electra would be the one to find the cookie trail. Then the girl would follow it out and proceed on their mission, alone. The trail markers would be gone, so Nada would not be able to follow her. Electra would marry Dolph, and live and be happy. Dolph would be happy too, for once he really paid attention to Electra—a thing he really had never done—he would discover that she was a far better match for him than Nada was. She was closer to his age, which counted for a lot, and seemed closer yet, which counted for more. She shared his juvenile enthusiasms. She loved to eat, and she could never refrain from laughing when someone blew on a stink horn, making a foul-smelling noise. That was something no princess could get away with, but a prince could and an ordinary girl could. Most important of all, Electra lived to please Dolph, and that was a quality any man could come to appreciate in any woman, once she got his attention. So Dolph would be happier with Electra, and everyone knew it except him. He just needed a situation where he could realize it.

The Crystal River wound its lovely way down to a strange
sea. It was red, and it seemed to be groaning. Well, not
exactly groaning; the sound was more like a whine.

She stopped at the beach, which was in the shape of a
great U. In fact there were many little metal U's on it,
instead of sand. They were the kind of things that centaurs
nailed to their feet to prevent wear. They were called horseshoes, because presumably horses could use them too. The
whole beach was made of diminishing horseshoes! What
bad dream was this supposed to be the setting for?

She went to the water, curious about its color. She looked
around, saw no human folk, and changed to her human
form. Then she stooped to dip out a handful of the water.

She saw eyes looking up at her, from under the surface.
Oops! Was someone there, spying on her human nakedness?
No, it was a shell with eyes. A see shell, of course.

She reached into the water, took the edge of the shell,
lifted it, turned it over, and used it to dip out some of the
whining red water. She brought it to her mouth and tasted
it.

Sure enough, it was a flavored alcoholic beverage. Red
whine. No doubt yet another prop for somebody's bad
dream.

Well, Nada didn't need it. She walked on along the beach,
away from the Crystal River, wishing she had her clothes.
She had forgotten about this detail when she separated from
Electra, and now could not go back to get her clothing from
her friend. She would just have to make do. Perhaps it
didn't matter, as she would not be emerging to normal
Xanth.

For that was the gist of Nada's notion: she would fail to
find her way out of the gourd, and Electra would marry
Dolph by default and live happily ever after. Nada could
not renege on her betrothal directly, but if she were lost
here she wouldn't have to. Maybe she could find work in
the dream realm, the way Girard Giant had three years ago.
Ivy had of course told her all about that: how they had
discovered a river of blood and traced it to its source, which

was the giant's injury, and managed to help Girard recover
and find his true love, Gina Giantess. Girard had been one
of the invisible giants, but now he was a visible one working
in the gourd. So there was a precedent, and Nada was ready
to work here if the Night Stallion had a use for her.

Then she saw the cookie. It was a delicious-looking pun-
wheel, the kind that was horribly tempting to princesses,
though they invariably made folk turn around and groan.
Ivy said she had loved them as a little girl, and she still
blushed and yielded to her desire to eat one, every so often.
After all, just how much could be expected of a princess?
There were limits.

Nada knew her plan was in trouble. She had thought that
the cookie trail was upriver, not down, because they had
fallen down to this region. Now she realized that the cookie
trail could go wherever it wanted, including down—and it
had done so. So she was the one who had found it, not
Electra. Her princessly sacrifice had been for nothing.

What was she to do now? She still knew that Electra was
the proper one to marry Dolph, and that would never happen
if Electra didn't find her way out of the gourd. Certainly
Nada didn't want to leave Electra here, because then she
would have no chance to marry Dolph, and would die within
the week.

Nada pondered, and considered, and thought, changing
forms for each activity, and finally realized that there was
a way out of this mess. All she had to do was avoid the
cookie trail, so that it didn't vanish, and hide. In due course
Electra, failing to find any cookies upstream, would come
downstream and find it here. She would assume that Nada
had already taken it, for she didn't know that it was a one-
use trail. She would follow it out, and the plan would be
intact.

Nada backed away from the cookie, trusting it not to
vanish. She was right: it remained in place, because she
had not passed it. She assumed her serpent form and slid
into the brush. When she was well hidden, she became
absolutely still. She intended to watch to be sure that Electra

did come. If she did not, Nada would have to go look for her, for at least one of them did have to make it on through the gourd. Che Centaur needed rescuing, after all.

Now that her notion was being implemented, Nada had a second thought. How could poor little Electra rescue Che from the mean goblins? She could shock one of them, but where there was one goblin there were always twenty more. Didn't Nada know that, from her father's endless war against the encroaching goblins of Mount Etamin! She was really deserting Electra, and that made her feel increasingly guilty. Yet this was her chance to do the right thing by Electra, and by Dolph too, and she really had to follow through. So she kept still, and waited.

Before long Electra did come. She hadn't found the cookie trail, so was trying to catch up with Nada, who she thought must have found it.

Nada watched as the girl ran by. Such vigor! Her light brown braids flounced busily, and her freckles seemed to bounce off her face. She had such joy of life, no matter what she was doing. She would be so good for Dolph, who had such little notion what life was about.

Yet Nada felt a tear flowing down across her snoot. That was odd, because as far as she knew, serpents didn't cry. This was the last time she would be seeing Electra. She hated what she was doing to her friend, though she knew it was best for her. Electra would never understand what had happened, and would be upset about taking advantage of the situation and marrying Dolph. Electra was horribly sweet about things like that. Yet at the same time Electra would be struggling to rescue Che without help, and that was almost as bad as the other part was good. Nada's emotions were getting so mixed up they were like scrambled spaghetti.

She watched Electra spy the cookie. "She found it!" the girl exclaimed, delighted. One of the qualities of Electra was the way she saw things: she had not been glad for herself, but for Nada. She was the best friend a girl could have.

But then Electra paused. "But maybe I shouldn't follow," she said. "It isn't as if I have a future, anyway."

Oh, no! Electra was getting the same notion Nada had! She thought Nada was headed out of the gourd, so she wanted to remain in and solve the Betrothee problem. That wouldn't do!

"But she'll need my help, handling those goblins," Electra decided, and ran on past the cookie, which vanished as she passed it.

Nada relaxed, but somehow she didn't feel much better. Electra had decided to go ahead because she wanted to help Nada fight the goblins. Nada had thought of that with respect to Electra, but had decided against it. That showed how much less caring she was. She felt terrible.

She slithered forward, tempted to follow the girl before she got out of sight. But by the time she reached the spot where the cookie had been, Electra was already out of sight. She moved so rapidly, with her slender, healthy body! One would never catch Electra languidly eating grapes on a couch; she would eat the grapes while zipping all around the castle.

Nada tried to see where the girl had gone, but it was no use; all directions were similarly unlikely. So she gave it up as a bad job. She would feel guilty no matter what she did, either for not making it possible for Electra to marry Dolph or for deserting her in the struggle against the goblins. Or both.

She turned and slithered toward the Crystal River. She moved right out onto it, not caring whether it was liquid or solid. Serpents could swim, after all.

It turned out to be in between; the crystals bobbed around when she touched them, floating individually on the water. They were cold, though. In fact, they were ice crystals. So she moved on through as quickly as she could. Her serpent body did not have a mechanism to maintain heat, and she could slow until she froze if she didn't get away from the ice soon.

She made it to the far bank. Here there were no horseshoes, just people shoes of all types and sizes, their tongues slurping around. This would be where the centaurs got their supplies for their game of people shoes. But Nada still didn't see how such things would make bad dreams. But of course there was a lot she didn't know about dreams.

She would have to learn it, though, if she worked here. First she would have to find the Night Stallion and ask for work in the dream realm. She did not expect to enjoy making sleeping folk unhappy, but she hoped to muddle through somehow. Now where would the stallion be?

She spied a city ahead. It seemed to be in the shape of a cross. Maybe there would be a night mare there, or someone else she could ask.

She reverted to her natural form, which was the best one for both travel and dialogue. It wouldn't be any good to turn human, because she might be mistaken for a nymph without her clothes, and anyway it just wasn't princessly to run around nude. When she had been younger she had done it, but her years at Castle Roogna had impressed on her the human way, especially with respect to panties. So her natural form was the one, until someone told her otherwise.

As she slithered closer, she saw that the city's buildings were all in the shape of crosses too. They had cross-shaped doors and windows, and cross-shaped chimneys. She wondered whether this was the place for cross people. Maybe this was where all the cross actors lived, for dreams where anger and meanness were required. She hoped she didn't encounter any of those!

She smelled something delicious: she was passing a patch of hot cross buns. But she knew that if she tried to eat one it would either burn her mouth angrily or try to switch her posterior.

The intersections were crosses too. Nada decided to slither straight on through; she would ask for information at some other place.

She entered the main intersection at the center of the city—and suddenly someone was charging toward her from the side. Nada hissed in surprise and drew back her head, fearing what this denizen of Cross City would do.

"Nada!" the other cried, gladly.

"Electra!" Nada exclaimed, instantly recognizing her.

Electra threw herself down and embraced Nada, not caring about either her form or the dirt of the street. "Oh, I'm so glad I finally caught up to you!" she exclaimed. "I was afraid something had happened to you!"

Nada opened her mouth, but nothing came out for a moment. *Electra didn't even realize what Nada had done!* Her innocence and goodwill was such that she had no suspicions of her friends. Nada was ashamed. "You're such a decent girl!" she said, her tears flowing again.

"No I'm not! I almost didn't follow you, because—"

"You weren't following me," Nada said, unwilling to have this lie between them any longer. "I didn't take the cookie trail. It was just coincidence we met here." But as she spoke, she realized that it might not be. This was Cross City, where all paths might cross, including theirs.

"But—" Electra said, round eyed.

"I deserted you, 'Lectra. I left you to face the goblins alone. I'm so sorry." Nada could hardly see, now, because of her tears of remorse.

"Because you wanted me to be the only one to leave the gourd," Electra said, "so I could marry Dolph."

"That, too," Nada confessed.

Electra squeezed her tightly around her serpentine neck. "Oh, Nada, how could I marry Dolph when you were lost? You were so generous, but I'm not worthy of it, honest I'm not! This isn't the way!"

"This isn't the way," Nada agreed, relieved.

"Promise me not to do that again!"

There was no help for it. "I promise." Then, after a pause: "But you *are* worthy of it, 'Lectra."

Electra shook that off as a kind overstatement. "Now we can go after those goblins together," she said enthusiastically, her bright spirits returning as if never dimmed. "And if anything happens to one of us then—"

Nada nodded. Sweet, innocent little Electra did understand the underlying reality. Perhaps their problem could be honestly settled, by chance. Goblins were mean creatures, and only an ogre could go into an encounter with them with any equanimity, and that was partly because ogres were so stupid.

They resumed their trek. The trail of cookies led them to a great wall, and to an alcove in it. When they entered the alcove, suddenly they were by another river, and there were cookies growing all along its banks.

"How can we find our way now?" Electra asked, dismayed. "There are so many!"

Nada was similarly baffled. She turned around, to check for the last vanished cookie, in case there was some misunderstanding. But there was nothing but the peephole of a giant gourd. She averted her gaze just in time to avoid being trapped in it.

Then she made the connection. " 'Lectra! We're out of the gourd! This is the With-a-Cookee River—the real one!"

"Oh!" Electra cried, thrilled. "Now we can rescue Che!"

"First we have to find him," Nada reminded her. "And watch for the goblins. We had better surprise them instead of having them surprise us."

Electra suffered a flash of seriousness. "Yes. I can shock only one. We'll need your jaws."

"I can bite only one at a time. What we'd really better do is find them, then blow the whistle to summon the others."

"But won't the goblins hear the whistle too?"

"Ulp! I had forgotten about that! We won't dare alert the goblins, because they might dump him into the pot immediately."

"Maybe the sparkleberries," Electra said. "It's pretty dark now, so they'll be visible. If the goblins don't realize what they are—"

"Yes, those will be fine. So now we had better move, because it is evident that Che isn't here anymore. The goblins must have taken him to their camp."

"Can you sniff out the trail in your serpent form?"

"I should be able to." Nada assumed full serpent form and flicked her tongue about. Immediately she picked up Che's scent—but also the scents of many goblins and something else. It was almost like elf, but not quite. She didn't think she had smelled that creature before.

She resumed Naga form. "Is there an elf elm near here?" she asked.

"I suppose there could be," Electra said, "since we don't know exactly where we are. But the elves wouldn't foalknap a centaur!"

"There's the smell of one elf, almost," Nada said. "But no elm tree scent. It's almost as if this elf didn't come from an elm."

"But that's impossible! All elves live in elf elms, and they get impossibly weak when they stray too far from them. If one did stray, his companions would bring him back; elves don't desert their own."

"Yes. That's why this is so odd. A funny elf smell, and no elm tree. I must be misinterpreting." Nada returned to serpent form and explored further.

Soon she was slithering along the goblin's trail. The evil little men had not even tried to conceal it; they had simply charged along to one of their trails, and then used that. The centaur and odd-elf smells continued, closely associated; it was almost as if both were captives.

Then Electra touched her back with a hand. "I see something," she whispered.

Nada lifted her head and peered around. She had kept her head low before, sniffing out the trail. There was a faint light off to the side.

She put on her human head. "That must be the goblin camp! We'll sneak up on it."

They did that, moving quietly. Nada had no trouble, in her serpent form, but Electra had to move very slowly in her human body.

They came to the edge of a little jungle glade. There were four goblins and a well-damped fire. Beside the fire was a little tent. Nada realized that Che must be tied in the tent. Could she slither silently in behind and untie him without the goblins knowing? It seemed worth a try.

She resumed naga form. "I'm going in that tent," she whispered.

Electra nodded. She would wait here and spring in when her help was needed.

Nada became a small snake and slithered around the glade toward the tent. The goblins seemed to be eating their supper. She hoped it wasn't boiled centaur! She was relieved that the party was so small; she could probably handle it alone, in large serpent form. One of them was female, which made it that degree less formidable, because lady goblins were much less nasty than males. But it would be better to untie Che first so that he could bolt free while Nada kept the gobs at bay.

The funny thing was, she didn't smell Che or the odd elf. The closer she got to the tent, the less likely it seemed that either creature was here. What could this mean?

She reached the tent and slithered under its back flap. It was empty. The only smell was that of the female goblin. Evidently she was in charge of this party and had the best facilities.

But why was this little party of goblins camping out here, apart from the main mass? And where was Che? The mysteries were deepening instead of fading.

Nada slithered back out of the tent, disappointed. They would have to resume the trail they had been following before; this was only a diversion.

Then Electra sneezed. Nada knew the sound the moment she heard it, and hoped the goblins wouldn't.

No such luck. "What was that?" the gobliness exclaimed, jumping up so quickly that her long hair swirled about her body.

"It sounded like a human sneeze, Godiva," one of the males replied.

"I know that, Moron!" Godiva snapped. She pointed to the sound with a wand she had.

"Eeeek!" Electra cried, rising into the air. Nada saw her clearly in the moonlight, flying without wings. It seemed that the gobliness had magic—in fact a magic wand.

Nada had to act. She assumed monster serpent form and launched herself at the goblins.

"Look out, Godiva!" a goblin cried.

Godiva whirled. She spied Nada. Her wand whipped around. In a moment Nada was lifted into the air, while Electra dropped to the ground.

"What have we here?" Godiva asked, keeping Nada suspended in the air.

Nada changed to human form, still floating. "You have a naga," she replied, hoping that would set them back or at least take their attention off Electra, so she could do something. This magic wand was another surprise!

"Look at that body!" a goblin exclaimed, ogling her. The other two males stared similarly.

Oops! In her confusion, Nada had forgotten her nakedness. She would have used her natural form instead, if she had taken more than half an instant to think about it.

"Idiot!" the gobliness cried. "Imbecile! Grab that other girl!"

Two goblins yanked their eyeballs back into place, turned, and charged Electra, but she dodged past them in her athletic way and went for Godiva. Electra, being human, was twice the size of the goblins, which helped. The charge caught the goblins by surprise; they might have expected her to flee. She touched the gobliness' arm and shocked her.

Godiva sank to the ground, dropping the wand. At the same time, Nada fell. She managed to twist around so as to land on her human feet, avoiding injury.

Electra dived for the wand. The goblins, stunned again by the sight of Nada, were slow to think of that. Electra brought it up and pointed it at one. "Now get back!" she cried. "Or I'll hoist you into the treetops!"

The goblins, amazingly, laughed. "You can't use that!" one said, advancing on her.

Nada resumed serpent form and hissed at him. He fell back.

"But it's true," Electra said, dismayed. "It isn't working for me."

Nada put on her human head. "Keep it anyway," she said. "That will stop them from using it. Now let's get out of here."

"Wait!" Godiva called, struggling to sit up. "Don't take our only magic!"

"Why not?" Electra asked. "You must've stolen it from someone else."

"No, it's mine," Godiva said. "My mother's actually, but I'm using it with her permission. Why did you attack us?"

"We didn't attack you!" Nada responded indignantly. "We were just checking to see if you had the centaur foal. Then Electra sneezed."

"You're looking for Che Centaur?" Godiva asked. "Are you with the elf?"

"You know about the elf? I smelled it, but there's something odd about it."

Godiva gazed at her a moment. "I think maybe we should talk," she said.

"Talk? We have to rescue the foal!"

"We may not be enemies," Godiva said. "Not exactly, anyway."

This was stranger yet! "Do goblins honor a truce?" Nada asked.

"Females do." Godiva turned to the three males. "Moron, Idiot, Imbecile—lay down your weapons and back off."

The three males did exactly that. Nada was impressed. "Truce, then," she agreed. "While we talk."

"While we talk," Godiva said. "Let me explain at the outset that we are not the goblins who have the foal. We want to rescue him before the Goblinate of the Golden Horde boils him and his companion, the elf girl."

"Elf girl!" Nada explained. She had assumed it was male. But that did not account for the whole of the oddity.

"Who is that elf, if she's not with you?" Nada asked.

They settled down by the warm fire, which was a pleasure. Nada did not fully trust the gobliness, but as long as Electra held the wand, and the goblins didn't know that Electra's charge was gone, perhaps it was all right. It was evident that Godiva had information they needed.

"We know little of her, and I will tell you what there is. But first I must explain our interest in the foal," Godiva said. "Have patience; I will make this brief, and I think the Golden Horde will not harm them until morning."

"I hope not!" Electra said.

"We are from Goblin Mountain in the east," Godiva said. "Some time back, an ogre passed by with an entourage of seven females. He was remarkably decent for his kind, and suspiciously unstupid, except with regard to women. One of the females was Goldy Goblin, daughter of Gorbage, chief of the North Slope Gap goblins. She was seeking to trap a husband in the approved fashion. The ogre managed to fathom the secret of the magic wand the tribe had stolen, and he gave it to Goldy, who then had power to snare the son of the chief. The ogre stomped on northward and was lost to history, but Goldy remained, and married, and the stork brought me. I am so named because of an obscure legend associated with hair and taxes; I need not bore you with that." Godiva tossed her hair, and they saw that she wore little or no clothing beneath it; the hair served as an effective cloak.

"In due course I snagged my own chief's son, who seemed to appreciate my costume," Godiva continued. "In due course the stork brought us Gwendolyn, who was as lovely and nice as any female child. But through a tragic mischance she was rendered lame, and can walk only with difficulty. Since I will not suffer my daughter to be humbled by circumstance, I determined to obtain a suitable steed for her to ride. Thus it was that I borrowed my mother's wand, and used a tunnel spell, and took the centaur foal."

"But Che's too young to ride!" Electra protested.

"He will grow," Godiva said. "Meanwhile, we shall tame him, so that he is safe for Gwendolyn. On such a steed, when she is grown, she should be able to achieve my hope for her, and our tradition will continue. Unfortunately our tunnel spell malfunctioned, and when we emerged we were not back at Goblin Mountain, but here on the wrong side of the Elements. That was the beginning of our problem."

"Murphy's curse!" Electra exclaimed. "It made the plot go wrong!"

"So there was hostile magic," Godiva said. "I suspected as much. At any rate, my point is that we mean no harm to the foal. He will be well treated, and my daughter will be as compatible a companion as he can find. But here in this hostile region we knew we would have trouble with the Goblinate of the Golden Horde, so we were hurrying north to avoid it. We hoped to cross the river and circle the Elements and return to Goblin Mountain from the north. But this strange elf appeared suddenly, spooked my men with cherry bombs, and stole the foal from us. Naturally we followed, but they fled to a raft on the river, and we could not reach them. It is important that no harm come to the foal, you see; that limited our options. But then the horde goblins got wind of the presence of the foal and advanced on the river, and we had to fall back; they are hundreds to our four, and the magic wand will not prevail against such odds. This is our present state: we must save the foal from certain death at the hands of the horde, but we lack the resources to attack. Only if I can use the wand to float the foal clear of them during the night can it be accomplished."

Nada nodded soberly. Now things were falling into place! She could not approve Godiva's abduction of Che Centaur, but she had to trust her motive now. If Che died, Godiva lost, just as did the centaur's friends.

"But the elf girl!" Electra said. "Who is she? Why did she come? Where is she now?"

"Apparently she is a friend of the foal," Godiva said. "She is a strange one, with oddly pointed ears and missing fingers, and she is twice the size of the elves we know. The horde took her captive and seems to be treating her no better than the foal; I suspect they mean to cook her also. She is only a child, and the oddest thing is that she does not seem to weaken away from her elm."

"But all elves are tied to their elms!" Nada said.

"As I said, she is a strange one. I have never before seen her like. She even wears spectacles and associates with an odd little animal of the feline persuasion."

"Chex Centaur must have found her on some distant mount, and brought her in for a companion to Che," Electra said. "She must have followed you when you stole Che and tried to rescue him." She frowned. "But it's funny Chex didn't tell me about it. I have played with Che often, and there's never been an elf there."

"We are all mystified," Godiva said. "But there you have it. I believe we should make common cause and try to rescue the foal from the horde. Thereafter we may settle our differences as to the foal's disposition."

Nada pondered, not completely at ease with this. She didn't trust goblins for one excellent reason: they were untrustworthy. It was true that Godiva had no wish to harm Che, but the moment he was rescued, she would probably try to spirit him away to Goblin Mountain. Still, it was hardly likely that one naga and one human girl could rescue Che alone.

"We have a whistle to summon other search parties here," she said. "Maybe—"

"The goblins aren't deaf," Godiva pointed out. "If they think others are coming, they will simply move up their schedule and boil their captives now. They don't know about us because we hid, but they would know if they heard that whistle."

She had a point. "We also have sparkleberries to summon help from the Good Magician," Nada said.

"The goblins aren't blind, either. They have sentries

posted. That is why we did not dare camp closer to them; we would have been spied and wiped out. After we rescue the foal, then you might summon your help.''

She did seem to be making sense. ''But how will we settle who gets Che?'' Nada asked. ''We don't want him captive at Goblin Mountain either.''

''We can settle that after we rescue him. We can hold a contest or draw straws or something, the loser bound to let the winner have him. In either case, he will be safe.''

Nada looked at Electra. ''What do you think? Can we trust these goblins?''

''I think we have to,'' Electra said, evidently no better pleased than Nada was. She handed the wand back to the gobliness.

''Very well.'' Nada faced Godiva. ''We'll act together to rescue Che and the elf girl. Once we have them safe from the horde, we'll decide who keeps Che. But you have to understand that no matter what deal you make with the two of us, Che's parents will not rest until they have him back. They are winged monsters, and I think you could find the winged monsters laying siege to your mountain.''

''We had really hoped that no one would know where he was,'' Godiva confessed. ''But I think that once it is clear how well we treat the foal, the objections will fade. I think you would rather see him with us than cooked, and we would rather see him with you than cooked, so let's deal with the present situation and leave the other till tomorrow.''

She certainly was practical! But so was Nada. ''Even working together, we can't match the power of the Horde. We'll need a ruse or some device to get him out without their knowing right away. Suppose I assume small snake form and sneak unobserved into their camp, and untie him and lead him out. If they spy us, then you loft us high out of their reach with your wand.''

''I can't loft two at once,'' Godiva said. ''Not of your size.''

''I was afraid of that. Then loft him alone, and I'll assume large serpent form and fight my way out of it as well as I can.''

"But you can't hope to—" Electra protested.

"Then you will make the deal to free Che from Godiva," Nada said. "Before you marry Dolph."

"Maybe I could sneak in to untie him," Electra said.

"No. You can't change size or form. But you can help by carrying me to the horde, so that I can rest and sleep and be at my best when I have to be."

Electra looked unhappy, but she had to agree that this was best. Still, she had an objection. "That wand can keep him high only while Godiva wields it. The goblins will soon see her, and if they catch her—"

"True," Godiva said. "Just as the two of you overcame me. I must concentrate on the wand when I am using it; I will be pretty much helpless. But I might hide in a tree, and they would not see me. My three henchmen could decoy them away."

"Awww—" one of the males protested.

"Quiet, Moron," Godiva snapped.

"It isn't nice to call him that," Electra said.

"That's his name," Godiva replied. "They are Moron, Idiot, and Imbecile—all stalwart examples of their kind."

"Oh." Electra was embarrassed. "But you can only loft Che so far, from one fixed place, and those goblins of the horde will be all over."

Godiva sighed. "I know. It is not an ideal situation. But we must do what we can. If it comes to nothing, then you must signal your friends, as there will by then be nothing to be lost by alerting the horde."

"I'm not satisfied with it," Electra said.

"If you can improve on it, welcome," the gobliness said. "I think now we should get started, as I believe the horde is some distance away. We must move as quietly as possible, hoping to approach them undetected."

"I'll look for a pineapple plantation or something," Electra said. "There has to be something to cause some extra mischief for those mean things."

"Good idea." Godiva turned to the three males. "Spread out, look for anything like that, and report to a female if you find it."

"But we'd rather use the path!" one protested.

"That's the first place the horde will set an ambush, Imbecile."

Imbecile dropped his protest.

"But how will we find each other?" Nada asked, still just a bit uneasy about Godiva's intentions.

"Idiot can whistle like a bird," the gobliness said. "Idiot, do the bird-in-hand call."

The male goblin pursed his ugly lips and whistled. The sound was a trilling cadence that sounded almost like "I got it! I got it! It's mine!"

Nada was impressed. "But suppose there's a real bird here?"

"There may be. It wouldn't make sense to use a call that the horde knew was foreign. But a real bird will not remain for the rendezvous, while Idiot will."

Nada nodded. It was a good device.

They spread out into the forest. Electra might not like traveling alone through it at night, but the moon was extra big and bright, so she could see well enough, and she realized that the horde would have cleaned out most predators, so it was probably reasonably safe. "If you have trouble, wake me," Nada said, then took her hand and changed to small snake form. Electra put her carefully in a breast pocket. Nada, of course, could not use breast pockets; not only were they unprincessly, there was no room in that region of her torso for anything like that.

Nada coiled into a disk and let Electra's motion lull her to sleep. It was comfortable here, and actually, when it came right down to it, Electra was far from flat chested. In the right gown she could show off to a certain advantage. It was just that she never bothered to, preferring to look tomboyish. Maybe she was afraid that if she looked as feminine as she could, Queen Irene would notice and make her stop dressing like a boy and running unfettered around the grounds. But that would come to a definite stop within a week if Dolph didn't notice. Nada resolved to take Electra in hand the moment they got back to Castle Roogna and put her in a low-cut gown. Of course that would still leave those freckles to deal with, but maybe some vanishing cream would make them vanish. There was a creamweed in the orchard with the milkweeds; that might have some of the right variety. The wrong variety would make Electra's whole face vanish, so some care was in order.

Lulled by the motion and her thoughts, Nada fell asleep. She was fortunate that in her reptilian mode she had cold nerves and could relax despite her knowledge of the deadly danger of her coming mission. A warm-blooded creature would have worried about the horde. If she helped rescue Che but didn't make it out herself, then Electra would not need the gown and cream. That seemed sensible.

Nada woke because Electra had stopped moving. She had become accustomed to the steady irregularity of the struggle through the jungle, so this abrupt stillness was alarming. She poked her head out of the pocket.

Ahead was a gulf like that of the Gap Chasm. No, it only seemed so; she had forgotten to allow for her small size. It was actually a cleft, a miniature Gap, too wide for a human being to hurdle and too deep to risk. The trees grew up to within a reasonable distance of the brink, but left a clear space at the edge, as if not trusting their roots too close to that emptiness. The moonlight wafted down, brightening the ground, but hesitating to plumb too deeply in the cleft.

Electra was hesitating, and Nada knew her well enough to know that something was on her mind. So she slithered out of the pocket. Electra felt the motion and put her hand up. Nada crawled onto it, and Electra set her on the ground. Then Nada assumed woman form. "What's up?" she inquired.

"This looks a lot like the Gap," Electra said.

"It's too small. The Gap is a hundred times this big."

"But could it be an offshoot of the Gap? A crack branching off?"

"I suppose. There are a lot of them. What about it?"

"Then one end must go to the Gap, and the other just gets smaller until it quits."

"Of course. What's your point?"

"It would be hard to cross, toward the Gap, but easy toward the end."

Nada was getting impatient. "So what, 'Lectra? Just walk along it until you find where you can cross."

"But if we rescue—*when* we rescue Che, the gobs'll be chasing us. So—"

"So we find a good crossing point first," Nada said. "Now I get your notion. Very well, I'll check one direction, you check the other, and we'll return here and compare notes."

"No," Electra said.

"Now look, I'm not going to jump in!" Nada said. "I promised, remember?"

"'Snot that," Electra said. Nada shuddered; she would have to get the girl to stop using such expressions, even if she wasn't a princess. It conjured a vision of a leaky nose.

"Isn't there time? The moon's still out, so it's not dawn yet."

"'Snot that either." Ouch! "If they're chasing us, we don't want an easy crossing."

"But we can't afford to be delayed, if—" Then Nada understood. "The goblins! To stop the goblins!"

"Yes. If we can get across, and they can't, we'll be safe or at least get a good head start. I thought with Godiva's wand—"

"'Lectra, that's brilliant!" Nada exclaimed. "This cleft can be better than pineapple bombs! So we need to find a good wide section they can't cross, and then come to that."

"But they probably know this cleft pretty well, and maybe they have crossing places," Electra said. "So maybe we need to find those and get rid of them, so they can't cross."

"Yes indeed! Very well, we'll split up and explore, and

see what we find. We have to move quickly, though, so we have time to get together with Godiva.''

''Right.'' Electra headed off along the cleft, running, though she must have been tired. Nada assumed the form of a black racer and zoomed in the other direction.

As it turned out, she had the Gap side. Before long the cleft joined another cleft, and Nada had to detour around that until she found a place narrow enough for her human form to hurdle. Then she snaked on down until she came to the Gap itself. She had observed no suitable crossings; the goblins evidently didn't mess with this portion of it.

She zoomed back, hoping she hadn't delayed Electra. She was heartened by this discovery. She could lead Che to this cleft, and Godiva could loft him across, and the gobs would be stuck on the other side.

So would Nada.

She pondered that as she sped along. But then she realized that it should be no problem, because no goblin could keep up with this racing form. She could get clear. In fact, she might not need to; she could assume small snake form, and Che could hold her in his hand, and take her across with him.

Then she remembered the elf girl. The one who had tried to rescue Che before and gotten captured herself. What would happen to her?

Maybe there would be time to loft her across after Che was safe. Nada hoped so, because she wanted to know more about that elf.

But where would Electra be, at that point? She couldn't change form and slither away. So—she would have to remain on the other side of the cleft to help guide Che while Nada slithered around. That would have another advantage: if the gobliness turned out to be untrustworthy, someone would be there to protect Che.

Reassured, Nada zipped on to her rendezvous with Electra. Soon enough she made it, somewhat to this side of their point of separation. Electra had evidently completed her survey and come back to find Nada.

She slithered up and assumed girl form. "My end is the Gap," she said. "No crossing places. You found one?"

"Yes—just a little way up," Electra said breathlessly. "It gets very narrow, and the gobs have made a log bridge— a tree fallen across it. I looked beyond, but it's a good long hike before it peters out. So if we can take out that bridge—"

"Good enough! Let me look at it."

They went to it, and Nada studied the situation. It looked as if a person with a lever could wedge the log off the narrow place, so it would drop into the cleft. It would take the goblins a long time to get another log for the crossing. It looked very good. They might even be able to use the crossing themselves, then push off the log before the goblins reached it.

They resumed their progress toward the horde camp. Now the first signs of dawn were just beginning to think about starting to show.

They were going to be late. "They must be ahead of us," Nada said. "Maybe Idiot is whistling, and we can hear it."

They listened, and after a moment heard the conservative cadence of the bird in hand. They hurried toward that, hoping it wasn't a real bird.

It wasn't. Idiot was hiding against the trunk of a tree, and Godiva was nearby. "I was afraid you were—lost," the gobliness said, relieved.

"Or had run out on you?" Nada inquired.

"It is true I do not know you well, and our relations with the Naga folk are not ideal."

Nada was getting to like Godiva better. The woman seemed to be playing things straight. "We found an offshoot from the Gap Chasm that we think will balk the goblins— if we destroy their bridge after using it. So if we can get that far without being captured or killed ourselves—"

"Wonderful! We found nothing; the horde seems to have scoured the region clean. We have been here for an hour, observing, fearing that you would not come. We believe the horde has the foal and elf locked in a hut together; there is a guard pacing near it. There are other guards elsewhere in the camp; if we took out one, the others would hear the commotion and rouse the rest. So we have been unable to act, but we fear they mean to do their thing at dawn."

"I can go in and free them," Nada said. "But it won't do any good, if the whole camp is roused."

"Agreed. So I think I had better distract them. It's a faint chance, but all we have."

"Distract them?" Electra asked.

"With a dance."

"How could a dance distract goblins?" Electra asked. But Nada had a notion, and gave her a let-it-be signal.

"When I do it, you slither in quickly and rescue them," Godiva said. "Perhaps you will get away."

"But what happens to you?" Nada asked.

"Oh, they will no doubt have a great deal of fun with me, before they kill me. But once the foal is safe, perhaps I can be rescued."

Nada was chilled by her realism. "Maybe we should summon our help now."

"And set off the horde for sure! No, we had better try it this way. If I don't make it, you must bargain in good faith with my henchmen for the disposition of the foal."

Nada sighed. She feared disaster for them all, but they seemed to be stuck with it. She turned to Electra. "If I don't make it, you must be the one to bargain. Stay clear, and lead the party to the crossing. Che will follow you if he sees you."

Tight-lipped, Electra nodded.

Godiva turned to the three males. "If I am lost, you support these two. If you win the foal, take him home."

The three nodded grimly.

Dawn was encroaching. But before Nada could go in, one who was evidently the goblin chief marched with a group of henchmen to the hut. The rescue effort was too late!

"We'll have to watch our chance," Nada said. "Maybe this isn't the end."

They watched as the two captives were led out. The gobliness was right: that was the biggest elf Nada had seen. Neither was tied, but the elf seemed to be gagged. That was curious. "Does she have spoken magic?" Nada asked.

"Not that I know of," Godiva replied.

The goblins clustered around the captives, but it wasn't clear what they were doing. Then Che reached out and yanked the elf's gag down. Immediately the chief drew back his fist and swung at her, but the elf ducked.

"She must have magic!" Godiva exclaimed. "See, most of the men are just standing around, not helping their chief. So we must not listen." As she spoke, she was stuffing hanks of hair into her ears, to dull her own hearing. "I'll distract them visually; you get in there and get them out."

Nada changed to small snake form and slithered toward the group. She saw Godiva step out into the camp clearing, dancing and swirling her hair around her body. She was good at it; that hair was like a living cloak, that allowed parts of her torso to flash into view briefly before disappearing.

A goblin spied Godiva. "Look at that!" he cried, staring.

Nada didn't look at that; she concentrated on Che and the elf girl. She would slither right in close, then assume human form, and tell the two to run. Then she would assume large serpent form and bite any goblins who looked dangerous. She might get killed, just as Godiva might, but between them they might indeed give Che his chance to escape.

An increasing number of the goblins were standing frozen, and not all of them were looking in Godiva's direction. Could it be true that the elf had some kind of spoken magic? If so, that made Nada's job easier. She continued to concentrate on the two captives, allowing nothing to distract her from her immediate mission.

The chief was still trying to punch the elf, but she was ducking out of the way, and the goblins who were holding her seemed to be in a daze. It must be magic, because normally goblins' first interest was in hurting others.

Nada reached the group. She assumed woman form. "Che!" she cried. "Run for the forest!" Then she became a monstrous huge-fanged serpent and reared up before the chief. If she took him out first, the others might be disorganized.

But the chief's face had also gone blank. There was no point in biting him if he wasn't functioning. She turned to look at the others, and found them all standing slackly, slight ungoblinish smiles on their ugly faces. What was going on?

Che and the elf girl ran, and the elf seemed to be singing. Nada could not distinguish notes very well in her serpent form, so judged by the girl's open mouth. Well, if that was doing it, good for her!

Che and the elf ran to the side, where Electra stepped out, calling something. They followed her into the forest.

Godiva stopped dancing. The goblins remained standing in place. Nada slithered after Che, and after a surprised moment Godiva wrapped her hair around her and followed.

Then the goblins came back to life. But for a moment they were confused. It was almost as if they had not seen the captives flee. Nada and Godiva hurried into the forest, in effect forming a rear guard.

The party kept moving. Evidently Electra was showing them the way, and Che trusted Electra, and the elf trusted Che. Good enough; if they stayed ahead of the horde long enough, they could cross the cleft, dump the tree down, and be safe while they signaled for help.

But now the goblins were getting organized. Godiva turned her head, evidently hearing them, and in a moment Nada heard it too, as a roaring noise.

They passed a narrow section of their path, where two great trees encroached from the sides. Nada whipped to the side, and curled around the tree, climbing in a spiral, while Godiva ran on.

In a moment the first of the goblins charged up. Nada

struck out from the tree, hissing fiercely. She knocked him back with her snout. The goblin wasn't really hurt, but he was terrified. He screamed and scrambled back—just as the second one was arriving. The two collided and tumbled in the path—just in time for the next one to plow into them.

In a moment there was a sizable tangle of goblins. Satisfied, Nada assumed black racer form and shot along the trail, gaining on the others. She had bought them a little more time.

It seemed to be enough, for the party made it to the log crossing before the horde goblins caught up again. Godiva's henchmen were prying at the log, and it was nudging over. They paused, seeing Nada coming. But the log was too far over; it continued moving. They jumped on it and ran across just before it fell.

Nada pulled up at the brink, too late. Behind her was the noise of the horde.

Then she found herself floating in the air. She wriggled violently, afraid she was falling into the deep cleft. Then she saw Godiva, waving her wand. The gobliness was bringing her across!

She floated over the cleft and landed softly. She assumed her natural form, with her human head on her serpent body. "Thank you," she said. "I could have gone around, but it would have taken time."

"You helped me by slowing the pursuit," Godiva said.

Now the goblins of the horde charged up to the other side of the cleft. Moron, Idiot, and Imbecile stood at the edge and made faces at them, while the rest of the party got organized. "Maybe we had better exchange introductions," Nada said. "Che, I believe you know us all."

"Certainly," the centaur foal said. He looked somewhat worn, unsurprisingly, but retained his composure. "This is Jenny Elf, from the World of Two Moons. These are Princess Nada Naga and Electra. I gather you and Godiva have made each other's acquaintance."

Nada looked at Jenny. "You are not from Xanth?"

"No," the elf said. She held up a four-fingered hand.

"See, my fingers are different from yours and my ears. But, please, have you seen Sammy?"

"Who?"

"Her cat," Che said. "He finds things, magically."

"No, we have seen no cat of any kind," Nada said. "Look, Electra and I came to rescue you, but we have learned that Godiva did not mean to hurt you, Che. She wants you to be her daughter's companion. We made a bargain to work together to rescue you from the horde. Now we have to settle where you are to go."

"But you can't keep Che from his mother!" Jenny protested. She was indeed the foal's friend. She was goblin size, which was still only half human height.

"We had to compromise," Nada said. "The alternative was to let the horde keep you."

Che nodded. "I understand. I must abide by your compromise."

"But first we had better get away from here," Godiva said, "before the horde moves around the cleft."

Indeed, the horde goblins were already running to the side in the direction of the next available crossing. It would take them a while, but not long enough to be ignored.

"Then we had better travel down to the Gap," Nada said. "That's in the direction each party is going."

"I'm not sure of that," Godiva said. "See, some of them are going that way too. There must be a crossing you didn't see."

Nada saw that it was true. "Then north," she said.

They formed a line and started north, through the jungle. They were all tired, but it was no time to rest. Nada led the way, in large serpent form, because she was able to force a passage best.

Then suddenly there was a roar ahead. Nada drew back, alarmed. It was a huge fire-breathing dragon, and it was bearing right down on them!

Chapter 8. Dolph's Direction

Dolph, in nighthawk form, flew west through the night toward the With-a-Cookee River. Unfortunately Metria had not told him exactly where along the river his Betrothees were. That left him somewhat at a loss.

Well, all he could do was start at the source, assume fish form, and follow the river down until he found them. There must be a goblin tribe along it somewhere. Then he could assume dragon form or ogre form and smash the gobs to smithers and rescue the damsels. The notion had a certain appeal.

With his nighthawk eyes he could see clearly no matter how dark it was. But not only did he not know exactly where the girls were, he also did not know where the river was. Except that it was west of here. He almost wished the demoness was along, in case she could give him a better direction. But she would probably just give him the wrong direction, out of mischief.

In due course he spied the river. At least he thought it was the river. He flew down close and saw a clump of ginger cookies that snapped viciously at him; one had to be careful of ginger snaps. But this verified that it was the With-a-Cookee River, flowing generally north and west.

Maybe he could just fly over it, along its length, until he spied the girls and goblins. No, the jungle overhung it in places and was so dense that he could not see the ground. He would be better off as a fish—a big fierce one with sharp spines, which an allidile wouldn't attack. But first he had to find the river's source, so he didn't miss anything.

He followed it up until it reached a big messy morass. He knew what this was: the Half-Baked Bog, that had not yet ripened into a full-fledged swamp. When it did so, the products that grew along the river would be adult breadfruit and butter, instead of juvenile cookies, and they would have to change its name. He hoped it never grew up!

He came to land where the first trickle of river leaked from the bog. The bog didn't like giving up its water, but the river demanded it, so this was where the issue was fought. Dolph knew that when it rained, the bog sometimes wasn't quick enough to incorporate all the new water, and the river managed to suck more of it away. Sometimes the river got so full of it that it swelled up over its banks. That was the nature of juveniles: they had no restraint. Dolph was sorry he would not be a juvenile much longer.

He assumed his human form for a moment, so as to use his most familiar senses just in case the girls were near here. It would be awful to miss them and swim down the entire length of the river, while they got boiled by the goblins!

"Well, look at this!" a raucous voice screeched. "A bare-bottomed young whippersnapper!"

Dolph whirled, startled. But it was only a harpy, one of the dirty-bodied dirty-mouthed birds of the wilderness. "Get out of here before you poison the water," he said.

"Oh is that so, stink-face!" she screeched, flapping up close. "I have half a mind to poop on you, son of a woman!"

"You have half a mind, period," he retorted, stooping to pick up a stick.

"Are you threatening me, Prince?" she screeched, outraged. "I'll bury you in spit!"

Dolph swung the stick at her, but she flapped out of the way. "Clumsy! Clumsy!" she screeched harpily.

But then something percolated through his mind. She had called him Prince—but he had never identified himself, and certainly his costume did not give anything away other than his masculinity. How did she know?

"Metria!" he exclaimed.

The harpy became the demoness. "Oh, heck, I was just beginning to have fun," she complained.

She certainly had been! She hadn't even used any useful fowl words, because she knew he was still technically a juvenile. A real harpy would have delivered a barrage of obscenities that might have represented an intriguing education. She had been teasing him on two levels, as was her delight.

"Get out of here, spook!" he yelled, swinging the stick at her. Naturally it passed right through her torso without resistance. But she obligingly disappeared. What was the point in her remaining, once he had discovered her identity? He was no fun, by her definition, unless she was fooling him in some demonic way.

He turned back to the river. What was the best fish form to assume here, where it was so small? He worried that a minnow might be snapped up by some unseen predator. Of course he would immediately change to some larger form and chomp the predator right back, but still it was an inconvenience. Maybe he could be a small water snake and become a larger one as the river got larger.

"Meow."

Dolph looked. It was a cat, an orange fluff ball, lying on the ground. What was it doing here? Xanth hardly had any straight cats—just odd variants—but Dolph recognized the type because he had seen pictures of the mundane breeds.

Oh—the demoness was still having her sport, trying to see if he could be fooled again. "Quit with the games, Metria," he snapped. "I'm not going to give you the satisfaction."

The cat merely looked at him, not moving. He knew it was the demoness, but somehow he had just a bit of doubt. So he called her bluff by assuming the form of another cat: a big black one. "Say something in cat talk," he meowed, suspecting that she couldn't. He was a Magician, and could speak and understand the language of any form he assumed, but she was a demoness, who merely imitated the forms.

"Something," the cat meowed clearly in cat talk, swishing his cat tail.

That surprised Dolph. But it occurred to him that Metria might have learned just a few feline terms to fool him. Maybe she had just imitated his last word. Well, he would require the cat to say something that wasn't that.

"What is your name?"

"Sammy."

Dolph was impressed. But still, he had asked an obvious question, so it could still be the demoness, bluffing. "Where are you from?"

"Home."

"You aren't much for dialogue, are you!"

Sammy merely shrugged, hardly moving.

"Why are you here?"

"Help."

"You're here to help me?"

"No."

"You want my help?"

"Yes." It seemed that the laconic animal refused to expend any more than the minimum energy on anything. This was not Metria's way. Dolph was becoming convinced that Sammy was real. But that only made a new mystery.

"Well, I have to go help someone else right now, so it will have to wait."

Now the cat showed some agitation. "But Jenny needs help!"

"Who is Jenny?"

"My person friend."

Now Dolph remembered something else Metria had said: that a foreign elf and a foreign cat had come through the hole in Xanth. And that the elf was trying to help Che. "Is Jenny an elf?"

"They called her that," Sammy said a bit defensively. "But she's really a person."

Yet Metria was the one who had told him, so this was

no verification. Still, his belief was overwhelming his doubt. "And you two came through the hole?"

"I didn't notice."

"Why did you come through it?"

"For a feather."

Metria hadn't told him that. Still, he wasn't quite sure. "What feather?"

"A big one."

Dolph resisted the urge to get annoyed, knowing that the demoness would like it if he blew his top. "How did you know where it was?"

"I just knew."

"But wasn't it hard to find a big feather?"

"No."

She was still testing him! "How did you know where to find me?" That should trap her into some giveaway response.

"I just knew."

Was he getting anywhere or just wasting time—exactly as the demoness wanted. "Do you know who I am?"

"No."

"Then why did you look for me?"

"I didn't."

"But you said you came to me to get my help."

"Yes."

"How could you do that if you didn't know who I was?"

"Jenny told me to find help, so I found it."

"You didn't know what you were finding, just help?"

"Yes."

Dolph was stumped. Every time he thought he was getting somewhere, he wound up nowhere. He suspected that he should just leave the cat and head down the river. But suppose the cat was legitimate?

Metria appeared. "I can't stand watching you fumble any more!" she declared. "I'll have to help you get on with it, or we'll be here all night."

"But I'm not sure whether he's you," Dolph protested,

forming his cat mouth into just enough of a human mouth to speak human words.

She stared at him. "Are you trying to fool me into think-ing you're even duller than you are?"

Dolph looked from her to the cat and back. How could she be the cat when she was herself? "How would you proceed?"

"I'd ask him exactly how he finds things."

Dolph looked at Sammy, but the cat just lay there without moving.

"Dumbbell!" Metria snapped. "*Ask* him!"

"But he heard you."

"I didn't speak in feline talk. I can't. You have to trans-late."

Oh. "Sammy, how do you find things?"

"I just do."

"He just does," Dolph said to the demoness.

"How does he just do it?" she asked.

"Sammy, how do you just do it?"

"If I'm interested."

"If he's interested."

Metria looked as if she were controlling a monstrous aggravation. It made Dolph's heart glad. "How else?"

"How else, Sammy?"

"Someone tells me to, and I do it."

"When someone tells him to," Dolph reported.

"Then tell him to find Nada Naga!"

"Sammy, go find Nada Naga."

Suddenly the cat was in motion. "After him!" Metria cried, floating in that direction.

Dolph started to run, but immediately slipped in the mud and took a resounding spill.

"You're such a grab!" Metria called.

"A what?" Dolph asked as he hauled himself sloppily up.

"Hold, snatch, grip, seize, entangle—"

"Embroil?" he asked.

"No! Gear, wheel, engage, limited-slip—"

Dolph had heard about something the Mundanes used. "Clutch?"

"Yes! You're such a clutch!" Then she paused. "No, I'm not sure."

"You mean you're not going to insult me?"

"WILL YOU GET MOVING, DOLT!"

Oh. Dolph assumed red racer form and slithered at top velocity after the disappearing cat. He knew the demoness was annoyed, because she had gotten his name wrong. That was some satisfaction.

It turned out to be some distance. Sammy, evidently tired, soon slowed to a walk, but remained intent on his objective, and Dolph was glad of that. This was certainly a better way to find Nada than swimming down the river would have been, especially since they were going directly away from the river. The cat must have had a difficult journey to find Dolph, and now was traveling again.

That was an interesting talent Sammy had. Dolph had not known of many animals with magic talents. It showed that just about anything was possible.

But this business of a foreign elf coming to Xanth—that was something he had never heard of before. What business could she have here?

Another thing bothered him. They seemed to be heading for the territory of the Goblinate of the Golden Horde. Dolph had encountered Chief Grotesk and his evil minions before. If they had captured the girls—

He shoved that thought away and let it drift off behind him. Fortunately his thoughts seemed even tireder than he was, so could not keep up with his body.

Dolph was as tired as the cat looked by the time dawn approached; they had been traveling most of the night! But they must be getting closer to Nada; and with luck Electra and Che would be with her, and Dolph could rescue them all. If the cat's direction was right. It had to be!

There were sounds ahead. The dim uproar of angry goblins and some nearer crashing, as of more goblins forging through the brush. Nada must be running from the horde!

Dolph changed into fire-breathing dragon form and summoned his last strength. He leaped ahead of the cat to intercept the charging party.

He encountered a huge serpent. Behind it were several goblins! This was worse than he had feared to hope! But if Nada was in danger—

He inhaled, about to scorch the serpent's head off its body.

"Dope!" Metria screamed. "That's Nada!"

Startled, Dolph choked back his fire and changed to serpent form, matching the species of the other. He felt backed-up smoke sifting between his teeth; he had changed form, but it hadn't. He coughed.

Nada appeared in her natural form: a serpent with her human head. "Dolph!" she exclaimed gladly.

He changed again, to his human form. "Nada! I almost—"

She became human. "I know!" Then they embraced.

Somewhere in the background he heard a lesser dialogue: "Sammy! You found help!"

"Meow." Dolph was no longer in feline form, so could no longer understand cat talk, but it wasn't hard to guess. Sammy never uttered two words where one would do.

Then he became aware of several things. The first was that they were both naked, because their clothes didn't change with them. The second was that Nada was the most wonderful armful of woman he could imagine, especially this way. He had never before gotten to hug her like this, for reasons that had to do with his mother's odd notions of propriety. The third was that they were not alone.

He looked around. He saw nine pairs of eyes focusing on him, belonging to four goblins, one Betrothee, one centaur foal, one elf, one demoness, and one cat. The eyes of the cat didn't bother him; he knew Sammy didn't care. That left—well, he wasn't sure how many eyes, math not being his strong point, but he knew it was about eight pairs too many.

"Uh, let's change to naga form," he murmured in her ear.

Nada glanced around. Her lovely lips pursed. She turned naga. He followed, so that they were twined together but relatively sanitary.

"Uh, what's going on here?" he asked, still somewhat at a loss, and not just because of the strangers he saw.

"The Adult Conspiracy forbids an answer," Metria replied. "If she had had panties on, we would have had to lock you up and swallow the key."

Nada's head turned to cover the demoness. "And who is she?"

"Uh, she's Metria," Dolph faltered. "Demoness Metria. She—"

"I see." For now the demoness had assumed a form even more luscious than Nada's, which was a feat only a supernatural creature could accomplish, and she surely couldn't maintain it for long.

"She just appeared!" he protested. "She said she needed—"

"I can guess."

"Oh come on, Nada," Electra said. "You know he loves only you."

Nada was taken aback. "You mean I was getting jealous? Woe is me!" Then she laughed.

Dolph suspected that she was teasing him, but he wasn't sure. He also didn't know how to respond to Electra's remark, because of course Electra was the one who loved him. So he got away from that subject as fast as his tongue could take him. "I mean, who are these goblins?"

One stepped forward. "I am Godiva and these are my henchmen, Moron, Idiot, and Imbecile. We abducted the centaur foal, but also helped rescue him from the horde."

"Well, I came to rescue Che," Dolph said. "And I know Nada and Electra did too. So you can go now, because we're taking him back to his dam."

"You've got it mixed up," Electra said. "We made a deal with Godiva. The horde is after us all."

"A deal?" he asked, befuddled.

"Arrangement, bargain, pact, pledge," Metria said.

"I know that! I mean, just which side are these goblins on, anyway?"

"Ours, now," Nada said. "We can't just take Che home. We have to settle with Godiva. But first we all have to get away from the horde."

"I can become a roc and carry you all away," Dolph said. "Except the goblins; four extra is too many. What deal did you make?"

"That we would work together to rescue Che and the elf from the horde, then decide who would get to take Che."

"What about Jenny?" Dolph asked. "Who takes her?"

"How do you know my name?" the elf girl asked, surprised.

"Sammy told me."

"But Sammy can't speak!"

"He can't speak *human*," Dolph told her. "I talked to him in feline."

"He does that," Electra told Jenny. "He can talk the languages of the animal forms he assumes. But it's a good question: once we decide where Che goes, what about you? Are you going back where you came from?"

Che turned to the elf. "Oh, please don't do that, yet, Jenny!" he protested. "You have been such a friend to me, I do not want to lose you so soon."

"She can't go home," Metria said. "We blocked the hole."

"The hole?" Electra asked.

"The hole in Xanth through which she came," Dolph said. "I had forgotten. Monsters were coming through, so Metria and I blocked it. Jenny can't go back, because we closed it. So I guess she'll have to stay with us for a while."

Jenny hugged Che. "I didn't want to leave yet anyway," she said.

"We can't stand around talking," Godiva said. "The horde will catch us."

"Let's settle this fast," Nada said. "We'll decide where

Che goes, and if we win, you goblins help us take him to his mother; and if you win, we'll help you take him to Goblin Mountain.''

"Now wait!'' Dolph protested. "We can't give him to the goblins!''

"We made a deal,'' Electra said. "We may not like it, but Godiva did help rescue him by distracting the horde.''

"Yes, she did,'' Che agreed. "I saw her dancing. When she distracted them, then Jenny's magic caught them and we were able to escape. I will go with whoever wins. It is fair.''

"But these goblins abducted you!'' Dolph said.

"True. But they did not harm me.''

"We can work out those details later,'' Nada said. "Right now we need a fast, fair way to decide. What do we do, guess numbers?''

"But we're all on one side or the other,'' Electra pointed out. "Someone could cheat.''

"I know a goblin game,'' Godiva said. "I think it would do, because it's clear who wins.''

Dolph realized that they were determined to settle this before running from the approaching horde. "What game?''

"It's called godo,'' Godiva said. "We make a little noose of string, like this.'' She brought out a length of string from somewhere in her long hair and nimbly twisted it into a loop. "Then one person buries it in sand, and others try to poke sticks through it. The one who first succeeds, wins.''

Dolph looked at the others. "Does that seem fair?''

"I think so,'' Nada said. "But the one who buries it shouldn't play. In fact, the one who buries it shouldn't be present, because he might signal a player.''

"I'll bury it,'' Metria said. "Because I don't care who wins. I just like to be amused by the action.''

"She's right,'' Dolph said. "She doesn't care about any of us. So who plays?''

"I will,'' Godiva said.

"I will,'' Electra said.

"Give me the noose,'' Metria said.

Godiva gave her the noose. The demoness took it, and turned into a dark small cloud. There was a stir of dust. Then she reappeared. "It's done. Choose." She presented small sticks to Godiva and Electra.

There was a smooth patch of sand; somewhere under it lay the noose. "Wait!" Dolph cried. "How do we know when someone pokes through it? Maybe she'll win and not know it!"

"She just lifts the stick and the noose is on it," Godiva said, making a gesture as of twisting and lifting.

"I want something more certain than that," Dolph said. "I mean, the noose could slip off or something."

"Sammy can find it," Jenny said.

Dolph looked at the cat. "How?"

"I'll tell him to find the noose with the stick through it. He won't move until it's there to find."

The roar of the approaching horde was getting louder. They did not have time to waste. "Okay, I guess," he said.

"Who tries first?" Nada asked.

"She does," Godiva said, "because I chose the game."

Dolph was impressed. Not only was the gobliness a remarkably comely example of her kind—he wished he could see more of her, but her hair somehow always managed to fall into the path of anything interesting, obscuring it—she seemed both sensible and fair.

Electra took her stick, pondered the dirt briefly, and poked it in. She glanced at the cat, but Sammy seemed to be asleep. So much for that aspect! Electra twisted her stick and brought up the end, but there was no string on it. The way she had done it, she probably would have brought up the noose, it she had speared it.

Godiva stuck her stick in another place, but came up similarly empty.

Electra tried again, and missed again. So did the gobliness. The smooth patch of dirt was getting messed up by the failed attempts, but that did not necessarily make future prospects easier, Dolph realized; the loop might be right alongside of a failed effort, under the stirred-up dirt.

As the game went on, and the hullabaloo of the approaching horde grew, Dolph had a disreputable thought: suppose Metria was having her idea of fun with them? Suppose she had put the noose somewhere else so that it would never be found no matter how long they dug—until, distracted by that, they allowed themselves to be caught by the horde? What a laugh!

Yet the demoness knew that Dolph alone could hold off the horde. He had done so before, by assuming the form of the Gap Dragon. He could do it by becoming a huge sphinx, threatening to step on them, or an invisible giant, whose mere stink would gag them, or a salamander, setting fire to them. So the horde was no longer a real threat. So it made no sense for Metria to do that. She would get more amusement from watching the party settle its conflict of interests in a civilized manner. Demons did not understand civilization, having none themselves. She would also be entertained if Godiva won, because then he would have to help take Che to Goblin Mountain, and he wouldn't like that at all, and she knew that. How fascinating she found his trials of conscience!

Could she have somehow rigged it so that Godiva would win, then? Dolph didn't see how. So he just had to assume that she was playing it straight, and hope.

Electra came up with something. She squealed with girlish excitement—she was sort of cute when she did that, he noticed with mild surprise—and brought up her stick. There was something hanging on it. But it was a root.

Play continued. Then Godiva put in her stick—and Sammy the cat jumped. It was so sudden that it startled them all. He landed on the stick, knocking it out of Godiva's hand. The end flipped up—and on it was the noose.

"See?" Jenny Elf said. "He only *looked* asleep. He doesn't move when he doesn't have to. He found the stick with the noose!"

He had indeed. And Godiva had won the game. They couldn't even signal the other search parties, because that would interfere with delivering Che to the goblin home.

"All right," Dolph said heavily. "It was the deal. We'll help you go to Goblin Mountain. But that was just the deal Nada and Electra made with you. Che's mother didn't, and she's going to be coming to rescue her foal, no matter what."

"That can't be helped," the gobliness said. "I will worry about it when we get to the mountain. Right now I have to figure out the best route."

"North," Metria said.

Godiva glared at her. "What do you care, demoness? What's your motive to help us at all?"

"She finds it entertaining," Dolph said. "So far she's told the truth."

"Why go north when Goblin Mountain is east?"

"Because the goblins of the horde are coming in from east and west, and there's more of them to the south."

Indeed, the noise was now almost deafeningly loud. "North it is," Godiva said curtly. "But we've been up all night and on our feet. We can't make good time."

"I could carry some of you," Dolph said. "If I assumed roc form, if I had clearance to fly. But I can't take off in this jungle."

"Turn sphinx, and we'll ride on your back," Nada said.

Anything she asked him made immediate sense. There were both winged and wingless sphinxes, as there were with the dragons, but the wingless ones were much larger. He changed to monstrous landbound sphinx form and lay slowly down, so that they could climb up on his back. Even so, it was a struggle. Nada finally assumed her largest serpent form, which was still much smaller than the sphinx, and coiled in such a way as to form a series of tiers that the others could climb until they stepped off on his back.

Che and Jenny went first, she carrying Sammy, followed by Godiva and her three henchmen. All of them stood about the same height, though they were centaur, elf, and goblins. Then Electra took hold of Nada's head and held it while Nada became a small snake in her hands. They were all aboard.

Just in time. The first of the horde goblins burst into view, screaming.

Dolph could not change, because he was carrying nine people, counting Sammy as a people; he didn't want to dump them. But it was no easy thing to get up suddenly, either, because he didn't want to cause them to slide off his back. So he labored slowly, and hoped that not too many goblins arrived too soon.

The first goblin charged right up to Dolph's haunch. "They're here!" he yelled. "Riding a stinks!"

"That's *sphinx*!" Dolph rumbled, annoyed.

"You heard me the first time, bulge-bottom!" the goblin said, holding his nose. Then the goblin flew into the air, waving his arms and legs. What was happening?

"Godiva's using her magic wand," Electra explained, evidently catching on to his confusion. "She can loft folk here and there."

A magic wand. That was interesting. How did a goblin come to have something like that?

Another goblin charged in. In a moment this one too was flying faster and enjoying it less. Godiva had no mercy on her own kind! But if she could handle only one at a time, that wand wouldn't help much when the main body of the horde arrived. That could explain how Che had gotten taken by the horde in the first place.

Dolph finally made it to his feet. Now he could do something about the goblins himself. But he didn't want to step on them; they would squish under his feet and be all messy. So he simply forged forward, shoving trees out of the way, and left the goblins behind.

The horde did not give up. The goblins followed, more and more of them appearing as they came in from left and right. Dolph could see them back there when he turned his head. But all they had was sticks and stones, and there were not enough to break his bones. So he moved slowly onward, though to the goblins it was a swift pace.

"Now we can sleep," Electra said. "What a relief!"

"What a relief!" Godiva echoed.

Soon all of them were silent. They were sleeping. Dolph had been up all night, too, but he couldn't sleep. Well, maybe his turn would come later.

"Pretty dull, eh?"

It was Metria. For once he was glad of her company. It would help keep him alert. But he knew better than to let her know that. "Are you still here?" he asked with simulated irritation. "Everything's been decided, so you might as well float off by yourself."

"Nothing's been decided," she asserted. "Once you deliver the sacrificial foal to the gobs, the real fun will begin. Just wait till the winged monsters arrive!"

"What winged monsters?" he asked, looking nervously around. A flying dragon could swoop low on a strafing run and toast his passengers. That would be a problem.

"The ones Cheiron Centaur is gathering to rescue his foal. They won't equivocate around, you know."

"They won't what?"

"Sidestep, hedge, weasel, shuffle, feline paws—"

"Pussyfoot?"

"Whatever. They will demolish that Goblin Mountain tunnel by tunnel. That's a show I wouldn't miss for anything!"

She was probably right. Chex Centaur was a relatively gentle creature, seldom getting her tail in an uproar. But her mate, Cheiron, was a stallion, and he brooked little if any interference in his business. His foal was certainly his business! "There will be abyss to pay!" Dolph muttered.

"What to pay?"

"Blazes, underworld, Hades—"

"Oh no you don't!" she said, laughing. "You won't get me to tell you that bad word you want! I know you don't know it."

"Darn!" he swore.

"Mend, sew, repair?" she asked solicitously.

"Will you go away, you—you whatever?!"

"Of course not, sweetie. I love tormenting you. I think

I'll drop in on your wedding night and watch you try to figure out how to summon the stork.''

"Stork?"

"That's how you consummate a marriage, innocent boy. It doesn't really count until you contact the stork."

"But I don't know how to do that!''

"That's why it should be rare entertainment."

Dolph lumbered on, no longer quite as satisfied with his success in making her stay. How he wished he could pass that magic barrier and become adult, so he could learn everything in the Adult Conspiracy! Then the demoness wouldn't be able to tease him so cruelly.

But first he would have to get married, and that was worse. Oh, he would like to marry Nada, but the thought of seeing Electra die appalled him. Yet if he married her and lost Nada, his heart would break. Time was crunching on as determinedly as his big sphinx feet, but he was no closer to an answer than he had been six years ago when he had first gotten betrothed to the two girls. This news about having to summon the stork just made it worse. Nada knew the secret, but not Electra. But he feared Nada wouldn't tell him. After all, she hadn't told him until now; why should she change her mind then? Assuming he found some way to get around the problem of Electra's situation.

It was solid day when he tromped up to the south bank of the With-a-Cookee River. He was going to splash on through it, but its bottom turned out to be the muckiest muck he could imagine, probably dough left over from the Half-Baked Bog, and he was afraid his legs would sink in like deep pilings and be permanently mired. So he ground to a slow halt.

Nada woke. "Oh, the river!" she said, surprised.

"What did you expect, a desert?" Metria asked in Dolph's voice.

"What?" Nada asked, surprised at hearing that tone from him.

"That wasn't me!" Dolph cried.

"That is, it wasn't what I meant to say," the demoness

said immediately, using his voice again. "I meant to say that only the very most stupid hammer would—"

"Stupid what?" Nada asked.

"Vice, clamp, pliers, grip—"

"Wrench?"

"Yes. No, not quite—"

"Wench, Metria?"

"Wench! That's it! Only the very most stupid wench would confuse a river with a desert. So you can just—uh-oh." For the demoness had realized that Nada had called her by name. She departed in a puff of irritated smoke.

"I knew it wasn't you, Dolph," Nada said. "I heard how she was teasing you, before."

"I'm glad," Dolph said, relieved. "Now I have to figure out how to cross the river. The muck is too deep."

"Did you get any sleep last night?" Nada asked solicitously.

"No." How nice it was to have her interested!

"Then I think you had better get some. So why don't you become a whaleboat and drift down the river for a few hours? I understand it flows generally northward from here, so your direction will be right, and we can all relax and still keep moving."

"That's a great notion, Nada!" he exclaimed. "Hang on!" He changed into whaleboat form, slowly, so as not to dislodge the others. Soon the new form was complete: a giant flat fish (or something; he had never been quite sure what a whale was) with a hollow back that floated serenely on the placid water. His side flippers and rear flukes enabled him to swim as rapidly as he wanted, but he didn't have to, because his nose was a hole in the back of his flat head that would never sink under the water no matter how hard he slept.

"You're welcome, Dolph," Nada said. "I'll stay awake now and keep an eye on our course; I got some sleep last night, so I'm better off than the rest of you. I'll wake you if anything happens."

"Thanks, Nada!" How he loved her! She was just the

most lovely and sensible and princessly person he knew,
always knowing the right thing to do, and doing it. It had
been a great day when he had gotten betrothed to her.

"You're welcome, Dolph," she said. She sounded a little
sad. That reminded him that she didn't love him. Oh, she
would marry him if he chose her, because she had given
her word and a princess never broke her word, but her heart
would not be in it. She was nice to him because that was
the proper thing for a Betrothee to be. He knew he should
do the decent thing and not marry her. But he wasn't sure
he could.

There was a clamor at the bank. The goblins of the horde
had arrived! Well, too bad for them; they could not reach
him or his passengers, out here in the middle of the river.
They could follow along the bank all they wanted; it would
do them no good.

Satisfied, he let himself drift off to sleep.

Dolph drifted down the river, guided occasionally by the
delicious touch of Nada's hand on his nose, so that he did
not get stuck in a cul-de-sac. Cul-de-sacs were nasty off-
shoots which ended in sacks; once something floated into
one, the drawstring would pull it closed, and it would eat
whatever it had caught. Of course Dolph could change into
something else and escape it, but then all the folk riding on
him would get dunked. It was better this way, even apart
from the simple delight of having Nada's attention.

Now and then he heard the clamor of the goblins as they
raged at the shore. The three male goblins with Godiva (and
wasn't she a fascinating creature, even if she was almost
old enough to be somebody's mother!) took pleasure in
standing halfway tall and making gestures at those on the
shore. Dolph, wafting in and out of his snooze, picked up
intriguing bits of dialogue.

"What does that gesture mean, Moron?" Jenny Elf inquired. It seemed that now that they were working together,
the elf and the centaur foal got along well enough with these
four goblins. Dolph gathered that though the goblins had

abducted Che, they had not really mistreated him, only hobbled him so he couldn't get away. He had been unhappy at the time, but recognized that they were just doing a job.

"Gesture?" Moron asked.

"With the finger. Like this."

Dolph hadn't realized that male goblins could blush, but this one did, for Dolph felt Moron's big feet turn burning hot. "Uh, I don't know," the goblin said.

"But you made that gesture to the goblins on the land, and they threw rocks at us," the elf persisted. "I'm glad we're out of reach of their rocks, but that certainly must have been a magic gesture, and I wonder if I could learn it."

"I don't think so," Moron said. "Girls don't use that magic."

"Oh, you mean it doesn't work for girls?"

At this point Godiva crossed over to join them. "Do you have a problem?" she inquired.

"I just wanted to know how to do this gesture," Jenny said innocently.

Godiva must have paled or at least become light-headed, because Dolph felt her weight diminish. "Don't use that gesture!" she snapped at Moron. "Don't you know this girl is underage? Do you think things are different in her tribe just because they have pointed ears? You're in violation of the Adult Conspiracy."

"But they were doing it to us first!" Moron protested. "We couldn't just let them get away with it!"

"Then answer them with this gesture," Godiva said. She faced out and made some kind of signal. Dolph couldn't see what she did, but he saw the effect. Twenty fierce goblins at the shore stiffened, and half of them fell face first into the water, where shellfish shelled them. The three male goblins on the whaleboat fainted.

"I didn't see that," Jenny Elf said. "What—?"

"You weren't meant to, dear," Godiva replied.

"But I certainly am curious what—" Dolph was curious

too. Whatever it was, it had twenty times the effect of what the male goblins had been doing.

"Not until you are adult," the gobliness said firmly.

Jenny sighed. So did Dolph. The Adult Conspiracy was a terrible thing.

Later they stopped at Lake Tsoda Popka, and the passengers dipped out cups of the fizzly sweet drink to go with the cookies they had picked. Dolph snaked out his tongue, trying to latch on to a cookie from a plant by the bank, but couldn't reach it, so had to be satisfied with a drink of the pop. Then Electra caught on, and started dropping him cookies. She was often thoughtful that way, always being a good companion and friend. He liked her a lot, but of course she was hardly the shadow of the romantic figure Nada was.

They drifted on. Lake Tsoda Popka turned out to be not so much a single body of pop, but a popped-apart cluster of lakelets, each a different flavor. Dolph made a mental note: he wanted to return here some time after this adventure was over and royally oink out. He knew Nada wouldn't do it, but Electra would come with him and even get into a cookie fight with him. Cookie fights were one of those pleasures only the young really appreciated. Maybe if they brought bottles, they could dip them full of tsoda, shake them violently, and squirt each other mercilessly. Oh, what joy!

The three male goblins recovered enough to play same games of godo with Che and Jenny, using leftover cookie crumbs in lieu of dirt. Nada and Godiva got into a discussion about the proper care of hair that Dolph tuned out; he liked to look at their swirling tresses, but its maintenance didn't interest him at all. Sammy Cat snoozed throughout, seeming to be dedicated to the proposition that speed killed and the less motion the better. Electra took the helm, guiding him, and he knew better than to object because she wasn't Nada. The demoness Metria faded in and out, observing and seeking to sow mischief in little ways, but the others had caught on to her and generally couldn't be fooled. Overall it was a peaceful and pleasant voyage.

When the river began turning grandly to the west, looking for the sea, because all rivers had a death wish and sought to drown themselves in seas or lakes, they had to leave it. They would have to go north, then around the top of the Elements, then south to Goblin Mountain. That was beside the Element of Earth. South of that, beside the Element of Air, was Mount Etamin, where Drago Dragon lived—and the naga folk. Too bad they weren't going to that mountain, for Dolph would have loved to meet Naga's folks again, and she would have loved to be reunioned with them.

"What?"

"Rejoined, rejunctioned, remerged—"

"Reunited?"

"Whatever." Then he snapped out of it and realized that he had daydreamed a dialogue with Metria. He caught a glimpse of invisible Mare Imbri galloping away. Her pranks were always harmless and usually pleasant. Imbri had been a night mare, but had lost the taste for it when she acquired half a soul, and now was happier as a day mare.

Dolph resumed sphinx form, now rested, and again trudged in his slow yet ground-covering way north, with the others on his back. Two small dragons spied him and looped down to investigate, perhaps thinking of entertaining themselves with some innocent strafing, but Godiva waved her wand at them and they almost fell out of the air. It seemed that her wand could make anything fly, and when directed against a creature who was already flying, it messed things up. Dolph remembered how Chex made herself light with flicks of her tail; if she overdid it, she could have trouble too. Light things didn't necessarily like to be made lighter.

They came in due course to the Ogre-Fen-Ogre Fen, which was pretty swampy, but his huge feet were able to handle it. He was moving much faster than he had in the night, because he could see where he was going, but still it was getting late in the day, and they had a distance yet to go. So he didn't stop; if he moved right along, they could reach Goblin Mountain by soon after nightfall, maybe. He wasn't keen on delivering Che Centaur there, but a deal was a deal, and he had to honor it, so he might as well get it done as fast as possible.

But that reminded him of the other aspects of this situation. What did the goblins want Che for? Godiva had said something about using him as a companion for her daughter. But that probably meant as a steed, and Che was way too young to be ridden. His legs would be ruined. So this did not sound good, even if the goblins had no bad intent. There was also the matter of the foal being away from his dam. Centaurs of any age were amazingly smart and competent; they did indeed seem to be a superior species. But Dolph knew Che, and knew that he wasn't ready for such separation, no matter how well he might be treated. Dolph also knew that there was no way Che's sire would allow it. So it would have been better—much better!—if Electra had won the game, and they had been able to take the foal home. As it was, Dolph didn't know what would happen.

Also, what about the elf girl? She was nice enough, but a strange one, because of her pointed ears and four-fingered hands and her size. What was to become of her? She had tried to rescue Che, but the Goblinate of the Golden Horde had been too much for her. Now she couldn't go home, which meant she was stuck in Xanth. Well, maybe they could take her to Castle Roogna.

One thing about this adventure: it was taking his mind off his problem of his two Betrothees. But he knew that as soon as this was done, he would have to buckle down and make his decision. He was still no closer to it than he had been six years ago.

An ogre loomed before him. Dolph kept moving. Ogres were big, but grown sphinxes were bigger. He hoped to avoid trouble with the ogres here, but if it came, it came, and he would just plow through.

The ogre fell back, a stunned look on his stupid face. What had happened? Dolph hadn't done anything.

"That did it, Nada!" Electra exclaimed.

Oh. Nada had stood up in the ogre's sight and inhaled. That explained it. Ogres weren't smart, but no brain was necessary to appreciate Nada's human qualities. That ogre would be out for the duration, smiling.

Then a female ogre showed up. Oops—she would be less impressed by Nada's inhalation, because ogresses were justifiably proud of their ugliness. The perfect ogre was stronger, uglier, and stupider than any other creature of the jungle. The males could be stunned by beauty because it was totally foreign to their experience, but the females did have a glimmer of its nature and labored hard to eradicate it.

Then the ogress sailed into the air. Godiva's wand was in action again! The ogress made an ugly somersault and landed on a rock on her face. The rock cracked apart, and the fragments shied away, horrified, but her face was unchanged. It still looked like sat-on cornmeal mush.

The ogress began to realize that something was up. Thoughts traveled slowly through an ogre brain, but in time some of them did get where they were going. Her skull heated, and the fleas jumped off as their feet were scorched. She was trying to think! But in a moment she gave up on that futile effort and simply charged in.

The wand lofted her again, higher and farther. This time it dumped her headfirst in a mud puddle. The mud petrified in the vicinity of her face, and merely curdled farther out. That made it difficult for her to get out. She bellowed, and the petrified mud exploded, sending rocklike chunks far, wide, and deep. The ogress got back to her feet and charged again. Once a thought got into an ogre's head, little short of an earthquake could dislodge it. Nobody in his right mind tangled with an ogre—except another ogre.

Fortunately, she was charging in the wrong direction.

Dolph plodded on, trying to lessen the impacts of his great feet so that the ogress would not catch on to his location. That wasn't hard, because the impacts were more like squishes, as he slogged through the slough.

Dolph slogged south, and soon came to the Region of the Birds. Most of them ignored him, but a roc circled, pondering. The sphinx was the largest landbound creature, and the roc was the largest flying creature, except for the Simurgh, who did not generally involve herself in ordinary matters. But she had when Chex and Cheiron got married; Dolph had been there, and he had agreed with the others to safeguard their foal. He was afraid he wasn't doing that very well now!

The roc decided to attack. Rocs tended to resent the size of sphinxes, and this one's beak was evidently out of joint because a sphinx was invading the kingdom of the birds. Dolph did not like this at all; should he change form, dumping his passengers, so as to avoid a confrontation?

Che Centaur climbed up on Dolph's head and waved his arms. "Get down, Che!" Electra cried, alarmed.

Then the roc shied away, with a deafening squawk. Dolph realized what had happened: the roc had recognized Che. The rocs were winged monsters, and all of them were sworn to protect Che. So when this one saw that the foal was here, and all right, it canceled its charge. There would be no further trouble in the realm of the birds.

But what would happen when some of these same winged monsters came to rescue Che from Goblin Mountain? Dolph wished again that the decision had gone the other way!

He came to the Region of the Griffins as dusk was falling. Every creature here was a winged monster!

Sure enough, in a moment three fierce griffins flew up to challenge the intruders. Che waved to them, and so instead of attacking they formed an honor guard through the region. They assumed that the others riding the sphinx were serving Che's interest. They were, in a way.

Metria reappeared, floating in her regular luscious demon form near one of his eyes. "It should get interesting soon," she said encouragingly. "Do you really believe those goblins are going to treat the foal well?"

Dolph could speak in this form, but knew better than to

answer her. She was just trying to make him think about
something he didn't want to think about.

"Of course, once he's inside Goblin Mountain, it will be
impossible to get him out again," she continued blithely.
"Because if anything attacked, they'd simply dump him
into the pot, and have him cooked and eaten before the
defenses were breached. So he'll be their hostage, for sure."

Dolph plodded on, knowing she was right. Yet what could
any of them have done in the situation? Electra had explained it to him: Godiva had played a key part in the rescue
of Che from the horde by doing a sexy dance to distract the
enemy goblins long enough for the elf's magic to take effect.
Godiva had risked her life to rescue Che, and Nada and
Electra had to honor the deal they had made with her. And
it did seem that she didn't want to hurt Che. That counted
for a lot.

But did it count for enough? Ill at ease, Dolph plodded
on.

Night fell without much of a crash, as the sun just barely
managed to escape getting caught by the darkness. Dolph
wondered what would happen if the sun played it too close
and got lost in the night. It would probably have a nervous
breakdown!

He tromped on through more muck and shallow waters.
This was where the loan sharks swam, who were bright
pretty colors but would take an arm and a leg if anyone let
them. The sphinx was far too big for them to bother, though.

At last he approached Goblin Mountain. He recognized
it by the glimmering lights along its surface, outlining it.
It had many little goblin caves and paths running between
them, so that it looked like a collection of anchored fireflies.

The mountain shook as the huge feet of the sphinx
tramped to its base. Goblins erupted and swarmed down to
meet the challenge, bristling with sharp sticks, dull clubs,
and guttering torches. Now the mountain looked like a
lighted anthill.

Godiva stood on Dolph's head and swirled her hair provocatively. "Tell Goldy I have returned with the foal!" she called.

There was a stir. A number of goblins charged up the nearest path and back into the mountain. Dolph waited, not ready to trust such a mass of goblins until he had confirmation that his party was recognized.

A female goblin emerged. She walked regally down the path until she stood before Dolph. "Loft me, Godiva," she said.

Then she rose into the air and came to land on Dolph's back. Dolph turned his head enough to cast one eye on the proceedings.

The two goblin females embraced, and Dolph saw how much alike they looked, except for age. The newcomer was like an older version of Godiva with shorter hair. "What kept you?" she asked.

"I have brought the foal, Mother. We had complications on the way, so had to improvise."

"That was because of Murphy's curse," Electra explained.

The woman frowned. Dolph now understood that she was Goldy Goblin, who had first gained power here by the use of the wand. He had seen her in the Tapestry, when he replayed the story of Smash Ogre. But then she had been young and beautiful; now she was old and grim. "I see. What is the status of these others?"

"We made a deal to bring the foal here. They will leave in peace."

"Very well. Loft me down, then the foal."

"And me," Jenny Elf said.

"Now wait!" Nada protested. "Jenny shouldn't be made prisoner!"

"Che is my friend," Jenny said. "I want to be with him."

Godiva looked at Che. "This was not part of the deal."

"She is my friend," Che said. "I would much prefer to have her with me."

No one else looked particularly pleased, but they understood that the elf belonged to none of their parties, and could choose as she wished. "We'll have to let her go," Nada said at last, and Electra agreed.

"We'll have to take her," Godiva said grimly. "She did enable us to save the foal."

Goldy faced the elf. "Do you understand that once you enter our mountain, you may not be allowed to leave?"

"Yes," Jenny said. She was evidently quite nervous about the prospect, but she wasn't going to leave Che. "I'll bring Sammy too." She picked up her cat.

"Then so be it." Goldy signaled Godiva and abruptly was floating up, across, and down to the ground.

Then Che Centaur floated similarly down, followed by Jenny Elf and Sammy Cat. Then Moron, Idiot, and Imbecile.

After that Godiva threw the wand down to her mother, who caught it neatly and used it to loft Godiva herself down.

The party filed into Goblin Mountain, walking between lines of armed goblins.

"Oh, I don't like this!" Nada exclaimed, her eyes overflowing. She spoke for all of them.

Dolph backed away from the mountain, then slowly walked around it, proceeding on south. There was nothing else to do.

Chapter 9.   Cheiron's Chaos

Cheiron walked along the rim of Mount Rushmost, ill at ease. The news Chex had brought was horrendously disturbing, but that was only the personal aspect. The political aspect was just about as bad. For he knew the moment he heard the news that this was no ordinary crime; Che would not have been abducted just by chance. No, this had the earmarks of goblin involvement, and that suggested that the war between the monsters of the land and the monsters of the air was about to be resumed.

It had started centuries before, even millennia before, when the goblins and the harpies had their falling out, because the harpy males were attracted by the goblin females' legs. Before it was done, the harpy males had almost disappeared, leaving the harpy females severely out of countenance, and the goblin males were as mean and ugly as the goblin females were nice and pretty. Their wars had involved their allies of land and air, and had contributed to the decline of civilization in Xanth.

Today the centaurs and even the human folk were restoring Xanthly standards, while both harpies and goblins were scarce, at least on land. But the old alignments remained, and there were ancient covenants that had never been vacated. That was where the political element came in: if the goblins had taken Che hostage in order to wrest some advantage from the monsters of the air, then Cheiron would have to negotiate with them on that basis. He had no intention of doing so.

It was night, verging on dawn, but he would not rest. Chex was sleeping, secure in the knowledge that he, Cheiron, would know what to do. He did not care to inform her of his private doubts. But perhaps it wasn't as bad as it looked. He could find out before taking action.

He flicked his body and leaped off the rim. In a moment he was flying powerfully to the lair of Hardy Harpy. It happened that Hardy's goblin daughter, Gloha, was visiting the harpies, and she was the one Cheiron wanted to see. The romance between Hardy and beautiful Glory Goblin had nearly ignited the war again; only the discovery that goblins and harpies together had magic talents had eased that crisis. But it could be that the goblins retained resentment, so had taken captive another land-air crossbreed. Gloha, with her goblin connection, might know.

He reached the harpy grove. "Whatcha up to, monster?" one of them screeched irritably, disturbed from her sleep.

"I come to see Gloha, monster," Cheiron replied, using the same courtesy title she had greeted him with. They were all monsters, and proud of it. She settled back, satisfied. As a rule, the harpies hated goblins, but Gloha was different. She was of course a goblin, but she was also a winged monster.

He reached Hardy's tall tree. Gloha could not clamp her feet on a branch the way a harpy could, so Hardy had made for her a fine and private nest, complete with a roof against the weather. "Gloha!" he called, hovering beside the nest.

In a moment the thatch door opened and a sleepy head poked out. "What?"

"It is Cheiron. I must talk with you."

"Oh. Of course. I will fly to ground." She was too polite to point out that it was still before dawn, the very awfullest time to wake a maiden from her slumber.

She stepped out onto the branch, pulling on her robe. She was a lovely little lady goblin with birdlike wings, now

fifteen years old. Soon she would have to decide what kind
of man to take up with; unfortunately there were no other
flying goblins.

They flew to the ground, where Cheiron could stand
firmly. "Che has been abducted by goblins," he said
abruptly. "Do you know anything about it?"

Her dainty hand went to her mouth. "Oh, no, Cheiron!
Are you sure?"

"I am sure he has been abducted, and the operation has
the goblin stigma. We have search parties out, of course,
but my concern is with the motive. It occurred to me that
there might be some residual animosity because of the liaison of your parents and that this is an expression of it."

"I know nothing of this, Cheiron," she said. "But I will
certainly find out! I will fly immediately to Glory's village
and ask."

"Thank you. Do you need a guard?"

She considered. "Ordinarily, no. But if this is the start
of something serious, perhaps it is better."

"Get on my back and I will take you there."

She nodded. She flew to his back and settled down, as
light as a bird. Then he leaped up and spread his great
wings, forging into the sky.

As dawn came, they reached the goblin village. Gloha
flew off to consult with the chief, while Cheiron planted
his feet and waited alertly, on guard against treachery. If
the war were being resumed, his trip here could even be
part of the plot: to lure him down so that he, too, could be
captured. But he had no fear of goblins; he could handle
his bow and spear as well as any centaur could, and that
meant that fifty goblins would die before he had to retreat.

Soon Gloha returned with the goblin chief. The man was
gnarled and ugly in the manner of his kind, but his approach
was not menacing. Perhaps this was because of Gloha, who
by the dawn's early light was as gorgeous a goblin as this
village was likely to see. Her wings, folded, formed a
feather cloak covering her backside, so that a stranger would
have to look two and a half times to realize that she was a

crossbreed instead of a rich gobliness. Even a goblin chief tended to behave halfway politely when in the company of a creature like this.

"We know nothing of this abduction, feather-snoot," the chief said halfway politely. "Gloha was at your mating ceremony six years ago, and joined the pledge to protect your offspring. We don't give a clod of dung for you, horse-foot, or your flighty mare, but we don't want the Simurgh down on us, so we're leaving all winged man-faced horse-rears alone."

"I appreciate your sincerity, clubfoot," Cheiron said in polite goblin protocol. "But what about other goblin tribes?"

The chief scowled. "I can count on the fingers of one hand how many of them you can trust to leave your foal alone, hoof-nose." He held up one dark fist.

"But Grandpa Gorbage," Gloha protested, "you can't count!"

"That's not so!" the chief retorted gruffly. "I can count none—and that's how many tribes."

"Agreed," Cheiron said. "But there is no goblinwide conspiracy, or you would know about it?"

"Right, tail-brain. It's probably the Goblinate of the Golden Horde. They're closest to you, and worst. Even we don't like them."

"Grandpa, you don't like any other tribes," Gloha said.

"Right. But we don't like the horde even more than we don't like the others. They're mean gobs!"

Cheiron knew of the horde. They certainly were the worst gobs. Princess Ivy had brushed with them more than once and dumped most of them into the Gap Chasm, but they regenerated like weeds and made trouble again. But though they were the most violent, they weren't the smartest of goblin tribes. Che had been abducted by smart goblins, with special magic.

Still, the news that there was no conspiracy was gratifying. That meant that it wasn't a land-air war in the making, but merely a foray by one tribe. He could deal with one tribe. "Thank you for your news, chief," he said. "I'm glad we have no present quarrel."

"Well, if it wasn't for Gloha and the Simurgh, we'd have one, sweat-flank!" the chief said defensively.

"To be sure," Cheiron agreed, placating him. "Perhaps some day that will change."

"Yeah," the chief breathed, forming his first smile.

"Bye-bye, Grandpa," Gloha said, kissing him on the cheek. The goblin glowered, but could not quite hide his ungoblinish pleasure.

Then Gloha flew to Cheiron's back, and he leaped into the air, flicked himself, and spread his wings. The downdraft blasted a cloud of sand into the chief's face. Cheiron pretended not to notice. After all, sandblasting would probably improve the gob's complexion.

"Don't take me home," Gloha said. "I'll go with you to Mount Rushmost."

"But you should not be involved in ugly business like this," he protested.

"Yes I should. If another goblin tribe did this, you will need someone to negotiate who they won't attack right away."

"But that would be risky for you, Gloha. You know that regular centaurs don't like crossbreeds; some goblins may not like them either."

"That may be," she argued, "but I run a worse risk if I don't get out and meet folk."

"A worse risk?"

"Old maidism."

Now more of her motive came clear. She was fifteen, and just about ready for romance. Her own tribe might be tolerant of a winged goblin, but goblins were generally exogamous, preferring to marry outside their home tribes. This could serve as an excellent pretext to meet many males from many tribes, and discover who was tolerant and who was not. Her decision to check the goblin tribes rather than the harpy flocks was sensible; there were still so few male harpies that she would make vicious enemies just by trying.

"Very well, if your father approves."

"He'll approve," she said confidently.

No doubt. Like most teenage girls, she could twist her father around her littlest finger, just as she did with her grandfather on the goblin side. Cheiron had to admit that she could indeed be useful, because most goblins were surly and guilty ones would be worse. How surly would they be when they encountered her? Several rungs, grades, and degrees less than otherwise, surely, especially if there were young young males who were interested in pretty young females. That was to say, all of them.

They flew on to Mount Rushmost. Cheiron felt marginally better, because the scope of the plot had been reduced. But the matter was still desperately serious.

A harpy flew up as he landed. "News, horse-bird!" she screeched. "I saw your foal!"

"Where?" Cheiron asked, excited.

"Trudging south with a funny big elf, captive of the Golden Horde."

Cheiron felt a terrible chill. "The horde? Are you sure?"

"Sure I'm sure!" she screeched. "That's my home territory. I snatch their leavings. That's why I watch them. When their spies reported fresh meat on the river, they hustled up there and nabbed it, with help from Fracto the cloud. I'll bet they're going to cook them both!"

Cheiron was seldom speechless, but for some reason he was this time. So Gloha filled in for him. "Thank you, harpy. We appreciate your information, and will go there immediately to rescue Che." Then she reconsidered. "Did you say an elf?"

"Yes, an odd one," the harpy screeched. "Pointed ears and four-fingered hands. A girl, bigger than any other."

"She must have gotten very weak, so far from her elm."

"She was tired but not weak," the harpy screeched. "She was helping the foal when he stumbled. They looked like friends." She laughed raucously. "Can you imagine! Friends!" She spread her wings and took off, her backdraft smelling awful, in the typical harpy way.

Cheiron remembered something Chex had said, as she had babbled out her message: she had briefly encountered an odd elf girl, and her orange cat. Could this be the same elf? How did this relate to the abduction of Che? And how could they be friends? Che had no elf friends; the elves generally kept to their own business, and there was no elm near the home glade. They were good enough folk and a bulwark against goblins in their territory. But Che must have met her since the abduction. Friends? Che was more choosy than that!

But the elf was captive too, evidently. Maybe she had been traveling alone and the goblins had captured her on the same foray, so had lumped the two together. That would not be friendship, but common misery. That made more sense. Nevertheless, he could afford to take nothing for granted. ''We shall have to rescue that elf, too,'' he said.

''Oh, good!'' Gloha exclaimed. ''I'd love to meet her. I get along well with odd creatures.''

He knew what she meant. There were a number of one-of-a-kind or few-of-a-kind creatures, often the results of crossbreeding. In addition to the winged centaurs there was Grundy the Golem, and his wife Rapunzel, who was a human-elven crossbreed who could change sizes and had the most marvelous hair in Xanth. There was Gloha herself. Naturally she related well; she knew what it was like to be unique in species.

But right now he had to take action. With Che the captive of the Goblinate of the Golden Horde—the very worst place to be—he had to take necessary steps immediately. He did not acknowledge that it might already be too late, that the goblins could have boiled the foal at dawn; that simply was not a viable option. He had to assume that the goblins would play with their victims a while, torturing them psychologically before proceeding to physical mistreatment and finally the boiling. He had to assume that he had at least this day to organize for the recovery.

For this was not a mission that could be simply accomplished. The horde was vicious, with its horrible hate spring, and any ill-planned effort would result in disaster. Oh, the winged monsters would gladly exterminate the entire horde, but that would be useless if Che died in the process. So Cheiron schooled himself to do what was most difficult at the moment: nothing. He had to get more information before he acted, and then act with extreme dispatch.

"Gloha, may I ask a favor of you?" he asked.

"Of course, Cheiron," she said. "I want to help."

"Go to Dragon Net and tell him I wish to organize a posse to rescue my foal," he said. "But not only must it be capable of handling the goblins of the Golden Horde, it must be highly disciplined and not strike until we are ready. Ask him to have it ready by day's end, if possible."

She considered, evidently worried about the delay, but deferred to his judgment. "I will tell him," she said, and flew away across the flat surface of the mountain.

Cheiron walked across to where Chex was sleeping, with Grundy Golem on her back, similarly asleep. What a wonderful thing it had been when Chex came into his life! He had been the only winged centaur in Xanth, then had heard of a young female. But a centaur did not develop an association with another centaur merely because the other existed. The situation and the other centaur had to be right. The female was young and inexperienced and had not yet figured out how to fly. She was a fine looking specimen, healthy and resolute, but inexperienced. The fact that she was beautiful and winged was not enough; did she have the character required of the species as he foresaw it? He would have to test her and find out.

As it happened, she tested well, and later she learned to fly. He had not told her how, of course; part of her proving of herself was in achieving this without help. Then they had married, and the Simurgh herself had overseen the ceremony and sworn all the monsters to safeguard their offspring. That had been a surprise; Cheiron had in mind a stable new species, but evidently there was more to it than that. What was Che's destiny? It had to be considerable, for never in known history had the Simurgh left her perch in the Tree of Seeds to participate in such an event.

Could that destiny be why Che had been abducted? Was someone aware of the future and determined to change it by eliminating the centaur before he came of age to achieve that destiny? If so, this was worse than a conspiracy to resume the war between monsters; this was an effort to change destiny itself. Cheiron would have found that chilling even if it hadn't been his beloved foal at stake.

Chex detected his presence and woke. She smiled. What a lovely creature she was! "Have you located Che?" she asked.

"Yes. There is a complication. I am handling it."

"Oh, good," she said, visibly relieved, and relaxed back into sleep.

He had done the minimum he had to: he had told her part of it. He saw nothing to be gained by telling her exactly where Che was. That would only send her into as close an approach to being hysterical as she could manage. He was indeed handling it, and with luck the rescue mission would be organized and on its way before she caught up on her sleep and demanded further information.

He saw swift little dragonflies taking off for points north, east, west, and south, leaving tiny contrails. Dragon Net was sending out his minions to summon the creatures of the posse. The dragonflies would know where to find the fiercest yet most disciplined monsters, and would bring them back here as fast as possible. Cheiron was satisfied; he knew he could leave the organization of the posse to Dragon Net, knowing that it would be competently done.

Indeed, already there was a medium-small dragon coming in. How fast word spread!

But this dragon sought Cheiron, not Net. "I have seen your foal!" he gasped, his fire almost out. He had evidently flown swiftly, gaining on the clumsy harpy, and had a significantly later report. "He was riding a sphinx in the company of girls and goblins, and one of them had a magic wand! They used the wand to twist my companion and me out of the sky, but not before we could see that something strange was afoot!''

Cheiron was amazed. Che riding a sphinx? Sphinxes cared little for the affairs of other creatures. Girls? What were they doing in this business? Goblins on a sphinx? That was strangest of all!

He got the dragon to describe the other folk as well as it could, and gradually he pieced it together. One girl was stunningly beautiful: that sounded like Nada Naga. Chex had said that a number of search parties had gone out, and the two Betrothees of Prince Dolph formed one party. The dragon had also noted the pointed ears of the elf girl. So the Betrothees could have rescued Che and the elf, and then Prince Dolph could have come and assumed the form of a sphinx, so as to carry them. The goblins must be prisoners, perhaps hostages. So Che had been saved.

But the dragon said the party was going north, away from Che's home. That seemed to make no sense! The sphinx could have crunched right through the goblin camp, gone directly home, and been there by now. Why was it going the wrong way?

"You look puzzled, centaur," a voice said.

He looked but saw nothing. "Who are you?" he demanded, in no mood for mischief.

A form appeared, vaguely human. "I am D. Metria."

"A demon!" he exclaimed. "You're no winged monster! You don't belong here."

"Yes I am," the figure said, sprouting wings and breasts. "Yes I do. I have come to impart olds that will interest you and cause you much perplexity."

"Impart what?"

"History, information, bulletin, communication, ancient or recent intelligence—"

"News?"

"Whatever." She flapped her wings in annoyance. "About your foal. But if you aren't interested—" She began slowly fading.

"I am interested," Cheiron said quickly.

"Well, you didn't act interested." She faded further.

Cheiron suspected that she was teasing him. He did not appreciate it. "Either impart your news or fade out entirely," he snapped, turning away.

"What will you give me for it?"

"Nothing, because I do not trust demons." He walked on ignoring her.

This evidently unsettled her. "Do you have a creature who can verify truth? Let me talk to that one."

"The zombie owl can do that," he said shortly. "Over there." He pointed to the perch where the decrepit bird slept by day.

The demoness flew to the owl. "Listen, you rotter," she said, "tell the centaur whether I speak truth. The Prince's Betrothees made a deal with Godiva Goblin of Goblin Mountain to work together to save the foal from the Golden Horde and then decide where he should go, because neither side wanted the foal dead. They saved the foal with the help of the foreign elf girl, and then played a game of godo to decide. Godiva won, so they had to help her take the foal to Goblin Mountain."

The owl opened one big rancid eye. "Trhoo," it squawked.

So it was true! This complicated things further. If a deal had been made to save Che, he could not in honor abrogate it. Goblin Mountain was bad, but not nearly as bad as the Golden Horde. "Why north? That's not the way to Goblin Mountain either."

"They had to flee north until Prince Dolph caught up to them," Metria said. "Then the horde had covered all points south, so they had to plan a route the other way around the Elements, traveling together. It seemed less risky. If the girls had won, the Prince could have taken the smaller party directly through the air to the foal's home."

"Trhoo," the owl agreed.

"So they are all traveling together," Cheiron concluded, "because all are bound to see Che safely to his destination."

"You got it, centaur," the demoness agreed. "Doesn't that make your tail feathers squirm?"

"Why does Goblin Mountain want Che?"

"I wasn't interested enough to investigate that."

"Fhalse," the owl said.

"Oh shut up, you odd bird!" the demoness snapped. Then, to Cheiron: "I just think you'll squirm more if I leave something to your imagination."

"Trhoo."

Cheiron knew he would not get any more useful information from her. "Thank you, demoness," he said. "I will take it from here."

"Aren't you going to go rescue your foal?"

"In due course."

"If you hurry, you can do it before they reach Goblin Mountain."

"I am aware of that."

Her demonic eyes glittered. "So?"

"So I'll wait," he said, wishing she would go away. But there was almost no way to make a demon depart short of an exorcism, and he lacked that talent.

Her eyes rounded in simulated surprise. "You mean you will let the nasty goblins get your innocent foal into their awful mountain, from which little short of all-out war will dislodge him?"

"Yes."

"But why, centaur? Isn't that foolish, even to your kind?"

He knew she was baiting him and getting her demonic jollies therefrom, but he had to answer. "No. It is a question of honor. A deal was made to save Che, and that deal has to be honored. So we shall rescue Che after that deal has been honored."

"But that will require a battalion of the most ferocious monsters you can muster—and then you'll have to dismantle the mountain level by level to reach the foal."

"Yes."

She shook her head. "That should be fun. I shall be sure to watch the show." She faded out.

Some show! But despite her cruel teasing, she was right: it would be one horrendous job to reduce that mountain, and it would expose Che to unconscionable risk. But what he had not told the demoness was that he had another way in mind.

It would be a while yet before the posse was assembled. Now he could relax, getting some necessary rest before the campaign began. As he saw it, the sphinx, traveling at normal sphinx velocity, would not arrive until evening. The night would not be good for an attack by flying creatures. So they had until the following morning to get there and get set up. Then they would see.

One thing was sure: Che Centaur was not going to remain prisoner in Goblin Mountain.

Cheiron slept on his feet beside Chex, waiting out the day. Periodically reports came in. A roc arrived, the hugest of birds, and squawked in its deafening language. Grundy Golem woke from his nap on Chex's back, and took the message, for Grundy's talent was language.

"He says the sphinx passed through the realm of the birds, and Che was there with the others and seemed healthy."

"Thank you," Cheiron said, and Grundy emitted a loud squawk, translating. Actually Cheiron could understand bird language pretty well himself, from long association, but he preferred to let the golem feel useful.

Later a griffin arrived, a handsome creature with the body of a lion and the head of an eagle, whose hide was the color of shoe polish. Grundy translated again, and so they learned that the party had passed through that region safely. Che still seemed well, and friendly with the odd elf.

By this time Chex was awake, and Cheiron updated her on developments. "So Che is safe, but we have to allow him to be taken to Goblin Mountain," he concluded.

"Yes, of course." she agreed, appreciating the necessity of honoring the deal that had enabled Nada and Electra to save the foal from the horrendous clutches of the Goblinate of the Golden Horde. "Then when the party goes on, we must question that elf, who is obviously the one I encountered. I believe her cat located Che, but she was then made prisoner by the goblins along with Che, and they have been companions in adversity. I suspect she has been a mainstay of support for him, because he has evidently borne up surprisingly well. This would not have been the case had he been alone."

Cheiron agreed. Che was bright in the centaur way, but emotionally remained a foal, and could not have handled the horror of captivity by the horde by himself. But with a companion to shield him from the full impact, he could have survived, and evidently had. That spoke volumes for the elf girl. Perhaps she had no special virtues, but she had been there at the critical time, and that made all the difference.

In the afternoon, Dragon Net's posse was ready. It consisted of one flying sphinx, two chimaerae, three rocs, four griffins, five flying dragons, and a flock of harpies. There were hosts of tiny dragonflies and fireflies as a support group, and a cockatrice for close work.

One of the dragons was Draco of Mount Etamin, immediately to the south of Goblin Mountain. He was a firedrake, not large for a dragon, but versatile, because he could traverse caves, even when they extended under water. He had attended Cheiron's nuptial ceremony, bringing Prince Dolph, who had assumed the form of a dragonfly for the occasion. Draco knew the region well, and would serve as a guide for the members of the posse who were from farther afield. Cheiron was glad to see him; there was no substitute for direct knowledge of the terrain.

Before they took off, Cheiron briefed them. "My foal, Che, will be the captive of the tribe of goblins residing at Goblin Mountain. We do not know why they abducted him, but the indication is that they do not plan to harm him. There is no present evidence that they intend to use him politically; apparently this is a private matter. It is possible that it relates to Che's identification by the supreme winged monster, the Simurgh, as one whose life will change the course of the history of Xanth. The goblins may believe that by controlling him, they control Xanth. We can not allow this, either in terms of the history of Xanth or as a personal matter, as he is my foal.''

He glanced around the group a moment before continuing. All the members of the posse were grim as they received the information. He was speaking in the human language, which many of them did not understand perfectly, so Grundy Golem was translating. First the rocs and griffins listened to the squawks, and ruffed out their feathers and flexed their claws. Then the dragons listened to the growls, and puffed out slow jets of fire, smoke, or steam, depending on their species.

''I will not attack the mountain at the outset,'' Cheiron continued as the translations caught up. ''I will deliver an ultimatum: they will have a set time in which to deliver Che to me, unharmed. If they do so, we will depart in peace.'' As the translations reached that point, the creatures showed disappointment. They preferred to fight. It was not that they didn't want to save Che, it was that it was more glorious to wrest him by battle than to have him handed over without struggle.

''If they do not do so, we will attack,'' Cheiron said, and at that point there were squawks of approval and fierce jets of fire, smoke, and steam. ''We will take out their guards at the surface and smoke out the deeper denizens.'' Here the smokers exhaled, for a moment disappearing in a cloud of smoke. Some folk thought that smoke was not as effective as fire, but the fact was that in an enclosed space, smoke was more deadly than fire. Those goblins would come out coughing! ''But we shall do so in an orderly manner, halting the moment they capitulate. This is a rescue mission, not a destruction mission.''

''But suppose they kill the foal?'' the sphinx inquired.

Cheiron saw Chex flinch. He wished that question had

not been asked, but he had to answer it. "Then we destroy that tribe completely," he said grimly.

They made suitable expressions of regret for the loss of the foal, but were thrilled at the prospect of mayhem on this level. It had been a long time since there had been a prospect like this. Cheiron was privately disgusted, but knew that his posse had to have the capacity to reduce that mountain to rubble; otherwise the goblins would laugh at the ultimatum. They might laugh anyway, until a demonstration of power was made.

"We expect to arrive at night," Cheiron concluded. "We will rest until morning, and then survey the situation while we negotiate. Remember: we may make a show of force, but we will not actually attack until they either refuse to yield the captive or show bad faith. Discipline is paramount."

They understood. They did not enjoy discipline, but it was the price of admission into the posse.

Grundy Golem joined Gloha on Cheiron's back, because he expected to use both of them in the negotiations. Gloha would talk to the goblins, and Grundy would translate for the benefit of the posse.

They took off. The small creatures hitchhiked rides with the larger ones, so dragonflies kept company with full dragons and the cockatrice rode with a roc. The harpies were relatively clumsy flyers, so they too had to hitch rides, promising not to befoul their steeds.

They flew in formation, north-northeast. The strongest flyers were the rocs, so they stifled their pace and formed a wedge in front, forging a channel for the others. The posse made swift progress to the Gap Chasm and beyond, as the day waned into dusk and then into night. They skirted the Kingdom of the Flies and the Element of Air, not wanting trouble on the way.

"I don't think I know you, Gloha," Grundy said. "I know *of* you, of course; when your parents came together, it almost made for a war. But you've been among the winged monsters, mostly, and not at Castle Roogna."

"Well, I *am* a winged monster," she replied.

"I never saw a prettier monster!" he exclaimed.

She grew hot, evidently blushing. Cheiron didn't mean to snoop on their dialogue, but there was little way to avoid it. "I wish there were a monster of my kind. But I'm the only one."

"I'm the only one of my kind, too," Grundy said. "But I found it didn't matter, when I met Rapunzel, the only one of her kind."

"But you're not a winged monster," she pointed out. "You don't have an obligation to establish a new species, without sacrificing its best properties."

"You've got a point," Grundy said. "The goblins and the harpies have been fighting so long that there hasn't been any interbreeding in centuries. But I guess there used to be, in the early days. I wonder if there are any winged goblins in the Brain Coral's pool?"

"The Brain Coral's pool!" she exclaimed. "I never thought of that! Oh, I wonder if it could be so? Maybe there's a man for me in there!"

"Who knows?" Grundy agreed. "Maybe you should go and ask the Good Magician."

"Maybe I should! After we rescue Che."

"You know, Che faces the same problem," Grundy said. "He's another winged monster, with no other of his kind. You might go together, and maybe one Question would answer you both."

"Maybe it would! Oh, Grundy, you've given me something to look forward to!"

The same applied to Cheiron. He had worried about the fate of his foal, knowing that there were none for him to mate with; even if there were one year a sister-foal, she would not do. If the species was to become established, they needed to find other winged centaurs—and as far as he knew, there were none in Xanth. He had looked for years, before Chex appeared. Only if there were other cross-breedings would there be others, and centaurs as a class were too conservative to permit that. Cheiron's own genesis had been because of a chance meeting of a centaur and a winged horse, both of whom had come unwittingly to drink at a love spring. They had mated involuntarily, then remained together long enough to see to the survival of the offspring. The equine element had been retained, and the other aspects had manifested, so that a winged centaur had resulted. The mare had suckled it until it could be weaned, then departed forever. The centaur had taught it in the centaur fashion, until it could pursue its own further education, and similarly departed. Thus Cheiron had been alone, more so than a normal orphan. Short of tricking centaurs and winged horses into drinking love potions together, he saw no way to bring others of his kind into being. Chex was unique in that her parents had not taken love elixir. But the normal centaurs shunned her and her mother, for bearing her.

But if there had been similar breedings in past centuries, as there well might have been, and the foals had been hidden away in the Brain Coral's pool—that was something that ought to be checked. Maybe that chaos that threatened the dawning species of winged centaur could be abated.

So Cheiron flew on, his thoughts drowning out the dialogue between the golem and the goblin. Rescuing Che was the immediate thing, but promoting the continuation of the species was the long-range thing. How wonderful if a feasible way was found to do that!

Draco took the lead in the darkness, his head, tail, and the tips of his wings lighted by fireflies so that the others could readily follow him. He brought them to the base of Goblin Mountain, at the east fringe of the Element of Earth. They landed safely in nearby forest, avoiding the treacherous swamp where the loan sharks lurked. It was about midnight.

Then fireflies brought a report: Prince Dolph, Princess Nada, and Electra were camped nearby. They were coming in for a rendezvous.

Soon Cheiron and Chex saw the huge sphinx loom out of the darkness. The girls dismounted, and Dolph resumed human form. There were satisfied greetings all around.

Now at last they were able to get the full story. There had indeed been a deal, and it had been necessary to save Che. The surprise was the part the elf had played: her magic talent was singing in such a way that anyone within hearing range but who was not paying attention got caught up in a communal daydream in the mind of the elf and lost interest in other things until that dream was interrupted or someone jogged he listener's attention back to reality. It was a bit like the hypnogourd, only more pleasant and less compulsive, and difficult to get into deliberately. So the elf had made the goblins pause long enough to enable the captives to escape. That was two favors the elf had done for Che.

"But where is that elf?" Chex asked.

"She went with Che," Electra explained. "She said he was her friend, and she wanted to stay with him. So she went, with Sammy."

"Who?"

"Her cat. He—"

"Oh, yes," Chex said. "He finds things."

"He sure does!" Prince Dolph said. "He found their party for me, so I could carry them away before the horde got them again. Otherwise it could have taken me too long, because that complaint Metria was bugging me."

"That what?" Cheiron asked.

"Carp, fuss, gripe—"

"Oh, you mean bi—"

"Wolfmate," Chex said, knocking his fore hoof with one of her own. He realized that Dolph was still below the age of consent, so was not supposed to know the proper term.

"Whatever," Dolph said, evidently disgruntled. "I couldn't be sure when she was telling the truth."

"Agreed," Cheiron said. "Metria came to tell me about your deal with the goblins of the mountain. But I had a way to verify her accuracy." He turned to Chex. "I think we owe even more to that elf than we thought. She helped Che in three ways, counting the activity of her cat, and chose to remain with him in captivity. That is one more way. We shall have to rescue her too."

"Of course," Chex said. "And that cat."

"So they will become part of the package," he said. "The ultimatum will cover the three of them."

That decided, they settled down to sleep for the remainder of the night.

In the morning, as the creatures of the posse saw about foraging for food, Cheiron advanced with Grundy and Gloha to the main entry of Goblin Mountain.

"Send someone out here!" he called.

"Go soak your tail in sludge, man-rear!" a goblin guard yelled, brandishing his spear.

Gloha flew down to face the guard. "What was that?" she inquired sweetly.

Few things could put a goblin's loud mouth out of gear, but the sudden sight of a beautiful winged gobliness turned out to be one of them. "Get the chief," he muttered to a lesser guard.

Satisfied, Gloha flew back to Cheiron. It was evident that "man-rear" simply did not fit her description.

In due course a fat middle-aged goblin waddled out. "What the dung do you want, crossbreed?"

"I am Cheiron Centaur. Who are you?"

"I am Gouty Goblin, Chief of Goblin Mountain. Now speak your piece, fur-nose."

"You have captives, Gouty?"

"What if I do, Charnel?"

"That's *Cheiron*, Pouty!" Grundy called.

"What business is this of yours, string-face?" the chief demanded.

"I'm a friend to one of your captives, bulge-foot! And we're here to roast you in spit if you don't give him back."

Evidently deciding that it was a losing game to trade insults with the golem, the chief addressed Cheiron. "Why don't you just state your business, centaur?"

Cheiron was glad to oblige. "You have until noon to

release your captives: Che Centaur, Jenny Elf, and Sammy Cat. If you do not, I shall demolish your mountain and destroy your tribe."

"Yeah?" Gouty demanded. "You and who else, hoof-head?"

Cheiron raised his right hand. Immediately several winged monsters showed themselves, eager to get to work. They looked very close, big, and fierce.

"I'll think about it." Gouty turned around and waddled back up the path. It was evident that his swollen legs were not good for walking.

"I don't think you should have given him until noon," Grundy said as Cheiron turned away. "It will just give him more time to work up mischief."

"I want the monsters to be at full strength," Cheiron said. "They flew a long way here, and rested, and now they need to eat plenty. Noon is the earliest we can mount a truly effective attack."

"Oh. That makes sense. But suppose they summon allies?"

"Then we'll do the same," Cheiron said. "I'm hoping that once Gouty thinks about it, he will realize that there is no profit in holding out and will deliver up the captives without a struggle. This is after all our objective."

They waited, gathering their strength. The rocs carried in boulders to drop on the mountain; the griffins sharpened their talons; and the dragons ate prodigiously, their bodies converting the food to internal fuel for their fire, smoke, and steam. They were all hoping that the goblins would try to tough it out.

Noon came, and the captives were not delivered. Instead, the tunnel openings were abruptly closed by rocks and doors from within. The goblins had chosen to tough it out.

Cheiron's heart sank. How he had hoped it would not come to this! It was not that his posse lacked the ability to demolish the mountain; it was that this enormously increased the risk to the captives. Probably the goblin chief thought that the winged monsters would not dare to press their attack too hard, because of that risk.

Well, there was no help for it now. They would have to proceed to the first stage of the siege of Goblin Mountain. The weird aspect of this was that he still did not know why the goblins had chosen to abduct his foal and what resources they thought they could call on to make it stick. For they had to have known that it would come to this. That unknown rendered Cheiron's confidence into chaos.

Chapter 10.   Jenny's Jam

Jenny followed Che down into Goblin Mountain, carrying Sammy. She had done what she felt she had to, but there was no doubt it frightened her. She was a creature of the woodland and of the holt; she hated the forbidding depths of caves. This was like a giant anthill, with passages branching out everywhere, all leading farther down. At every intersection was another goblin guard, glowering with his spear as if he'd like nothing better than to poke a hole in someone to see how much he hurt before his blood welled out. She felt as if she couldn't breathe.

But how could she have let poor Che go in here alone? She had known the foal only less than two days, but already she understood that he hated captivity and would be horribly tormented if there were not someone to shield him from it. So she had to remain with him so she could sing to him and make him feel better when his eyes started getting wild. There just wasn't any other way.

The goblins carried guttering torches, whose grudging flames seemed to issue more smoke than light. The smoke bumbled up along the ceiling, searching blindly for some way out. Jenny knew how it felt.

At last, when it seemed they couldn't go any deeper, they were rudely shoved into an empty chamber. The door was slammed behind them. They were alone.

At least they had light: a goblin had jammed a torch into a notch in the wall. Otherwise it would have been pitch black, for not only was it night, there were no windows. This was an ant nest, where sight wasn't all that important to the denizens.

Jenny wanted to collapse into a huddle of fear, but she didn't dare do that because of Che. So she pretended to be unconcerned. "Well, at least we have a room to ourselves," she said brightly. She set Sammy down, and he promptly settled by the wall and went into an orange snooze. If he was bothered by any recent developments, he did not deign to show it. "Let's see what's in it." She walked around the room, though she expected to find nothing.

She was surprised. There was an alcove with shiny stone that served as a mirror, and there was a crock full of clear water, a basin, and a sponge. "Why this is a washing chamber!" she exclaimed. "We can get cleaned up and look nice!" She did not bring up the subject of the seeming pointlessness of washing, in an awful covered pit like this.

She poured some water into the basin and dipped the sponge into it. "Would you like to be first, Che?" she asked. "I can sponge you off, if you like. Your hide is pretty dirty."

"Yes, thank you," he said, evidently distracted by her positive attitude. It was hard to believe that anything was really wrong, when a person was doing something as routine as cleaning up.

She sponged him off, and indeed his hide was dirty, through no fault of his own. Their trek through the jungle and that night in the horde village had coated them with layers of grime. She had to rinse out the sponge repeatedly, and the water in the basin turned brown, then black, before she was done. In fact, she had to empty it into the drain trench and fill it again with clean water from the crock.

After she had him pretty well clean, she used the remaining water to sponge herself. Her clothing was a total loss, so she got out of it and dumped it into the basin. She couldn't get it all the way clean, but it would be better than before. She hung it up on snags on the wall, hoping it would dry before she had to put it on again.

There was a sound at the door. Someone was unbarring it. Jenny, having noted that the human and similar folk always were clothed, was alarmed. She didn't want to dive into her wet clothing, but if she didn't, she would be exposed. So she hurried to stand behind Che, so that whoever came in would not see the central part of her body.

The door squeaked open. A woman stood there, outlined by the glow of the torch behind her. She was lovely, her slender body garbed in a perfect dress, her face shrouded by the darkness.

She stepped inside, and the door closed. There was the sound of the plank falling into place; the visitor was locked in with them. Was she another prisoner? Surely she was a princess, for her raiment was elegant.

"Hello, Che," the woman said. "Hello, Jenny."

It was Godiva! "I didn't recognize you!" Jenny exclaimed. "Are you prisoner too?"

Godiva laughed. "No, dear. I had them lock me in with you so we could be assured of absolute privacy. I know you wish to rest, but there is something I must explain to you, which I could not before, and a commitment I must have from you."

"We honored the Betrothees' deal with you and came here," Che said. "I believe that expiates our obligation."

"Yes, it does, Che," she agreed. "Indeed, Jenny had no obligation to me, and she is here by her own choice. Now we must forge a new deal."

"I honored the deal only because it was made by others on my behalf," Che said. "I am under no obligation to make a new one."

"Nevertheless, one must be made," the gobliness said grimly. "Now that Jenny is here, she must become party to it." She glanced across Che's back to Jenny. "But we must get you some clothing. Just one moment." She went to the door and rapped on it with a knuckle. "Bring one of Gwendolyn's outfits," she called.

"Yes, lady," a goblin answered.

Godiva returned to Che. "I am prepared to offer commitments of my own in return for yours. First, a comfortable mode of life, including the best food, clothing, and entertainment, along with security. In return for your commitment never to tell another person what I am about to tell you now."

Jenny was astonished. "If you want to keep a secret, don't tell us at all!" she said. "I don't think we're your friends." But she regretted that, because Godiva had impressed her during their journey here.

"But I think we have seen enough of one another to know that we can trust one another," Godiva said, "if we give our words. Therefore we can deal."

"This is true," Che said. "But I see no reason to give our words."

"Because if you don't, I can not tell you why I abducted you," Godiva said evenly. "The entire mission will become pointless, and that will profit none of us."

"Then perhaps you should let us go," the centaur said.

"I am not prepared to do that. And I think that you will understand, once I tell you why you are here."

"I do not care to understand," Che said, his little jaw setting.

Godiva sighed. "Centaur stubbornness is legendary. But you do not need to agree to fulfill the role I have in mind for you, only to agree to listen—and not to tell others. This is not unreasonable."

"You abducted me," Che said, showing that stubbornness she had described. "You have no right to ask anything of me, only to return me to my dam."

Godiva considered. "Suppose I tell Jenny Elf, and then she can tell you whether to make the deal?"

"Now wait—" Jenny protested.

But Che considered it. "Jenny was not abducted by you. She came here by her choice. She may deal with you if she chooses."

"Then come with me, Jenny," Godiva said.

"But I came here to be with Che!" Jenny said. "I don't want to leave him."

"I promise to return you to him the moment our dialogue is done," Godiva said. "He will not cooperate with me until he hears what I have to say and until you return, so I have no motive to keep you from him, only to protect the privacy of my statement."

That seemed to make sense. "I'll do it," Jenny said. "But I can't promise to tell Che to do anything."

Godiva rapped on the door again. "Pass in that outfit," she called.

The door was unbarred. A goblin hand poked in, holding a dress. Godiva took it, then took a pair of slippers and other material. The door closed again.

"Now, Che," Godiva said firmly. "Face the door and close your eyes."

"Why?"

"Because we are about to dress Jenny Elf, and this is a process no male is allowed to witness."

"But—"

"Including panties."

That did it. He knew about panties. He faced the door and clamped his eyes absolutely shut.

Godiva approached Jenny and held out the panties. They were pretty and pink, much nicer than seemed likely for a goblin stronghold. Jenny put them on. Then another item of apparel that it seemed was even less mentionable, about halfway between the panties and her head. Then the dress, which was also pink, and fit her almost perfectly, and was quite the nicest one she had encountered. Finally the slippers, which were made of stretchy stuff that expanded to fit her feet without pinching. She looked at herself in the stone mirror and was amazed; except for her tangly hair, she looked almost like a princess!

"Where—how did you get—" she started, as she took the brush Godiva presented her and worked on her hair. It would never come within even the thought of a suggestion of anything like Godiva's own glorious hair, but she might as well get it as unmessy as she could. Her hair had fallen to her waist, before this adventure started, but it had gotten so tangled that it might as well have been cut off.

"The outfit belongs to my daughter, Gwendolyn," Godiva explained. "She is about your size."

Evidently so! And that explained the quality of this apparel, because Gwendolyn *was* a princess, or the goblin equivalent. The outfit had enabled Jenny to be transformed much as Godiva herself had been by her change of clothing. Jenny had thought that Godiva always wore mainly swirling hair, but apparently that was only outside the mountain.

"Now you may look," Godiva told Che.

The foal opened his eyes, turned, and looked at Jenny. "You are beautiful," he remarked.

Jenny blushed hard enough to obscure her freckles. "I am not!" she protested.

Che turned away.

"You should not have said that," Godiva murmured. "A centaur speaks only the literal truth. You have hurt his feelings."

Jenny was appalled. "Oh, Che, I'm sorry," she cried, dropping the brush. "I didn't mean to—I misunderstood! Please forgive me!"

"Of course," he said, brightening. "I should have realized. I apologize."

She decided not to argue with that. She just hugged him. Then she turned to Godiva. "I am ready to go with you."

She glanced down at Sammy, who had not moved since entering the chamber. "Sammy will keep you company, Che, while I am gone. He won't move or speak, but he can understand you, and if you lose something, he can find it."

"I think I have lost my confidence," Che said with a weak smile.

Godiva rapped on the door again, and it was unbarred. It opened, and they stepped out into the hall. The goblins barred it again behind them.

Godiva led the way along the passage. Soon she came to

another chamber. She opened the door and ushered Jenny in.

This chamber was quite different from the last. It had rugs on the floor and carpets on the walls and a painting of the sky on the ceiling. It had soft-looking chairs. It was the kind of chamber that could make a person forget all her problems.

"This will be yours to share with Che, if you wish," Godiva said. "If you get him to consider my proposal."

Jenny had heard the demoness Metria struggle to find a word. She felt like that now. There was surely a word that covered this situation, but she didn't know it. The gobliness was offering her something nice to do what she probably should not do. But she had agreed to listen. "I will listen and not tell anyone else except Che, if I decide to," she said. "That is all I promise."

"That is enough. I want Che to be companion and steed for my daughter, Gwendolyn. I knew he is not yet of age to be a steed, for his bones are not yet grown, but he can be her companion until they both are of age. That will be some years. How old are you, Jenny Elf?"

Jenny saw no reason not to answer. She showed three hands of four fingers each.

"Twelve, by our reckoning. That is Gwendolyn's age. It is perhaps a fortunate coincidence that you match her so closely. She is a child, like you, but will not remain so much longer. She is my only offspring, and the first heir to the chiefship. It has not before passed to a woman, but this time it shall, for Gwendolyn will have the magic wand."

Jenny appreciated the difference that made. She had seen that wand in action. "But why should she need a steed, when she has that?"

"She is lame. This is the first aspect of her situation. But with a steed, that need never be a problem. I need her to have that steed by the time Gouty passes, which I fear will be sooner than might ordinarily be the case. His illness is progressive, and when he can no longer walk he will be deposed. This I can not prevent."

It was evident that goblin politics were as fierce as their natures. They required a fit and active leader. Jenny had seen what happened to her own folk when they became incapacitated. They usually chose not to remain as burdens on the holt.

"But this is perhaps the lesser of Gwendolyn's problems," Godiva continued. "She is also virtually blind."

Jenny jumped. "You mean nearsighted, like me? These spectacles have made me see so much better! Maybe if you get her a pair—"

"We may not do that. Her deficiency must not be accommodated in this manner. If others of the mountain discovered that her vision is impaired, they would make her life a short one. So she must conceal her liability. She can see only general shapes, but not well enough to recognize faces or the detail of tapestries. I have kept her isolated so that the others are not aware of this, but it will be far more difficult as she matures and is required to take greater part in the activities of the tribe. The centaur can serve as her eyes, too, advising her of those things she needs to perceive."

"But surely other goblins will help her!" Jenny said, beginning to feel for the goblin girl. To be lame and nearly sightless—what an awful thing for a princess!

Godiva frowned. "I see you do not understand the way of goblins," she said.

"Well, I'm not from here," Jenny admitted. "You call me an elf, but where I come from I'm just a girl. I've never been to Xanth before, and it's strange seeing cookies growing on plants, and having cherries explode. So I guess I don't know much about anything here."

"But you did see how it was in the Golden Horde."

Jenny shuddered. "They are mean folk."

"Goblins generally are mean folk," Godiva said. "This dates from a long time ago, when a curse was put on us so that the women preferred the worst of men. This resulted in a degenerating species, at least with respect to the male persuasion. That curse was finally eliminated, so that now we can choose good men, but there is great inertia.''

''Great what?''

''Things are slow to change. This is because there are so few good men of our kind that we are constrained to pick the marginally less bad. It will be a long and frustrating climb back to decency, and I suspect that some tribes will not make it.''

''Like the horde,'' Jenny said, understanding.

''Yes. The goblins of the mountain are not that bad, but remain bad enough. My husband, Gouty, does have certain qualities of leadership, though he does his best to conceal them. But he has done this tribe one signal favor, though he does not see it that way. He sired as his legitimate heir no male.''

Jenny's brow furrowed. ''You do not choose your chiefs according to who is best?''

''We do not. The son of the chief will be the next chief. That is one reason I married Gouty: he was the son of a chief. My mother, Goldy, married a lesser chief, one high in the hierarchy but not the leader. She was beautiful, but it was the magic wand that gave her extra appeal, because it enhanced the power of her husband. She passed it on to me so that I could nab a full chief. Thus my son would have been the next chief. Only Gouty dissipated his waning energy with mistresses and lost his ability to summon the stork before providing me with a son. So Gwendolyn is heir to the chiefship and has the chance to improve things greatly in this tribe, because, of course, the goblin women have always been everything the goblin men are not: intelligent, attractive, and decent.''

Jenny had seen the difference between Godiva and the goblin males. She had no argument. ''So that's good, then.''

''I see you still do not appreciate the difficulties. Perhaps there is no concept of infidelity among your people. Do you know what a mistress is?''

''A person who is in charge of something or very good in her work,'' Jenny said promptly.

Godiva nodded sadly. ''I do not like doing this, but I

must encroach on the tenets of the Adult Conspiracy in order to make something clear to you. It is forbidden to tell a child how to summon the stork, along with certain related matters. This is why Che Centaur, who is a male child, is forbidden to see your panties."

"But what do panties have to do with storks?" Jenny asked, bewildered.

"I may not answer that. Just accept the fact that no male of any age may see any woman's panties, with the single dubious exception of his wife's. This is not merely goblin protocol, it is Xanth protocol. As for the storks: they bring babies, and no child is permitted to know the mechanism by which the stork is signaled for this purpose."

"But this seems like nonsense to me!" Jenny protested. "Where I come from, there are no—"

"You are not where you came from," Godiva reminded her.

Jenny nodded, realizing that there were whole hosts of ways in which she was ignorant of the ways of this land.

"So I will merely advise you that a mistress, in the sense I am addressing, is a woman who consents to signal the stork with a man who is not her husband." Godiva frowned, and Jenny could see that this was no pleasant matter for her. "My husband indulged himself with several of these women, and the stork, being blind to propriety, brought sons to two of them. These are known as illegitimate offspring, and their place in our society is secondary. But in the absence of a legitimate heir to the chiefship, the older boy would become eligible."

Jenny began to get a glimmer. "You mean, if Gwendolyn wasn't—?"

"If Gwendolyn did not qualify, she would be dispatched, and the boy would assume the chiefship after Gouty."

"Dispatched?"

"The tribe will need a chief. If the leading candidate is not qualified, she must be eliminated so that a better candidate can be considered."

"Eliminated?" Jenny was still missing something.

''Killed.''

Jenny gazed at the woman in horror. The way of goblins was abruptly coming clear. ''And if she can't see well—''

Godiva nodded grimly. ''A lame chief might be tolerated; after all, Gouty does not walk well. But a blind one would be out of the question. Unless she compensated so well that it made no difference. Spectacles could compensate, but that would not be allowed.''

''And a centaur companion would compensate,'' Jenny said, seeing it. ''But why a winged one?''

''That was coincidental. Most centaurs are in Centaur Isle, and there is no hope of getting one from there. They hardly deign to associate with non-isle centaurs or with human beings, and have no truck at all with goblins. Most remaining centaurs live in villages and guard their premises diligently. Che was alone. He was the only one we could reach who was young enough to be trained. The fact that when he matures he will be able to fly is a bonus; Gwendolyn could achieve real success among goblins with such a steed. That can certainly be presented as a rationale for his presence. But the real reason is to compensate for Gwendolyn's sight. With such a creature at her side, no matter how young, she can participate actively in goblin affairs and demonstrate her competence. That will not only enable her to become chief, it will save her life.''

Jenny now saw why Godiva had made such a great effort to abduct the foal. Her daughter's life and fate were at stake! Still, she wanted to be quite sure she understood, because she would have to tell Che about this and her own judgment had to be sure. ''If one of those other goblins becomes chief, will it make the tribe more like—like—?''

''Like the Goblinate of the Golden Horde? Indeed. You will have a chance to meet that other prospect for the chiefship in due course. But if a woman assumes charge, there will be much improvement. This would be true for any woman, but Gwendolyn is the only one who has the chance, because she is the chief's daughter. There will be considerable resistance to that, because there has never before been a female chief, but with the centaur and the wand I believe she can succeed.''

"Why—why can't *you* become chief?"

"I am not the daughter of the chief, only of a subchief. I am the wife of the chief, but when he dies I will be only a widow, which is no qualification. Only Gwendolyn can do it.''

Jenny had seen enough already to be satisfied that what Godiva had in mind was best for her tribe, and probably best for all the creatures in the vicinity of the tribe. "I will tell Che,'' she said.

"Thank you. Remember, he must agree, as you have, not to reveal Gwendolyn's liabilities. I will move both of you to this suite when he agrees to listen. His decision will be a separate matter; such a thing is not lightly undertaken by a centaur, and we must have his word. When he gives it, he will be completely free, for there is no binding as firm as a centaur's word.''

"Um, could I—could I see Gwendolyn?'' Jenny asked. "I will tell Che, but it would be better if I could tell him how Gwendolyn is, if he asks. I mean, if he has to decide whether to be with her—''

"Of course.'' Godiva got up and walked to a door in the wall, not the one through which they had entered. She opened it and ushered Jenny through.

Beyond was another chamber, decorated with girlish things. There were pictures of trees and flowers and animals and clouds. There were cushions. There was a feather bed, and on it lay a beautiful goblin child, asleep. Her dark hair spread out against the pillow and around to form a kind of coverlet. It was obvious she was Godiva's daughter.

"Gwenny,'' Godiva said gently.

Jenny felt a start, for that version of the name was so similar to her own. But of course it was the nickname for Gwendolyn, just as hers was for Jennifer.

The eyelids flickered. Gwenny woke and looked up. "Hello, mother,'' she murmured.

"This is Jenny Elf, who may become your companion," Godiva said.

Gwenny sat up, blinking. "Hello, Jenny Elf. I did not see you." She extended her hand in the general direction of Jenny.

Jenny took it and squeezed it for just a moment. "I just wanted to say hello," she said. "I did not mean to disturb your sleep."

"That's all right. It wasn't much of a sleep."

Jenny found herself liking Gwenny Goblin. That was dangerous, because she had to be objective. "Maybe I'll see you in the morning," she said, backing away.

"I'd like that," Gwenny agreed. She lay down again and closed her eyes.

Jenny went out the door, and then Godiva took her back to the bare chamber where Che remained. "I will talk to him," she said.

"I will wait a moment outside," Godiva said. "If he agrees to listen, knock, and I will convey you both to the other suite."

Jenny entered. Che smiled as he saw her. "Sammy found my confidence!" he exclaimed. "I feel much better now!"

"How did he do that?" Jenny asked, amazed. She had not realized that such a thing could be found in that way.

"I asked him, and he came and rubbed against my leg and purred, and my confidence was back. He must have brought it."

Oh. Sammy had done that for Jenny in the past. She just hadn't seen it quite that way. "Che, I have talked to Godiva. She—please, I think you should listen to her. You don't have to make her deal, just agree not to tell."

He looked at her. "If you tell me, I will listen."

"I will tell you. But first we must go to a more comfortable chamber." She knocked on the door.

It opened. Jenny led Che out, and Sammy came along, knowing that something was up. Without words they filed into the suite. "Food will be delivered if you ask," Godiva said as she closed the door behind them. "I will come when you ask for me. perhaps in the morning."

"Thank you," Jenny said.

Sammy promptly found a suitable cushion and settled down for the rest of his orange snooze. Che stood for a moment and looked around, plainly awed. "I did not realize that goblins had such accommodations."

"They do for princesses, or whatever," Jenny said. She saw that he was tired, so she decided to abbreviate the discussion. "Let me tell you the essence now, and in the morning I'll tell you as much else as I know, if you want."

"I appreciate that."

"Remember, you must not tell anyone else, regardless what you decide about the deal she offers."

"Of course. I did not want to be compromised by something extraneous, but since you have ascertained that it is not, I accept the terms."

"She wants you to be the companion for her daughter, Gwenny, who will be the next chief if you help her, and will die if you don't—because she's lame and mostly blind. A female chief would try to make this a better tribe."

Che had evidently been braced for something of significance, but this surprised him. "But females aren't goblin chiefs!" he protested.

"This one can be, with your help."

He pondered. "What kind of person is this goblin girl?"

"I saw her only briefly. She's sleeping in the next chamber. She seemed nice, but of course I don't really know her."

"Perhaps I can see her."

"Oh, I don't think the door would be unlocked." Jenny said, trying it. It opened. She stared at it, dumbfounded. How could Godiva be so trusting?

They entered. There by the dim light of the torch lay Gwenny Goblin. lovely in her sleep.

"She is very like you," Che said.

"Oh, no, she's—" But Jenny caught herself. "She is

my age and size, but of course her ears are round and she has five fingers.''

"These hardly matter.'' He retreated. his hooves landing very lightly so as not to wake the girl.

They returned to their own chamber and closed the door. ''This alters the complexion,'' he said. ''I must consider.'' Then he settled down on the carpeted floor, leaned against the carpeted wall, and went to sleep.

Jenny gathered cushions and formed a bed beside him. She lay on it, and

The light of morning woke her. She had not even been aware of falling asleep. She had been so tired, but now felt much refreshed. She blinked and stretched, and one hand encountered something furry and warm. Oh, yes, that was Che Centaur. He—

She blinked again. Morning? How could that be, way down here in the anthill?

She sat up and saw that the light was coming from an alcove. It seemed to be a well, with the chamber at the bottom, so that the light could come down. She saw that its sides were shiny, so that the light reflected. How nice! She had not noticed it at all in the night, but of course then it had been dark and would have looked like just a blank niche.

By daylight the room was brighter and nicer than it had seemed by torchlight, and it had seemed nice enough then. This was evidently Gwenny's playroom that they were sharing.

Gwenny! Was she still there? Jenny walked to the door between chambers, but hesitated. It wasn't her place to disturb the chief's daughter, after all. Besides which, she had something to do.

She explored the chamber, and found a curtained compartment with a shiny stone surface, a basin, a crock of water, a sponge, two brushes, and a pot with a lid. She picked up the pot and sniffed it, then wrinkled her nose in disgust. That was what she was looking for, all right. She used the pot, then put the lid back on. Then she used the water and basin and sponge to clean herself again, getting rid of the faint lines of grime that had escaped her before. She brushed her hair, working out the tangles that had sneaked back in overnight. Not only did she feel better, she now felt quite good.

She stepped out of the curtained alcove. Sammy was up, and pacing the floor. Oh.

She went to the outer door and knocked. In a moment the bar lifted and it opened. A goblin face peeked in.

"Oh, Moron!" Jenny said, recognizing him. At first all goblins had looked alike to her, but that was passing. "Can you get us a box of dirt?"

He seemed surprised. "Not cookies?"

She laughed. "Not to eat, silly! For Sammy." Then she reconsidered. "But bring some cookies too, or whatever is good for breakfast. For two." She re-reconsidered. "For three. And a dead rat, if you have one." For she realized that Sammy might not have much luck hunting, down here. Actually she wasn't sure what Sammy ate, because she never saw the results of his hunting.

Moron smiled. He turned to the goblin behind him. "Three piles of cookies, a dead rat, and a box of dirt. They are hungry."

Jenny bit her lip. It seemed that goblin males were not entirely sour.

She turned back into the room. Che was awake now, and getting to his feet. He looked around. "There's a curtained place," she said, anticipating his need. She hoped he knew how to use the potty himself.

It seemed he did. But meanwhile there was a sound from the next chamber. Jenny went to the door, and it opened as she reached it. Gwenny Goblin stood there, blinking in the way Jenny had. She was just Jenny's height. "Hello?" she said uncertainly.

"Hello, Gwenny," Jenny said. "I am Jenny Elf. We met last night."

"Oh. I thought I had dreamed it!" Gwenny said. "I was just going to the—"

"It's being used right now."

Gwenny tried to look across the room. but it seemed that her vision did not reach that far. "There's another girl?"

"No, Che Centaur. He—your mother brought us here last night."

"She did? Why?"

"She would like Che to be your companion."

"She would? Why?"

"You mean you don't know?"

Gwenny shook her head. "I don't know anything much. I get lonely, sometimes."

Surely she did! Jenny had thought that Che was coming here to be a prisoner, but she realized that Gwenny always had been a prisoner. Godiva didn't want anyone to know of her infirmities, so she would have had little company. How awful!

Che came out. "Hello, Gwenny," he said politely.

Gwenny peered intently in his direction. "Are you really a centaur?" she asked, seeming doubtful.

"Yes, albeit a small one. Didn't your mother—"

"No," Jenny said quickly. Then, to Gwenny: "It's empty now. Let me walk across with you."

"Oh, I can find it," Gwenny said. "I know where everything is, here, if it isn't moved." She walked across the room confidently enough. But she limped, for one leg seemed not to function perfectly. It looked all right; in fact it was a well proportioned leg, but it seemed not to bend the way it should.

Then Jenny saw Sammy, who was lying in his bump-on-the-ground mode in the middle of the room. "Wait!" she cried. diving for the cat.

Gwenny stopped. "Is something there?"

"Sammy. my cat. He doesn't realize you can't see him." She picked Sammy up.

Gwenny peered at Sammy. now at close range. "Oh, orange!" she exclaimed. "How pretty!"

Jenny could tell that these two would get along. "Sammy, she can't see you well from a distance," she told him. "So you will have to find a place where she won't step." She set him down. She hoped that would work. He could find anything, but she hadn't tried this before.

There was a sound from the outer door. "Oh, that will be breakfast," Jenny said. She was feeling quite organized, now. She crossed to it.

Moron was there, with the box of dirt and a yellowish chunk of cheese in the form of a rat. Evidently they had found rat cheese instead of a rat. Maybe that would do. "Oh, thank you, Moron!" Jenny exclaimed, taking the box. She carried it to a corner near the curtained alcove and set it down. "There you are, Sammy; you know what it's for. The rat's yours, too." She hoped he would like the cheese; she really preferred it to a real rat.

Sammy headed for the box. Meanwhile, Jenny returned to the door, where Moron had three piles of cookies. They were big cookies and tall piles; they filled Jenny's arms. She brought them into the center of the room, then wondered where to set them down.

"I believe I saw a table in the other room," Che said.

"Oh, good." Jenny lumbered through the door and dumped the cookies on the table.

Gwenny emerged from the curtains and walked toward the sound. "I smell cookies," she said.

"Yes, I got them for us," Jenny said. "Is it all right? Do you like cookies?"

"Oh, yes! But Mother never gave them to me for breakfast."

"Oh? What does she give you?"

Gwenny scowled. "Pease porridge hot."

"Oh, is that good?"

"No. It's awful. But it's supposed to be good for me."

"The Adult Conspiracy!" Jenny exclaimed, laughing.

"Did you ever doubt?" Che inquired innocently.

"Maybe Moron didn't realize," Jenny said.

"Oh, you asked Moron!" Gwenny said. "He's not bright."

"Why, who do you ask?" Jenny asked.

"Mother usually brings it in."

"That explains it. She's smart."

"I think I wasn't smart, not to do what you did."

"I just didn't know any better."

"You see, Jenny is from another land," Che said. "She does not know local customs."

"Oh, that must be fun!" Gwenny exclaimed. "I've never been out of the mountain."

Jenny considered and decided not to argue the case. She missed her holt, but it would be awful to be confined to it all the time. So she ate her cookies, which were very good, and the others ate theirs. She hoped Sammy liked his cheese, but didn't care to call attention to it, lest he change his mind.

"What is it like in your land?" Gwenny asked.

Where should she begin? "It's a little like Xanth, but there aren't goblins or dragons, and most folk don't have magic talents. All the folk I know are like me, I mean with pointed ears and four-fingered hands, except for the human beings."

"You have pointed ears?" Gwenny asked, peering at her closely. "Why so you do! I didn't realize! And you say your hands—are you sure?"

Jenny held up a hand. Gwenny held up her own. They touched. Sure enough, they were of similar size, but the goblin girl had one extra finger.

"Unlike the Xanth elves," Che said. "I think Jenny is unique in Xanth."

"Unique?" Gwenny asked.

"I mean that there is none other like her here."

Gwenny clapped her hands. "Isn't that nice!"

Jenny was getting thirsty. "I should have asked for something to drink."

"Mother brings plain old wholesome milk pods," Gwenny said, wrinkling her nose.

"I wonder if—" Jenny started.

"It seems reasonable—" Che continued.

"Let's try it!" Gwenny concluded.

They got up and hurried to the outer door. Sammy was sleeping halfway there, but he was in Jenny's path, not Gwenny's. Evidently he had known where to find the spot where Gwenny wasn't going. Jenny jumped over him, as she was used to doing. He must have liked his cheese, because he hadn't protested. That was a relief.

Jenny knocked on the door. In a moment it opened, and Moron's face appeared. "Some Tsoda Popka water, please," she said. "Any flavor, so long as it's good."

He nodded. Soon it arrived: purple fizz flavored, in three bottles. Jenny took it and thanked him.

Jenny, about to sip hers, paused. "Have you ever—?" she asked, putting her thumb over the top of the bottle. Electra had told her about this, and she was curious. According to Electra, Tsoda Pop got angry when confined and shaken, and swelled up in protest.

"Covered the bottle?" Gwenny asked, peering at her hand. "No. Why?"

"I am not certain this is proper," Che said.

"But you're only five years old," Jenny reminded him. "You shouldn't know any better."

"True."

"What are you talking about?" Gwenny asked, perplexed.

"This," Che said, giving his bottle a shake. The Popka frothed up and squirted Gwenny in the face.

"Oh!" she exclaimed, astonished. "How did you do that?"

"Like this," Jenny said, touching Gweny's hand and guiding her thumb to the top. "Shake."

Gwenny shook, hard. The Popka swelled up furiously and blasted out, spraying everything.

In a moment they were all doing it, firing away until the bottles were only half full and too tired to froth any more. Then they drank what remained. It tasted awful, yet good, because of the fun they had had. They were all soaking, their dresses and fur ruined.

"What has happened here?"

All three jumped. It was Godiva!

"I fear we have misbehaved," Che said contritely.

Godiva frowned. But as her eyes focused on Gwenny, who was trying to be properly chastened but not succeeding very well, they softened. Jenny realized that Gwenny probably had not had many good times before. "Well, you will have to clean up and change your clothing. You reek of Tsoda!" Her gaze focused on Jenny. "Have you spoken with Che?"

"Yes," Jenny said.

The eyes focused on Che. "And have you come to a decision?"

"No," Che said.

Without a word, Godiva departed.

"What did she mean?" Gwenny asked.

"I guess we'd better get cleaned up," Jenny said. "And I guess I'd better tell you. Come on, I'll sponge you off, and you can sponge me off, and we'll talk."

"But who will sponge me off?" Che asked, disappointed.

"We both will," Jenny said.

"Excellent."

They had to send out for more water, and while they were at it they sent out the brimming potty for emptying. Soon they were cleaning up, while Che dutifully faced the door and closed his eyes.

"Your mother says you can be chief, one day," Jenny explained to Gwenny. "But not if anyone finds out that you can't see very well."

"That's true. They would dump me out as dragon bait, and Gobble would become chief."

"Gobble?"

"Gobble Goblin, the eldest half-son of my father."

"Is he nice?"

Gwenny grimaced. On her it looked cute. "He's the brattiest ten-year-old brat who ever existed."

"Well, your mother thought that if she got you a centaur to ride, you could get around better, and he could watch out for things and tell you about them, so that no one would know you couldn't see them yourself. Then you could be chief."

"Why, I never thought of that!" Gwenny exclaimed. "Maybe it's true! Centaurs are very smart."

"So she brought Che. But it won't work unless he agrees."

"But I thought you said he's only five years old!"

"Yes. But by the time the time comes, you might be adult and so would he, so you could ride him."

Gwenny considered. When the two of them were clean and in nice new dresses, and it was time to do the centaur foal, she asked: "How did she bring you here, Che?"

"She abducted me."

"I was afraid of that. It's the goblin way. So you didn't want to come here."

"That is correct."

Gwenny shook her head. "I'm sorry about this, Che. I didn't know. Of course you shouldn't stay here. I will tell Mother to let you go."

"But what will become of you, Gwenny?" he asked.

She shrugged. "Well, it's not much of a life anyway."

Jenny felt her heart sink. The goblin girl would survive only as long as her secret was kept, and she would never be able to go out among the goblins. That meant that eventually her condition would be discovered, and then it would be over. That probably wouldn't be good for the tribe, either, if a bratty brat took it over.

"I have not decided," Che said.

"But it isn't right to keep you away from your dam. I don't want to hurt you. I—" She paused. "What's this?"

"One of my wings," Che said.

"You have wings?"

"I am a flying centaur. I can not fly yet, but in time I will."

"I didn't know! I never heard of a flying centaur!"

"I believe there were none in Xanth, before my sire and dam appeared," he said. "At least, not currently. We are trying to become a new species."

"That makes it even worse! You can't be a new species if you're captive!"

"Untrue. Were I to agree to be your companion in this fashion, I would no longer be held captive and could go where I wished, as long as you were with me and agreed to go."

Gwenny nodded. "Because a centaur never breaks an agreement. Still, it isn't right."

"I am not certain," Che said. "In fact, I am unable to come to a decision. So I shall delegate it to another."

"Who?"

"Jenny Elf."

Jenny jumped. "No! I can't decide for you, Che! Not on something that affects your whole life like that!"

"I think you shall have to, for I can not, and a decision needs to be made." And his little jaw set in that way she recognized.

"All right, Che, I'll decide," she said. "But not right now. I'll have to think about it. A lot."

"But while you're thinking," Gwenny said wistfully, "can we be friends?"

"Yes, of course," Jenny said, touched. "In fact, while I'm thinking, I will try to help you see things, so you can go out among the goblins."

"Oh, thank you!" Gwenny cried, jumping in joy. "I've always wanted to go out, but except when my mother took me, I couldn't."

Jenny nodded, understanding exactly how it was. She had no idea how she was going to decide, but at least this meant she didn't have to rush. It occurred to her that this was like Prince Dolph's dilemma, in which he had to choose between Betrothees and one would die if he chose wrong. Gwenny would die if Jenny chose wrong.

She played with that notion, intrigued by it. Of course it really wasn't the same, because the three of them were younger and were of three different species. But the parallels were sharp enough. One male, two females, both of them older than he. He had to choose one to be with, and couldn't. They all liked each other.

The difference was that this wasn't marriage but a different kind of association. And that Che would not choose; Jenny had to choose for him. And she had no interest in the outcome.

No, that wasn't true. Now that she worked it out, she saw that she was in a real picklement of a jam. She had to make a decision that would affect the life of one friend and the freedom of the other, and it did affect her. Because she had come here into Goblin Mountain because she knew that Che needed her, being too young to survive the horror of isolation from his kind without the support of a friend. But now he could have a friend. Gwenny Goblin needed him and would be his friend; and she was not only a nice girl, she was a princess, or at least a chiefess. So Jenny wasn't needed. She was sort of the odd one out, like Electra, if Dolph married the Princess Nada. She was no princess, either in nature or role, just a girl who had been wrenched out of her former life to come to this strange one. How she wished she could return to her holt in the World of Two Moons and to her family, who surely missed her and wondered what had happened to her. But the hole through which she had come was plugged, and she didn't know the way anyway, and Sammy could not find it, because home was the one thing he could not find.

"Why are you so sad?" Gwenny asked.

Should she answer? Her situation really did not relate to the problem.

"She is far removed from her home and folk," Che answered for her. "Just as I am. It is not an easy situation."

"I wish you could both go home," Gwenny said. "And that I could go with you."

"But you are to be a chief!" Jenny protested.

"I'd rather have friends."

Jenny saw that the goblin girl needed a friend as much

as Che did. Che had many friends, back at his home, and so did Jenny at hers; their only problem was that they weren't home. Gwenny was home, but without friends. Her situation was just as bad as theirs.

"Let's go exploring," Jenny said, changing the subject, because there really wasn't anything she could do with the subject. "I can tell you what I see, and you can tell me what or who it is."

"I am not sure that is wise," Che said. "Others will hear you talking, and will realize that Gwenny is not perceiving things directly."

Jenny hadn't thought of that. "Maybe I could whisper." But she saw that it was still a problem. "Or if we could work out some code the others wouldn't know. Only I don't think I could remember anything very complicated."

"I could," Che said. "That is evidently part of the reason Godiva chose a centaur. It would be relatively simple to devise a mechanism amounting to a veritable language of signals known only to us. They should be auditory or tactile rather than visual, since Gwenny can not see well at a distance. I think tactile would be best, were she riding a centaur; simple flicks of the tail or twitches of the skin could signal affirmative or negative, and more sophisticated combinations for other communications."

Gwenny considered. "I think that's too complicated for me right now. I do want to go out, but I think I'd feel better waiting until I'm sure I can handle it. If Gobble ever caught on to my infirmities, I would be doomed, and he's so sneaky that I fear he would."

"Perhaps we could remain here and play with magic," Che suggested. "Do you have a magic talent, Gwenny?"

"No. That is, not by myself. Goblins only have half talents, and harpies have the other halves, so it's not easy for us to do magic. I will have the magic wand, of course, but not yet." She peered in his direction. "But you do? I thought centaurs didn't."

"It was thought that centaurs didn't," he said. "But it turned out that we do. My talent is making things light by flicking them with my tail; that is why I must be careful what I flick. I can turn it off when I choose, but if I forget it can be awkward.''

"Oh, that seems like fun!" Gwenny exclaimed. "Can you make me light?"

"Certainly. But what is the point?"

"The point is I think it would be fun," she said. "Mother sometimes lofts me with the wand, but if I had another way to float, I'd like that."

"Very well. Stand in the middle of the chamber."

Gwenny went to the middle. They had long since finished brushing Che off. He stood beside her and flicked her on the shoulder with the tip of his tail.

"Oh, it works!" she exclaimed. "I can jump so high!" She bent her good leg to jump.

"Don't do that!" Jenny cried, grabbing for her. She was almost too late; Gwenny was in the process of jumping. Jenny grabbed her arm as she rose.

It was well that she did so, for otherwise the goblin girl would have launched herself headfirst into the stone ceiling. As it was, her body rose and was stopped only by Jenny's hold on the arm. She spun around, squealing and kicking her feet, before Jenny managed to wrestle her back to the floor.

"Oh, that was fun!" Gwenny exclaimed.

"Fun!" Jenny said severely. "You almost banged your head!"

"But I'm so light, it wouldn't hurt."

"Not so," Che said. "Your inertia remains intact."

"My what?"

"Slow to change," Jenny said, remembering what Godiva had said.

"My slow to change remains intact?" Gwenny asked, confused.

"Not precisely," Che said. "Inertia can be used in either the social or the physical sense. I mean that your body has the same mass as ever, but feels light, so you can jump higher. But if your head hit the ceiling, it would be like landing on the floor head first."

"Oh," Gwenny said. "I wouldn't like that. I'll be careful. But maybe if you flick me again, I could just float. That would be fun."

"Not in that dress," Jenny cautioned.

"Why not?"

"Someone might see your panties."

"Oh!" Gwenny flushed, which was impressive on her dark face.

Jenny had underestimated the seriousness of the warning. She had not meant to embarrass the girl like that. "I thought of another thing to try," she said, hauling Gwenny down.

"Another thing?"

"Try my spectacles." Jenny removed them from her face and put them carefully on the goblin girl's face. They looked funny on her, but they curved around to fit her head.

"Oh!" Gwenny exclaimed. "I see you!"

"So they do work," Jenny said, satisfied. "Except—"

"Except that I don't dare been seen in them," Gwenny said, taking them off.

Jenny accepted them back. She had been just about blind. She had gotten used to the spectacles, and now felt lost without them. "Maybe we can do something else," she said quickly. "Like telling stories."

"Oh, I love stories!" Gwenny agreed. "They are the only way I can travel."

Jenny realized that with her own magic talent, which she had discovered with Che, she might help the girl travel in a very special manner. But right now she thought that a regular story was enough. "Let's settle down, and I'll tell a tale," she said. "Then you can tell one, and Che can."

"Oh, how nice!" Gwenny cast about, finding scattered cushions with her feet and picking them up to form into a pile. She covered quite a bit of territory, but somehow never encountered Sammy, who was sleeping in the very spot that she didn't go. She piled them up in a corner, and they plumped down on them, Che lying on one side, Jenny on the other, and Gwenny in the center.

What tale should she tell? Jenny had heard a number of nice tales of the history of her folk, such as the ones about the former chiefs and their friends, but she wasn't sure a goblin of Xanth would understand these. For example, there was the one about Prey Pacer and Softfoot, who was lame. Gwenny might think she was being mocked. There were the tales of the wolf friends, but Jenny didn't know whether there were wolves in Xanth, and she was pretty sure that if there were, they did not have riders, so that might only confuse the girl.

So she settled on one that was more like Xanth, adapting the terms to fit. Instead of High Ones she could have—what? She wasn't sure what in Xanth would fit.

So she tried something foolish. "Sammy, find me what fits," she said.

The cat woke, looked around, and went to Che, settling down against the centaur's side. So much for that.

"I think that means I should answer your question," Che said. "What is it?"

"I need to know the Xanth equivalent of the High Ones."

Che looked perplexed, but offered an answer anyway. "The Muses, perhaps."

"Is there a Muse of beauty?"

"They aren't of that type. They are patrons of the arts. But perhaps Erato, the Muse of love poetry, would do."

"Does she get angry with mortal folk?"

"I don't think so. Maybe Melpomene, Muse of tragedy. She has a tragic mask, a club, and a sword."

"Maybe she's the one," Jenny agreed. "Well, one day Melpomene was annoyed, because a woman named Willow had a baby—I mean the stork brought her a baby girl who was so pretty that everyone knew she would grow up to be as beautiful as any Muse. She named the baby Lily, because she was as fair as that flower.

" 'We'll see about that,' Melpomene said. 'Lily shall not see the flower after which she is named. No mortal may look as good as a Muse without suffering tragedy.

"Willow went out in a field of flowers near the mountain of the Muses, where a flock of birds flew, holding Lily. 'Oh, Muses,' she said, and the tears flowed from her eyes, 'you have given me such a beautiful child, but why have you made her blind?' Then the Muses were sorry, but there was nothing they could do, for once a thing was done it could not be undone.

"Lily grew up to be a fine girl, but she never saw a flower or anything else. She walked out in the field and touched the flowers, including the one for which she was named, but this was not good because flowers could not survive well when they were handled. She began to cry.

"'Why are you crying?' Willow asked her.

"'Oh, Mother, you have taught me right from wrong and to appreciate what I have, but how can I appreciate the flowers you speak of so fondly, when my touch hurts them?'

"The flowers listened and were sad. 'She likes us so much,' they said to themselves, 'and she is named for one of us. We must find a way for her to appreciate us without hurting us.'

"They discussed it among themselves, and they asked the Muses to help them; and the Muses remembered that they were at fault and agreed. They could not make Lily see, but they could help the flowers change. They gave the flowers the power to describe themselves in odor.

"Each flower assumed that fragrance it felt best described it. Some flowers, like the roses, believed they were extremely beautiful, so they adopted scents that were delightful. Others thought they were ugly, like the geraniums, so they took unpleasant smells. It didn't matter whether they really were beautiful or ugly, only how they thought of themselves, and some had an unrealistic view of the matter. Some were bold and had strong smells, while others were very shy and had little or no fragrance, though a person looking at them might have thought they deserved more. Thus it was that though some fragrances were not very accurate, at least they helped define the flowers and distinguished one from another.

"So it was that Lily at last came to appreciate the flowers, and could tell the rose from the daisy without touching them; and she was happy, and the flowers were happy, and even Melpomene was less tragic. Ever since then, flowers have had different smells, so that anyone can know them by either sight or scent."

There was a silence as Jenny finished her story. Then Gwenny spoke. "Oh, Jenny, I wish I could see that! I think that must be why flowers have fragrance, but if only I could see Willow and Lily . . ."

"I believe you can," Che said. "If Jenny will sing for you."

"Oh, I couldn't!" Jenny said, abashed.

"Then sing for me," he said, "and Gwenny can ignore us."

Jenny understood what he meant, and knew that it was right. She nerved herself and looked at him, for she knew she could sing for him. She knew that though he had suggested it for the goblin girl, he really wanted it for himself, for he was still a foal and a captive deep in the mountain; and no matter how educated he seemed, he was afraid inside.

She hummed a little, and the room slowly faded out. Then she sang, and there was the field of flowers and the mountain of the Muses in the background and Willow holding her baby Lily, the tears on her face. Her hair spread out around and behind her like a soft cape, the way Godiva's did. Indeed, she looked a lot like the Lady Godiva, caring so much for her daughter but helpless to give her the thing she lacked.

Then the baby turned, and Jenny knew it was Gwendolyn, though the name was different here. Gwenny was in the scene!

In the background a centaur appeared, watching but not interfering. Che was here too, now. Near him was a sleeping orange cat.

Time passed in an instant, as it could in a dream or a

vision, and the baby grew to look a lot like the goblin girl, but she still could not see. But the flowers changed for her, and assumed their fragrances, and the girl came to know them and was thrilled.

The scene shook. Suddenly it fell apart and dissipated, and they were all back in the chamber. But the shaking continued. Indeed, the whole mountain seemed to be rumbling. "What is that?" Jenny asked, alarmed.

"I don't know," Gwenny said. "That's never happened before. Something must be wrong!"

There were sounds in the passage outside. "We'd better ask," Jenny said.

They went to the door and knocked. After a moment Moron opened it. "What's happening?" Jenny asked.

"The winged monsters are attacking the mountain," he replied.

"My sire!" Che exclaimed. "He has arrived!"

"He sure has!" Moron agreed. "He gave Chief Gouty until noon to give you and the elf back, and when Gouty didn't, the monsters started the siege. Rocs are dropping boulders on us. You had better stay in there, because the tunnels may not be safe." He closed the door.

"I forgot about your folks!" Jenny said. "Of course they didn't just forget you! What are we going to do?"

"You had better tell my mother to let you go," Gwenny said sadly. "I shall be sorry to lose your company, but I'm sure your dam cares for you, Che, as much as my mother does for me. They should stop the attack when you are out."

"They surely should," Che agreed. "But we must not decide on that basis, for that is duress. We must decide on the basis of what is proper." He looked at Jenny. "Have you decided yet?"

"No," Jenny said. She looked at Gwenny. "If we told your mother no, would she let us go?"

"She might. But I'm not sure my father would. He doesn't know why she brought you here—not the real reason, I mean—because he doesn't know I can't see well.

He thinks it's just for company. And he doesn't like anyone telling him what to do. So when your sire came, Che, and demanded your release, Gouty probably—well, there's something he does with a finger, I don't know what it is, but—''

"It's part of the Adult Conspiracy," Jenny said. "I think it's an impolite way of saying no." But she suspected it was more than that, remembering what had happened on the With-a-Cookee River.

"It must be. So maybe you can't just leave now. I'm sorry."

Jenny turned to Che. "Would your sire stop the siege if you agreed to be Gwenny's companion?"

"I fear he would not," Che said. "I can speak for myself, but I can not speak for him. I believe he would conclude that my agreement was made under duress and was therefore invalid."

"So whichever way it goes, the siege is going to continue," Jenny said. The strange thing was that she was almost relieved, because it took much of the pressure off her decision. She could afford to wait and take her time to make up her mind. As long as it didn't make any difference.

The mountain shook again, as another boulder landed. Some sand sifted down from the ceiling.

Jenny realized that her decision might be the least of their problem. They were in the midst of a battle, and who could know how it would end?

"Let's go back to the cushions and sing," she said, frightened.

The others were quick to agree.

Chapter 11. Electra's Empathy

After the preliminary bombardment, Goblin Mountain was pocked with dents, and several goblin tunnels now were open that had been closed. But before he sent in the smokers, Cheiron chose to negotiate again. "Gloha, do you think you can go there without being attacked?" he asked.

"I think so," she said. "I am a goblin, and my Aunt Goldy is there. She's my mother's big sister, and though she did not approve of my father, I think she has come to accept me."

Electra stepped up. "Godiva is Goldy's daughter!" she exclaimed. "I talked with her and learned that. So Godiva is your cousin, Gloha!"

"Yes. She is older than I am—in fact she has a daughter almost as old as I am, though we were never allowed to play together. So maybe they don't accept me after all."

"Oh, Godiva's not like that!" Electra protested. "I mean, I knew her only briefly, but it was pretty intense, because of the horde. I'm sure she has nothing against you."

Gloha's eyes flicked toward her wings, but she didn't speak. Everyone knew how crossbreeds were treated in some cultures.

"Let me go with you!" Electra said. "Maybe I can talk to Godiva, if—"

" 'Lectra, that's dangerous," Nada warned her. "We were under truce with Godiva, because none of us wanted Che to be hurt, but now that truce is over. You can't presume on your two days' acquaintanceship."

"I have little to fear from danger," Electra said.

Nada did not reply. Neither of them had forgotten that if one of them were taken out of the picture this week, a problem would be solved next week. She had to let Electra go.

Gloha looked relieved. She was ready to go, but evidently preferred company.

The two of them walked to the mountain, carrying white bits of cloth to show they were under truce. They knew that the goblins could attack them, but hoped they wouldn't.

They reached the nearest blasted tunnel. The stone that had sealed it shut had been dislodged and rolled down the slope. There was rubble piled at the entrance, but it looked clear farther in.

"Hello!" Gloha called. "We would like to talk."

. "Go fly through a fire, birdbrain!" a goblin called from the depths.

Electra became annoyed. "Listen, dope, we came to parlay. You know the winged monsters will destroy the whole mountain if this goes on. Get someone up here to talk."

"Like who, freckle-brain?"

Electra stiffened. She did have freckles. So did the elf girl; that was one of the things Electra liked about her. As far as she knew, there was nothing wrong with this. But the goblin made it sound as if it were a crime.

It was Gloha's turn to be annoyed. "Like Godiva, dim-wit!"

"I'm not Dimwit, I'm Scrounge," the goblin replied.

"Then tell Godiva, Scrounge," Gloha called.

"Tell her yourself!"

"Is she coming here?"

"Naw! Har, har, har!"

Gloha looked at Electra. "They are my own kind, but sometimes they get so annoying," she said.

"Maybe we should go look for Godiva," Electra suggested, though the idea of going unguarded into the mountain frightened her.

"Maybe so," Gloha agreed. "I know my way around here pretty well, though they're always making new tunnels. I know where she lives."

"Let's do it!" Electra said, before she could freak herself out of it. She knew that if they did not succeed in negotiating, the attack would resume and there might be no turning back.

"All right. I'll tell Cheiron." Gloha spread her wings and flew quickly back. She flew like a bird, not like a bug; she moved quickly, because otherwise she would have fallen to the ground.

In a moment she was back. "He says it's better to take the chance if we're ready for it, knowing the risk."

Electra wished he hadn't phrased it quite that way, but she kept her doubt to herself. "Then let's go find Godiva!"

They entered the tunnel. There was a light in its dim reaches, which turned out to be one of the smoky torches the goblins used for light. Electra lifted it out of its socket, so that they could have light where they went. The smoke did its best to choke them, but soon gave it up as a bad job and wrestled its way along the tunnel ceiling, looking for someone else to suffocate.

"Hey, whatcha doing in here?" a goblin demanded, giving Gloha a good look and Electra a cursory one.

"We're going to tell Godiva ourselves, Scrounge," Electra said bravely, "just as you suggested."

Goblins weren't capable of looking disgruntled, but this one made the effort. "Well, see that you do," he mumbled, stepping back.

They went on, following the tunnel as it wound around and down. "We'll have to change passages at the base," Gloha said. "But any of these will take us to the base."

Electra was glad Gloha knew where she was going! Electra by herself would have been lost after the first turn.

"What are you up to?"

Electra turned, startled. There was the demoness Metria, surely looking for more interesting mischief. It was probably best to answer her question and hope she lost interest. "We're trying to negotiate to get Che and Jenny free. You know how the goblins got them."

"Yes, it would have been dull if you had won that game! No captivity, no siege of the mountain."

"It's still pretty dull," Electra said.

"Oh, I don't think so. You don't have a chance of getting the foal back. So Cheiron will just have to demolish the mountain. That's interesting."

"Well, we'll see," Electra said shortly.

"Meanwhile, what about your own situation?" the demoness asked.

Electra didn't want to answer but still hoped that if she played along the demoness would go away. "What about it? Dolph will choose, and that will be that."

"But everyone knows he will choose Nada Naga. What happens to you then?"

"I die," Electra said.

"You do?" Gloha asked, dismayed. Evidently she had not been aware of that aspect.

"I have to marry the prince who woke me from my discounted thousand year sleep, or die," Electra said. "I knew that when I got into it. Since he won't marry me, that's it."

"I'm so sorry!" Gloha said. "I thought I was not well off, with no male of my crossbreed, but your case is worse!"

Electra really did not want to talk about it, but didn't want to let the demoness know that. "Maybe so."

"How will you feel, when you see him marry the naga princess?" Metria asked persistently.

"Glad for her. She's my friend and a wonderful person."

"But she doesn't love him. Don't you mortals put great store by love?"

"Yes. But she can take a love potion."

"How will you die?"

"Must we have this conversation?" Gloha demanded, distraught.

Electra appreciated her support, but knew it would only make the demoness worse. "I don't know," she said, answering both of them. Actually she did know how she would die, but did not like to talk about it.

"I can show you wonderful ways to die," Metria said. "Suffocation, stroke, rupture of—"

"I suspect I shall just expire in a maidenly manner," Electra said. "It will be most dull."

"No, wait, I remember!" the demoness exclaimed. "There was a story—when you went to Mundania, didn't you age rapidly? So probably that's how it will be. You will get older all of a sudden, and become mature, and then a hag, and then a bag of bones, all in a few minutes."

Electra gritted her teeth, fearing that it would be exactly like that. She was actually around nine hundred years old; only the magic of the enchantment kept her as young as she should be. Once that enchantment was broken, she would revert to her proper age, which was about eight hundred and fifty years dead. But she refused to give the demoness the satisfaction of seeing her faint with horror, no matter what. "You may be right," she said.

"We've got to get Dolph to marry you!" Gloha said.

"No!" Electra protested. "It has to be his choice."

"I could surround you and give you Nada's aspect," Metria said. "You could marry him, and he wouldn't know the difference until it was too late."

"No!" Electra was trying not to cry, knowing that the demoness would like that.

"You would rather die, and see him marry the one who doesn't love him and isn't right for him, rather than do what is necessary?" Metria inquired, interested.

Electra really didn't have much of an answer for that, but she did the best she could. "I just want him to be happy."

"How happy will he be, with the wrong woman, even if she takes a love potion?"

"Nada's not wrong! She's a princess! She was betrothed

to him before I was!'' Despite her best intention, she was arguing the case and playing into the demoness' trap.

''If you marry him, and he becomes king, you will be queen,'' Metria said. ''Won't that be right for him?''

''Only if he chooses it!'' she protested, not really absorbing the demonic logic.

''But he's a boy!'' the demoness said derisively. ''What does he know about choosing well? He can't see farther than the naga-woman's bosom.''

''That's not true!'' Electra cried. ''He can see to her—'' But she realized that she was only getting deeper into trouble.

''Her panties,'' Metria finished triumphantly. ''He sets great store by those, doesn't he.''

''Well, all men do.'' But it seemed awfully lame.

''And after he's finally seen them, what will remain of that marriage for him? Life with an older woman who's a real reptile?''

''That isn't fair!''

''And by the time he realizes his mistake and comes to appreciate you,'' the demoness continued inexorably, ''you will be dead. You could hardly have a neater revenge than that.''

''Get out of here, you—'' But Electra, being still most of a week under the magic age of consent, did not know the word. ''You intemperate complaint!''

''What?''

Electra blinked. The demoness had faded away, and she stood before Godiva. She was appalled.

Gloha stepped in. ''The demoness was here, teasing her cruelly,'' she said. ''She didn't mean you, Cousin Godiva.''

Godiva frowned. ''The demoness. It figures. But what are the two of you doing down here? Don't you know that the mountain is under siege?''

''We're here to bargain,'' Gloha said. ''We want the violence to stop.''

''Come in,'' Godiva said, showing the way into her suite. ''Gouty is indisposed, so I am handling things for now.''

Inside was a very nice apartment, with tapestries and cushions and daylight from a shaft leading up. There was some rubble and dust in the bottom of the shaft that seemed to be of recent origin, but the goblin woman ignored it.

They sat on cushions. "I have asked Che Centaur to be a companion for my daughter, Gwendolyn," Godiva said. "He is considering his response. Until he makes it, we can not end the siege, unless the winged monsters withdraw."

"But Cheiron will destroy the whole mountain!" Electra protested. "He will not let his son be captive!"

"That is a risk we must take," the woman said evenly. "But I think it will not come to that."

"But I tell you, Cheiron—"

"Let me introduce you to someone, so that you can report to Cheiron," Godiva said. She reached up to pull on a tasseled cord, and a gong sounded elsewhere in the mountain.

"You have other captives?" Electra asked. One thing about this business: it did take her mind off her own problem.

"No."

In a short time there was a knock. "Enter," Godiva called, rising from her cushion.

The door opened, and a man crawled in. No, it was a snake. No, it was—

Electra's mouth dropped open in amazement. *It was a naga!*

"Prince Naldo, meet Gloha Goblin and Electra, who is Prince Dolph's Betrothee," Godiva said. "Girls, meet Prince Naldo Naga, Nada's brother."

Electra had never met Prince Naldo before, but she recognized the resemblance to Nada. Now he assumed his human form and made a formal little bow. He was almost unbelievably handsome. "I am glad to meet you at last, Electra and Gloha. I have heard much of you, having just been talking with your King Dor and Queen Irene at Mount Etamin."

Both girls found themselves tongue-tied. This seemed

impossible; the naga were hereditary enemies to the goblins.

"I shall explain," Godiva said. "There are covenants which extend back more than a thousand years, to the years when the war between the monsters of the air and the monsters of the ground was fresh. Anticipating an attack by the monsters of the air, we invoked such a covenant, and summoned our allies. Goblins and naga have differences between themselves, but these are superseded by the covenant. The naga of Mount Etamin are here to support our effort."

Aghast, Electra finally got her mouth going. "And the—the ground dragons, and—"

"And the callicantzari," Godiva agreed. The callicantzari were horrendous underground monsters. "And the elves."

"That can't be!" Electra exclaimed. "I mean, they—"

"Come with me." Godiva led the way out of her suite.

"It is true," Naldo murmured. "We can not claim to be delighted by this development, but we are required to honor the covenant and must support the goblins against the winged monsters. The local elves are similarly bound."

Numbed, Electra followed the goblin woman to a chamber farther down the tunnel. This business had abruptly escalated beyond her worst possible fears! What was Cheiron going to do, when he learned of this?

Godiva opened the door. This appeared to be an infirmary, with a bed and a goblin nurse. There was a patient on the bed, small and wan. Not a goblin, not a child, but—

"An elf!" Electra exclaimed. "But his elm must be far away!"

"Beyond Goblin Mountain," Godiva agreed. "But not far as we think of distance. He prefers to recline, because his strength is low, here, but he is in good health." Then, as they stepped close, she introduced them: "This is Bud, of the tribe of Flower Elves." The elf nodded. "And these are Prince Naldo Naga, Gloha Goblin-Harpy, and Electra, betrothed to Prince Dolph of the human folk." They nodded in turn.

Bud Elf looked surprised. "The human folk are allied with you too?"

"No," Electra said quickly. "They aren't in this quarrel, really. Just a few of us who know Che Centaur personally. Gloha and I are here on behalf of Cheiron Centaur to see if we can get Che and Jenny released before the winged monsters destroy the mountain."

"Who is Jenny?" he asked.

"Jenny Elf. She's—" Electra paused, realizing that this was another oddity. "She's not from an elm or from Xanth. She doesn't get weak away from her tree. She's twice your size, and her ears are pointed. But she's definitely an elf, I think."

"I should like to meet her."

"I will bring her here," Godiva said. She stepped out.

"How can you help the goblins, so far from your elm?" Gloha asked Bud. "I mean—"

"I am just here to arrange details," Bud said. "We shall defend one side of Goblin Mountain from intrusion by the winged monsters on that side. That will relieve the goblins of the fear of a flank attack."

It certainly would! The elves were small, but their strength and expertise near their elm was such that no monsters would pass that way.

"I never thought the elves would be in this," Gloha said unhappily. "But I suppose elves have to keep their word, and a covenant is a word."

"You are on the side of the winged monsters?" Bud asked her. "Isn't there a certain ambiguity in your position?"

"No. Che Centaur is a winged monster, and I am too."

"To be sure," he said, indulging in the very most circumspect of male glances at her petite body. Electra knew that glance; it was the kind no one directed at her.

While they talked, Prince Naldo approached Electra. "My sister—where is she now?"

"Nada's with Cheiron," Electra said. "We joined with him after delivering Che here."

"You delivered the centaur here?" he asked, surprised.

"It was a deal. The Goblinate of the Golden Horde was

going to cook him, so we joined forces with Godiva to save him. Then we had to decide which group got him, and she won. We don't want him here, but we didn't have a choice. It was—"

"A matter of honor," he concluded. "How well I understand. Tell me, how are matters between the two of you?"

"Nada and I get along fine. We just wish Dolph wasn't going to marry her."

"It was another deal," he said. "A political betrothal. We had thought the prophecy referred to me and the Princess Ivy. We were in error, so Nada took the lead."

Electra wondered what would have happened had it been Ivy on that quest, instead of Dolph. Ivy might well have married Naldo; he was indeed a prince and a handsome man in his human form. But that would have meant that Ivy would never have met Grey Murphy—and that Dolph would not have met Electra.

"Well, Nada means to see it through. She doesn't love Dolph, and I do, but it's his choice."

"It is an irony. My father would direct Nada to break the betrothal, but it is not his right. We have accepted the benefits of the political liaison with Castle Roogna, and can not in honor renege."

"I know. Just as you can't renege on the covenant with the goblins."

He grimaced. "Just so. We find both situations awkward, but our course is clear. The Flower Elves are similarly caught."

The door opened—and there was Jenny Elf. But of course she couldn't be a true elf, really, because—

"Oh, I'm so glad to see you, 'Lectra!" Jenny exclaimed, running up to give her a hug. Electra was suddenly aware how much they differed in size; Jenny was barely half her height. "Che and Gwenny and I had a Tsoda fizz fight, just the way we wanted to at the lake!"

Then she became aware of the others, and was abashed.

"I'd better introduce you," Electra said. "Folks, this is

Jenny, from the World of Two Moons. Jenny, this is Gloha, and Prince Naldo, who is Nada's brother, and Bud of the Flower Elves.''

"You can fly?" Jenny asked, looking first at Gloha.

For answer, Gloha spread her wings and flew toward the ceiling. But there wasn't room to go anywhere, and she landed almost immediately.

"You must meet Che!" Jenny said. "He doesn't fly yet, but—"

"I know," Gloha said. "I came here with Cheiron."

Then Jenny focused her spectacles on Bud. "An elf?" she asked, looking surprised. "But you're so small!" Indeed, he was only half her height.

Bud smiled tolerantly. "Just as the human folk have giants, such as the ogres, and the goblins have giants, such as the callicantzari, it becomes evident that we elves also have giants. By the look of you, you are young; others of your kind must be larger yet."

"Yes, I'm small. Maybe there's a mistake, because my people never called themselves elves. We must be another species, that just happens to resemble yours in some ways."

Bud smiled. "This interests me. Let's explore it further, if you will." He glanced at the others. "If I am not interfering with business."

"My business is introducing you to each other," Godiva said. "So that when Electra and Gloha return to the surface, they can made a competent report."

"So that Cheiron will believe that you really do have these allies," Gloha said. "I suppose that means that you don't intend to give up Che Centaur or Jenny Elf."

"Jenny Elf may go," Godiva said. "She is not captive." She glanced at the girl. "But I expect you to keep your word."

"I will," Jenny said. "But I'm not going until Che does." She turned back to Bud. "You really think we are just variants of the same species?"

"I suspect we are equivalents for our respective lands. Do you have other creatures on yours?"

"You mean like trolls?"

"Ah, you have trolls! Are they point-eared like you?"

"No, they're round-eared and ugly. They don't stand much taller than we do, but they are way more massive."

"Interesting. Our trolls are tall and thin. How many fingers on their hands? Ours have five, unless some have been bitten off."

Jenny smiled briefly. "Four, when they're all there. Yours do sound similar after all."

Electra listened with growing interest, and realized that the others were doing the same.

"Are there human beings there?" Bud asked.

"Some. We really don't have much to do with them."

"Neither do we. Electra is the first I have had contact with in years. Your humans' ears are pointed?"

"No," Jenny said, growing excited. "They are round— and they have five fingers too. I mean, I never actually saw one, but I remember the stories. Round ears and extra fingers. And they're big—half again as tall as we are." She looked at Electra. "In fact, the same size as the ones here. They're the same, except—" She looked away from Electra.

"They're not friendly?" Electra asked.

"Not with us," Jenny agreed. "We're enemies, mostly. We have a long history of fighting, and our kind is seldom friendly with their kind. It started when we first came to their world, and we were civilized and they were primitive; and they attacked us and slaughtered us, and they were so big and strong and vicious that despite our magic and organization we suffered terribly and had to flee to the forest and hide, and form into scattered tribes, and ever since then—"

She broke off, looking around. "Oh, I'm sorry! It's not like that here, I think."

"It has been like that, sometimes," Electra said, and Bud nodded. "When I was young—I mean, around nine hundred years ago—" She faltered as she saw others staring at her.

"She slept for a number of centuries," Godiva explained,

"owing to an enchantment. She is no older than she looks, in terms of the life she has lived."

"Yes," Electra said, grateful for the woman's clarification. Somehow it sounded normal, when Godiva said it. "There was more fighting between human beings and other creatures. I don't know about elves, specifically, but—"

"They wanted to clear land for their villages," Bud said. "They wanted to cut down elms."

"They wanted to burn our holt," Jenny agreed. "That— it's a tree we live in, but we don't get stronger near it, except that we fight harder to save it, because—"

"I think we have affinities," Bud said. "Perhaps, when this ugly business is done, you will visit our Flower Elm, Jenny."

"I—I'd like that," Jenny agreed.

"Now would you like to see the foal?" Godiva asked Electra. "Before you return to the surface."

Electra had almost forgotten her mission, distracted by the developments. "Yes, we'd better."

"I regret meeting you in this circumstance, Electra and Gloha," Naldo said.

"I feel the same," Bud said. "But perhaps a compromise will be worked out."

"I hope!" Electra said fervently. What would Nada say when she learned that her brother was on the other side?

Godiva led the way out of the chamber, and Jenny, Gloha, and Electra followed. Naldo remained, perhaps to talk further with Bud Elf. The naga and the elves, supporting the goblins—this changed things!

They came to another chamber, guarded by a male goblin. "Idiot!" Electra exclaimed, recognizing him.

"Hello, 'Lectra," the goblin said. "Who's your friend?"

"Gloha, meet Idiot," Electra said, smiling. She had never liked goblins, but the females had impressed her, and the three males in Godiva's party had turned out to be all right too, once allowance was made for their ugliness.

"Hello, Idiot," Gloha said, smiling shyly.

"Open the door, Idiot!" Godiva snapped.

The goblin hastened to lift the bar. They trooped in, and the door closed behind them.

Inside stood another goblin girl, beside Che. "This is my daughter, Gwendolyn," Godiva said. "Gwendolyn, these are Electra and Gloha, from the surface. As you can see, Electra is a human girl of about your own age, and Gloha is a winged goblin girl of fifteen. Gloha has been here before, but you have not actually met before; she is my first cousin. They are here to verify the status of Che Centaur."

"Hello, Electra," Gwendolyn said. "Hello, Gloha."

Jenny crossed immediately to join Gwendolyn. "Yes, those wings of Gloha's really work," she said. "She's like Che, only older, so she can fly. A crossbreed."

"Oh, how nice," Gwendolyn said, a bit vaguely.

"I have asked Che Centaur to be my daughter's companion," Godiva said. "As you can see, he is not being mistreated, and I believe they are getting along well."

Something was slightly odd here, but Electra couldn't pin it down. Gwendolyn seemed like a nice girl, and both Jenny and Che seemed to like her. But why did she need a winged monster for a companion? Why this particular one, who was bringing war to Goblin Mountain? It just didn't seem to make sense to go to such extraordinary trouble for such a minor thing. There were surely plenty of goblin girls available and plenty of harmless animals.

"Che," Electra said, "your sire is preparing to destroy the mountain, level by level, if he doesn't get you back. I'm sure Gwendolyn is a nice girl and happy for your company, but how do you feel about this captivity?"

"I had some trepidation about entering the mountain," Che replied. "But my concern has been abated. I am being well treated, and I like Gwenny. I am in the process of deciding whether to agree to be her companion."

"But that doesn't count, when they are holding you captive!" Gloha protested. "Cheiron won't accept that."

"It is a problem," Che said. "Because it proved to be beyond me, I have delegated the decision to another."

Godiva was startled. "You have? Who?"

"Jenny Elf."

Electra, Gloha, and Godiva stared at Jenny. "*You* are deciding for him?" Godiva asked.

"Well, he asked me to," Jenny said, abashed.

"And what do you propose to tell him to do?" Godiva asked.

"I don't know. I haven't decided either."

Godiva shared a look of bafflement with Electra. They were on opposite sides, but neither saw much sense in this.

Electra returned to Che. "What happens to you if you agree?"

"I will remain here as Gwenny's companion, but we may travel outside if we wish, later."

"But she can go outside by herself or with another goblin!" Electra protested. "She doesn't need *you*!"

Che shrugged. "That is as it may be. Jenny will decide."

"How can you be party to this, Jenny?" Electra demanded. "I thought you were his friend!"

"I *am* his friend," Jenny replied.

Gloha was equally baffled. "What happens to you if you say no?"

"I am uncertain. It may be that I will be released."

Electra turned grimly to Godiva. "What happens if he says no?" she repeated.

"I haven't decided," the gobliness said.

"Mother!" Gwendolyn said angrily.

Godiva paused. Then, reluctantly, she answered. "I will release him."

"Good!" Electra said. "Jenny, tell him to tell her no, and we'll all leave now, and the siege will be lifted and no one will be hurt."

But Jenny shook her head. "I can't tell him that. I haven't decided."

"Which side are you on?" Electra demanded, baffled and upset.

"Why don't you marry Dolph?" Jenny asked her in return.

"Because I can't just—" Electra broke off and regrouped. "That has nothing to do with this!" But she was shaken, for it was the last response she had expected from Jenny. Was the elf in some similar situation?

She pondered. Suppose the goblins had threatened to kill them all, Electra and Gloha included, if Che refused what they demanded? But Che didn't want to do it. Then he would be unable to say either yes or no. So he would say he hadn't decided. In which case Electra and Gloha had better get out of here as fast as they could.

But that question about marrying Dolph. Jenny knew the decision wasn't Electra's to make. Maybe the decision on staying wasn't Che's to make either, but that was only because he had passed it on to Jenny. That wasn't any good parallel. The whole situation of the marriage was complicated, and no one would know how it would turn out until it happened. Though they all had a pretty good idea.

Was there something more complicated here? Not a threat but some other factor? For Godiva simply did not seem like the kind to break her word, which was what she would be doing if she dishonored the truce and did anything to Electra or Gloha. In fact, it was Electra's definite impression that Godiva was telling the truth: that she would let Che go if he refused to be Gwendolyn's companion.

Then why was Che balking—and Jenny too—despite what they knew of the siege and Cheiron's determination to free his foal? If Che agreed, it seemed he would be well treated and even free to go outside, because a centaur's word was his bond. If he declined, he would be freed. So he had every reason to decide promptly. Yet he was not doing so—and neither was Jenny.

Electra shook her head, unable to make sense of it. She would just have to go back out and make her report.

"I guess that's it," she said. "We'll go now."

They moved to the door. "Tell Cheiron of our allies," Godiva said. "The land dragons too are coming to support us."

Worse and worse!

They walked up the tunnel and finally emerged into bright

daylight. Squinting. they walked to the winged monster
camp.

Cheiron met them there, with Chex beside him, and
Prince Dolph and Princess Nada in human form. They all
looked grimly hopeful.

"It—it's complicated," Electra said heavily. "They
aren't letting Che go, exactly, but they aren't exactly holding
him either. They want him to decide whether to be the
companion of Godiva's daughter, Gwendolyn, and he hasn't
decided."

"A decision made under duress would not be valid,"
Cheiron said. "He knows that."

"Yes. But this doesn't seem to be that, exactly. He—
he's having Jenny Elf decide for him, and she hasn't made
up her mind. They'll treat him well if he agrees, and let
him go if he doesn't. He—seems satisfied. Just not decided."

"There has to be duress," Cheiron said grimly. "We
know how to deal with that."

"But there's more," Gloha said. "They have allies."

"Allies? Who? More goblins?"

"The Flower Elves," Electra said, hating it. "The callicantzari. The land dragons. And the naga."

"What?" Nada demanded, shocked.

"Your brother, Prince Naldo, was there. There's an ancient covenant. They have to help the goblins against the
winged monsters." There: it was out.

"My own people!" Nada cried, appalled. "I forgot about
that covenant!"

Cheiron turned to her. "There is such a covenant?"

"Yes. But it's never been invoked in our time—not for
centuries, in fact. We hate the goblins! That's how I got
betrothed to Dolph!"

Chex shook her head grimly. "It seems we have a problem."

Electra had to agree, feeling empathy for them all. She
knew about difficult situations!

Chapter 12. Dolph's Diagnosis

Dolph was stunned. Not only were the goblins intent on holding Che, they had summoned Nada's people to help them. That meant that if Cheiron's forces attacked again, they would be going up against folk who were allied to Castle Roogna. He could see how shocked Nada was. He wanted to cheer her up, but couldn't think of anything sensible to say.

"We had better verify this," Cheiron said grimly. "We should be able to spot land dragons on the move."

"Yes," Chex agreed. They walked toward the clearing being used as a runway for takeoffs and landings.

"I'll go with you!" Gloha exclaimed.

Dolph was torn. Should he change to a winged form and go with them or remain to console Nada? He turned to Nada—and saw her tearfully hugging Electra.

Nada was closer to Electra than she was to him. Why did that jar him so? Electra was always sympathetic to the problems of others.

He decided to go with the centaurs.

Cheiron ran onto the field, leaped, spread his wings, flicked his tail, and flew up. Chex followed, but paused as a roc came in. It was best to give the big birds plenty of room, because they didn't always see small creatures, and their downdraft could be horrendous.

Gloha went out, then turned back to Dolph, who hadn't yet decided what form to assume. "Prince Dolph, I don't feel easy in the air with the larger monsters, and I can't keep the pace. May I go with you?"

"Oh," he said, surprised. "Sure." So he assumed the form of a winged centaur, because that would be easiest for her to ride. Also, he could talk with her in that form. He had practiced it, after attending the wedding of Cheiron and Chex, and now could handle it well enough. He could assume any living form—and on occasion a borderline form, like that of a ghost—but it took practice to make each form function perfectly. Thus his repertoire was limited, but growing. However, there was one extra thing he needed in this form.

Gloha hopped on. She was a light little thing, and as shapely as a nymph in her goblin aspect. She evidently knew how to ride, for her position was secure; he didn't have to worry about her falling off.

He trotted up to join Chex as she waited, the wind from the landing roc blowing back her brown mane. "When we get to take off, will you make me light?" he asked her.

Chex glanced at him, noting his change of form and his rider. "Of course, Dolph."

The roc touched ground, bounced, and slid along the hard surface, its claws sending up sparks as they braked against rocks. A small brush fire started, but a steamer dragon was ready to douse it with several well-aimed bursts. The roc finally came to a stop and hopped off the landing strip. It held a small beerbarrel tree trunk in its beak: evidently this bird was on the beverage committee.

"Go ahead," Chex said, touching Dolph and Gloha with two flicks of her tail. Immediately both Dolph and the goblin girl became light. Dolph trotted onto the field, spread his wings, and jumped into the air. He was airborne, not as neatly as the real winged centaurs managed it, but well enough. He flew up to join Cheiron, who was circling overhead.

In a moment Chex was coming up behind him. When the

three were at a suitable elevation, they spread out and flew south, watching the ground.

"I think it's true," Gloha said. "We really did see Prince Naldo and Bud Elf down there, and they told us about the covenant."

"But that won't make Cheiron give up his foal," Dolph said. "More likely, he will launch a desperation attack to get Che back before any more goblin allies come."

"But with the naga there—"

Dolph sighed. "I guess that makes it my problem. I mean, it already was, but now even more so. We can't start killing naga! Especially not Nada's brother!"

"Or elves," she said.

Dolph remembered Jenny Elf. "I don't think that's the same. Jenny's not the same kind of elf."

"But humans have never warred with elves!"

Oh. "Yes, not that I know of. They keep mostly to their elms, and once our kind learned to leave the elms alone, that was that. About four hundred years ago Jordan the Barbarian made a deal with Bluebell Elf—I don't know exactly what it was, but the stork brought her a crossbreed baby, and Rapunzel is their distant descendent. So I guess humans and elves can get along when they try. Certainly we don't want trouble with them. But if we support Cheiron, and the goblins won't let Che go—"

"I'm not sure Che wants to go," Gloha said.

"Well, as Cheiron said, if there is duress—"

"I'm not sure there is. For one thing—well, how well do you know Jenny Elf?"

"Not that well, really. But she seems all right, and Che really seems to like her. She didn't have to go with him into Goblin Mountain, but she did."

"So if it's a hard decision for him to make, because maybe there's a threat or something." she said carefully, "what about Jenny? Would it be hard for her too? I mean, if she doesn't have to stay there?"

"I guess if she really likes him, and doesn't want him hurt, then maybe it could be pretty hard for her too."

"And Jenny—when Electra asked her why she couldn't tell Che to just say no and she said she couldn't and Electra asked her which side she was on, she said 'Why don't you marry Dolph?' and that sort of floored Electra. So maybe there's an answer there, if we can just figure it out."

Dolph was amazed. What did his possible marriage to Electra have to do with whether Che remained with the goblins?

"It doesn't make sense to me," he admitted.

"I guess maybe it's because Electra can't just decide to marry you," Gloha said. "Because you're the one who has to decide."

"Right. So if Jenny couldn't decide, because it was Che's decision, that would make sense. But if he told her to make it, then she can make it, can't she?"

"I would think so. But something must be stopping her." She pondered. "Dolph, suppose you told Electra to decide? I mean, you wouldn't decide, she would, and she would tell you which of them to marry? Her or Nada. Would that be the same?"

"Well she'd just tell me to marry her. Everyone tells me to marry 'Lectra!"

"Would she really?"

"Wouldn't she?" What was Gloha trying to get at?

"I don't know. But I think maybe Jenny Elf knows. It sure set Electra back! So if you can figure out what Electra would say, maybe you can figure out what Jenny's saying. Why she's not deciding about Che, yet, despite everything. And why Che lets her."

"That's another mystery! Why doesn't Che make his own decision, before things get really bad?"

"Why don't you?"

"That has nothing to do with it!"

"I think maybe it does," she said. "I think maybe it was such a tough decision that Che couldn't make it himself, so he asked Jenny to make it, and it's still so tough she can't make it either. Just as maybe it would be too tough for Electra, if you told her to decide. Maybe it's not quite the same problem, but maybe close enough so the same principle holds. All we have to do is figure out what it is.''

She was making more sense. ''How come you're making better progress on this than I am?'' he asked.

''Well, everyone knows that girls think better than boys do,'' she said shrugging.

''I didn't know that!''

''Well, you're a boy.''

Why did that seem to make so much sense? ''Okay. So maybe there is a similar principle. But I don't think they have any love triangle.''

''Not a marriage triangle,'' she agreed. ''But it could be love.''

''How could it be love? They're children!''

''And we're not?'' she asked archly.

''Well, I'm not! I'm going to be married within a week!''

''I'm the same age as you, you know. If you cared to assume winged goblin form, I could show you a thing or two.''

Dolph realized that she was indeed a fine figure of a goblin girl. He was tempted to do just that: become a winged goblin, and see what she looked like then. ''How about showing me your panties?'' he asked.

She kicked him on the ribs. ''Those aren't on the list for showing. Only if you wanted to marry me.''

''But I already have two Betrothees!'' he protested.

''I was being facetious,'' she said. ''Even though there is no boy of my kind. I was just making the point that age is no barrier to love. We're all children, according to the Adult Conspiracy, but we can love.''

''Oh. I guess so.'' The Adult Conspiracy was the bane of his life, with its ridiculous tenets. ''But Jenny Elf and Gwendolyn Goblin and Che Centaur don't—''

''They love their families, and maybe each other. Not all love relates to the stork, you know.''

Dolph hadn't known, but let it pass. ''So maybe they care about each other. But why would that make it so hard for Che to decide what to do?''

"I don't know. That's what we're trying to figure out. If you don't marry Electra, she dies. Could there be something like that with Gwendolyn Goblin?"

"Did she seem ill to you?"

"No, she seemed perfectly healthy. And nice. I could see how well both Che and Jenny liked her. But there must be something odd about her, because that's the first time Godiva ever let me meet her. I'm sure we could have been friends, if we had met earlier."

"Well, as you said, your wings—"

"But Che has wings!" she said sharply.

"That's right! So it couldn't be the wings. Maybe it's that he's male?"

"Male? How could a male be better than a female?"

"Well, Electra had to be kissed awake by a prince. Maybe Gwendolyn Goblin has to have a male companion."

"But I'm sure there are plenty of male goblins who could have been her playmate."

"Would any of them have been as nice as Che?"

"Well, you don't expect a goblin male to be nice," she said reasonably. "All the niceness is in the females."

"So if she wanted a nice companion male, it couldn't be a goblin," he said. "Still, there must have been some other companion they could have gotten that wouldn't bring the winged monsters down to besiege their mountain. Why didn't they look for one of those?"

"That's the mystery," she agreed. "Or half of it. Why did they take Che—and why can't he make up his mind about it? All we know is that maybe it's like you and Electra in some devious way."

He sighed. "You know, if it was exactly like that, it wouldn't be easy to solve. I can't make up my mind which girl to marry. Maybe Che can't make up his mind which girl should be his companion."

"Maybe," she said doubtfully. "But I should think he would do it quickly enough, if he knew that goblins and monsters would be fighting and dying if he didn't. He's a centaur, after all; he has logical thought processes, unlike the rest of us."

"Maybe we should ask a centaur!" Dolph exclaimed.

But then a motion on the ground caught his eye. "Oops—there's a dragon!"

She peered down so avidly she almost fell off his back. It didn't matter, for she would merely spread her wings and fly back. "Oh, yes! A big smoker!"

"A smoker? I saw a steamer!"

In a moment and a half they had spied a whole slew of dragons. A slew was a measurement that applied only to big fearsome things, and was a standard unit for monsters. Normally it was sufficient for whatever purpose was intended; Dolph had never heard of a situation requiring two slews.

The dragons were tromping north from the land of the dragons, toward Goblin Mountain. There was no doubt about it: the goblins' claim was true.

"Aren't you flying rather low, Dolph?" Gloha asked.

Dolph discovered that he was. He flapped his wings harder, but continued to descend. "Oops—my lightness is running out!" he exclaimed, realizing.

Then Cheiron spied what was happening and swooped down. He flicked Dolph with his tail as he passed, and suddenly Dolph lurched up, light again. As he chased down his equilibrium, he saw tiny Grundy Golem clinging to Cheiron's mane. Grundy was serving as translator for the assorted monsters.

"So it was no bluff," Cheiron remarked, unsurprised. "Well, we had better consider what to do while we fly back to the mountain. Those dragons won't arrive until tomorrow, so we have some time to play with."

"We think there's something funny about Che's position," Dolph said. "That there's some reason he can't make a decision, maybe like the way I can't decide between Betrothees. If we knew that reason, maybe we'd be able to help him decide."

''There is only one decision,'' Cheiron said. ''He is not remaining captive in that mountain.''

''Uh, we're not sure he is captive,'' Dolph said. ''I mean, if he tells them no, they'll let him go.''

Cheiron glanced sharply at him. ''Then why doesn't he tell them no?''

''There's something, some reason—we thought maybe you would be able to figure it out.''

''It seems like duress to me. Perhaps they have threatened to kill the elf girl if he says no.''

Gloha made a horrified peep, and Dolph was taken severely aback. They had not thought of that!

''And so he told Jenny Elf to decide, because it affected her,'' Gloha said. ''And she doesn't want to decide, because she doesn't want to die—but she doesn't want to make him prisoner either.''

''And maybe they told her they would kill them both, if they told,'' Dolph said, his horror growing. ''So she couldn't tell. But she asked Electra a question, and nobody knew what it meant, so the goblins didn't realize.''

''What question was this?'' Cheiron asked alertly.

''Why didn't Electra marry Dolph,'' Gloha said.

Chex, flying on the other side of them, nodded. ''If Electra doesn't marry Dolph, she will die. If Che does not agree to be Gwendolyn's companion, Jenny Elf will die. It seems a reasonable parallel.''

''The case is not tight,'' Cheiron said. ''But it will do as a working hypothesis. If we proceed on that assumption, it is definitely a case of duress. In which case the reason they are not making the decision is to provide us time to free them. An agreement made under such duress would not be binding on Che, but perhaps he doesn't properly appreciate that, so believes that his choice is between slavery and the life of his friend. We shall have to act swiftly, reducing the mountain before the land dragons arrive.''

''But if you attack, won't they kill them anyway?'' Dolph asked.

''I think not. They will know that their only hope of

reprieve is to return foal and elf unharmed. They will keep them as hostages, hoping in the end to bargain for their lives, if they are not able to hold out until the dragons come. As I judge it, it will be extremely close, but we can do it in time.''

Dolph was bothered by the prospect of such a life and death struggle, but also by something else. He had gotten to know Godiva Goblin during their trek to Goblin Mountain by overhearing her conversations with others in the party. He remembered how she had honored the Adult Conspiracy, refusing to show Jenny a devastating gesture because she was a child. While he chafed at the Adult Conspiracy, it hardly seemed that a woman who honored it so carefully would be the kind to kill a girl just to make someone else do something. Adults, whatever other awful things might be said about them, usually tried to protect children, rather than hurt them. Godiva had seemed very much like a protective mother.

''Gloha, you saw Che and Jenny with Gwendolyn, didn't you?'' he asked as they flew back, a little apart from the centaurs. ''How did they seem to get along together?''

''Very well, actually,'' Gloha said. ''In fact—'' She paused, as if remembering something significant.

''Goblin girls are nice, aren't they? Was Gwendolyn nice?''

''Yes. And she—when Electra asked what happened if Che said no, Godiva said she hadn't decided, and Gwendolyn said 'Mother!' and then Godiva said she would release Che.''

''Well, that could mean she would release him and kill Jenny,'' Dolph said. But Godiva had not seemed like that kind of person. She had been tough, but true to her word.

''I don't think so. Jenny didn't seem frightened, just undecided. And Gwendolyn liked her. I could tell. When Gwendolyn challenged her mother, Godiva backed down. I don't think Gwendolyn wanted Jenny killed, and I don't think she would be killed if Gwendolyn didn't want it. She's in line to be chiefess, you know. She has power, even now, as a child. So it must be something else.''

''What about Che? Was he frightened?''

''No. He liked Gwendolyn too. The three of them really seemed to be friends. In fact, he *said* he liked Gwenny, as he called her, and that he was being well treated.''

''If he said it, it was true,'' Dolph said. ''Even a young centaur would not tell an untruth. He might say nothing, but he wouldn't lie.''

''That's what I thought. Dolph, I don't think anyone was threatened.''

''Then why wouldn't they decide?''

She shrugged. ''That baffles me.''

''I think we haven't solved the mystery yet,'' Dolph said. ''and I guess maybe we'd better, before there is bloodshed.''

''Yes. But how?''

''I'll go in there and find out.''

''But you're not a goblin, Dolph!''

''I can become one.''

''But you don't know the mountain! You don't know the goblin ways.''

She was right. He could get into deadly trouble, blundering around in there. ''I could become an ant, or something, and sneak in.''

''And somebody would step on you!''

Right again. ''Then maybe as myself. Gloha, I've got to go there and find out what's going on, before horrible things happen, maybe from some misunderstanding.''

''I'll go with you.''

''But you've already risked it once!''

''I can take you right to Che and Jenny Elf.''

He nodded. Then he angled his flight toward Cheiron. When he got close, he called ''Can you hold off your attack a little longer? I think I should go in there and see if I can bring Che out. I think maybe there's something we don't understand.''

Cheiron was grim. ''There is too little time. I must commence the attack in time to complete the reduction of the mountain before the land dragons arrive or the siege will fail."

But Chex had closed on them. "Dear—"

"But we can hold back on the smoke and fire for an hour, to give you time," Cheiron said.

"See? Females rule," Gloha murmured with satisfaction.

They reached the mountain and came down in single file for the landing: Cheiron, Chex, and Dolph. Immediately Cheiron set about organizing the attack, while Dolph changed and approached Nada and Electra. "Cheiron's resuming the attack," he said tersely, "because land dragons are coming, and the mountain must be reduced before they get here. But we think there's something we don't know, and maybe I can get Che and Jenny out. So Gloha and I are going in, for an hour."

"I'll go with you!" Electra said immediately.

But Nada drew her back. "My turn, 'Lectra," she said with a dark glance.

"But it's dangerous," Gloha protested.

"We know," Nada and Electra said together.

"I guess you want to see your brother," Dolph said to Nada. She didn't want just to be with Dolph, he knew, though he delighted in the prospect of her company.

"That too," she said. "Let's go."

Now Dolph realized what they were doing. They were taking turns in danger, so if one died, the other could marry him. It was a grim business, but he couldn't fault it. Except, suppose the wrong one . . . ?

The three of them advanced on the mountain. Already the rocs were taking off to seek more boulders to drop on the mountain, and the steamer dragons were warming up. They would steam the surface, so that it would soften and the boulders would break it down faster. Once more of the inner tunnels were exposed, the smokers could make the goblins retreat, choking, and the harpies could lay explosive eggs and set them rolling down the passages. But if those eggs started catching nagas—brother! Specifically, Nada's brother. Ouch! So Nada was coming along to see personally.

Gloha led the way. Nada changed to her natural form, a woman-headed serpent, which she found more comfortable for tunnels. Dolph considered, and matched her form. He remembered when they had first met, six years before, in this form. They had become betrothed, and kissed, banging noses before getting it right. He hadn't realized it, then, but he had fallen in love with her at the moment of that kiss. Of course he hadn't realized that she was five years older than he; she had seemed his age or even slightly younger. What times they had had, then!

They moved down into the mountain. A goblin appeared, challenging them. "We're coming to parlay again," Gloha called. "This is Prince Dolph and Princess Nada."

The goblins recognized those names. They made way. In half a dozen moments they were at the base level.

Godiva awaited them at the door to her daughter's chamber. "What is your mission, Prince Dolph?" she inquired, recognizing him.

"The winged monsters are going to reduce this mountain to rubble before dawn tomorrow," he replied. "Your land dragon allies won't get here before then, so you can't stop it. We want to take Che and Jenny out of here and stop this battle before anyone is hurt."

"You will not be able to reduce this mountain that fast," Godiva said. "Our other allies will see to that." She glanced at Nada. "You may verify this with your brother, if you wish."

"Maybe I'd better," Nada said.

Godiva snapped her fingers. In a moment handsome Naldo Naga slithered up. "Nada!" he exclaimed, surprised and delighted.

"Naldo!" she cried. They slithered up to each other and kissed. Dolph wished she would kiss him with similar joy.

"Oh, isn't he handsome!" Gloha whispered to Dolph. "I didn't see him in such good light, last time."

Naldo heard that. He looked at Gloha, who blushed almost black. "So glad to meet you again, lovely creature," he said handsomely. Gloha's blush assumed a purplish tinge, with heart-shaped squiggles of red.

Nada rolled up her eyes. She had remarked before that her brother could charm any female. She had not exaggerated. Dolph understood how it was; Nada herself could charm any male. How well he knew!

"Tell them of your efforts, Naldo," Godiva said.

Naldo nodded. "As you know, sis, we don't like this situation, but we are bound by the covenant and will acquit our obligation honorably. We brought a supply of pineapples, cherries, and popcorn, and will assume serpent form of the size required to carry these into key crevices by key tunnels. They will detonate when any invaders come, causing the tunnels to collapse on them. It will not be possible to penetrate to the base without collapsing all the tunnels— by which time the defensive forces will have exited with their captives to the nether world of the callicantzari. Assuming that proves necessary. More likely, this tactic will slow down the advance enough to allow the land dragons to arrive before the reduction is complete. So the chances of the winged monsters prevailing are remote."

"But the smokers can smoke you out," Nada said.

"Not if we collapse the tunnels before the smoke gets through. And of course you would not want the captives to get smoked, so I doubt it comes to that." Naldo shook his head. "Sis, you had better go back and tell Cheiron that his effort is hopeless. This stronghold will not be forced. The decision will be made by the foal or the elf, and then violence will be pointless."

Nada was silent. So was Dolph. Naldo's case was persuasive. It really did not look possible for Cheiron to rescue his foal by violence.

"We should talk to Che again," Gloha said.

"By all means," Godiva said. She opened the door.

Foal, elf, and goblin girl stood within, together. "Hello, Prince Dolph," Jenny said. "Hello, Princess Nada. Hello again, Gloha."

Why was she so formal? There was indeed something

funny about this, but Dolph still couldn't fathom what it was. Well, he would just have to do what he could.

"Che, your sire is set to bring this mountain down into rubble," he said. "And the Nada are set to do the same, in defense of it. There's going to be a whole lot of trouble, and many creatures may die. You can't allow this to happen. You must decide."

Che nodded. "Yes, I must." He looked at Jenny. "What will it be?"

"Oh, Che, I'm sorry," Jenny said, looking as woebegone as an elf could, which was extremely so. "I don't see any other way. You must agree to be Gwenny's companion."

"I am relieved, not sorry," Che said. "I so agree."

"Oh, Che!" Gwendolyn exclaimed, hugging him. "Oh, thank you, thank you! It means so much to me!"

"But your sire will level the mountain!" Dolph protested. "He says a decision made under duress is not valid!"

"There is no duress," Che said.

"But—" Dolph started.

"Do not affront him," Naldo murmured behind him. "You know a centaur's word is inviolate."

"Uh, yes, of course," Dolph said, flustered. "But, Che, can you tell us why? I mean, after these goblins foal-napped you and kept you captive."

"No," the foal said firmly.

Dolph looked at Jenny Elf. "Then you, Jenny. You're his friend. Why—?"

"I'm sorry," Jenny said tearfully. "I can't tell you either. Just that it's best."

Dolph dreaded returning to tell Cheiron and Chex this, but saw nothing else to do. His mission had failed miserably.

Nada came to his rescue. "Che, your sire and dam will have trouble understanding this. They suspect you are too young to fully appreciate the ways of centaur honor. Could you come to the surface and tell them yourself?"

"Why, I don't know," Che said, confused. "I really should stay with Gwenny." He looked at Godiva.

"You are free to go where you will, Che," Godiva said.

"We accept your word, and your sire and dam should also, once they hear it from you directly."

Che turned to Gwendolyn. "Do you feel up to making the trip to the surface, Gwenny? I think you will not want to talk very much with others, in this confusion, but you could at least look outside."

"I'd love to, Che," the goblin girl said.

Che turned to Dolph. "Then go tell my sire and dam that I am coming," he said. "We will follow shortly."

Dolph was relieved. "I'll do that." What a pass this was!

Nada lingered to talk with her brother. Gloha and Dolph proceeded up the tunnel toward the surface. "Why do you think he's doing it?" Gloha asked when they were alone. "If there's no threat, why won't they tell?"

"I think if I knew that, I'd know how to make my own decision," Dolph said heavily. "I just can't figure it out."

"Gloha's right," Metria said, appearing between them. "Boys are duller than girls."

"That isn't what I said!" Gloha protested. Then, belatedly, "Who are you?"

"She's the demoness Metria," Dolph said. "She likes to drive folk crazy."

"Oh, D. Mentia," Gloha said.

"That's D. *Metria*," the demoness said sharply.

"So why are you here this time?" Dolph asked, deciding to get it over with.

"I thought you might just possibly figure out what's with the foal, if I gave you long enough to stew over it," Metria said. "But since you're not figuring well, I'll have to give you a hint."

"I don't want your hint!" Dolph exclaimed, because at this point he did want it.

"Think about the parallel," Metria said. "If you don't marry Electra, who dies?"

"She does. But what has that to do with—"

"If Che doesn't become Gwendolyn's companion, who does what?"

"But Gwendolyn's healthy!" he protested. "And if she

isn't, just having a companion won't help her."

"What do you know of goblin society?"

"It's vicious," he said. "They kill each other to get ahead. None of the males dares show any weakness or decency, because it'll be the end of him. But that doesn't count for Gwendolyn, because she's female, and they aren't like that."

"And what kind of a position is she slated for?" the demoness asked.

"She'll be the first female chief," Gloha said. "It's always been a male job, before." Then she put her little fist to her mouth. "Oh, my! Competing with males!"

"Which means they'll kill her, if they spy any weakness!" Dolph exclaimed. "But Che couldn't possibly protect her from them!"

"Unless he provided her with something to eliminate her weakness," Gloha said. "But what could that weakness be?"

"I don't know," Dolph said. "She seemed all right to me. Her eyes didn't quite focus, but—" He stopped, a monstrous conjecture looming.

"She could be almost—" Gloha said.

Suddenly Dolph was able to make his diagnosis. "Metria—" he started. But the demoness was gone.

"If—" Gloha said.

"Then—" Dolph continued.

"To save her life," she concluded.

"And they wouldn't tell, because—"

"And we mustn't either."

"Except for Cheiron and Chex."

"After they give their word."

"And no one else," he said.

"And no one else," she agreed.

But he wondered about the demoness. She honored no human scruples and could blab the secret throughout Xanth. Would she? She hadn't yet, so maybe she didn't intend to. It couldn't be that she had any compassion for the goblin girl or any interest in better relations with the goblins. But maybe she thought it would be more entertaining to have a goblin chiefess, some future year. Or maybe she had lost interest entirely. That last would be best.

They arrived at the surface and quickly moved down to talk with Cheiron and Chex. Dolph resumed his natural form.

"We must have your word not to reveal what we have learned," Dolph said.

"Does it concern the welfare of my son?" Cheiron demanded.

"Yes."

"Then I will not give my word."

"But—" Gloha said to Chex.

"Dear—" Chex murmured to Cheiron.

"Until you tell me why this is necessary," the centaur said to Dolph.

"Che has agreed to be Gwendolyn's companion, and—"

"*What*?" Cheiron demanded, outraged.

"And we think he has reason," Gloha said to Chex.

"But we can't tell you, unless—" Dolph said to Cheiron.

"Dear—" Chex murmured.

"Is there duress?" Cheiron demanded.

"No," Dolph and Gloha said together.

"Ha!" Grundy Golem said from Cheiron's mane.

"Not him!" Dolph said. "Grundy's got the biggest mouth in Xanth."

"Go elsewhere for the moment," Chex said to Grundy.

"But—" Then the golem translated the nature of her glance, and hastily departed.

Chex rotated the glance and brought it to bear on Cheiron.

Cheiron considered. "We will not speak your secret," he said at last. "But I make no commitment about my actions."

Dolph glanced around to make sure that no other creature was in hearing. "We think Gwendolyn goblin is blind, or close to it. If the goblins learn—"

"They'll kill her, so she can't be chiefess," Gloha said.

"So Che—" Dolph started.

"Will help her—" Gloha continued.

"I can see that the goblin girl has a problem," Cheiron said. "But that does not justify foal-napping our kid." He was evidently upset.

Then Chex touched his arm as she looked toward the mountain. They all looked. Che had arrived at the surface, with Gwendolyn Goblin and Jenny Elf.

Chapter 13.   Chex's Choice

Chex was thrilled to see her foal again, but she knew that the situation had not been resolved. For one thing, Cheiron had not made a commitment about his actions, and that meant he still intended to get Che back.

"Oh, we forgot to tell you," Prince Dolph said. "Che said he would come up to tell you himself. That's Gwendolyn Goblin with him."

What an omission! But of course Dolph remained pretty juvenile. Marriage would cure him of that.

They trotted up to the tunnel opening. Chex reached down to hug Che! "You're all right!" she exclaimed, almost painfully relieved.

"Of course, Dam," he replied. "We have been treated very well. I have decided to remain as Gwenny's companion, so will not be returning with you."

"But why?" she asked, for she knew that she must not reveal her knowledge of the answer.

"I weighed the considerations, and consulted with Jenny, and made the appropriate decision."

He had indeed! But how could she give up her foal to the goblins?

"If you will not give adequate reason, I can not accept your decision," Cheiron said carefully. "I must recover you from captivity."

Che, with an aplomb that made Chex proud, avoided responding to that. "Sire, Dam, allow me to introduce my companion, Gwendolyn Goblin, daughter of Chief Gouty and Godiva."

"Hello, Gwendolyn," Chex and Cheiron said together.

"Gwenny, these are Cheiron and Chex Centaur, my sire and dam," Che said.

"Hello, Cheiron and Chex," the girl said shyly, blinking. She was pretty in the gobliness manner, in a bright red dress and red slippers and with a red bow in her hair. With other species, appearance was no necessary guide to character, but with goblins it was. The ugly males were brutish, and the pretty females were nice.

"And my friend Jenny Elf," Che said, turning to the elf girl. She was in a blue dress, slippers, and ribbon, a perfect complement to the goblin's outfit. She had brushed the snarls from her hair so that it hung long, as the goblin's did; she seemed like an elf sister, except for the pointed ears and huge spectacles. "She helped save me from the Goblinate of the Golden Horde and has been a great comfort to me in my hours of need."

"Hello," Jenny said, almost as shyly. "We met before, Chex Centaur. You gave me these spectacles."

"Yes, of course, dear," Chex said. "I am glad they have served you well."

"And Sammy Cat," Che concluded, indicating the orange speed bump now snoozing at Che's front feet. Sammy twitched an ear.

"Hello, Sammy Cat," Cheiron said formally. "Now we must talk with the goblin chief, because this matter has not been resolved."

An older gobliness appeared at the tunnel opening. With her were Nada Naga and a male naga.

"This is Godiva Goblin, who is handling business while the chief is indisposed," Nada said. "And my brother, Prince Naldo. Godiva, these are Cheiron and Chex, Che's sire and dam."

"As you have learned, Che has agreed to be my daughter's companion," Godiva said. "Your continued hostile activity seems pointless, in the light of that decision."

"You abducted our foal," Cheiron told her. "The fact that you subsequently prevailed on him to accede to your purpose does not absolve you of guilt or justify his continued presence in your mountain."

"I did what I had to do," Godiva said.

"And I will do what I have to do," Cheiron said.

"Oh, Che, I did not know it would be like this!" Gwendolyn said to the foal. "I don't want all this trouble."

"And it's all my fault!" Jenny Elf said, tears on her face. "I must have made the wrong decision!"

"No," Che told her, before Cheiron could speak.

Cheiron was silent, because he was not going to challenge the word of his foal.

"We are on different sides," Chex said. "It is a situation that can not be resolved by the decision of any one person. We shall have to work out some compromise."

Cheiron could not oppose that, either. But he was by no means daunted. "I bear no animosity to your daughter," he told Godiva. "But I will not give up my foal. He is unique in a way your daughter is not, and necessary to our species in a way your daughter is not, and he must be with his own kind. You must find some other companion for Gwendolyn, for Che will not remain in your mountain."

"Then I think the proof must be in violence," Godiva said, undaunted. "We shall retire and await your onset."

"But I don't want this!" Gwendolyn protested, crying. "Che, you must go back to your folks!"

"No." Che looked desperately unhappy, but his jaw was set in the same way as Cheiron's. He took her hand and turned to the tunnel. They entered, and Jenny Elf followed.

Chex knew she could not let this happen. She had to find some way to resolve it without violence. Che and Cheiron were both set, and neither would change his mind, for centaur character (some said stubbornness) was legendary. But Chex was not only centaur but mother, and she saw in Godiva a mother, and knew why the gobliness was doing this. She saw also that Che and Gwendolyn Goblin really did like each other, and that the elf was friends with both. The key might lie in the elf.

"Jenny!" she called.

The elf paused at the dark hole of the tunnel, turning back. "Yes, Chex Centaur?"

"You are not bound. Come with me."

Jenny was flustered. "But—"

Godiva, evidently recognizing Chex's concern, interceded. "Go with her, Jenny. We will allow you to return to us, if it can safely be done."

The girl remained confused. "But I can't—I mean—"

"I think she already knows. Talk to her."

Jenny hesitated a moment more, then turned back to the tunnel. "Che!" she called. "I—I will join you later." Then she picked up her orange fur ball and came down to Chex.

Cheiron turned away. "The barrage will resume in a moment," he said.

Nada bid parting to her brother, and walked down the slope. Chex knew that she was suffering similarly, not wanting to be on the other side from Naldo. This was all so difficult, and it threatened the welfare of Che. Chex wished that for once centaurs were not so resolute. But she knew better than to argue.

The elf came to her. "Get on my back," Chex said. "We must get away from here and talk. Perhaps we can find some way through."

The girl set the cat on Chex's back, then scrambled up herself. It was obvious that she had never been on a centaur before, but she seemed to have a touch for riding, for her balance was sure once she got settled.

"Hold on," Chex said. Then she flicked them with her tail, spread her wings, and leaped off the mountain.

She saw, as she moved past the camp, that Nada was hugging Electra, being consoled. Gloha, the winged goblin girl, was standing beside Prince Dolph, looking forlorn. And Cheiron was directing the rocs and dragons in the renewed attack. It would be a savage one, Chex knew, because of the time limit: whatever was to be accomplished had to be done before the land dragons arrived. The irony was that Cheiron now understood why the goblins needed Che, and that they would not mistreat the foal, but could not retreat from his position. Cheiron was a male centaur: that said it all.

Then they were up above the trees and sailing into the sky. Chex did not want to watch the bombardment; she knew that little good would come of it, no matter how things turned out. Violence was the way of males, and it seldom benefited anyone, but they kept right on with it. She could not tell Cheiron no, but she could signal her distress by absenting herself from the proceedings.

"Oooo, this is fun!" Jenny Elf exclaimed. She definitely knew how to ride; her balance was excellent. The cat seemed to be having no trouble either; by the feel of him, he was asleep again.

"How is it that you know how to ride, Jenny, when there are no centaurs in your land?" Chex inquired.

"We're wolf riders," the girl explained. "We have wolf friends, and when we have to go somewhere fast, we ride them. I don't have a wolf friend yet, but I guess we all know how to ride, just naturally. This is like being on a wolf when it makes a huge leap."

"Those must be big wolves!"

"How big are wolves in Xanth?"

"Too small for you to ride! Actually, the straight wolves are in Mundania, but if they came here, they would be too small to ride. But your wolves—do they fly?"

"No. They just run fast, and protect us, and are our friends."

"Did that make it easy for you to be Che's friend?"

"Maybe it did," the girl said, surprised. "But mostly, Che just needed a friend."

Chex reviewed what Che and Jenny had been into: the deep jungle, the goblins of the horde, a long trek around the Elements, and captivity in Goblin Mountain. She shuddered to think how Che would have fared alone! "He needed a friend," she agreed. "And you have been a good one. But now it seems he has another friend."

"Oh, Gwenny's not exactly a friend. Well, she is, but that's not the point. He's her companion."

"And she needs a companion who can see for her."

Jenny didn't answer.

"I called to you, Jenny, because I believe you have the best understanding of the situation," Chex said. "We believe we have come to understand enough of it to enable us to appreciate Godiva Goblin's motive in abducting our foal. Gwendolyn will be killed if she evinces any significant weakness, and a centaur companion can both alleviate and conceal that weakness. Cheiron and I have undertaken not to tell. Isn't it true that Gwendolyn is blind?"

"No. She can see. Just not very well, no better than I can, and they can't put spectacles on her because then the goblins would know. But Che really can help her, and—oh, I didn't want to tell him to do it—I knew he should come home—but I just couldn't let Gwenny die, and neither could he! We just couldn't!" She was crying again, tormented by the difficulty of the decision even after it had been made.

And Gwendolyn's mother could not stand by and let her daughter be killed, either. Chex knew exactly how that was. That was what made it impossible to hate Godiva. She had indeed done what a mother had to do.

"You don't see well without your spectacles, Jenny," Chex said. "How did you manage, back in the World of Two Moons? Weren't you almost blind, there?"

"Well, yes, with my eyes. But it didn't matter so much, because of the sending."

"The what?"

"The sending. It doesn't seem to work in Xanth."

"Exactly what is it, Jenny?"

"It—it's sort of a mind connection. When there's an emergency, the chief can call everyone in the tribe, without making a sound. Sometimes in past generations that's been the only thing that saved us from disaster."

"We would call that mind reading," Chex said. "Some folk have it as their magic talents. But most of us have no mental connection with others."

"Isn't that awful lonely?" the girl asked wistfully.

"It doesn't seem so, perhaps because we have never experienced it. So you were able to know people because of your contact with their minds?"

"Yes, pretty much. And Sammy helped, in his way; I sort of could see him, I guess by his mind, though I couldn't really talk to him. I did trip and bang into things a lot, but outside in the berry patches there wasn't much to bang into, so it was all right."

Chex saw how the girl put a positive face on something that must have been a continuing burden to her. It was also clearer now why she kept the cat so close, though she could no longer tune in to his mind. Jenny was from a far, strange world, but she was a good girl, and she had helped Che immeasurably.

"How do you feel about Che?" Chex asked.

"Oh, I like him!" Jenny exclaimed. "I never met a centaur before, except for you, I mean, but he's nice."

She was absolutely correct. But Chex knew that Che, young as he was, was highly discriminating about friendship. He would not have been her friend without good reason. That was the best recommendation Jenny Elf could have had, though she did not know it.

"Yet you gave him up to Gwendolyn Goblin."

"Oh, I didn't do that!" Jenny protested. "I'll always be his friend! But she—she really does need him for her companion, and she's nice too, and—"

And Jenny was crying. She could have had Che to herself, as it were, but had done what she felt was right, knowing that there would be a smaller place for her in his life because of it. She also surely hurt to think of him remaining tied to the depths of Goblin Mountain. But since he could leave it, in the company of the goblin girl, that was the lesser concern.

That explained why Che had asked Jenny to make the

decision. He had known that she would be making as much
of a sacrifice as he. Gwendolyn's gain was Jenny's loss.
Che had not felt right about deciding that for Jenny. So
Jenny had decided it for Jenny. Now she was on the way
to being bereft of her only real friend in Xanth.

Chex was not satisfied with that, but in the complex
situation they faced, she had no ready solution.

She looked down and spied the land dragons, now significantly closer to the mountain. They were big ones, without even vestigial wings, which meant they were in no way
bound to see to Che's safety. The smaller winged dragons
would not be able to oppose them. Once the land dragons
arrived, they would guard the mountain, and only the rocs
would be able to attack. That would not be enough. Cheiron
was right: whatever he did had to be done promptly. He
surely had a stratagem to bring the mountain down faster
than the goblins thought it could be done, and force their
capitulation before the following morning. But there was
so much danger to Che in that violence!

"Here is the problem," Chex said after a bit. "Cheiron
simply is not going to allow our foal to be held in this
manner. If Che has a commitment to the goblins, Cheiron
is prepared to void it by eliminating the goblins."

"But that's worse than ever!" Jenny protested. "They
aren't such bad folk, really, not like the horde, and Gwenny
truly is nice. And so is Godiva, when you get to know her.
And this way the goblins will get better. It's not just
Gwenny, it's that it's right to do."

"I think perhaps it is," Chex said. "But Cheiron is right
too. Do you see any way out of this impasse?"

"I just wish they could all be friends and not fight any
more," Jenny said tearfully.

"So do I!" Chex agreed fervently. "So it is up to us to
find a way to make that possible. Now Cheiron will not
relent until Che is home with us. While Godiva—"

"It's not her, really," Jenny said. "I mean, it was,
maybe, because she started it by foal-napping Che. But she

gave him his choice, after we met Gwenny. He could have gone home then. But . . ."

"But Gwendolyn would have died, in due course," Chex said. "So it was Che's decision, even if you made it. He wanted someone older and more objective than he was to make it, so he could be sure it was right. And perhaps it was right, for him. So now it is Che on the other side. We have one male centaur against another, and we as females must find a way to resolve it."

"But how can we?" Jenny asked plaintively. "Che has to be either with you or with Gwenny."

"Unless we went to join him in Goblin Mountain!" Chex said, with a short and not very mirthful laugh.

"You wouldn't fit in there," Jenny said, with a trace less unmirth. "But you know, Che can visit you. Once he gave his word—"

"True. But he would have to return, and it is obvious that he will have to spend a lot of time with Gwendolyn, because any slip would be disastrous. Cheiron wants him free of Goblin Mountain entirely, because there is a great deal of education he must have. There simply isn't time to accommodate both Che's centaur heritage and full-time companionship with Gwendolyn."

"I guess not," Jenny agreed sadly. "Unless she could come along."

"Come along?"

"And be with him while he learned," she said. "She wants to get out and see things, only she can't. She's never been out of Goblin Mountain. Because she can get by in her room, alone, or maybe in a tunnel where she knows exactly where everything is. But outside it would be hopeless."

"Unless she had a competent companion." Chex sighed. "I do see the problem."

"Of course, with Che she could do it, because he would tell her what to see. Only he wouldn't tell her, he'd have some sort of signals only a centaur could memorize, that nobody else knew about. That's why it has to be a centaur; they have mental powers others don't.''

''True,'' Chex said. ''I could do it. But of course a grown centaur wouldn't. We have other business. So does Che, actually.''

''Other business?''

''He is destined to change the course of the history of Xanth. That's why he has to be free, even if he wasn't a centaur and our foal. We cannot allow the goblins to interfere with that. Indeed, we feared that his abduction was a plot to prevent his destiny from being achieved.''

''But if Gwenny gets to rule the goblins, wouldn't that change things? I mean, there's never been a female goblin leader before. With the magic wand she could do it, if she could see well enough to use it, or have someone tell her.''

Chex was stunned. She almost fell out of the sky. She had to pump her wings vigorously to recover equilibrium, while Jenny hung on.

''To change the history of Xanth—by enabling a goblin woman to become a chief!'' Chex said after she got straightened out. ''We assumed it was human history or centaur history. We never thought of goblin history!''

''Well, maybe it isn't,'' Jenny said. ''Or maybe the goblins will do something that will affect the others.''

''All this time we were trying to protect Che for his destiny—and we may be interfering with that destiny now!'' Chex said. ''I must tell Cheiron!''

''Will that change his mind?'' Jenny asked.

Chex, making a sweeping turn to go back to Goblin Mountain, paused. ''No. He is already committed. It is just one more reason to find some peaceful way through this picklement.''

Jenny considered. ''You said that any centaur could help Gwenny, outside. But they wouldn't.''

''That's right. We centaurs are busy with our own concerns. Cheiron and I are trying to raise Che, for example.''

''But suppose Gwenny visited you. Would one of you help Gwenny while the other educated Che?''

"We could. But for what reason?"

"In case that's his destiny. Then you could keep his destiny. and educate him, and Gwenny wouldn't suffer."

"Do you mean, bring her to live with us?" Chex asked, astonished.

"I guess it wasn't a good idea," Jenny said, abashed.

Chex considered it rationally—and suddenly everything fell into place. Cheiron could be satisfied, and Che's destiny would not be compromised—whatever it was—and the goblin girl would be safe, for none of them would betray her secret. It could be done—if Godiva let her go.

"I think it's an excellent idea," Chex said. "I'll go tell Cheiron right now." She resumed her turn and winged powerfully for the mountain.

Then something else fell into place in Chex's mind. "Jenny, you will have to go in and talk to Godiva, because the rest of us are fighting the goblins. But you will need to talk to Che and Gwendolyn too."

"Yes," the girl agreed faintly.

"I want you to take a message to Che that perhaps will help him understand."

"Oh, of course!"

"It is this: remember the Night Stallion's creed."

"Remember the Night Stallion's creed," she repeated. "I'll tell him. But what does it mean?"

"That would be complicated to explain, for I suspect you do not have night mares in your world. But I think he will fathom it, and then tell you."

"Oh. All right."

The girl did not push for further clarification, and Chex was glad, because she wanted this decision to be Che's.

As they approached the mountain, they saw the rocs circling. carrying boulders. Each would swoop low, release its boulder at high speed. then fly up while the boulder crashed into the mountain at an angle. The mountain would shudder, and several tunnels would be crushed in. Then the first roc would head off for another boulder. while the next swooped in.

Meanwhile the dragons were hovering. When all three rocs completed their runs, the fire-breathers swooped in for strafing runs, sending flames shooting into the exposed tunnels. The steamers did likewise, only their steam was intended to soften the substance of the mountain so that the boulders did more damage. Finally the smokers approached. Their attack would be the worst, because their smoke would penetrate far into the mountain, bringing misery and even death to those it caught. The other winged monsters were relaxing, waiting for their turn. Some were licking their chops, evidently having a taste for smoked goblin.

"But the naga are collapsing the tunnels, so nothing can get through," Jenny said. "The smoke won't smoke them out."

"Cheiron will send in the cockatrices," Chex said. "They will freeze the goblins and naga with their glares, and the tunnels will not be collapsed. Cheiron has studied siege technique; he will counter all their ploys. That's one more reason I don't want this to continue; I know how bad it will be for all concerned."

"The goblins will retreat to the caverns of the calli—calli—"

"Callicantzari," Chex said. "They are like exaggerated goblins, grotesque monsters with some of their limbs installed backwards. Only desperation would make the goblins go there."

"But they are allies now, because of the covenant. And I guess they'll take Che along with them."

"We have to stop that. The callicantzari will be treacherous allies. They could put them all into the pot." Actually, Cheiron had probably anticipated that ploy also, and would send the cockatrices first to the lower chambers to prevent the goblins from moving anyone out.

Chex folded her wings and angled down, her increasing weight lending her velocity. If she didn't flick herself with her tail every so often, she eventually became too heavy to fly. But it was a good thing, because otherwise she would never be able to be comfortable on land. She zoomed down toward Cheiron, then spread her wings and braked abruptly just before lowering her hooves.

"Cheiron!" she said. "Stop the smokers! There is another way."

Cheiron paused, as he always did for her. "I shall be satisfied with no less than the return of our foal, unharmed. If the goblins think that night will stop us, they are mistaken; we have fireflies to illuminate the scene."

"We can bring them both to our residence," Chex said. "Che and Gwendolyn. He can be her companion in our glen."

He was startled. "Why I suppose he could. But we would then be obliged to take care of her, which could be a burden."

"Che's destiny," she said. "It may be to enable the goblins to have a female chief. That could change the history of Xanth."

That made him pause. He realized that his efforts might be counterproductive. "Very well. I will suspend the attack for an hour. If Godiva will let her daughter go, we will do it. But she must answer promptly, for I will not be stalled." Horses could be stalled, but not centaurs.

"Jenny has access to the mountain. She can go in and ask. This could solve everything and make the entire course of this incident have meaning."

"Let her go in, then," he said. "But she must have an answer. If she does not return within the hour, the attack resumes, and it will be swift." He leaped into the air and flew off to attend to the halting of the attack.

"It's up to you, now, Jenny," Chex said. "You will do us all a phenomenal favor if you bring this to pass."

The girl looked scared. "I'll try," she said. "I'll try my very best."

Chapter 14. Jenny's Judgment

Jenny was terrified as she approached the mountain, carrying Sammy. She had been with company before, but now she was alone except for the cat; and the surface of the mountain was mostly rubble, and the feel of warfare was in the air. Suppose the goblins thought she was an enemy invader and threw stones at her?

Then she had a moderately bright notion. "Sammy, find a safe way in," she said, setting the cat down.

Sammy seemed irritated to have his snooze interrupted, but he picked his way to one of the smaller tunnel holes and went in. Jenny had to get down on her hands and knees to squeeze past the rubble partly blocking the hole, and she got her nice blue dress—actually it was Gwenny's dress—smudged in the effort, but she made it.

Inside it was terrifyingly dark. She should have thought to bring a torch! How was she to find her way in such blackness? "Sammy, wait for me!" she called, fearful of being left behind. The cat would surely find a safe way in, but that wouldn't do her any good if she didn't keep up with him. It was so much harder here in Xanth, where she could neither send nor receive Sammy's mind.

There was a faint meow. Jenny went toward that, and her foot caught a stone and she almost fell. Then she stepped over an edge and did fall. Screaming, she slid into some sort of slick pit, unable to catch herself.

Then she realized that it was not a sheer drop, but a steep tunnel. In fact it was a slide! She was sliding down and around and around, swiftly but not horrendously. This was the safe way in!

After a while her descent slowed. She was sure the back of her dress was horribly soiled, but at least she was all right. Now she saw light, and in two and a half moments came to rest by one of the guttering torches. Sammy was waiting for her there, licking the dirt off his fur.

"Now find Godiva," Jenny told him. "Slowly!" She took the torch out of its holder and followed as the cat set off again.

A male goblin intercepted them. "Hey, schnook! Where you going?"

Jenny adjusted her spectacles and looked at him. She did not recognize him. "Who are you?"

"What do you mean, who am I?" he demanded. "I'm the one doing the asking here! Where are you going, glass-eyes?"

"I'm going to see Godiva," she said. "Now get out of my way, because this is important."

"Oh, yeah, elf?" he demanded, making the "elf" sound like an epithet. "Why you wanna see that female dog?"

Jenny realized that this was a juvenile goblin. Not only was he smaller than she was, he didn't know the terms forbidden by the Adult Conspiracy of this world. "I don't have to tell you anything."

"Is that so, point-ears!" he said belligerently. "Well, I'm Gobble, son of the chief, and I want to know what you have to say to that, hair ball."

So this was Gobble Goblin, the ten-year-old son of Gouty! According to Gwenny, the brattiest brat who ever existed. She could believe it. She remembered that he would become chief if Gwenny didn't.

Ordinarily Jenny tried to be polite to folk, but she was

in a hurry, and this one was just not worth it. "Disappear, brat!" she said, and pushed past him.

"Oh no you don't, freckle-bottom!" he cried, grabbing her spectacles from her face.

Suddenly Jenny could hardly see. "Give those back!" she demanded, grabbing for him.

"Nyaa, nyaa, you can't get them!" he cried tauntingly, staying out of her reach.

Jenny lurched after him, but only banged into a wall. It scraped the side of her face and hurt horribly.

Gobble laughed uproariously. "Hey, your snoot looks better already, furriner! Why don't you do the other side too?"

Jenny was furious and humiliated. Worse, she knew she could not catch him, and she could not see where she was going without those spectacles. She was in real trouble. But she knew that if she started crying, the brat would be even happier.

"What's going on here?" a voice demanded. Jenny recognized it. It was Godiva! She must have been close to the woman's chamber when she ran into Gobble.

"Aw, nothing," Gobble said, his voice developing a whining tone. "Just playing."

"You have her spectacles!" Godiva said severely. "Give them back this instant!"

There was a faint crash and tinkle of something breaking. "Oops, dropped 'em!" Gobble said. "Oops, stepped on 'em too, by accident. I guess they're broke."

He had deliberately broken her spectacles! How could she get around now? What a calamity!

"I will deal with you later, Gobble," Godiva said, and there was that in her voice that made Jenny wince. She heard the brat fleeing; evidently he recognized that tone too. "Come with me, Jenny."

Godiva's hand took Jenny's elbow, and guided her firmly. Suddenly Jenny didn't have to worry about where she was going: Godiva knew exactly how to help her. She must have had plenty of experience with Gwenny

In three quarters of a moment they were in Godiva's nice suite, and the woman was sponging off Jenny's face. It stung, but in a good way, for Godiva had a mother's touch. "Why did you return, Jenny?" she asked gently.

Suddenly Jenny remembered her mission. "Chex Centaur says can Gwenny come to live with her!" she burst out. "She—she knows—I didn't tell her but—"

"I understand. I knew she had something in mind. She's a mother."

"If you could let Gwenny go there, then Che could still be her companion, and they wouldn't tell—"

"Give up my daughter?" Godiva asked, dismayed. "But she must be chief, otherwise—"

"Otherwise Gobble is," Jenny said, making a face. "But Chex isn't trying to stop that. She understands. She can teach her—I mean Gwenny can learn while they're teaching Che—and when it's time for her to come back here and be chief—Che will come too. They want Che with them, they don't mind if he's Gwenny's companion, and this is a way—"

"It is a way," Godiva agreed. "They want their child, as I want mine. But mine can have more freedom with them than theirs can have with me. They are centaurs; they can be trusted. Perhaps this is best."

"Then you'll do it?" Jenny asked. "You'll let them go?"

"I will do it," Godiva said.

"Oh, thank you!" Jenny exclaimed, hugging her.

"You will have to get another pair of spectacles," Godiva said, turning businesslike. "But what will become of you, Jenny?"

"Become of me?" Jenny asked blankly.

"You came, as I understand it, into Xanth by chance, and can not return to your world. You have helped Che Centaur, and perhaps helped my daughter too. What will you do with your life, now that they will be secure in theirs?"

"Why—why I don't know. I wasn't thinking of myself. I just did whatever seemed best to do."

"Perhaps it is time you did think of yourself."

"First I have to tell Che and give him his mother's message."

"Oh? What is that?"

"Remember the Night Stallion's creed," Jenny said before she thought. Then: "Oh, I don't know if I should have told you. I mean—"

"It is all right, Jenny," Godiva said gently. "I understand that message." She seemed sad.

"What does it mean?"

"That is for Che to decide. Come, I will take you to them now."

They went to Gwenny's chambers, Godiva's firm hand making it easy for Jenny. Godiva opened the door, moved them in, and closed it behind them. "Here are Che and Gwendolyn, and your cat seems to be settling down on a cushion," she said.

Jenny appreciated that, because the room was just a blur with vague shapes; she couldn't recognize any of them.

"Jenny—where are your specs?" Che's voice came.

"I ran into Gobble," Jenny said.

"That explains it!" Gwenny's voice came. "I didn't see they were missing, until Che commented, but I know what Gobble is like. Now Che will have to help you too."

"I shall be glad to," Che said.

"Give him your message, dear," Godiva murmured to Jenny.

"Che, Chex says Gwenny can come to your home with you," Jenny said. "So you can be home, and still be her companion."

"Oooo!" Gwendolyn exclaimed, delighted.

"Why that is very nice, Jenny," Che said. "It does seem to solve our problem nicely, if the Lady Godiva is amenable."

"I have agreed to allow this," Godiva said. "With the understanding that the same strictures apply to your family, Che."

"Oh, my sire and dam would not betray a confidence."

Che said. "But do you wish to do this, Gwenny?"

"With you, yes," Gwendolyn said. "I would be afraid otherwise, but already you are helping me to see, and if your folks are like you—"

"They would not have extended the offer, were they not prepared to meet the attendant commitments," he said. "They will treat you well and prevent your private situation from being known. I assure you that you can trust them in this regard as you do me. They are centaurs."

Gwendolyn must have looked at her mother, for Godiva spoke. "This is true, dear. You will be secure with them."

"But you, mother—won't you be lonely?" Gwendolyn asked.

"Yes, dear, I will. But I would be more lonely if anything were to happen to you. I think you will be safer with the centaurs than you will be here, until you are of age and experience to handle the magic wand. Perhaps you will visit regularly, with Che."

"Oh, yes, mother, of course we'll visit!" Gwendolyn said. "Just the way Che would have visited his folks. Oh, this is wonderful! I must pack some dresses."

"I don't think there is time," Jenny said. "We have to be back at the surface within an hour or the attack will begin again."

"I will bring your dresses out later," Godiva said. "Once you emerge, the siege will stop, and it will be easy to complete arrangements."

"Oh, good. Then we can go now."

"Give your other message, Jenny," Godiva murmured.

"Oh, I forgot! Che, your dam says to remember the Night Stallion's creed."

There was a pause. Then Che spoke, subdued. "I shall do that. That aspect had not occurred to me."

"What does it mean?" Gwendolyn asked.

"It is a certain code enforced in the realm of dreams, but relevant here," Che said. "I think my dam thought I would neglect it, and perhaps I would have. I must consider its application carefully."

Jenny was frustrated. What was the mystery here? Why should Che keep it secret? But if he didn't want to tell what it meant, then he didn't have to. Right now they had to get on up to the surface, before the attack resumed.

"I will lead you out, Gwendolyn," Godiva said. "Che will walk with Jenny."

"Yes, mother." There was motion in the room. Then a shape loomed near Jenny. It was Che. He took her hand.

"Sammy!" Jenny exclaimed. "Where's Sammy?"

A ball of fur rubbed against her legs. She stooped to pick up the cat.

They trooped out the door and into the tunnel, two by two. It was a great comfort to have Che guiding her, for Jenny knew he could see perfectly and would not lead her into any mischief. She understood more clearly how important his companionship to Gwendolyn was. When a person couldn't see, trustworthy guidance was essential.

They came to the bright surface. Jenny blinked. The fact that she couldn't see well did not mean she wasn't sensitive to light; it just meant that shapes at any distance were blurred.

"I think we understand the nature of the agreement," Godiva said.

"We do," Cheiron's voice came.

Jenny knew why they weren't saying more. Goblins and winged monsters were surely within hearing range. Jenny's incapacity of sight was known, but Gwendolyn's had to remain secret.

"Gwendolyn will ride on me," Cheiron said. "We shall be afoot, because Che will walk, but there is no need to tax your daughter with a long walk."

"Understood," Godiva said, and helped the girl get on him. Jenny realized that this made it clear to monsters and goblins alike that Gwendolyn was under Cheiron's protection and that the siege was over. It would also make it impossible for others to tell that Gwendolyn could not see.

So it was done, and all was well. Jenny suddenly realized that her part in this was done. She was no longer needed.

It was time for her to say farewell to her friends. She fought
back her tears, not wishing to embarrass herself or them.

Then Che was beside her. "And you will ride my dam,
as I believe you did before," he said.

"Me? But that was just to—"

"Do we not remain friends?"

"Yes, of course, Che!" she exclaimed. "But now you
are safe, and you have other things to do."

"I would like to have you remain with me, until you are
able to return to your home."

"But Che! You have a companion, and your folks—"

"I have a companion and a friend. I do not wish to lose
my friend."

"I would just be in the way! Your sire and dam will be
so busy, and—"

"When a person challenges a decision of the Night Stallion in his realm, he dictates that the one who takes the part
of another shall share the fate of that other. This is part of
his creed, and it is a formidable one."

"Share the fate?" she asked blankly.

"When Prince Dolph tried to protect Grace'l Ossein from
the punishment of the Night Stallion, he had to share her
fate. She was vindicated, and so was Dolph. When Grey
Murphy tried to help Girard Giant, they shared fates. My
dam reminded me of this policy in the realm of dreams,
and I agree with it, though it is only an analogy. It was her
way of alerting me to the appropriate procedure and signaling her acquiescence."

"But what has that to do with me?"

"You took Gwenny's part, though perhaps you felt it
weakened your position. Now Gwenny is coming to my
home. I would like to have you share her fate."

Jenny was nonplused. "But that's not bad, that's good!
Gwenny will be happy with you."

"Will you not be also?"

He was finally getting through to her. "You mean—me
too?"

"That is what he means, dear," Godiva said. "You

would have been welcome in Goblin Mountain, but I think you will be better off with the centaurs, with your friends."

Jenny just stood there, unable to speak.

Chex spoke. "Ride me, Jenny. We welcome you."

"Thank you," Jenny said, somewhat choked.

Godiva lifted her, and she was on Chex's back, still holding Sammy.

"I am glad that we were able to settle this matter amicably," Cheiron said to Godiva. "We shall be in touch."

"Agreed," Godiva said.

Then the centaurs walked down the slope and away from the mountain.

It was a long walk, for they were limited by Che's pace. Jenny knew that Prince Dolph could have assumed a large form and carried the foal quickly there, while the two grown centaurs flew, but evidently they preferred to go at their own pace, and by themselves. They stopped to pick fruit and eat it, and to see the sights of Xanth; indeed, their course seemed to weave around somewhat. Jenny wondered why—and then she found out.

"There is one, dear," Chex said.

"Very good," Cheiron said. "Che, please lead your companions to the spectacle bush."

A spectacle bush! That was what they had been looking for! Jenny got down and found Che's little hand. In a moment Gwenny had his other hand.

"The ground is rough," Che said. "You must step cautiously. I will guide you by small pressure on your hands." And he did so, so that neither of them had any difficulty.

"I think this pair would look good on you, Jenny," Che said, picking a pair and giving it to Jenny. She put them on her face, and suddenly the world came clear again. It was wonderful!

Che picked another pair, and put them on his own face. Jenny laughed. "You look so funny, Che!"

"And this pair should look nice on you, Gwenny," he said, picking a third pair.

"But I can't—" Gwendolyn protested.

"It is not nice to express it, but the spectacles make Jenny Elf look odd," he said. "It would be courteous to don a similar pair, to share her oddity and make her feel more comfortable, as I have done. My spectacles have no effect on my vision, of course; they are merely decoration."

"Oh, I don't mind—" Jenny protested. But he made a NO signal that Gwendolyn could not see, and she stopped. What was he up to? His sire or dam must have told him to do this, somewhere along the way.

"I don't want Jenny to feel odd," Gwendolyn said. "No one knows me out here, so I suppose I can wear a pair." She put the spectacles on her face.

She stood for a moment, her mouth slowly dropping open in amazement. "I can see!" she exclaimed. "I can see everything, no matter how far away!" She tilted her face up. "Is—is that a cloud?"

"Yes," Jenny said, now understanding. They had given Gwendolyn a reason to wear the spectacles without commenting on what the lenses did. Now she could see as well as they could, without having to admit how it was without them.

"But if we encounter goblins, we may all remove our spectacles," Che said. "Until we are away from them. So that they will not make fun of us."

The two girls nodded, understanding very well.

They returned to the adult centaurs, wearing their spectacles. Even Sammy had a pair, now. "I see you children enjoy playing games," Cheiron remarked. "Perhaps the two of us should complete the effect by donning similar pairs."

"No, Sire," Che said. "Only children are permitted to be childish."

"I stand corrected," Cheiron said, making a droll face.

Jenny did not know Cheiron well, but she could see already that she would like him well enough.

"If you must indulge in such foolishness," Chex said severely, "at least indulge in it while we travel, so as not to waste more time."

They quickly agreed. Gwenny scrambled onto Cheiron's back, and Jenny onto Chex's. The centaurs started off again.

But now it was different. Jenny could see all Xanth, and so could Gwenny. Gwenny's head was constantly turning that way and this, as if she wanted to cram everything into her eyes before it disappeared. Then she faced Jenny, and Jenny winked, and Gwenny broke out laughing, mostly from the sheer joy of being able to see such an expression at this distance.

Later in the day they encountered a giant land serpent. The creature lifted its head, hissing hungrily—only to discover itself bracketed by two arrows that thudded into a tree on either side of its body. It gazed at Cheiron, whose bow remained in his hands, and decided to hiss at some creature far away. In a moment it was gone.

Jenny had assumed that the flying centaurs escaped threats by flying away from them. Now she saw that this was not always the case. Cheiron had not missed the serpent, he had warned it. A centaur's arrow went as true as his word.

They came to a stop beside a pleasant pool. Jenny suddenly realized how thirsty she had become. "Oh, I could drink half of it right now!" she exclaimed.

"Me too!" Gwenny agreed.

"Caution," Cheiron said. "One must never take an unfamiliar pond for granted."

Jenny remembered the hate spring of the horde, and shuddered.

Cheiron looked around, and found several ladybugs being pestered by several gentlemenbugs. He caught two of the latter in his hand and carried them to the pool and dropped them in. They splashed, then began swimming for the bank. Cheiron lifted them out and looked at them. Both were wet, but otherwise unharmed.

He set them down beside a pennypede. They ignored it, instead scrambling back toward the ladybugs, eager to pester them some more. "This water appears to be neutral," Cheiron remarked. "No love, no hate, no poison."

So it seemed. Nevertheless, they sipped it cautiously at first. It was sweet and good.

It occurred to Jenny that Cheiron had known the character of the lake before coming to it. But he had wanted to make a point, so that children excited about being able to see did not take foolish risks. This was part of centaur education. Che had remained silent throughout. He must have known.

"Dear," Chex said, "I believe I would prefer to spend the night in our own cottage, rather than in the field. It has been a wearing occasion."

"Very well," Cheiron said. "Girls, we shall need your help. Che can not ride readily, and can not yet fly, so you will have to hold him while we fly."

"But—" the two said together.

"In this manner," Chex said. "Get on us, and take his hands."

Baffled, they did so. Now each girl was riding a centaur, reaching down to hold one of Che's hands.

Then Cheiron flicked Che with his tail. Che became so light that the pull of their hands on his drew him into the air. "Don't let go!" he exclaimed.

The two centaurs flicked themselves, spread their wings, and jumped together into the air. Suddenly they were flying, perfectly synchronized, with Che floating between them.

Jenny realized that they could have done this anytime, but wanted to give the girls some experience on the ground, and with the spectacles, first. And perhaps they wanted to let the group get comfortable with itself, before risking such a maneuver. She was learning a lot about centaurs, already.

Chapter 15. Electra's Election

Electra watched the centaurs go. Gwendolyn Goblin was riding Cheiron and Jenny Elf was riding Chex, with little Che prancing along between them. Their family of three had become a family of five, and they all looked happy, and Electra was glad. She knew the centaurs would take excellent care of the girls; in fact, not only would they be happy and healthy, they would receive the best education available in Xanth.

And the siege of Goblin Mountain was over, before lives had been lost. Goblins were not Electra's favorite creatures, but she had come to respect long-haired Godiva. If a woman were to become a goblin chief, the goblins would become much better neighbors!

The winged monsters were departing. Some were evidently disappointed that they had not gotten to use their horrible weapons, but most seemed glad to be away from here before the arrival of the land dragons. That left Godiva and Nada and Nada's handsome brother, Naldo, and Dolph. Nada and her brother were talking, renewing their family ties, and Dolph was seeing the monsters off.

Electra approached the gobliness. "I guess it's hard to lose your daughter, even if it's for the best," she said.

"I would have lost her in a worse way, if this had not happened," Godiva said, but she did look sad. "At least they will be visiting.'' She shrugged. ''But I don't see this type of solution for you, Electra. What will you do, this week?''

''What can I do? Che could be a companion to both girls, but Dolph can marry only one. Maybe if I looked like Nada—''

''You girls helped save Che Centaur, and that helped save my daughter,'' Godiva said. ''Let me see what I can do for you.''

''Unless your wand could make me beautiful—''

''Stop it, girl. Beauty is not the problem. It's just an aspect of it.'' She inspected Electra shrewdly. ''You don't have a family here, do you.''

''No. My family is centuries gone. But King Dor and Queen Irene have been very good to me.''

''They have a conflict of interest. They have to look to the welfare of their son. I have no such conflict. Come into the mountain with me.''

''But—''

Godiva smiled. ''Not to stay, Electra. I want to try some dresses on you.''

''Dresses? But—''

''My daughter is gone. I have to fuss over someone.''

''Oh.'' Electra could appreciate that.

Godiva glanced to where the two naga were talking. ''Naldo, may I have a moment with you before you go?''

''Of course, lady.'' Both naga slithered over.

''Naldo, we have resolved a crisis here, and I express my appreciation for the support of your folk. Your kind and ours are not normally allies, but you honored the covenant. We shall do the same, when the time comes. As goblins, we can not oppose our own kind in Mount Etamin, but when my daughter is grown and assumes power, we shall see what can be done politically to alleviate your situation.''

Electra recognized the significance of that commitment. If Gwendolyn later became chief here, and married a chief there, she would be in a position to stop the goblin aggressions against the nada of Mount Etamin. It might indeed turn out to pay the naga well for their honoring of the covenant. because the goblins there were their worst nemesis. Indeed. it was the reason Nada had been betrothed to Dolph: to make an alliance with the human folk and gain power to push back the goblins.

"Thank you, lady," Naldo said. "I am glad to have come to know you."

"But you may be able to do something more immediate for your sister," Godiva said. "You know she doesn't want to marry Dolph, and not just because she doesn't want to void your alliance with the human folk. You know Electra must marry Dolph or die within the week, and furthermore, she loves him. Now you are an astute observer of creature nature. I want you to put your mind to this problem and come up with a devious solution that will serve all parties best."

"But—" he protested.

"Within the hour," she said. "While I dress Electra." She took Electra's arm and guided her into the tunnel. With her free hand she lifted a smoky torch from its holder to light their way. The funny thing was that Electra, being human, was about twice as tall as the gobliness, but she felt like a child with this adult.

"He can't solve the problem that no one else has solved in six years," Electra protested belatedly as they wound down into the depths. "There *is* no solution! I mean, even if I didn't die, he wouldn't love me, and I don't want him to be unhappy."

"There are ways to solve any problem," Godiva said. "It's just a matter of finding them. Naldo has a clever mind; I have seen it in action recently. He will find a way, though the rest of us may not properly understand it."

Electra did not argue. She knew this was an impossible dream. Unless the Good Magician had an Answer. That was her only real hope.

Godiva brought her to her nice suite. "I make my daughter's dresses myself," she said. "Because it isn't convenient to go out and harvest from clothes hangers or dress mannequins. I get material and I cut and sew. I believe they suit her well enough.''

"They make her beautiful," Electra said. "And the elf girl—that blue dress made her beautiful too. It was amazing.''

"It's just know-how," Godiva asserted. "A woman can be beautiful in just a hank of hair, if she drapes it correctly. It's all in the technique.''

Certainly Godiva could! She had the most lustrous black tresses Electra had seen, reaching down to her knees. Her hair flared out and around, constantly caressing her. But Electra had no such asset.

Godiva brought out white material. "This will be your wedding dress," she said.

"But—"

"Any woman looks beautiful in her wedding dress," Godiva said. "It is part of the enchantment.''

"But I can't wear that if I don't get married!''

"Of course you can. Naldo will figure out how." The woman worked busily, measuring Electra here and there, then cutting the material and tacking it together with quick temporary stitches. Soon she had it ready to try on. "Strip.''

Electra gave up protesting. There was a hope and fascination about this business that she could not resist. Of course she would not get to marry Dolph, but for this hour she might pretend. She removed her shirt and jeans and heavy shoes.

Godiva studied her with embarrassing directness. "You are grimy from the siege. Go to the alcove and sponge yourself off.''

Obediently, Electra went. The voice of a mother was not to be denied.

There was a polished stone mirror, but Electra did not look at herself, knowing that there was nothing to be gained. She cleaned up, dried, then turned to put on her panties. But they were gone. In their place was something else.

She picked up the satiny bit of material. It was a pair of delicate pink panties! "Oh, I can't wear these!" she said.

"Do you think I want you trying on a wedding dress in grimy off-white panties?" Godiva demanded.

Embarrassed, Electra capitulated. She donned the pink panties, then the pink bra, feeling wicked. She stepped out, knowing that her blush just about matched the color of the forbidden items.

"Very good," Godiva said briskly. "Now this." She held up the dress. It was thoroughly evident that it was not lack of dressmaking expertise that caused Godiva to wear her hair instead. She must have had much practice with her daughter.

Electra climbed into it, almost afraid to touch it. The material was wonderfully light and frilly. Godiva made quick adjustments, then had her step into white slippers.

"Unbraid your hair."

Electra did so, and fluffed it out. Finally she had to don a translucent veil and put a white flower in her hair. She felt totally foolish.

"Now look in the mirror," Godiva said, pushing her back toward it.

Reluctantly Electra went. She nerved herself and looked.

Before her stood a vision of absolute beauty, a veritable princess of a bride. The woman in the mirror was tall and slender, yet full above and full below, and her thinly veiled face was lovely. It couldn't possibly be her!

"Yes, I think it will do," Godiva said. "Now we must hide this until the occasion, and see what Naldo has devised."

Electra was sorry to return to her old, grimy clothes, but she realized that this was best. It had been a wonderful vision, but that was all it was.

Soon she was her normal shabby self, with a package under her arm. She had never felt as negative about herself as she did now. That was the trouble with a vision: it made the reality seem so much worse.

At the surface, Naldo was ready. "I believe I have found the way," he said. "Prince Dolph must marry Electra—" Electra's heart jumped foolishly. "The day before she is eighteen, and divorce her the next day so he can marry Nada," he concluded. "That will save her life without depriving Dolph of his desire."

Electra couldn't bring herself to comment. He had indeed found a technicality that should save her life—but what was the point? Without Dolph she didn't want to live. Nada looked no more pleased.

"You do want Dolph to be happy?" Naldo asked Electra.

"Yes, of course," Electra said immediately, realizing how selfish she was being. Dolph would not be happy if she died because of him or if he did not marry Nada.

"You can take a potion to nullify your love for him, after your life has been saved," Naldo said.

Electra nodded. She could hardly imagine not being in love with Dolph, but of course that would ease her own pain.

"And you do want not to void the alliance between our kind and the human folk?" Naldo prodded Nada.

"Yes, of course." Nada agreed, her voice the echo of Electra's.

"And you can take a love potion with him," Naldo said. "Then when you marry him, you will love him."

Nada was silent in the same way as Electra. Naldo had indeed come up with an answer, and the fact that neither of them liked it was irrelevant. The fact that it was as cunningly sinister a device as anyone could imagine was also irrelevant. It would work.

"So let's tell Prince Dolph," Naldo said, setting off at a brisk slither. Nada followed less briskly.

Electra started to walk, but Godiva held her back. "If you have to, you can ask the Good Magician," she reminded her. "He may have a better Answer."

"I hope so!" Electra said.

"But Naldo is cunning enough to make a good goblin leader," Godiva continued. "I don't think we appreciate the ramifications of his ploy. I think you should play it through."

Electra sighed. "If it makes Dolph happy," she said.

"You are a generous person. That's a good quality, in folk other than goblins."

It was a poor consolation. But Electra couldn't afford to start crying, for now Dolph was coming toward them, smiling. Evidently he was thrilled with the idea.

Electra knew she loved an idiot.

This time there were no challenges at the Good Magician's Castle. Grey Murphy was ready for Electra's Question. He thought.

Ivy greeted them both with abandon. "We saw that siege on the magic mirror!" she said. "I was frightened, but we couldn't interfere. I'm glad it turned out all right. Gwenny and Jenny seem to be doing nicely at the centaur's glade."

"Now for your Question," Grey said.

"Oh, we don't have a Question," Electra said quickly. "Just a favor. We'd like to get two vials from you. One to nullify love, and the other to make it."

"Two vials?" Ivy asked blankly.

"We're following my brother's suggestion," Nada said. "Electra will marry Dolph first, then divorce him, and I will marry him the next day. So she'll live, and Dolph will be happy. But we won't be happy unless we change our own emotions. So we aren't asking you for an Answer."

Grey shook his head, bemused. "Just as well. That was the answer I was going to give you. I don't like it much, but I found it in the Book of Answers, so it must be right."

Ivy went to the storeroom and fetched the vials. "These will be our wedding gifts to each of you," she said. But she did not look happy.

"Make sure you use these correctly," Grey cautioned. "The nullifier is no problem: it simply cancels the magic love, such as the enchantment that caused you to love the prince who woke you, Electra, without touching any other magic. So it won't cause you to age abruptly or to be free of the need to marry Dolph. But there's no need for you to take it until the divorce anyway." He turned to Nada. "But you must be careful to be looking at Dolph when you take this, because if you see another man first, you will love him instead. This is not the type of potion found in some springs, that causes instant, ah, activity; it will just make you love him. But it would be awkward if—''

"I understand," Nada said.

"There's one other thing," Electra said somewhat diffidently. "I don't know how to—to signal the stork. I understand that the marriage won't count until we do that."

Grey shook his head. "You're still technically under age. The Adult Conspiracy—"

"But Dolph doesn't know either," Electra said. "So how do we—?"

Ivy spread her hands. "We're not allowed to tell you. But surely you will be able to figure it out when the time comes. Most folk do."

Electra didn't argue, but she had her doubts.

They held the wedding on the Isle of View, of course. That was where Electra had slept for her thousand years (with time off for good behavior), and where Prince Dolph had kissed her awake. King Dor had arranged to have a pavilion that could be enclosed at night erected on the beach, so that they could consummate the marriage right here on the island of love. In fact the isle had become popular since its rediscovery, and not merely for young couples. It was a beautiful region. The centaurs had even sent an expedition at one point to dig in the sand to see if they could find the ruins of the Sorceress Tapis' old residence. That expedition had been headed by centaurs named Archae and Ology, and they had surely known what they were doing, but no one else did. They had not bothered to consult with Electra, who had actually lived there and could have told them all about it. But this was the nature of the folk of Centaur Isle.

Electra took her package into a closed chamber to don her wedding dress. She had not been allowed to see Dolph this day, to her dismay; it was part of the ritual of the occasion. Nada was to be her maid of honor, which meant that it was her job to see that Electra did things the right way. That was just as well, because Electra knew she would have botched it on her own. She was horribly nervous and guilty and depressed and hopeful all at once. She would have one day and night married to Dolph, and her sheer joy in the notion was countered by her knowledge that it would be awful for Dolph. She would do anything to make him happy, but this was not what would do it. This would only save her life so that he would not suffer guilt when he married Nada.

"I just had an idea," Nada said as she fussed with the dress, getting things fastened and adjusted. "Suppose we pour the love potion into Dolph's drink? So he takes it when he's with you, and—"

Electra was obscenely tempted. She cursed herself for that. "No. It wouldn't be right."

Nada sighed. "I thought you would say that. Your life and happiness are on the line, but you insist on doing what's right."

"I'm sorry. I know it's stupid."

"That wasn't the word I had in mind." Nada went on with her business, briskly. She set a fragrant red rose of love in Electra's unbraided hair, and put the veil on Electra's face, adjusting both.

Finally it was done. Nada stood back to look at her. "It's amazing!" she breathed.

"It's a nice dress," Electra agreed.

"You are suddenly the loveliest woman of the day," Nada said.

Electra laughed, somewhat bitterly. "Godiva said that wedding dresses have magic. Think what it will do for you, tomorrow!" For they would let out the seams here and here and particularly there, so it would fit.

"I can only see what it does for you, today. 'Lectra, you've always had an inferiority complex about your appearance, but believe me, you are stunning now. Take my word: when the others see you, they will be astonished. They will not be mocking you. You are queen for the moment. Make the most of it!"

"The only one I want to impress is Dolph," Electra said regretfully. "And he—" She shrugged.

"This time his eyes will pop out of his head!" Nada said. Then they both laughed, picturing that.

It was time. "Oh, Nada, I think my knees are going to melt!" Electra exclaimed.

"And there's a butterfly in your stomach," Nada said.

"How did you know?"

"Open your mouth and stand still," Nada said.

Surprised, Electra did so. Nada whacked her on the back. The butterfly flew out of her mouth and fluttered around the room. It was bright yellow, of course.

Nada opened a window and the butterfly flew out. "You feel better now," she said.

Electra nodded. It was true.

"Now you must go out there and do it. My brother will guide you down the aisle. Just go where you're taken, and when someone asks you a question, say 'I do.' Then kiss Dolph. After that it's just a matter of listening while folk congratulate him for marrying you."

"Yes, it's a real sacrifice for him."

"Now stop that!" Nada opened the door and shoved her out.

Electra was suddenly in front of an audience. Everyone was there: King Dor, Queen Irene, Dolph's grandpa Bink with his wife, Chameleon, in her neutral stage, King Emeritus Trent with Queen Emeritis Iris, Magician Murphy with Sorceress Vadne; Grey Murphy with Ivy; the Zombie Master with Millie the (former) Ghost and their grown children Hiatus and Lacuna; Cheiron, Chex, and Che Centaur, and with Che was Gwenny Goblin and Jenny Elf and her cat Sammy, all four wearing spectacles and looking happy with the joke; Godiva Goblin with Gloha beside her; Grundy Golem and Rapunzel; Marrow Bones the walking skeleton, and Grace'l Ossein, his female friend with the nice bones; even Draco Dragon quietly smoking in a corner, keeping his fire damped, for he was Dolph's friend too; and any number of other folk Electra had come to know in her six years in this time. Everyone was there, looking at her.

Electra felt herself reeling. She knew she was about to faint.

Then a firm hand caught her elbow. "No you don't, beautiful bride!"

It was Nada's handsome brother, Naldo Naga, in full human form. The one who had suggested this way through their impasse. She wasn't sure whether to bless him or curse him for that, but his presence was reassuring. He surely knew what he was doing.

"Why are they staring?" Electra asked faintly.

"They hardly believe it is you," Naldo replied in a low voice. "You have been transformed, Electra."

"No," she said doubtfully. But somehow she did feel prettier than ever before, except for that moment before Godiva's mirror when she had first tried on the dress. She knew it was illusion, but it was a precious one. She was thankful for the veil, which at least hid her freckles.

Then two trumpet swans stood in a garden of red, green, and bluebells. The swans lifted their flaring bells and played, and the flowers rang their colored bells in accompaniment. Electra realized that Queen Irene must have taken great care with those plants, so that they would be tuned just right. It was the "Wedding March." It was the loveliest music she could imagine, though it mocked her.

In fact this whole elaborate ceremony mocked her, because everyone knew it was only for a day. Yet Electra knew that it was her only possible chance for joy; if she wasted this, she would have nothing on the remaining days of her life. So she straightened her back, faced forward, and let Naldo guide her down the aisle while the beautiful music played.

There seemed to be a murmur of awe as she passed the various folk of the audience. They were probably admiring the dress. Electra was really thankful that Godiva had made it for her, because otherwise she would have been ashamed to be here at all. She had had no idea that it would be such a fancy occasion!

Then she saw Prince Dolph, standing at the far end of the aisle at the edge of the pavilion. He was in a suit and his hair was combed, both of which she knew made him really uncomfortable. He was taller than he had been. When they first met, they had been the same height, though she was two years older. But recently he had grown, and now he was taller than she was. He was also halfway handsome. He was facing her, and absolutely still; he seemed to be in a trance. Her heart went out to him; she knew he didn't want to marry her, even for a day, and she was sorry to be putting him through this. But it was the way it had to be.

Beyond the end of the aisle was a huge hypnogourd, angled so that its peephole faced away. Before it stood what appeared to be a big wooden horse.

That was the Xanthly representation of the Night Stallion, she realized—the head of the realm of bad dreams! She had encountered him briefly when she first woke from her long sleep after being kissed by the Prince, and she had been terrified. But now she was outside the gourd, where the Horse of Another Color did not have power, and she was more curious than afraid. What was he doing here?

But further consideration gave her the answer. Prince Dolph had a special relationship with the gourd; he could go there when he chose and be well treated, because the Night Stallion liked him. Naturally the stallion was here for Dolph's wedding. He was Dolph's best man—or best creature.

King Nabob Naga, Nada's father, was here to perform the ceremony. Naturally he had an interest, too!

Naldo placed her beside Dolph, facing the King, and stepped back. But Dolph remained fixed. It was as if he had been turned to stone, which was impossible, because the Gorgon, Magician Humfrey's wife, was no longer in Xanth, and nobody was getting stoned.

Turn him.

It was the stallion. Electra understood that he could speak normally when he chose when he was in the gourd, but this wasn't the gourd, so it was more mental, like a dream voice.

It didn't matter, as long as he could be heard.

So Electra put her hands on Dolph and gently turned him to face King Nabob. She had thought that she was the one freaked out by the ceremony, but now she saw that Dolph was worse than she, and she had to help him get through it. She was glad to do it. She would have been glad to help him through the rest of his life, if only he had wanted that.

King Nabob was saying something. Electra tried to pay attention, but she was worried about Dolph, who might as well have been a zombie for all the animation he had. He must be utterly terrified! She took his hand and squeezed it reassuringly; this would soon enough be over.

Suddenly she was jolted to awareness of her own situation. King Nabob had asked her a question! She remembered what to do. "I do," she said.

". . . pronounce you man and wife. Kiss the bride."

Dolph remained in his trance. So Electra lifted her veil away and kissed him. Then at last he began to recover. His arms tightened around her, and he kissed her back. That was a relief; she had been getting quite worried about him.

Then they were in the reception, and the folk were filing by, congratulating Dolph. Electra would have been disgusted, but she realized that this was all show, in an effort to make the man feel good about being caught by the woman.

There was a wonderful big wedding cake, too. Dolph was supposed to cut it, but he still seemed a bit vague, so she guided his hand for him. Her own nervousness had disappeared in her effort to get Dolph through. She would have to warn Nada about this, so that she would be prepared to get him through tomorrow.

Finally it was all done, and they were alone in the pavilion for the night. The others had all gone home, or wherever wedding guests went.

The chamber was beautiful. It had a monstrous feather bed, and pillows and cushions all over, and not much else. It seemed that couples were not expected to be interested in other things on their wedding night.

Dolph seemed vague. "What now?" he asked.

"Now we have to consummate the marriage," Electra said. "Because it isn't final until we do. And it has to be final, because you can't divorce me until it is."

He gazed at her as if still not quite understanding. "Oh."

Electra began removing her dress, because she didn't want such a lovely outfit to be damaged in any way. She would never use it again, but Nada would, and Nada would surely be twice as beautiful in it as Electra could ever dream of being.

"Maybe you should take off your clothes too," she suggested. "You have such a nice suit, you don't want to sleep in it."

"Uh, yes, I guess." He looked helplessly at her. " 'Lectra, I—I think I never saw you before."

She laughed, perversely enjoying this. "Of course you have, Dolph! I've been with you every chance I could possibly get, ever since you kissed me awake six years ago."

"I mean, when you came down that aisle, I didn't recognize you. You were beautiful."

"It's the dress. That's its magic."

"Oh." He started removing his clothing. "Um, should we—I mean, mother says folk shouldn't be undressed together—"

"We're married now, Dolph," she said brightly, though the truth was that she was having a qualm or two of her own. Was he supposed to be allowed to see her panties now? She concluded that it was now or never, because after tomorrow it would be Nada's panties he would be seeing, after six years of trying. If Electra's own panties were to have any chance at all, it had to be before Nada's.

She nerved herself and drew the dress off over her head. Suddenly she was in her wonderful pink underclothing. She hoped Dolph would have the grace to be impressed. She turned to face him.

Dolph was now in his underpants. He looked at her—and went straight back into his trance. He just froze in place, not moving a muscle. Oh, no! He had Freaked Out.

She went to him, determined that this night, of all nights, would not be ruined. "Snap out of it, Dolph!" she said. "It's all right! We're married!"

"P—p—p—" he stuttered.

"Panties," she agreed firmly. "I know they aren't the ones you really wanted to see, but maybe they'll help prepare you for tomorrow."

But he remained entranced. He just stood there, staring.

"Oh, mice!" she snapped. "This isn't getting us anywhere!" She picked up a pillow and threw it at him. It bounced off the side of his head.

That registered. Dolph picked up a cushion and hurled it at her. Electra threw another back at him. Soon they were in the middle of the biggest, wildest pillow fight ever, for there were many pillows and cushions, and there was no one to stop them. Electra had had some pillow fights with Nada and Ivy at Castle Roogna, but these had been restrained because they hadn't wanted anyone to overhear. Now, with Dolph, there was no restraint. What delight!

She got hold of the biggest pillow she could find, swung it around her head, and whammed him on the rear. "Oho!" he cried joyfully, and got another to wham her with. She fled, screaming happily. Now Dolph was acting normal, and that was the way she liked him.

"Eeeek!" she screamed as she tripped over a cushion and fell headlong on the feather bed. Dolph whammed her directly on the panties while she was down. She rolled over and caught his ankles and yanked, making him fall too. In a moment they were wrestling, jamming cushions at each other, and tickling ribs. They clasped each other, trying to get into better whamming position, rolling over and over. Dolph got a knee over her body, pinning her down, and reached for a pillow so he could wham her on the head. But she cheated: she sat up quickly, caught his head in her hands, and kissed him.

She expected him to make an exclamation of disgust and go to wash off his mouth. But he seemed to lose his strength, and his eyes went vacant.

"Oh, I'm sorry, Dolph!" she said. "I should have let you hit me with the pillow! Don't go into a trance again!"

"K—k—k—kiss," he said.

"Look, I *know* I'm not Nada, and you don't like me doing that," she said, frustrated. "But Dolph, this is my only night to—to be with you, and I wish—"

He caught her shoulders with his hands and hauled her face down to his. "I never kissed you before," he said. "Do it again."

"You mean you *liked* it?" she asked incredulously. "Oh, Dolph, you can have all you want!" She kissed him again, and again, and again ten times, getting in as many as she could before he got disgusted.

But he didn't get disgusted. "Oh, 'Lectra," he breathed. "I never knew it would be like this with you!" He kissed her back.

"You mean you like mushy stuff with me?" she asked, afraid to be too thrilled for fear he didn't mean it.

"I guess I do," he said. Then they hugged, and kissed, and hugged again, and kissed again, the pillow fight forgotten.

"But how come?" she asked when they paused for air. She was gaining confidence; it seemed he really did like this.

"When I saw you in that dress, I didn't even recognize you," he said. "I thought it was some other girl, and I got scared, because I didn't know what had gone wrong. You were so beautiful!"

"Was I really?" she asked, hardly believing that he could have seen her that way.

"Really! They told me the dress would make a difference, but 'Lectra, it made so much more than I knew! Then you came closer, and I saw a freckle under your veil, and I knew it was you—"

And that was the end of the illusion, she thought.

"And you were still so lovely I could hardly stand it," he said. "All this time I've been betrothed to you, and I never realized how beautiful you could be!"

Electra was elated. "You mean that's why you were in a trance? Because of me?"

"Yes. I never truly saw you before, 'Lectra. I was such a fool! Not until that dress—"

"And then I took off the dress," she said with resignation.

"And I saw your panties. And your—your—I don't know the word."

"Bra?"

"I guess. I never saw that before. I didn't even know it existed. And you were still so beautiful, and I knew it wasn't just the dress."

"Pink panties are special," she agreed. One thing she knew: having discovered their magic, she was not about to take them off! She wanted him to go right on thinking she was beautiful, even if it was only the magic of the panties and bra. Nada might not need such magic to be beautiful, but Electra did.

"Then you kissed me, and—"

"Oh, Dolph, it's kind of you to say you liked it!" she said, bursting with appreciation.

"To think I could have been kissing you all this time, instead of trying to kiss Nada when she didn't want to be," he said. "You would have kissed me anytime, but I—"

"You can catch up now," she suggested.

"Yes!" He kissed her again, and then she kissed him, and then he kissed her. Electra's fondest dream was coming true. "Oh, 'Lectra, I just didn't know!"

But after a time they were sated even with that, and just lay beside each other staring at the ceiling. Electra realized that there must be special magic associated with the entire wedding ceremony to make him love her for the moment, and she hated to break the enchantment. But there was business that had to be accomplished. "You know we have to consummate this marriage," she said, finally.

"I'd rather just look at you, and hug you, and kiss you," he said.

"That, too. But still we have to signal the stork."

"But how do we do it?" he asked plaintively. "I never found out."

"Neither did I." For they both were still victims of the Adult Conspiracy, being underage. They had married because they had to, but had to discover the secret themselves. If it had been possible to wait one more day, Electra would have been old enough to learn it, ironically.

"I think it has something to do with mushy stuff," he said. "But *what*?"

"I guess kissing isn't it," she said. "Because if it was, it would have happened by now."

"And I guess hugging isn't it," he said.

"And pillow fighting."

"And looking at panties."

They considered everything they could think of, but nothing seemed to be it. The secret remained impenetrable.

They realized that they just weren't going to figure it out. Dejected, they hugged and kissed a few more times, then got serious. "Maybe I can sneak out and ask Nada," Electra said. "She's staying in a cave on the south end of the island with Naldo and King Nabob, because it's easy for them in snake form. I think she'll tell me, if I beg her."

"Promise her you'll never tell she told," Dolph said, awed by the prospect of violating the Adult Conspiracy. "They have to think we figured it out for ourselves."

"Right," she said. She got up, then found that she didn't have anything to wear. She refused to use the lovely wedding dress for this, and her regular clothing was in the other chamber where she had changed. But maybe the door wasn't locked.

She wrapped a sheet around her, and Dolph wrapped another around himself. Then, feeling mutually guilty, they sneaked quietly out, looking like two ghosts.

No one was around, which was fortunate, because they were about as inconspicuous as the sun and moon on a dark night. More so, in fact, because the moon seldom appeared on a dark night, and the sun had never been known to do it.

They slunk around to the bride's changing chamber. The door was unlocked, to their relief. They went in, and Electra found her yellow shirt and blue jeans and put them on. "You had better go back to the bedroom," she whispered to him. "If someone comes, you can say 'Go away!' and throw a pillow at the door."

"Right." But he lingered. "Would it be all right if I kissed you again?"

"But I'm in my blah clothing!" she protested.

"But *you* aren't blah," he said.

Her heart was catching fire. "Oh, Dolph, I'll always love you!" she said, and kissed him with as much passion as she dared risk without turning him off.

Then they left the room, Dolph slunk back toward the bedroom to guard the fort, and Electra set off through the moonlight for the naga camp.

The beach was gorgeous in the night. The sand was soft and bright, and the waves of the sea lapped gently up to smooth out the disturbances of the day. The moon was using the water as a mirror, reflecting itself in every wave. Everything was lovely, and everything loved its neighbors, for this was the Isle of View.

"Well, now, bride pro tem!" a voice exclaimed, causing Electra almost to jump out of her skin. Fortunately she was able to clap her hands to her bosom and hold herself down in time to save her skin. She had thought she was alone.

"Who—?" she gasped.

"We've met. I'm the demoness Metria. Remember?"

Oh. When it came to folk Electra did not want to meet at the moment, this demon was two places ahead of the very top of the list. Metria could take great pleasure in blabbing about this embarrassing mission to all and sundry and everyone else. But it would be impossible to get rid of her merely by being hostile. Electra wasn't sure she was up to being hostile anyway, right now, even to Metria, because she was still glowing from Dolph's kiss. He had actually *asked* her, when she had been in her blah clothing! So she tried to be neutral. "I remember."

"What's on your freckled mind?" the demoness asked.

"Dolph kissed me!" Electra said. "I mean, even in this clothing!"

"Of course. You still have your pink panties on underneath."

Electra's heart descended from the clouds. That was true. The magic of those panties was still operating. Had she changed back to her old ones it would have been different. "I guess so," Electra said dully.

"Where are you going?"

What use to lie, even if there were any point in it? The demoness probably had already guessed. "We can't figure out how to signal the stork. I'm going to ask Nada."

"Oho! So you're going to do that tonight! Maybe I'll watch."

"If you do, we won't do it!" Electra said defiantly. But it was a bluff, because they had to do it. If they didn't, the marriage would not be consummated, and it wouldn't count, and Electra would die the moment she turned eighteen, tomorrow. Well, not right at the moment; actually she would start the process, with her heart bleeding and her body aging as the enchantment expired, and she would age and weaken into oblivion within hours. Then Dolph would be free to marry Nada anyway, but he would be unhappy because of having let another person die. She did not want him to be unhappy.

"And if you do it," the demoness said relentlessly, "then Dolph will be free to divorce you and marry Nada tomorrow. That must make you feel great."

"At least he'll be happy," Electra said shortly.

"He's an idiot."

"Right!"

Metria, taken aback by Electra's ready agreement, faded out. That was a relief.

She was now at the south end of the isle. Where would Nada and Naldo be? Then she spied them in the sea. They were swimming in their natural forms, laughing as they used their tails to splash water on each other.

"Nada!" Electra called.

Nada's head whipped around. " 'Lectra! What are you doing down here?"

"Oh, Nada, please, it means my life! Tell me how to signal the stork."

Nada and her brother were forging to the shore. They hit the beach and slithered up to Electra, their serpent bodies moving in perfect parallel. "But, 'Lectra," Nada protested. "The Adult Conspiracy—"

"But I'm married now! And I have to do it! Please—"

"Tell her," Naldo told his sister, and slithered back to the ocean.

Nada had respect for her brother, and of course he was the one who had suggested this two-marriage course. So Nada told her.

"You mean that's all there is to it?" Electra asked, amazed and somewhat disappointed.

"Not much of a secret, is it!" Nada said. "You must promise not to tell any children, because if they ever found out how little there is to know, they would laugh the adults right out of the picture."

"I can see that," Electra agreed. Then she hugged Nada, and set off up the beach. Now at last she knew how to do it. Now she could save her life and free Dolph for tomorrow. Her feelings remained oddly mixed.

Back at the bedroom, she found Dolph waiting anxiously. "I was afraid something had happened to you," he said.

"No, it's perfectly safe here, now," she said. "Remember, this is the Isle of View."

"Isle of View too," he said, laughing.

She whammed him with a pillow.

He grabbed her and kissed her.

They got into another hugging and tickling fight. It was great fun. But finally they had to get down to business.

"We have to embrace each other very closely," Electra said. "But there's a catch."

"We've been hugging." he said. "I don't mind that. What's the catch?"

"No clothing."

"You mean—?"

"No undershirt. No shorts for you. No panties for me." That was the awful thing about it. Without the fabulous pink panties she would lose what remained of her attractiveness.

But he seemed to handle this unfortunate aspect pretty well. "How do we know when the signal goes out?"

"We see the ellipsis."

"The what?"

"It looks like three dots. It always marks the signal to the stork. Nada told me."

"So we just keep hugging until we see dots?" he asked, having trouble with this notion.

"That's it."

"It seems too simple to work."

"It's magic." What was the point in admitting that she hardly believed it either? It *had* to work.

"Oh. Yes. Well, we'd better do it."

They took off their underclothing and hugged. "This close?" Dolph asked.

"Closer."

He squeezed her so that her ribs hurt. "This close?"

"That's hard, not close," she gasped.

He eased up immediately. "I'm sorry, 'Lectra. I never want to hurt you! I'd rather kiss you."

"We can do that too."

"We can? Gee, that's great!"

He kissed her, and she kissed him. They rolled over and hugged some more and kissed again, and the more they did it the more fun it became. The lack of clothing didn't seem to be hurting, surprisingly: Dolph seemed to like her just as well this way. Soon they forgot about what they were supposed to be doing, and just kissed and kissed and hugged and hugged and got closer and closer. They were so close it was hard to tell where one of them left off and the other began. Like ghosts or demons, they seemed to be overlapping each other. But it didn't bother them at all. Electra knew that eventually they would have to get back to the business of signaling the stork, but that could wait; this was too much fun. She was loving Dolph, and he was loving her back!

She felt an electrical thrill, and realized that she was losing control of her magic talent. The current was leaking out, mildly electrifying them. She hoped that was harmless, because she just couldn't stop kissing him.

Then Dolph's body got hot and his eyes stared glassily past her face. "Dolph! What's the matter?" she asked, afraid he was going into another trance or that her current had tingled too strongly and hurt him.

"I see them!" he gasped, shuddering.

"See what?" she asked, really worried. His whole body was shaking.

"I see the Dots!"

Electra turned her head and looked where he was looking. There they were: three dots floating just above their bodies:

. . .

The dots paused to get their orientation, then lined up in a row and took off through the wall, heading for the stork.

"We did it!" Electra exclaimed. "We got to the ellipsis!" She had elected to do it right, and they had made it.

Dolph kissed her, relaxing. Then he lay back and closed his eyes. "Oh, Nada, I'll always love you . . ." he whispered.

Electra felt her wildest hopes collapsing. Her fond dreams dissipated like the smoke of the demoness. Her heart began to bleed.

Chapter 16. Dolph's Decision

Afterward, Dolph lay beside her. His mind and heart were spinning. Today he had not only gotten married and learned how to signal the stork, he had discovered Electra. Three great shocks had come to his indifference: he had seen her beautiful in her wedding dress, as lovely a creature as he could imagine. He had seen her in panties, and that had excited him in another strange yet wonderful way. He had kissed her, and discovered to his astonishment that her kisses were just as thrilling as Nada's were. After that, the idea of summoning the stork with her had become interesting instead of burdensome.

But that brought another burden he had never thought he would have to handle. How was he going to do it?

Oh, Nada, I'll always love you!

But as he pondered it, the answer fell into place. He knew it was right.

Satisfied, he fell asleep.

In the morning he woke and kissed Electra, but she was strangely subdued. Maybe all their pillow fighting had worn her out. He considered telling her what he had in mind to do, but feared she would object, so he didn't. She would learn soon enough, anyway.

They dressed. Dolph had only his good suit, so he got

into that. Electra got into her marvelous panties and bra, then into her dull everyday clothing, leaving the wedding dress hanging in the closet. It was true she had no further need of that, though he was sorry not to see her in it again. But even in her ordinary clothing she was a wonderful girl. It had taken him six years to realize that, but he would never forget it.

Electra helped get his buttons in order, and she combed his hair and dusted off his shoes. "You're quite handsome, Dolph," she said sadly.

What was wrong? "'Lectra, I—"

She forced a smile. "It's all right, Dolph. I know what to do."

He concluded that he did not understand women. "We'd better get breakfast, then."

They went out to the main pavilion. There were assorted fruits and pastries that someone had obligingly set out. Dolph picked up an eclair.

Electra walked to another table, where the two vials of potion had been put. She picked up the null potion.

"'Lectra, wait!" he cried. But he was too late. She drank the vial in one gulp.

He went to her. "'Lectra, I didn't mean for you to—"

"It's all right, Dolph," she said. "My love would only get in your way at this point."

"But—"

"If you don't mind, I think I'll sit down. I think I have a headache."

"Well, of course, then. But—"

She was already walking away. Baffled, he chewed on his eclair. Each time he took a bite, it made a little "Eeeek!" because that was its nature.

The demoness Metria appeared. "Well, Prince, how are you feeling?" she asked.

He gazed after Electra. "Sort of confused," he confessed.

"Really? Now you've had your one night stand, you've had your fun, and it's time to run. Time to dump Electra, who still loves you, and go for the one who doesn't love you. Why should you be confused?''

''But she just drank the null-love potion!'' he exclaimed. ''I would've stopped her, if I'd realized, but—''

''Why should she wait?'' the demoness inquired. ''The longer she went on loving you, the more she hurt. Now she's cleared the way for you, just as she promised, fool that she is.''

''Your teasing won't work, Metria. I made my decision last night.''

''Yes, I heard, when I snooped on your oval. So did she.''

''Snooped on my what?''

''Your circle, loop, omission—''

''You mean those three dots?''

''Right. Your ellipsis. But here's something that should really delight you, Dolph. You know that potion she drank?''

''Yes. I didn't want her to—''

''It didn't work. At least not the way she thought it would.''

''But the Good Magician's potions are guaranteed!''

''Oh, it abolished the love spell on her,'' Metria said. ''But that's immaterial.''

''Why?''

''Because her magic love faded out years ago. It was replaced by natural love. So the potion had no effect. She still loves you, dope.''

''But why didn't she tell me that?''

''I presume because she wants you to be happy and doesn't want to spoil it for you. It's a kind of generosity no demon would indulge in, but human beings aren't up to our standard.''

''That's great!'' he exclaimed.

''I thought we demons were callous. You have real potential, Prince.''

Dolph ignored her, for he spied Naldo and Nada slithering toward the pavilion from the beach. With them was another person, a human woman of middle age, in a full-length white robe. Her dark hair was neatly pinned back, and her nose was straight. He had never seen her before.

"Prince Dolph," Naldo said. "Please meet Clio, the Muse of History, who has come to record the details of this unusual event."

The Muse of History! "But the Muses stay on Mount Parnassus!" Dolph said.

"Normally we do, Prince Dolph," Clio said. "But this is an extraordinary situation, so I came to make sure I had it right." She entered the pavilion and took one of the empty seats, writing busily on her notepad.

"Uh, sure," Dolph said, disgruntled. He hadn't realized that this would be an occasion warranting recording in a history tome! The Muse had not attended the wedding yesterday, after all. How could this be more important than that?

"I suppose we had better get on with this," Naldo said. "Most of the others have chosen not to attend, but the centaur family will be here, and my father, King Nabob, to handle the formalities." He and Nada went to the changing rooms, where they evidently had sets of clothes stored. Soon they emerged in human form. Naldo glanced back the way they had come. "Ah, yes, there they are now."

Dolph looked. In the sky were two centaurs flying side by side, somehow supporting a third between them. As they came in for their landing in the sand he saw how they did it: a girl riding each big one was holding a hand of the little one, Che. They sent up a waft of sand as they touched; then the centaurs folded their wings, the girls jumped off, and all five of them and a small orange cat came in. All of them were wearing big spectacles, apparently enjoying some family joke.

Dolph turned—and there behind him was King Nabob. "Do it," he said.

Dolph realized that the stage was his. "Um, 'Lectra," he called.

Electra got up and came to him. "Of course, Dolph,"

she said. She brought out a small handkerchief and used it to wipe his face; he had a bit of eclair on it. "May I kiss you one last time?"

"No," he told her gently.

"Beautiful!" Metria murmured.

Electra turned away. She wanted him to be happy, so she was not making any scene. She was dutifully giving him up because she loved him. So many aspects of her were coming into focus now that he should have seen long ago!

Nada was not in a wedding dress, but it didn't matter; she was beautiful in ordinary clothing. She took a step toward the table where the vial of love elixir was.

"Please, no," Dolph told her. "I—I have something to say, and I hope you will understand."

"Of course, Dolph," she said, exactly as Electra had.

He took a breath, nerved himself, and spoke, as he had rehearsed it to himself in the night. "Oh, Nada, I'll always love you. But I can't marry you."

Electra's face turned to him, expressionless.

Nada blinked. "What?"

"Oh, for censored's sake!" the demoness snapped, fading out in a cloud of deep disgust.

Dolph gulped. "I—I am breaking our betrothal, Nada. Because the fault is mine, the forfeit is mine. The alliance between my folk and yours must be honored as it has been. You may—may marry whom you choose. I hope always to be your friend, and the friend of your folk. And—but—may I kiss you one last time?"

Nada was recovering her wits, which had scattered somewhat. "Not till you tell me why," she said as she caught the last one.

"Because I won't divorce 'Lectra. I—I know her better, now, and she loves me, and she's doing everything she can to make me happy no matter how it hurts her, and she's really more my type—I mean, she likes pillow fights and things, and she's closer to my age, and you—I guess I thought no one else could have what you have, but 'Lectra does, and freckles too, and I can drink that vial of love potion and look at her, and it's just better this way."

"So you're dumping me," Nada said.

Dolph scuffled his feet. "Yes."

"So that's the meaning of the Answer!" King Nabob said. "The Good Magician Humfrey told us to 'Marry what Draco brings'—and Draco brought Dolph, and yesterday I married Dolph to Electra!"

"I'll kiss to that," Nada said. She took hold of Dolph and gave him a kiss that reminded him of the past night. Oh yes, he loved her—but not quite the same way as he had before. He had learned some things, and matured, and he knew what he had to do.

When she let him go, Dolph turned and took a step toward the table with the vial. Then he paused, turning to Electra. "No, I don't think I'll need it. 'Lectra, you can't kiss me one last time because there isn't going to be any last time. Not for as long as I can imagine. But if now you want to get on with one of the middle times, or if you want to be mad at me for being so stupid about you—"

"I do!" she exclaimed, and stepped into him. Her face was tear-streaked, but her electricity tingled the way it had during the night, and her kiss practically sent him floating. "I love you as you are, stupid," she whispered tenderly.

"I—I guess that's it, then," Dolph said when his head steadied somewhat. "I, we—I don't know what we'll do, except to stay married. Thank all of you for being here."

"You're welcome, stupid," King Nabob said gruffly, and slithered away, seeming quite satisfied.

Dolph looked around the pavilion, dazed by the neatness of the resolution. But when he saw Clio talking to Jenny Elf, he realized that of course it had worked out, because the Muse of History had been here to ensure that it was correctly plotted. Magician Murphy's curse on Che's abduction could have messed up other aspects of Xanth history, so it had required personal intervention to get it all straight again.

"Clio is explaining to Jenny about Muses, I suspect," Chex remarked. "The elf has been telling stories, and her details have not been completely accurate. Also, she is from another land, and perhaps has not before been written into the books of the Muses. I can appreciate why Clio decided to give this matter her personal attention."

So it hadn't been because of Dolph's undivorce! He was glad of that.

"Nada and I will return to Mount Etamin," Naldo said. "But we shall certainly be in touch." Somehow Dolph had the impression that the naga prince wasn't much surprised by this outcome. Maybe he had a notion what it was like spending a wedding night with a woman. He had been the one to suggest this marriage and divorce, and he had wanted to spare his sister grief; it seemed he had found a way. If so, Dolph was grateful, because it had led to his discovery of Electra. It wasn't that Nada was in any way diminished in his eye or heart, but that he did after all have an alternative that he knew would keep him happy.

"Wait a bit, Naldo," Cheiron Centaur said. He did not seem surprised either. Perhaps none of the menfolk at the wedding were surprised. "We would like you to foal-sit our family this afternoon."

Nada was surprised. "You mean Che and Gwenny and Jenny?"

"And Sammy," Che said. "The spectacles spectacle."

"But why?"

"Because we have to take Prince Dolph and Princess Electra to the far side of the moon," Cheiron explained.

"What?" Electra asked.

"Your honeymoon," Chex clarified. "It's traditional."

"I mean—you called me—I'm no—"

"You married the Prince," Naldo said. "You are the first princess in memory to wear blue jeans."

"That's right!" Dolph agreed, realizing. "And when I'm king, you'll be queen."

Electra began to wobble. Naldo caught her and supported her before she fell. "Princesses swoon rather easily," he said. "Especially when they are new. You will have to stay very close to her and keep an eye on her for the next few days, Prince Dolph.''

"For the next few *weeks*," Nada said. "But princesses mend readily with affection."

"Months," Chex said. "Perhaps years." Her voice was authoritative, in the adult manner, but somehow Dolph no longer found that annoying. He would do his best.

Dolph felt a bit dizzy himself. Before he knew it, he was on Cheiron's back, and Electra was on Chex's back, and they became light indeed as the tails of the centaurs flicked them. Then they were in the air, rising above the beach and pavilion, headed for the moon, wherever it might be at this hour of the day.

Dolph looked down. The children were already running to the water's edge to build sand castles around the cat, who did not deign to move out of the way. Except for Jenny Elf. She was standing by herself, looking somewhere. Dolph knew it was toward her home, the World of Two Moons. He knew how she felt, losing one thing she loved while finding happiness with another. Her story was not yet done, he suspected. But he knew that the Muses were on top of the situation now, so they would see her story through, as they had seen his own through.

"Look!" Electra cried, pointing down.

Dolph looked where she pointed. Beyond the central ridge of the Isle of View were two unicorns, a male and a female, walking toward the place where Jenny Elf stood.

"Why, I believe I know of those unicorns!" Chex exclaimed. "They were in a dream we made!"

"Che spoke of a dream he had with Jenny," Cheiron said. "Do you suppose—?"

"With that talent of hers, it could be," Chex agreed.

"Look, Clio is finishing the chapter!" Electra said, looking to where the Muse was putting away her notepad.

"She's finishing the whole volume," Cheiron said. "I'm afraid this honeymoon isn't going to be recorded."

Dolph looked across at Electra, who smiled. The Muse of History was not putting their next week's activity into her book? It was just as well. They were now, after all, part of the dread Adult Conspiracy.

Author's Note

This is not an ordinary Xanth Note. Do not read beyond this page if you are squeamish.

Oh, there are some credits for puns and notions, but I discourage these now, as Xanth is not quite as punny as it once was. As Xanth enters its teens—this is number thirteen—it is maturing, developing new awarenesses, touching on more serious matters, and putting aside some of its childish things, though with luck it will never grow up enough to join the Adult Conspiracy. So fans who send in puns are unlikely to see them in Xanth. But some did appear in this novel.

Arthur Hoover fired off the .22 and other caliber shells. Bob Leonardi had the heart attack. Chris Cha stuck me with the traffic jam. Margaret Drennan got the stage fright. Chris Swanson saw the see shells and got bogged down in the corkscrew swamp, Plant City, Crystal River, horseshoe beach, and Cross City, all of which strange places show up in Mundane Florida by a suspicious coincidence. Becky Shoenberg and Asia Lynn drank the red whine. Shelly Poirer unwrapped the cheesecloth. And Ramiro Gonzalez, Jr. interpreted the Good Magician's Answer for the naga folk, just barely in time; I had already recorded the scene the wrong way when I received his letter.

I have regarded Xanth as the least consequential of the

writing I do. It's easy, fun, and popular, but the critics revile it, and it's hard to find anybody who likes it except the readers and booksellers. I have been told that I should never have done more than the first Xanth novel, and disgust abounds about this business of having as many as nine novels in a trilogy. I guess I thought a trilogy was three multiplied by three. So here I am with the fourth novel of the second Xanth trilogy, not having learned better.

But there have been some slight indications that there is more to Xanth than meets the Mundane eye. One naturally expects great literature as defined by the critics to achieve permanence and be read by following generations, while the junk is quickly forgotten. But Xanth is violating that rule too, and refusing to be forgotten. Every Xanth novel remains in print and continues selling well, and Xanth-related things like calendars and statuettes and game books are appearing. Some day there could even be a movie, if the motion picture companies ever catch on to what folk like. Also, there seems to be some genuine human benefit deriving from Xanth. So if literature were to be defined not by the critics, but by permanence and relevance to the interests of real people, Xanth might score better than it has.

For example, there has been more than one person who read Xanth to alleviate the discomfort of illness, including chemotherapy treatments. There was a girl who was taken into a barn, attacked with a hammer, and raped. She didn't dare tell, but the experience shattered her. Then someone showed her *Ogre, Ogre*, which addresses a similar problem, and where the girl finds comfort at last with an ogre. This Mundane girl found an ogre (they aren't nearly as horrendous as they look, when you get to know one), and her life mended, and she wrote to tell me about it. There was the girl who survived an auto accident but lost her ability to remember things; she was a Xanth reader, and I attended her birthday party, and I think it helped her to remember. There are the mothers who have written to tell me that their children had no interest in reading until introduced to Xanth. There are the teachers who have told me similar things. I suspect that literacy is the most important skill for today's person; learning to read is vital, and it's getting harder to get folk to read. This sort of thing is causing me to reconsider the value of Xanth; it may be more than just passing entertainment.

And Jenny—yes, there is a real girl, Jenny Gildwarg, twelve years old, whose ordinary life abruptly became extraordinary, but not in a nice way. Jenny has a separate story, which for our purpose begins Dismember 9, 1988. Jenny is much like Jenny Elf in the novel, only her ears are round and her hands have five fingers. On this day she was walking home from school with several of her friends. She stopped at an intersection, looked both ways, and waited for a car to pass. The car slowed and stopped, and the driver motioned to the children to cross. They did so. Another car was approaching the intersection, but the driver was intoxicated and impatient; he passed the stopped car and took off. He struck Jenny and hurled her a fair distance. That was almost the end of her life.

A driver behind that one witnessed the accident, radioed for assistance, and ran out to help. The police and ambulance arrived promptly. They arrested the drunk driver, who was belligerent and had to be handcuffed. They administered first aid to Jenny and made ready to rush her to the hospital. The mother of one of the other children saw the whole thing, and came to tell Jenny's folks. A family friend went to the scene and identified her for the police and ambulance crew. He came home to report that there was a lot of blood, but that she was still breathing.

I am trying to restrain myself, but it's difficult to stifle my attitude about drunk driving. That man was convicted on all counts, including reckless driving and nonappearance (bail jumping); he paid court costs, and got a suspended sentence. Chances are that by the time this sees print, that driver will have forgotten this episode; with luck he may already have notched another pedestrian on his bumper. Who can measure the grief brought to innocents because this soused burro-sphincter couldn't wait his turn?

Jenny's folks scrambled to get to the hospital, where they learned that Jenny was in critical condition and comatose. The doctors worked on her for several hours to get her stabilized. Then she was flown by helicopter to the emergency ward of another hospital, where they worked on her for another several hours and transferred her to a children's hospital. At this point Jenny's folks were told that she would probably die; she had only a 15 per cent chance of survival. Her father had a heart attack, which he survived; her mother hung grimly on, helped by the support of good friends and family, but months later she was suffering things like bleeding ulcers and staying out of the hospital herself more by defiance than sense.

Jenny made it through the critical period of seventy-two hours. After those three days they increased her chances to 50 per cent, but not much was said about the state of her brain. The specter that can haunt such cases is brain damage, which the surgeons can't repair. Physically she was in a sorry state. Her lovely waist-length hair had been cut short and half her head shaved. Perhaps it was just as well that she remained unconscious, for her awakening would have been a horror at this stage.

About three weeks later she was transferred to another hospital, still in a coma. She remained there six more weeks, barely responsive to outside stimuli. Occasionally she would wiggle her big right toe, lift her head a little, and track with her eyes on request. Her mother showed her pictures of her cats—Jenny rescued every homeless cat she encountered, and there were eleven cats at her home—and read notes from her friends to her. Jenny's eyes widened and she sighed heavily. This suggested that her nervous system was there and that her mind remained. But that was all. They had tried to tell her what had happened, and perhaps then she had spoken her only word, if that was the meaning of the sound she made: "No!" She did not cooperate with therapists. It was as if she was deep in a pit, and only the most evocative things could reach her at all, and then only briefly. She did not seem to want to live. What was the point, with her body paralyzed? Weeks passed without change.

At last Jenny's mother, grasping at straws, wrote to me. She thought that maybe a letter from the author of Xanth would strike some spark and motivate Jenny to come out of the coma. Jenny had read the first ten Xanth novels; the accident had cut her off from the eleventh, published not long before. The things of Xanth were common in Jenny's house. The Spelling Bee was as balky as ever, forcing them to use the mundane dictionary; Agent Orange sometimes wilted their plants (that turned out to be their big orange cat, using the pots in lieu of kitty litter); the Gap Chasm had an extension past their backyard; the Forget Spell frequently caused things like homework and room tidying to be forgotten; the Monster Under the Bed made things disappear; and the hypnogourd-TV tended to trap her father after his hard day's work. So maybe Xanth would have the magic needed to wake Jenny from her long sleep.

Jenny's mother happened to know a novelist of the genre, Andrea Alton, whose novel *Demon of Undoing* featured civilized catlike creatures. She asked Andrea about this business of writing to me, and Andrea suggested that she ask me to name a character of Xanth after Jenny, as this could be done without reference to Jenny's real nature and might encourage Jenny to take notice. At worst, I would say no.

As it happened, when I received the letter in FeBlueberry 1989, I was about three weeks from starting this novel. I knew how it would begin and how it would end, and I knew about Che Centaur needing help. But much of the rest was inchoate; I would figure it out when I got there. So I wrote a letter to Jenny for her mother to read to her, and I told her of the novel and offered to put in a character with her name. Would she prefer an elf girl or an ogre girl? I asked whether she liked ElfQuest, the series of novels in comic form—many of my younger readers do—and mentioned that her Bed Monster had gotten lonely at home without her so had moved in under her hospital bed. But he was in danger there of having a nurse give him a loathsome shot in the rump. Monsters don't much like shots, for some reason.

I really had my doubts. I hoped my letter would help, for I have raised two daughters, and by an odd coincidence each of them was once twelve years old, and to me there is nothing more precious than a little girl. But by the time my letter could reach her, Jenny would be almost three months in her coma, and that was no positive sign. So I schooled myself not to hope too much, like Electra with Prince Dolph.

I should say that I am not eager for a deluge of requests for characters named after readers. This was a special situation. I would rather have every young reader live safely and never suffer any pain or even a low grade at school. One character can be named after a reader, but I have half a million readers. So if you're not in a coma, don't ask.

Jenny's mother read my letter to her. It brought a great widening of Jenny's eyes and her first smile since the accident. She became responsive. She would squeeze someone's hand on command. They used flash cards saying YES and NO, and Jenny's eyes would track to one or the other in answer to questions. By such means her mother ascertained that Jenny definitely preferred to have an elf girl, not an ogre girl. Big surprise! I was teasing her, of course.

After that Jenny cooperated with the therapists, and each week saw improvement. She remained largely paralyzed, and was in a body brace, and unable to move her left side or to talk. She could not close her mouth; a smile was about the limit of what she could do. She had to have nerve blocks to free up her limbs. She was, we suspect, in pain at times. But Jenny is a cheerful girl, and her smiles became more frequent, and then her laughs, and then she managed to say the first word we are sure of: "Hi." It's hard to speak when your face is paralyzed. So she had miles to go, and how far she would get no one could say, but now she was in motion. She was climbing out of the pit, an inch at a time.

I wrote again, and again, on a weekly basis. Jenny became a major correspondent, though she could not answer. Her mother reported on Jenny's reactions to my letters, and interpreted. The blinking of eyes could be a signal, and a kind of game of "twenty questions" could run down what Jenny had in mind. She was so responsive now that it was easy to forget that she remained mostly paralyzed. I learned that she is a vegetarian, like me, and I saw the drawings she had made before the accident, for her story about the flowers and the blind girl. Yes, that was Jenny's story that Jenny Elf told; this is my listing of credit for that. As I write this, they are shopping for a wheelchair, looking forward to the time when Jenny can come home. I joked about how she would zoom down the halls, setting the nurses spinning, and be known as Spinning Jenny. I will, if you wish, make a report in the next Xanth novel Note about Jenny's progress. As for Jenny Elf, we don't yet know about her either. She may remain in Xanth, or she may return to the World of Two Moons. Only the Muses know for sure, and they don't seem too certain. Any of you who haven't visited that world may do so now, to check it out for her: ElfQuest graphic novels are in your bookstores. For now, take my word: they aren't junk, any more than Xanth is.

Meanwhile, back in Mundania: what would I do with that drunk driver, if I ruled the universe? I'd sentence him to three months in a coma, and a possible lifetime crippled. It is past time to start taking action with teeth in it to stop such brutal idiocy. For this was no isolated event; every day, other drunk drivers are doing this to other innocent children. Why should they stop, since punishment is a joke?

So I got into the novel, and Jenny Elf took form as a cross between Jenny of Mundania and a visitor from ElfQuest. I wrote to Richard and Wendy Pini, who record ElfQuest, and they gave me permission to make Jenny an ElfQuest elf rather than a Xanth elf. In fact they also got in touch with the original Jenny, sending her things of their realm. I understand that at one point Jenny, annoyed by the rock music of a boy in the ward, turned up her ElfQuest tape to drown it out. Should we call that spar

wars? So it was that an ElfQuest elf came to Xanth, making
this novel unique. The rest you know.

After I completed the novel and the Note, back in Mayhem, something came up. I discovered that Jenny lived close
to a science fiction convention that was scheduled for
NoRemember 1989. So I told her folks about it and said
that if it turned out to be possible for Jenny to attend, I
would go too. I hate to travel, but this was special, and
anyway it seemed unlikely that the hospital would let her
go that soon.

Surprise! It could be arranged. The hospital gave Jenny
a one-day pass, and she came with two therapists and her
family. Thus it was that I attended Sci-Con 11, in Virginia,
and met Jenny, who was now thirteen. She was still unable
to move well, or to talk, and could not remain sitting in her
wheelchair for long. But I took her hand and talked to her
intensely for about half an hour, tuning out the rest of the
world. The essence of what I said to her was that maybe
she had decided to wake from her coma on her own, then
learned of my first letter, and said "How nice. What's for
lunch?" At that point she began to smile; we both knew it
hadn't been that way. Then I got serious: "But maybe you
were walking through the valley of the shadow of death,
and you faced resolutely toward that other world, until my
hand caught your hand, and held you, and turned you back
to face this world." I explained how I had been just the
final person in a long chain of her parents and friends reaching for her, and so I had been able to stretch the last bit of
the way and finally catch her hand. But I hoped that what
I had brought her back to was more than paralysis. This
convention was part of what the world offered for her.

Then I introduced her to another person who had come:
Richard Pini of ElfQuest. At this point she broke into a big
smile. Richard gave her Wendy Pini's painting of Jenny
Elf, looking just like her only with pointed ears. They will
make a graphic—that is, pictures—version of this novel,
published more or less concurrently, so those of you who

prefer exciting pictures to dull print may throw away this book and go for that one.

Jenny got to tour the art show at the convention, in her pretty purple gown and matching shoes, in her wheelchair. Art Guest of Honor Ron Lindahn, who does the Xanth Calendars, showed his paintings personally for her. The folk of the convention came up to meet her, some in costumes, ignoring Richard and me. We were happy to have it that way. It was Jenny's hour.

But that was it. Jenny was very tired. She had to return to her room, and lie down, and then she was taken back to the hospital. I visited her there the next day and read a story to her and her similarly paralyzed friend Kathy. Next day I returned to Florida, with a red artificial rose from Jenny's corsage. I still have that rose.

So that's an update, taking Jenny through 1989. How far she will progress hereafter we do not know. But she has now met the public, and many Xanth fans have met her. My experience with "Ligeia," the suicidal girl some years back, tells me that some readers will want to write to Jenny. I will give you the address, with this caution: Don't expect Jenny to write back. She can't hold a pen well enough to write, and they are still figuring out how to hook up a computer that she might direct by head motions. In fact, she won't actually read letters, because she can't hold them up to see; her folks will read them to her. So don't say anything really private. You can write to her in care of Jenny Elf, P.O. Box 8152, Hampton, Virginia 23666–8152.

And if you want to get on my mailing list for autographed pictures, catalog of books and sample copy of my personal newsletter, call 1-800-HI PIERS.

PIERS ANTHONY

MAN FROM MUNDANIA

Three years have passed since Prince Dolph returned
from his search for the Good Magician Humfrey who
disappeared from his castle in a cloud of holy smoke.
Electra has finished Electra-plating the Heaven Cent.
Now that it is fully charged, the Heaven Cent will take
its invoker wherever he or she is needed most. So it is
time for Prince Dolph's elder sister Ivy, the future king
of Xanth, to complete the Quest.

The totally unexpected is the only way in Xanth, but
even Ivy is surprised to find that the Heaven Cent has
taken her to Mundania, an extraordinary city not unlike
New York in our world. There she meets Grey Murphy
whose computer has been setting him up with the most
unsuitable girls, like the lovely Salmonella whose food
is delicious but causes problems later.

Grey thinks Ivy is the nicest girl he has ever met, but
he can't become her queen unless he has a magic talent.
Is he a real Mundane or, worse still, could he be
connected to the Evil Magician Murphy?

Post·A·Book

A Royal Mail service in association with the Book Marketing Council & The Booksellers Association.

Post-A-Book is a Post Office trademark.

MORE BOOKS BY PIERS ANTHONY

The Magic of Xanth

☐	58150 0	Demons Don't Dream	£15.99
☐	58135 7	The Colour of Her Panties	£15.99
☐	55361 2	Question Quest	£7.99
☐	55099 0	Man from Mundania	£3.99
☐	53719 6	Heaven Cent	£3.99
☐	50533 2	Vale of the Vole	£3.99

The Apprentice Adept

☐	52471 X	Out of Phaze	£3.99
☐	56004 X	Robot Adept	£3.99
☐	55202 0	Unicorn Point	£4.99
☐	56246 8	Phaze Doubt	£4.99

All these books are available at your local bookshop or newsagent,
or can be ordered direct from the publisher. Just tick the titles you
want and fill in the form below.

Prices and availability subject to change without notice.

HODDER AND STOUGHTON PAPERBACKS, P.O. Box 11, Falmouth,
Cornwall.

Please send cheque or postal order for the value of the book, and add
the following for postage and packing:

UK including BFPO – £1.00 for one book, plus 50p for the second
book, and 30p for each additional book ordered up to a £3.00
maximum.

OVERSEAS INCLUDING EIRE – £2.00 for the first book, plus £1.00
for the second book, and 50p for each additional book ordered.
OR Please debit this amount from my Access/Visa Card (delete as
appropriate).

CARD NUMBER ☐☐☐☐☐☐☐☐☐☐☐☐☐☐☐☐☐☐

AMOUNT £...

EXPIRY DATE...

SIGNED..

NAME...

ADDRESS...